THE WINDSMITH ELEGY

Volume II

Windsmith

Kevan Manwaring is a writer and storyteller based in Stroud, Gloucestershire. *The Windsmith Elegy* is grounded upon his practice-based research into the Bardic Tradition and inspired by his deep love of the land and the lost of history.

To Terry,

Happy Exploring,

Kevan
Asylum
2017

Also by Kevan Manwaring:

Fiction
The Long Woman
The Well Under the Sea
The Burning Path
This Fearful Tempest
Ballad Tales (editor)
Northamptonshire Folk Tales
Oxfordshire Folk Tales

Non-fiction
Desiring Dragons
Turning the Wheel
The Way of Awen
The Book of the Bardic Chair
Lost Islands
The Bardic Handbook

Poetry
Silver Branch
Lost Border
The Immanent Moment
Green Fire
Waking the Night
Immrama
Spring Fall

WINDSMITH

being the second part of
The Windsmith Elegy

Kevan Manwaring

with illustrations by the author

AWEN
Stroud

First published in 2006 by Awen Publications and Sulis Underground
Second edition 2012

This third edition published by Awen Publications 2017
12 Belle Vue Close, Stroud GL5 1ND, England
www.awenpublications.co.uk

ISBN 978-1-906900-47-2

For more information about Kevan Manwaring visit:
www.kevanmanwaring.co.uk

For the ancestors
and
all my brothers

Whoever hears my bardic books
shall have entrance to the otherworld.

Taliesin, sixth century

Hyper-Eurus

TUNDRA
TAIGA
TUNDRA

STEPPE
STEPPE

EAST LANDS

BADD LANDS

FORBIDDEN KINGDOM

TAIGA

NORTH SOUTH ROAD

BARBARIC PLACE

FORT V?

THUNDER

SWORD ROAD VINEYARD PASS

SLAVE VILLAGE

WOLF FOREST

THE RED HILLS

BRENNUS RD

LAKE MANDORLA

WIND-EYE

MANDO-BAY LAKE VILLA

AUTHON CHASM

WIN DARK SEA

DOWNLANDS

DOWNLANDS

N

HILLS OF PEACE

ORE HILLS

VALLEY OF THE CHALKPOLL

ORE

SOURCE OF THE DARRU

BARROWS

DARK FRIERN

ORE HILLS

WULDER-NESSE

WIGHT WOOD

TANT ANLL

BONE MOUNTAINS

BONE MOUNTAINS

A realm of SHADOW WORLD

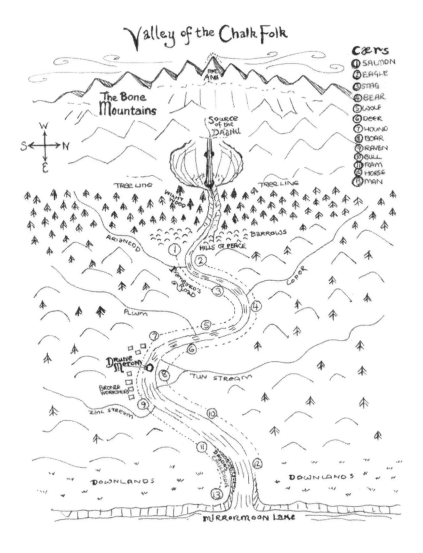

Prologue

The Angel of No-Man's-Land

23 August 1914, Franco-Belgian Border

Wind keened like a banshee around the biplane. The bitter dawn air numbed cramped limbs. Smoke and sweat half blinded both pilot and passenger. Sitting in the crow's nest designated for observers and bombers, Isambard Kerne, officer of the Royal Flying Corps, lifted smeared red rubber goggles and wiped them with a cotton handkerchief. His fingerless leather gloves traced the monogram his wife had embroidered on the corner. For a moment dark eyes lingered on the initials. From the edges of his leather flying helmet, his clipped black hair was showing grey, like flecks of cloud in the fleeing night. He thought of Maud back home, brushing her teeth, boiling an egg or taking Nubi for a walk on the Downs.

Reality rattled around him, breaking his reverie. He checked the box camera fitted into the floor of the passenger cabin. And then he tested the telegraph attached to the outer fuselage, sending a message to the radio operator. *Approaching front line ... Visibility good ... Merlin out,* Kerne tapped in Morse code.

All was ready for the surveillance shots they had orders to take. Ordnance needed enemy positions and numbers. The gun batteries would use the information to place their shells. He tried not to think about the consequences. 'Just follow orders and keep your head down,' they all said. That's all he could do. He wasn't a soldier by nature, but he'd had to enlist – before he was called up. It was the honourable thing to do, his brother Archibald, veteran of the Boer War, had insisted. He would have never let him live it down otherwise. It was his turn to do his duty for King and Country. *Dulce et decorum est pro patria mori* and all that John Bull. Archibald had survived. Surely Isambard would too – the Kerne luck had to hold.

This is not the way for a forty-four-year-old to go about life, Kerne reflected. His peacetime occupation, as a railway surveyor, was a far more sedentary affair; except for the odd wrangle with

1

awkward landowners life had been pretty harmonious. It gave him time to pursue his main interest – his research into ancient alignments. Yet his lifetime obsession with prehistory had been overwhelmed by the present.

They'd soon be at the target zone. The spotter plane spluttered along at barely seventy miles an hour but it felt too fast for him. Kerne produced a silver hip flask from the breast pocket of his fleece-lined flying overalls. His cold fingers brushed the GWR engraving on the side – a gift from his work colleagues. He debated about offering some to the pilot, then thought better of it. Harry 'Mad Duck' Mallard was probably still reeling from last night's session. And the G and T he always had before take-off. Kerne took a shot of brandy, felt the slow fire burn through him, taking away the chill and steadying his shaking hands. The adrenalin surged through him like lava. Things were happening too fast. He felt swept along on an inexorable tide. War had caught them all by surprise. Nation after nation was being pulled into its vortex. Within a month the peace of the world had been blown to smithereens. Into its vacuum they were all being sucked.

Kerne took deep breaths to try to steady himself. He had a job to do. Slipping the flask back into his breast pocket, he set to work with grim resolve.

Peering through the view finder, Kerne surveyed the flat world below, trying to focus, ascertain the depth of field, the correct exposure. Features emerged from the morning mist, but no discernible landmarks. Not like dear old England – every hill and vale distinct. Yet surely to a Belgian even such a monotonous landscape must have character, evoke strong memories, associations, nostalgia, like Logres did for him.

Dawn cast its pallor on the unfamiliar world beneath, the lights of farms snuffed out. 'All over Europe ...' murmured Kerne, remembering the broadcast. 'We shall not see them lit again in our lifetime.'

The daylight was as cold and stark as a surgeon's lamp, revealing the vulnerable flesh of the land. The virgin fields of Belgium spread out below – roads, ditches, hedges, brakes of poplars, lines intersecting, vanishing, like the cables between the wings. The Breguet buzzed slowly over the fields, its thin membrane catching the morning sun like a dragonfly in a pool of light. It was mid-August; the crops were high, but would go unharvested. Every available man was at the front. The women would eventually take over the farm work, but for now the ears of wheat stood tall and silent, catspawed in the warming breeze, poppies swaying.

The biplane passed over the broken bridges of the Mons–Condé canal – recent handiwork of Royal Fusiliers sappers. The map of Europe was being rewritten.

They were passing over Mons itself. Kerne recognised the slag heaps of the mining town. He checked the Ordnance Survey chart attached to the side of the cabin in its glass case. Tapping Mallard on the shoulder, he pointed downwards. This was their spot for today – 'a bit of photography and back for lunch at the base', as Mallard had said. *Tickety bloody boo.*

Mallard gave the thumbs up and grinned, his Viking eyes gleaming with berserker fanaticism. With a sickening lurch he took the plane down couple of hundred feet.

He's loving this, thought Kerne. It's all a game to him, like a bloody pheasant shoot.

At first he thought they were cattle. Then glints of rifles, insignias and pale faces showed them to be rows of mounted troopers waiting in the twilight fields like redundant chess pieces.

'Allenby's cavalry,' shouted Mallard over his shoulder, growling the vowels, his Yorkshire accent deep. 'Waiting for the Boxing Day hunt by the looks of things. Tally-ho!'

They passed lines of British troops digging in with dogged solemnity. Noticing the biplane overhead, they waved, or saluted with two fingers – that ancient insult of the British archer. They wouldn't do that to General Smith-Dorrien, the general who was leading the 70,000-strong infantry corps of the British Expeditionary Force east and west of Mons on a fifteen-mile front. The living lines of soldiers stretched like ants on the African plains – no difference from the air between the Allies and the enemy.

And, suddenly, they were over the German lines.

The biplane sliced through shrouds of smoke. The pounding started, audible even through the din of the engine. Howitzers punctured the sky. Explosions flamed all around them like burning eyes. The aircraft shuddered and groaned. Kerne held on tight to the delicate camera equipment and prayed that it would survive, that *they* would survive.

Below, a rent in the clouds revealed a new hell – a quagmire of tangled carnage. Amid shattered trunks and twisted limbs, the whistle and boom of shells, strikes that vomited mud like geysers, old craters filled with muddy water and bodies, the death rattle of machineguns carried like Morse code. Kerne's head buzzed. He blinked

3

and looked again. How had the flat fields of Mons been turned into such a Hades so soon? The battle had only just begun. Yet already it looked like it had been raging for years.

The arclight flickered around them – licking the edges of the wings. Between the shreds of smoke the scene below alternated between a late summer of burgeoning wheat and the wasteland of winter, like the flickerbook of a train window. Was he seeing things? Certainly, seeing the land from the air was a disorientating perspective. Kerne had spent his adult life measuring solid earth. Aerial surveillance was a new science and they were the guinea pigs. Yet he'd rather be in the sky then down there any day. Kerne spotted a soldier crucified in a skein of wire, half his face missing. Hard to tell if he was British or German. *There but for the grace of God.*

He clicked the shutter release. I'm like the Recording Angel, witnessing history, brooded Kerne. Or an Angel of Death. Kerne was all too aware that his intelligence-gathering would result in fatalities. As he went to reload the camera a shell burst directly below a wing, making the biplane buck. Cursing, Kerne fumbled with the icy photographic plate. In slow motion he watched it shatter. Frozen shards showered the cabin.

In front, an explosion ripped a tear in the smoke and mist, revealing a vast horde of German soldiers.

'Christ, there must be twice as many Huns!' Mallard bellowed back, baring teeth. 'Kluck's got us outmanned! We haven't got a snowball's chance!'

Frantically, Kerne started tapping out a warning message. His hand couldn't stop shaking. He tried to concentrate as the bombardment increased.

Light flashed off the biplane's wings. Then the air seemed to peel away like flayed skin.

Mallard was screaming at him. 'Eyes to the front! Twelve o'clock, twelve o'clock!'

The enemy fire coalesced before them into an otherworldly vision. In the flak Kerne thought he saw flashes of archers, a knight shining, raising his sword … They were bathed in a preternatural light. Time dilated … Kerne felt detached from his body, from the events. In a pattern-recognising part of his brain not frozen by fear he observed distantly, 'An avenging angel with outstretched wings, holding spears …' He breathed a prayer to the sky, yet the heavens seemed empty. Then it struck him: 'Like the Long Man!' he shouted into the void, the wind stealing his words.

'Hell's teeth! It's Saint George himself!' cried the pilot. Inspired by the vision, Mallard gunned the engine and swooped down.

Christ! He's going for a bombing run, thought Kerne, his stomach lurching. Mallard had insisted they carried a couple of hundred-pounders, even though it was only meant to be a surveillance mission. He had been one of the first to practise the hazardous method of dropping them over the side, using haystacks for targets.

Well, Kerne wasn't going to get his head blown off.

Suddenly, they were in firing range of the rifles below. Bullets started to whip and ping about them, tearing into the canvas of the wings, splintering the props, puncturing the fuselage.

'Get the hell out of here!' Kerne roared, but Mallard was oblivious, lost in the delirium of battle. He seemed on fire, the tendrils of uncanny light playing over his broad-shouldered form, the bulky black leather jacket accentuating his powerful frame, like some armoured warrior from another time.

'Cry God for Ha—aagckkk!' Mallard's battle-cry was cut short by a bullet in the throat from below. Gurgling blood, he let go of the controls to clutch his spurting neck. The Breguet plummeted. Cables thrummed, snapped, as the flimsy machine started to nose-dive.

Pitched forward, Kerne fell towards Mallard. He reached over to grab the pilot and thrust his handkerchief against the wound. The wind sprayed blood over him, smearing his goggles with a red mist. Mallard's hands flailed about – the controls moved by themselves.

Then Kerne remembered: no parachute – to stop them from bailing out.

The biplane tumbled drunkenly across the blasted charnel house of no-man's-land, straight into the cloud of fire.

Book One

The Bone Mountains

1

The Lost Journal of Isambard Kerne

And so we died. That was how it started.

Half-blinded by Mallard's blood, through the red mist, smoke and fire I saw a swirling tunnel in the sky – a sight that will stay with me until the end of my days. It was no archangel or Saint George, but a vortex into which we were sucked, lock, stock and biplane. The Breguet strained under the heavy turbulence. Wing wires snapped, the fuselage groaned … I thought it was going to buckle and crush us completely. It was like no storm I've ever experienced. Yet the wood, canvas and metal frame miraculously held. I screamed to Mallard, who still seemed to be alive: he was holding his throat, flailing about, choking. My words were snatched by the wind. That wind – it scoured the very fibre of my being! It seemed to come from the dawn of the universe, chilled with the ice before existence. Yet, strangely, there was no sound, as though we were in a vacuum. The biplane spun around and around, as if down a plughole, but each orbit of the Void seemed to take an aeon. Time and light dilated on its extreme edges. The world blurred. As our craft pitched and yawed I was shaken out of my passenger seat. I tried to grip hold of the wings, but my arms were yanked away. And my grip on reality slipped with it as I was left swirling in a sea of stars. Lost to life, lost to the world …

My consciousness was engulfed by shadow as I was swallowed by the night-black Void. It was as if I had ceased to exist. The sensation was almost comforting – and that feeling alone reassured me I was still alive, at least. But I was nowhere: in a limbo without form, without foothold. Was this to be my fate – an eternity of nothingness? A ceaseless oblivion?

I tried to shout but the Void sucked up my cries. Any movement seemed only to reinforce my inertia. I struggled against a prison with no walls, cursing against my captor – if indeed there was one. I dared not entertain the notion that no one knew I was there, that the universe was indifferent to my fate.

Suddenly there was a hideous shrieking and fiery demons emerged from the aether, ripping the shadows with their flickering limbs, screaming about me insanely, threatening to tear me apart with their talons and fangs of infernal fire.

I thought I was doomed, that this was how it ended, the soul torn to shreds. But something pulled me back; a keening that pierced even the demonic howling. It became a sobbing, raw and ragged, a woman's grief. I recognised it instantly. My darling Maud, mourning for me. I wanted to tell her I was alive, I was alright, but I was unable to reach her. Yet her sorrow reached me and seemed to drive away my attackers. The demons withered, vanished, and my prison transformed around me.

I found myself in a deathly cold cell without doors and windows. I beat upon its crystal walls to no avail. Beyond was the Void. I think that I spent nine days there, although how I could gauge the passing of time I do not know – only my internal rhythms reminded me of the diurnal round. Yet I did not hunger or thirst, nor could I sleep. I gazed into the abyss, lacking anything better to do, and slowly I began to discern glimmers of light, of stars. It was as though I was looking up into the night sky through a telescope. The more I looked the more I could see. A depthless field of stars opened up before me, and I had to clutch the sides of my invisible prison through fear of plummeting for eternity. When my head stopped spinning, I started to notice regular movements in the firmament. Did I see the movement of the planets about the sun? It was as though I was trapped in a revolving castle at the centre of the solar system … The silence, the darkness, was terrible.

Time stretched around me like a vast ocean in which all of history was contained. I gazed into its waters and seemed to see all of my forty-four years reflected back, with all of its mistakes, regrets, contentments and little triumphs. My mother and father, Archibald, school, college, meeting Maud, working for the GWR, researching alignments, enlisting, training with the Royal Flying Corps. I saw the patterns in my life like alignments between the stars; constellations of significance. Seemingly random episodes, but seen with the perspective of hindsight, meaningful.

After what seemed an eternity in the Void I began to see flickers of light, geometric shapes forming on my retinas. And with each came a sound, expressing the quintessence of that constellation – epitomised in that note, that frequency – which resonated within the very fibre of my being. An alphabet that encapsulated the archetypal patterns of existence. I was just on the point of articulating this occult alphabet when a singing called me back down to Earth, to the green mound of Glastonbury Tor. A doorway opened. I saw myself standing beside my beloved. Yet she did not recognise me and was startled – indeed, I seemed a stranger to myself, dressed in a hooded cloak, wielding a staff. Perhaps I imagined the reassuring grip of my old stang, my thumb resting in its Y. The black cloak hung about me like a cloud. Maud screamed and recoiled. I was pulled back into the chasm.

Time passed tracklessly in my prison. How long I languished there I do not know …

Then I heard a ragged female voice singing, frail and broken, but to me it was like a nightingale in that lonely, desolate place. The sound broke my shackles and I was released from the limbo, called across the abyss, summoned by song – this time to what seemed to be the interior of a long barrow. Maud stood there. Her singing had taken me by surprise, so rarely had I heard it. She had been shy of singing in our home, though I'd encouraged her. I managed to communicate with her on this second attempt, a little more used to my condition and my surroundings. I tried to explain my predicament to her. Maud had aged – nine days for me had been nine years for her. She had to let me go. And I knew where this final release could be accomplished, as though guided by an inner voice: at the Long Man at Samhain. Samhain – the word seemed to rise from an ancestral memory, and I knew it meant Summer's End, when the veil is thinnest. The chalk giant of the Long Man of Wilmington was of significance to us both and symbolically presented the ideal portal. I had always suspected the ambiguous figure held not staves in his hands, but held open a doorway. The hill he stood sentinel on was scattered with burial mounds. If he was guarding the hills of the dead, I intuited, perhaps he would be a suitable gatekeeper. I had glimpsed him above the fields of Mons. He had been the gateway then. He could be again.

I returned to the Void. The days passed imperceptibly until I was called back one last time. All went, somehow, to plan. Maud made the rendezvous. And, strangely, Archie was there also. Perhaps they both had to let something go … Together they released me from Purgatory. And I released Maud from her duty as grieving widow. She needed to move on – find a new love. She could not mourn me for ever. I had to move on as well. Released from my past, from Maud's love, I finally escaped my cell of stars.

Before me I saw a swirling window of sigils, five concentric circles like the rings of a tree, flickering with letters of flame. I plunged once more through the vortex, falling, falling down the cosmic axis, the sigils swirling around my head, burning into my skull like cattle brands.

Screaming, I fell, into a world of jagged shadows and ice, and awoke.

2

Opening of the Mouth

Kerne's head was full of light. He opened his eyes to let it out, but his consciousness was flooded with an even more intense radiance. And his ears were filled with a roaring, as though from a seashore. But it was the wind. From the distant corners of the universe it seemed to blow, across fathomless tracts of stygian fastnesses, carrying with it the song of stars, of dead suns, alien tongues, the keening of black holes. It coursed through his skull, scouring away any sense of self, of past or future. Only the endless present.

He could no longer remember his name.

Blinded and deafened, Kerne tried to stand up. He felt icy rock beneath his hands, half-protected by fingerless leather gloves. It was freezing, wherever he was. He blew on to his fingers, then, as feeling stirred in them, he ran them over his person, to check what he wore, what skin he inhabited: fleece-lined overalls, a leather headpiece with raised rubber-rimmed goggles, finely made brown leather boots that came to his knees. A black utility belt hung heavily about his waist, a diagonal strap supporting it over his right shoulder. Around his waist hung various leather pouches. He was glad of their weight. It was the only thing keeping him anchored.

So, he seemed to be in the military. Beneath his overalls was a grey woollen jacket which buttoned up one side. He checked the insignia on its breast. Crowned wings with letters in the centre he couldn't read upside down at first. They swam like runes before his eyes. Finally, his vision adjusted. R ... F ... C ... *RFC* ... Suddenly he recalled. *Royal Flying Corps.* Yet he knew he was no pilot. The memory of Mallard clutching his throat came back to him. Where was the pilot? Where was the biplane? Battered field glasses swung about his neck. Wiping the lenses clean of frost, he looked through them. One eyepiece was shattered. With a grunt, he broke the ice-brittle metal apart – one half would serve as a small telescope. He cast the other aside. As he looked at the dark tube in the snow a word came back to him: *surveillance.* That was it. He was 'in' surveillance. An observer. Not that he was much of one now, half blinded by the snow glare, and by his days in darkness.

Vision swimming, he checked the pouches around his waist and found a box compass. He flipped it open and tried to level it to get a reading. The needle spun about. Where the hell was he?

And who was he? He tried to remember his name. It felt like his lips were sealed shut, his throat clogged with dust. He desperately needed a drink. He couldn't remember the last time he'd had one. His body felt paper thin, like it would blow away at any moment.

He scooped up some snow and placed it in his mouth. It made him cough, his head and teeth ache, but it had the desired effect. The moisture that he sucked from the snow allowed him to speak.

And a name formed on his lips.

'Is … am … bard,' he whispered.

He shivered. He was *Isambard*, and he was alive. Slowly, like melting pack ice, his memory ebbed back. By some miracle he had survived the perilous journey through limbo. And now where was he? He tried to examine his surroundings but the light dazzled him at first. Then shapes started to form as his eyes adjusted: tall figures, cloaked in feathers, surrounded him, watching in silent sentinel. They startled him, he'd grown accustomed to his solitude, but then the spindrift cleared momentarily and he saw they were no more than forms sculpted in the snowdrift by the wind. They seemed to form a circle, surrounded by taller pinnacles. He was on a snow-covered mountain. Rocky crags towered behind him. Wind whistled between the pinnacles, biting into him like cold fire. He could not dally any longer; his overalls would not keep him warm for long. He fastened them tight to his neck, wishing he'd had a scarf like he had seen some of the other pilots wearing. He began to move, to get his limbs warm before the numbness made him seize up.

There was only one direction he could go – down, out of the wind and light, into the shining lands below …

In the back of his mind the sigils from the Void flashed and whispered. If only he could recall their sound. They were on the tip of his tongue, but he had pressing matters at hand: survival.

Searching beyond the circle, Kerne found a path leading down. The world below was anonymous with mist. One path was as good as another until he got his bearings. All he knew was he had to get off the mountain before he froze.

All morning Kerne negotiated the narrow track as it followed a ridge plunging from the summit. Cliffs fell away either side, a thousand feet into the mist. Finally, he reached a safer zone – a saddle of flatter space between the two peaks looming either side like stern gods. The wind had scoured this plateau of any features, but at least it was firmer ground. He was exhausted already, weak with hunger and fatigue, but he could not stop. He shielded his eyes and tried to see a way down. The snow glare was dazzling, even through his flying goggles obscured by frost. Dazed and directionless, he let the wind push him towards one side of the saddle. He staggered through the rising snowdrift until he could go no further – the lee of the hill was impassable. Digging his way out, and retracing his steps, Kerne walked into the wind, head down, arms in front of his face to stop as much of the stinging snowdrift as possible. He slogged ahead, but felt like he was making no progress, with no features to gauge his movement by. Then, suddenly, the plateau dipped and he was stumbling down scree. Rocks clattered about him, dislodged by his clumsiness. He had to be careful, this was treacherous terrain, but his legs were too tired to care.

The momentum alone kept him going, until his descent was checked by a line of boulders. They seemed to delineate a path of sorts. It was the best he had, and so he began to follow it. The way was steep and precarious. Sometimes the path was little more than a goat track. He edged nervously around the sides of a vast gulley, at the blind end of which a mile-tall horse-tail of waterfall tumbled into the chasm below.

At one point the path passed behind the thundering deluge. Kerne had to cling to the cliff-face lest he slip on the slick, slimy rocks. Loose stones scattered below into the churning waters, quickly absorbed into oblivion.

With relief, he made it behind the roaring wall of water. Past the veil of white a black emptiness gaped. Kerne probed it with his outstretched hand. Deep shadows, nothing. As his eyes adjusted to the gloom a cave was revealed, gouged out by the ceaseless action of the waterfall. He ventured into it, carefully testing his footing. Water dripped from fanglike stalactites on to the frozen ooze of stalagmites. There was a sharp tang of minerals in the dank air. Crystal fissures glistened in the darkness. From the back of it, in a moss-lined cleft, gurgled a spring. Around the clear water a halo of small pale five-pointed flowers with black hearts glowed in the gloom.

By this time his exertions had made him thirsty – though he was drenched from head to foot from the incessant spray. He could not remember the last time he had had a proper drink. Was it nine days

14

ago, or nine years? His mouth felt like parchment, his skin like sand. He fell on to the moss-covered rocks. Raw and cracked lips slurped greedily the icy water. He could not stop himself. If it was poisonous, or some kind of Lethe of forgetfulness, so be it – it was too late. The water tasted good and refreshed him, waking him up inside. He filled the tin cantina hanging from his belt.

Alert again, he began to question his surroundings. Where was he? He gazed through the curtain of water. He was certainly no longer in England, or anywhere he recognised. The landscape seemed Alpine, but that might just be the altitude. It could be any mountain range on Earth.

Or perhaps he was somewhere else entirely.

Too many questions … And he was not at his best to answer them. He felt the aches and grubbiness of his body. Warm fatigue washed over him all of a sudden and he felt incredibly weary. The toll of his incarceration and descent caught up with him.

The idea of a cold shower suddenly seemed appealing. He plucked off his flying helmet and goggles, but as he went to put them down he noticed they were caked with a dark substance. Licking his finger and tasting it confirmed that it was blood. He checked his head, and felt no lesions, but his wet hands picked up the blood also smeared over his face. He must have looked a fright.

Flickers of a biplane rocked by flak came back to him. The Morse code of bullets. A gargled cry of pain. A shower of blood.

As if peeling off layers of memory Kerne stripped off his belt and boots, overalls, uniform and long johns. His winter-pale body shook. It had seen better days – he'd always had a naturally good build but was no sportsman like his brother. And after the ordeal of the limbo he was 'all skin and bone', as his Ma would have said.

Taking a deep breath, he stepped into the icy deluge and let out a cry of pain.

The shock of the water blasted the last remnants of grogginess from him. Singing a barrack room song as loudly as possible, as if the din would drown out the agony, he braced himself and showered in the waterfall's spray, taking care not to go too near the edge. Then, shivering uncontrollably, he pulled on his clothes, letting the woollen long johns dry him. The undergarments scratched and the uniform didn't feel right, as though he was pulling on someone else's skin, another life – not his own.

In another breast pocket was a hip flask. On it was inscribed:

To Isambard Kerne, for excellence of service.
Godspeed. GWR MCXX.

He had to assume that was his name. He tried to speak it, but only uttered a dusty croak. Unscrewing the pewter flask, he took a sip of the burning liquid. Coughing, he felt false warmth flood through his veins. Dangerous, so high up, his instincts told him. It would make him unsteady on his feet.

He made a quick audit of his equipment: Sam Browne belt with holster and pistol, munitions pouch containing a box of bullets, hip flask, officer's handbook, ID, small wax-covered notebook and pencil, small knife, compass, a box of Swan Vesta matches and a pack of emergency rations – dried biscuits and bully beef in a tin, loose tea and a little bar of chocolate.

Not much to go far in foreign country.

Finally Kerne handled the cold iron of the Webley, warily, as though it was the cursed artefact of a savage civilisation. And perhaps it was. It felt heavy in his hand, and he hoped to God he would never have to use it.

He flipped open his wallet, laughing at the large damp English pound notes. What use would they be here? As much use as his officer's papers and orders, their ink running in the waterfall's spray. Then a dog-eared print caught his eye. He wiped his hand on his knee and slowly pulled out the sepia photograph of Maud.

For a long while he just stared at her gentle face, the aquiline nose she hated, the dark almond eyes he adored. It had been taken soon after they were engaged. She must have been, what, twenty? She looked so … pure. The last time he had beheld her, she had looked so much older, weary with grief, with the burden of the years. She had always been his 'little flower' – ten years younger than him. But now she was nearly the same age, because of the differences in time. They had finally caught up with one another – his heart with hers, her mind with his – but now they were worlds apart.

Kerne packed all the items away, arranging them around his person equally. Then he sat and stared at the flowers, wondering what to do.

Their pattern triggered something in his memory from the Void. Quickly, he seized the stubby pencil and notebook from his back trouser pocket. The sigils flashed in his mind, and quickly he scribbled them down, one on each page of his notebook.

When he had finished, his head hummed and his hand was shaking.

He tried to mouth the sigils, but the waterfall drowned out all sound. What did they mean? He needed answers. He wouldn't find them here. The only choice was to descend the mountain in the hope of finding human life. Kerne hoped it would be friendly.

Before he left, he picked one of the glowing flowers and pressed it between the pages. He needed some proof of this strange place.

When he had finished pulling on his boots Kerne set off once more, feeling a little more composed. He had his props and he had a role to play, though it was not one of his own choosing.

Proceeding along the cliff-path on the other side of the waterfall, he passed under a rainbow, through the mist of spray into the dazzling light once more.

He carefully continued his descent. Loose chippings fell away with every step, clattering into the chasm below. He watched them topple, bounce, spin and disappear. The sickening sound echoed about the gorge, announcing his presence to all. Not that there was a living soul in sight. How far he was from civilisation, from his fellow man, he had no way of gauging. He felt utterly alone. If anything were to happen to him here, no one would find him. The chances of rescue were nil.

Then, perhaps unsteady from the slug of brandy, the inevitable happened. He slipped and plunged down the scree. He flailed for handholds, grazing the skin from his palms and knuckles. Roots pulled away with his weight and velocity, like wishbones snapping. He fell about two hundred feet towards the gaping chasm, then came to a juddering halt, his descent stopped by a boulder. There was a sharp pain in his leg – it was jammed under the rock. On the other side of the boulder the gorge churned where the spring stream had become a young mountain river, fierce and fast. He could hear its sickening thunder.

Painfully, he extricated himself, screaming as he did so. The cry threatened to dislodge the mountainside. Sweat broke out in his effort to right himself. He dragged himself along the edge of the gorge. He probed his ankle, lifting back the crimson rags of his trouser leg. Wincing, he plucked out the bloody bits of stone. Despite the pain, it didn't seem broken, just bruised – nevertheless, an injury like that up here could be fatal. How was he going to get down safely now? He found a fallen branch and used it as a crutch, hobbling along as best he could. There was no way he could ascend back to the path – a couple of hundred feet above. His only option was to try to get down to the river below and follow its path. It cascaded into a dark pine forest, down ranks of wild foothills, snaking along a distant valley towards the hazy horizon east. No obvious sign of human habitation was visible.

His heart beat faster with the fear that he would never find help, that he was irredeemably lost.

'Where am I?' he cried out in despair.

The mountains mockingly echoed back his words. The cliffs loomed over him like stern giants, indifferent to his fate.

He could die here.

If he wasn't already dead.

3

The Feathered Magician

This was not an auspicious start. Stuck on a mountainside with a damaged, twisted ankle, limited supplies, no idea where he was, or indeed whether he was still alive. And what of his gung-ho pilot, Mallard? Hadn't the Breguet been consumed in a cloud of fire? Hadn't Kerne languished in a nightmarish limbo for nine days? If that was Purgatory then what was this?

Before Kerne could work out an answer his concentration was broken by a piercing cry. Amplified and echoed by the gorge, it sounded unearthly – like the call of a Valkyrie. Whatever it was, it sent a chill to his bones. Stuck in the stark canyon with nowhere to hide, he was easy meat. He loosened the Webley in his holster, although he had only fired it in target practice, and then only under duress. He loathed guns. And all the trappings of war he had on. His dress uniform never seemed to fit comfortably; the collar was always too tight. He lived in another man's skin. He didn't want to die in it.

Kerne shielded his eyes and looked up.

Out of the sun came a bird sharp-angled like an arrow. It looked like a bird of prey of some kind. Did it think him carrion? He wouldn't go without a fight, he thought, an instinct for self-preservation momentarily overriding his pacifism before he could check himself. What right did he have to shoot such a beautiful bird? He hated his brother's fondness for pheasant-shooting. Archie had boasted about the big game hunting he'd enjoyed in the Transvaal, but had come back without a trophy.

Kerne clicked the pistol back into its holster. The bird of prey approached. What was it? Not a buzzard or a red kite. It was smaller. A peregrine maybe? No, he could see now it was smaller still. He wished he had studied birds more carefully … It seemed to be a small falcon. Then he could make out its plumage: its shoulders were slate blue, its breast buff, streaked with black. The tail, with its broad black band, was the giveaway. Just as Kerne recognised it, the bird swooped past, flicking his face, making him flinch and nearly lose his balance, uncertain as it was. For a moment he wavered over the chasm at his back. Rocks clattered down and were swallowed in the churning water below. Then he lunged forward, gripping the rock, sweating, seething at his own disadvantage.

'Damn you!' he called out, shaking his empty fist.

At the edge of the treeline the falcon cried out and arced back. Once more it swooped. Kerne flailed out with his stick, but as the bird passed it shrieked: 'Follow, you fool!'

Stunned, Kerne dropped his temporary crutch and watched as the bird floated to a graceful rest on a dying branch at the edge of the pine trees a hundred yards away. It turned its imperious head almost one hundred and eighty degrees to look scornfully back. Once more, it cried out, 'This way, you idiot!' but it was in his head the voice rang out – sonorous, aloof and short-tempered like a Scots professor.

Kerne shook his head. Was his mind playing tricks? Perhaps he had concussion. Or had the spring been polluted? Yet the predicament he was in seemed real enough. Whatever the bird had, or had not said, his way was clear. He edged his way awkwardly along the side of the ravine, conscious always of the death waiting inches away. The sixty-degree slope, the flinty crumbling surface and his damaged ankle did not make the going easy. Beads of sweat broke out on his head. He took off the flying helmet, tucked it into his belt, and mopped his brow with the back of his overall. Grunting, he carried on hobbling towards the bird. In his pain he hated its arrogant ease. Finally, out of breath, he collapsed at the foot of the tree, immersing himself in its delicious shade. The resinous smell of the pine forest soothed him.

'Took your time.' Once again, the voice jarred in his head, an intruder.

Kerne gritted his teeth and lifted his head from the bed of needles.

The falcon glared down at him with yellow black eyes. Kerne glared back.

'Am I going mad?' he asked rhetorically.

'Going? That depends whether you were sane in the first place.'

Kerne shook his head in disbelief. 'I'm talking to a bird!'

'Are you?' riposted the falcon. 'Not everything is what it seems.'

'Well, to me you look like a merlin.'

The falcon looked at him fiercely. 'At your service,' he said almost resentfully.

'Pardon?'

'You have spoken my true name, and, in this world, names have power, *Isambard*.'

He tried to comprehend what the bird had just told him. He'd said his true name was *Merlin*. And names had power. The falcon seemed to know his first name. And 'Merlin', coincidentally, was also Kerne's RFC codename, chosen on a whim, because of his fondness for the Arthurian legends as a child.

'It seems also you know my name …'

'It was hard not to know it, when you shouted it from the mountaintop!'

Kerne remembered speaking his name when he'd first arrived. 'Shouted? I barely whispered it!'

'Whispers carry far on a mountain.'

'So it seems, but … Hang on a minute! I called you "merlin", the type of falcon. Are you claiming to be *the* Merlin the magician?'

'Do you know of any other falcons who talk?' the bird squawked impatiently. 'Let me explain – and I'll make it simple so even you can understand. Here, the real name of something is the thing itself. I am called Merlin, because I *am* Merlin. QED. This pine tree *is* a pine tree. If you knew its unique name you would be able to control it. Below us is the Da'anu. If you knew the full name of the river you would have some power over it. You would know its source and destination. Fate is locked in a name. When Adam named the creatures in Eden he gave them their destiny.'

Kerne tried to take it all in, but his head swam. His hand shaking, he unscrewed his canvas-covered cantina and took a draught of the spring water. It cleared his head again, and a sudden revelation came to him. 'So, are you saying that because my name is Isambard I was destined to work for the GWR, like Brunel?'

'That may have been your father's intention, but there is often serendipity in our actions. Names can become self-fulfilling prophecies, or reveal dormant aspects of our personalities we didn't know were there. Every David meets his Goliath, every Helen her Paris, or Menelaus. In your case, it couldn't have been more appropriate.'

'Meaning?'

'Think, damn you! You are not without wits, if you but apply them! How often has your antiquarian field research confirmed what you suspected in the place name; a spring, burial mound, hill fort, old straight track? Names contain the ghosts of the past – or the seeds of the future.'

Kerne pondered on this. What was Merlin implying? What secret was locked in his name? He knew 'Kerne', his father's surname, derived from a light-footed Irish infantryman. He saw no possible connection in this, other than being stuck in a war. But he was an airman. What about his Christian name? Isambard, Isambard … He said it out loud – and suddenly it came to him.

'Is … Am … Bard. I am … a bard?'

'We shall see. No one said fulfilling your destiny was easy. Come.' Merlin stretched his wings and flitted between the branches, down into scented shadows the pine forest.

'Wait! What about free will? Don't we have a choice?'

'We create our own choices,' Merlin called back, camouflaged by the speckled sunlight and shadow. 'But they are determined by our destiny. We chart our trajectory by will, desire and fear. You would call them alignments, I believe.'

Kerne looked at the faint path before him, snaking through the pine trees, following the edge of the ravine, but not too closely. The trees muffled the river's roar. He couldn't stay there for ever, and his guide was getting further away.

'Wait!' He cursed under his breath, and hobbled after the falcon as best he could. His guide let him catch up. He had caught a vole and was holding it between his talons. It was squirming, wide-eyed and terrified.

'Excuse me while I have breakfast.'

Kerne watched in disgust as the bird jabbed it with his beak, killing it in one blow, then began to tear it apart.

'So this is Merlin the Great?'

The bird gave him a hooded glare. 'That is the name I am known by in your land, in your day. I am known by others. Myrddin Wyllt in your mother's tongue – Merlin the Wild, so be warned! Anyway, even magicians need to eat.'

'But you're not what I was expecting.'

'What were you expecting, a wizard in a pointed hat?'

'I wasn't expecting anything … but, a bird?'

'It's a sore point,' muttered Merlin through a beakful of vole.

'Ah.' Kerne chuckled ruefully, suddenly getting the measure of his mentor. 'A woman, was it?'

A gore-filled beak spat a gobbet of rodent out. 'Do you want to find your own way out of this wilderness?'

'Sorry.'

Kerne let him continue chewing in peace. Realising he was now famished, he decided to break his own fast. He broke open the bully tin, and cut out a slice with his knife. It had the texture of boot leather. He quickly munched on a biscuit to take the taste away, and washed it down with a tinny draught of spring water.

'Merlin?'

'Mm.' If his mouth was full of food, or whether he was just being taciturn, it was hard to say.

'What is this place?' Kerne gestured at the forest with his stick.

His guide looked at him inscrutably, as if deciding what to tell him. 'Where do you think?'

'Not France.'

'Obviously.'

'Somewhere on the Alps?'

'Keep going.'

'Switzerland, Austria?'

'You're heading in the right direction – but you're in the wrong world.'

'What do you mean?' asked Kerne with a growing sense of unease.

'How many birds speak on the Earth you know?'

Kerne choked on his bully beef. He didn't like where this was going. 'You're not saying we're on ... another world?'

'In, not on.'

Kerne sat down. The rock he sat on seemed real enough. The forest looked Alpine. None of it was alien. He remembered the novels of Jules Verne and H.G. Wells, Haggard and Doyle that he and his brother enjoyed so much as children.

'So.' He tried to frame his question carefully. 'Are you saying this is another planet?'

'No. It *is* the Earth you know and love, but *more* so. It is its quintessence. In the way a tree has its dryad, so the Earth you know has its true self: unsullied by man, unravaged by time. But the two are inextricably linked. Whatever happens *there* creates repercussions *here*, and vice versa – as though this was the world's shadow.' Merlin brooded over the correct analogy, as Kerne struggled to understand. 'Like a coimimeadh, a co-walker.'

'Co-walker?'

'Every human has one. They are in every way like the man, as a twin-brother and companion, haunting him as his shadow. Sometimes they are called the "fetch" and are seen before the person's death.'

'A doppelganger...' Kerne shook his head in disbelief. 'A shadow world…' He tried to comprehend what Merlin had told him, looking at the pools of light and dark before him, the shafts of sunlight through the pine trees.

'How did I get here?'

'Through the Angel Gate.'

'The "Angel Gate"?' Kerne thought of the fleeting image of the figure he had seen in the cloud of fire above the battlefield. It had looked like an angel for second, then had seemed like the Long Man to Kerne, Saint George to his pilot. 'Do you mean the gateway we passed through over Mons?'

'Yes. It was opened up by the commencement of the Great War.'

'The Great War?'

'That's what the conflict you fought in became known as, an iron-ic title for so terrible a war … It lasted four years. Millions died needlessly. Mons was the first battle, and the last chance to stop the juggernaut of war. Such a devastating conflict creates a vast build-up of energy.'

In a dizzying flash, Kerne recalled the swirling horrors of the Void. 'A vortex…'

'Yes. It was a doorway of possibility. The threshold – it could have led to peace. Instead, Europe chose war. You were unlucky enough to be caught in the cross-fire.'

'Please, tell me straight, Merlin. Did we die that day?'

'You … passed over while the veil was thin. It was an accident, or perhaps not.'

'So, am I in Hell?'

'No, I think you left that behind. These are one of the Afterlands – your ancestors thought of them as the Summer Country, as their paradise.'

'My ancestors?' Kerne thought of his Irish father and Welsh mother, of the generations stretching back. 'Am I dead?'

Merlin eyed him closely. 'No.'

The revelation hit him like a bullet. Not dead? After all the grief Maud had gone through – unless, unless her inability to let go was because she had intuited he was still alive. And then he had *made* her release him because he believed himself beyond the veil … Instead, he could have gone home. The thought sickened him. His chance of escape had been wasted. The door had closed. He had doomed him-self.

Kerne roared, striking a tree with his branch, shattering his make-shift crutch. Crumpling on to the pine-needle carpet, he sobbed in silence, crushed by the vast gulf between him and his darling Maud, between a forest of death and the green hills of England.

Merlin settled back on to the swaying tree, smoothing his feathers. 'You crossed over by mistake. This is a great transgression. The presence of a living man in the land of the dead is disrupting the equilibrium of the worlds. It will widen the longer you stay here. You must repair the rift! Otherwise, the dead will walk the Earth, and the living will be sucked into the land of the dead. The vortex is ravenous. Death must have his due.'

Then Kerne remembered what he had said to Maud in the long barrow: *'Death is our ticket from this world ... I have not the coin to pay for my return.'* He could not have returned to the land of the living after all, except with his death.

'What ... what can I do to make amends?'

The falcon preened himself. 'Heal the wound. Find your friend.'

'Harry? He's here? He's alive?'

'Yes, but he was wounded. He has ... changed. He has infected the Summer Realm. He has brought the iron poison.'

'The iron poison? What's that?'

Merlin grew impatient. 'The technology of your world. The technology of war.'

Kerne shook his head, looking down at his uniform. Slowly, he got to his feet. 'Where is he?'

The falcon paused. 'In the Forbidden Kingdom.'

Kerne gritted his teeth. This was not getting easier or clearer. He took a deep breath, gripped the tree for support as pain flashed up his leg. 'How do I get there?'

'You must travel through the Valley of the Chalk Folk. They will help, though at first they will fear you.'

'Why?'

'Because you fell from the sky like Taranis.'

'You use words I do not understand! *Taranis?*'

'Speaks-with-Thunder he is kenned by the Chalk Folk. You know him by another name ...'

Kerne shook his head in disbelief. 'I know him?'

'Yes. Your friend, the enemy.'

'Do you mean Mallard? My enemy?'

'Yes – his time here has ... corrupted him.'

'His *time* here? But surely he hasn't been here more than nine days? How could he have changed so quickly?'

'Time runs differently in this world. You are in a crossing place where the fast and the slow currents balance themselves out, but the further into HyperEurus you go, the quicker the days pass, in relation to the outer zones.'

Kerne brooded on this, remembering how his nine days in limbo were nine years for Maud. How much more time had elapsed for Mallard? He had thought his pilot lost, yet it seemed it was him who had been AWOL. The years had left him untouched.

'He has journeyed deeper into the Shadow World and succumbed to cythrawl – the source of darkness and chaos,' Merlin added, as if hearing his question. 'He has taken the night road to Annwn, to soul-death. You must balance this by walking the light. He uses weapons. You must use words. To fight the Iron King you must master the way of the windsmith.'

'The *windsmith*?' Kerne whispered. '… I have heard of that name before … In another life …' The names *Wilmington*, *Dru*, echoed in his mind.

'Yes,' agreed Merlin, again hearing his thoughts. 'He was a wood-priest. A master of the winds.'

'But I thought he was just a character from folklore?'

'As you will discover, such tales have grains of truth. Things cross over. Myths, legends, artefacts, ideas … The windsmith is adept at walking between the worlds. You must study their lore. Find the one-eyed man. He will teach you – for a price.'

Kerne asked where he would find him, but Merlin flapped his wings and flew on. 'Enough prattle! Follow swiftly. We must reach charmed halls before twilight!'

'Merlin! Why are you helping me?' Kerne called out, but the mysterious magician flew on into the forest of light and darkness.

4

Chalk Folk

Kerne followed the falcon down the wooded mountainside, trying his best to keep up, his sprained ankle sending shockwaves of pain up his body with every step. He had found a dead branch with a Y-shaped end, reminiscent of his old stang, and used it as a makeshift crutch. Pine branches scratched at him, resisting his passage. He felt like a trespasser, like he did not belong. The land was unwelcoming, perhaps sensing his otherness.

He was still reeling from the notion that he was alive in the land of the dead, and from the revelation about Mallard. 'Taranis', Merlin had called him. 'Speaks-with-Thunder' – 'the enemy' … Yet how could that be? Mallard had been in this world no longer than him, surely? Well, no more than nine days. How could he have become known by such strange names in such a short period? How could he have become 'the enemy'? Had he been driven mad by this maddening world, a world of shadow where nothing is what it seems? Or perhaps it was a case of mistaken identity.

Yet how many men would have 'fallen from the sky' recently?

There was no time to dwell upon the matter. Kerne had to concentrate not to fall on the steep slope, slippery with pine needles. His boots sank up to the ankle in the many winters of mulch.

To his left, where the forest thinned to a precipice, the river roared in its gorge, angrily coursing to its fate. Nothing could check its descent. The ridges and folds of the mountain proved no obstacle as it gouged out its own headstrong way from the white chalky rock.

He could have ended up there, in the Da'anu, if it had not been for – what? Destiny? Which course was he taking? His own? There seemed to be limited choice – either get down, or stay on the mountainside and freeze to death.

Kerne pondered what Merlin had said about destiny. How much was predetermined, how much desire? Certainly the idea of becoming a bard, from what he knew of bards from the Welsh Eisteddfod, and from Celtic history, appealed to him. But more so did the mys-

tery of the windsmith. He had encountered such a figure in his antiquarian studies at Wilmington: in the curious legend of Dru the
Windsmith, surveyor of windmills and summoner of winds. Had
Dru been a remnant of the Celtic druids, the men of oak? Had he
been the last of his kind?

Kerne had also discovered that a windlass was needed to unlock
the gateways. Too late had he realised Maud had been his – until he
made her let him go. Now he would have to find his own way to
unlock the gateways between the worlds. He was no singer, that was
for certain. But he did like to write – the small, wax-covered journals
had been his touchstone, his sanity, in England. And perhaps they
would be in this strange land. But there was no time to reflect now.
Questions and confusion over the nature of this other world, and of
his strange guide, were overridden by the primary concern of self-
preservation. Besides, being lost on an alien mountain with a badly
sprained ankle, Kerne was in no position to look any gift-horse in
the mouth.

Despite his querulous nature Merlin was an effective guide: the
feathered magician knew the area well and picked the easiest route
down for his crippled charge. Nevertheless, it was still a painful descent. Every step for Kerne was jarring. The route down the mountain seemed little more than a goat-path.

They descended all day, heading east, and as the day progressed
past noon the shadows began to lengthen behind them. They had to
make haste to avoid being engulfed in them. Merlin advised this
would be for the best, although he wouldn't specify why.

Kerne was only allowed to stop for water breaks, and these were
brief. The rations he chewed on as they went, which was fine by him
– they were not meals to be savoured. Fat white mushrooms caught
the airman's eye, but Merlin advised against eating them.

'Were you reading my thoughts?' Kerne accused, indignant at this
continual invasion of privacy.

'I could hear your stomach rumble. Come, we must not dally in
these woods at dusk!'

As the shadows lengthened about them, nipping at their heels, the
air cooled dramatically, making Kerne's arms become gooseflesh –
he had long since rolled up his sleeves. He must have looked quite a
sight, a dishevelled itinerant, with nine days' growth of beard upon
his face, which itched annoyingly, and mud smeared with sweat on
his brow and bare forearms, which were lacerated with crimson runic scratches from the pine branches. The pain from his right ankle

had become intense, and he'd had to loosen the laces on the backs of his boots as the swelling increased. His right shoulder ached from the extra weight it carried, propped up by the Y-shaped crutch. Yet even in such a state as that Kerne still felt the hairs on the back of his neck stand up as the shadows came.

A panic started to rise in the airman. Wild-eyed, he looked back over his shoulder. 'Merlin, what is this place?'

'You're on the Bone Mountains. You arrived on Mount Anu, its highest and most sacred summit. This is Wight Wood. The Hills of the Twice-Dead. You do not want to meet them ...' The way Merlin spoke the warning chilled his soul.

'*Wight* Wood ...' As Kerne spoke the word it dislodged a distant memory, of Nine Barrow Downs on the Isle of Purbeck, said to be haunted by a wight. He recalled a man called Foss, the shop-owner he had bought his stang from, warning him and Maud. How far away that midsummer honeymoon seemed now, yet even then he had talked of death on the chalk cliffs.

The forest, which had been deathly silent, stirred ... It was hard to describe in a rational way, but the trees took on a malevolent aspect, seeming to delight in tearing at him. The silence was penetrated by ... whispers, from no discernible source. Whenever he turned, there was no one there, but movement flickered at the edge of his vision – blurs of white in the gathering gloom. It became suffocating. Kerne felt an icy grip on his heart, willing him to stop, to give up. His limbs became leaden the more urgent was his pace. It was akin to the sleep paralysis he had heard of, which is accompanied by an overwhelming terror, in those who wake while still dreaming.

'Quickly, they are nearly upon us!' cried Merlin.

There was a frenzy of pushing through the lashing branches, heedless of their toll, as Kerne stumbled blindly through the forest, aware all the time of the *creatures* behind. The white shadows strived to grab him with icicle fingers, to pull him back into the hungry forest.

Then Kerne burst through the treeline, into open hills. Beyond these undulating ripples of the mountain, carved by the river, there stretched before him a darkening plain.

Kerne collapsed, exhausted, sensing himself outside the reach of the terror. For a long while he savoured the coolness of the snow-dappled grass.

'Get up – you're not out of danger yet!' commanded his guide.

Kerne groaned, but staggered painfully to his feet. He looked around: row upon row of round barrows stretched across the bare hilltops. It reminded him even more strongly of the barrowed downlands of England, and for a second he felt strangely at home, but Merlin would not let him rest. The feathered magician seemed agitated by some great peril close at hand, and ushered Kerne along, between the burial mounds, insisting on haste, and forbidding him to stop and investigate.

'Whatever you do, don't step on them!'

They weaved their way among the beshadowed barrows, which were constructed of compacted chalk, like miniature Silbury Hills. Stark, though oddly beautiful. They seemed to sing to the airman, and he had to use all of his will to walk past them.

'What were those ... things in the forest?' Kerne asked in hushed tones.

'They are wights – the twice-dead: those who died here without tribute, without proper burial. They are murderers and misers, those who did not love or were not loved. They are jealous of the barrow-dwellers, whose inhabitants have found peace because their souls are honoured by their loved ones. Dying the second death without an honourable grave means a soul will never find rest or rebirth.'

Kerne wished to ask Merlin about the idea of rebirth. He had heard of the Pythagorean concept of metempsychosis – the soul's migration at death – and he'd heard of a similar belief in the Far East; but this was neither direct reincarnation nor eternal life as promised by the Christians. This seemed more like a Celtic notion of the afterlife, and indeed the druids must have had a system mapping out the soul's journey, but, alas, they never wrote any of their teachings down, relying on bardic memory which largely died with them. The Roman historians had never discovered exactly what it was either, only that the Celts believed in the afterlife so strongly they were careless with their lives in battle, were buried with all they needed for a good life beyond, and even deferred the repayment of debts until the next life.

Before Kerne could formulate a question they had emerged on to the brow of the main ridge. A spectacular view greeted them, half in twilight. They looked down on to a series of hill forts stretching into the hazy east, separated but interlinked by the Da'anu as it wove about them like a silver dragon. Fires were glowing from the round huts within each compound, ever brighter in the gloaming. Sounds of life carried across the valley: dogs barking, the clang of metal, horses whinnying, a baby crying. And in the dusk, shining from the flanks of the hill forts, were figures carved into the white rock. Stylised, elegant and economical in form and execution, a pantheon of figures from prehistory – salmon, eagle, stag, bear – like earthbound constellations. A wave of déjà vu swept over the airman. They reminded him of the Long Man of Wilmington and the White Horse of Uffington. Yet how could that be? Chalk figures were unknown outside Britain. Yet stretching out beyond the shadows of the Bone Mountains was no downland of England.

Before Kerne could question Merlin, the bird had swooped down the ridge towards the nearest settlement and Kerne had to follow.

An unearthly sound split the gloaming, and Kerne knew – every sense of his body told him – it was the howling of the wights, their cries full of angry hunger.

The hills of the dead were no place to be at night.

The path down to the hill village was easier going than the forest track; a deeply cut processional route lined by white quartz megaliths that glowed in the dusk. It had been well trodden for centuries by the looks of things.

Ahead, by a cataract of white water, where the steep-sided gorge widened out into the green-hilled valley, there stood a circular enclosure, delineated by a raised bank, which seemed to suggest a sacred compound more than a defensive structure, reminding Kerne of the henge at Avebury. Within its circle stood a cluster of round-shaped huts with conical roofs, some connected by covered passageways. Hazel trees grew among them. In the centre there was a long hall shaped as a vesica piscis with intricately carved beams like ribs, making it appear like a beached whale. Indeed, its entrance seemed to be between a pair of gigantic jawbones, like Kerne had once seen at, of all places, Glastonbury Abbey.

Above the gateway to the enclosure gazed strange figures with large heads and tiny bodies, arms held aloft in greeting. Pendants fluttered in the chill breeze, bone chimes clattered together, echoing the music of the river as it descended over the ledges of rock carved into a thousand shapes.

The compound seemed to be a gateway, either into the gorge or into the valley. There was a feeling of peace and sanctuary about it.

Gentle robed figures moved gracefully about, collecting water, chopping firewood, tending the goats or lighting the pungent fish-oil lanterns.

An old man in a long silvery robe, with watery green eyes, wearing a scaled skullcap, emerged from the long entrance passage, hazel staff in hand. He bowed and smiled. 'Welcome to Caer Fintan. I am Partholon, chief of this caer, and you are my most welcome guest.'

5

The House of Partholon

The Journal of Isambard Kerne
Date unknown

I find myself in a Celtic paradise. The House of Partholon is a place of peace, of sanctuary, where I am starting to recover from my recent ordeals. The head of this household is a wise and hospitable man. Before asking who I was or where I hailed from he welcomed me in and commanded helpers – they look and bear themselves like monks and nuns, for both genders are here – to bring me to a warm chamber, where hot water simmered in a cauldron-shaped bath. Still jittery, at first I thought they were going to cook me, but their gestures informed me it was meant for a bath, much to my relief! I was left in peace to wash myself and dress in the soft clean robes they had left me. And then my nose and my hunger led me to the main hall. The smell of freshly baked bread and stew drew me in. The members of the mysterious order, its church unknown to me, were sitting down at semicircular benches and eating in silence. I was welcomed in and bid to help myself to the steaming broth, warm bread, goat's cheese and mugs of dark flat ale.

It was only after the meal had finished that Partholon bid me join him by the central hearth on fur-covered chairs while the monks and nuns left and serfs cleared away the dinner. Of those serfs, more later … Not a paradise for all, it would seem.

I was feeling warm, clean and well fed – a stark contrast to my previous nine days in Hell, or my time on the Bone Mountains. Of winged Merlin there was no sign. I half wondered if in my disorientation I had imagined the talking falcon, but it was thanks to him that I had made it here. He seemed to have vanished when Partholon appeared.

The kind-faced leader, if he could be called such, since I never saw him giving orders, sat in silence and waited for me to speak. I looked into his green-grey eyes and saw such compassion, such understanding. The chief reminded me of my Da, whom I miss so. How long has it been since I've been able to talk with him? He was always the one I was able to turn to for impartial advice, seemingly above the petty feuds of family life. He would tell it straight when no one else would. And his unshakeable stoicism taught me how to endure life's vicissitudes. I have been shouldering the burden of my responsibilities ever since I became a man. Da taught us to be strong, because the world was tough. But he wanted us to do well. My Grand-da, on the Kerne side, had been a navigator on the canal-ways – an Irish navvie, a trade that my Da had inherited as the railways took over. He had worked his way up through the GWR and had managed to get an education for Archie and me – the first of his family to have the privilege. We proved adept, winning places at grammar school. Archie was always more into sport than I. He loved the rough camaraderie of the playing field, while I preferred reading and walking. Sometimes Da would bring home maps from work and I would pore over them, deciphering the marks with the key, seeing how signs on the page could translate into physical features. From this developed the fascination with the landscape that would become my lifelong obsession. While Archie went for a career in the military, I followed my father into the railways, becoming a surveyor and, eventually, civil engineer. But with the assassination of Archduke Ferdinand all hell broke out in Europe and my surveying skills were needed in the skies above Mons. My career with the Royal Flying Corps was short-lived. Mallard and I were shot down in the first battle of the Great War, as it's become known – for as I spent nine days in limbo nine years passed by in the land of the living. Maud's grief, her refusal to give up hope that I was still alive, trapped me in that Purgatory. Her love wanted to bring me back, but my love made me let her go – so she could enjoy life while she could. I could not have returned through the Long Man portal: I could not cross over unless I paid with my life. And it seems it works both ways. The ferryman must be paid … I became separated from my pilot and somehow survived.

And now I am here, recording how I poured out my heart to a stranger, though even now I am not sure whether I spoke these things or Partholon plucked them from my mind in the way Merlin seemed to.

Whether my confession had been words or thoughts, Partholon accepted what was on my mind with gentle reassurance, although some of the names and references were unfamiliar to him.

I had not shared my heart like that with anyone, not even my wife. I regret bitterly not being more open with her. I kept my research to myself, my quest for the windlass that would unlock the worlds – yet *she* was the windlass all along, if I'd had but eyes to see it. But I was a fool, a blind fool, and now it is too late: I am trapped in another world. To my shame I found myself crying – a grown man – but Partholon let me. It seemed the last few days had taken their strain, reducing my resistance, making me too emotional, yet it felt the right thing to do. No one was judging me – except myself. Partholon put a firm hand upon my shoulder and made me feel that it was alright to show my emotions. This was not the done thing in England. I did not find camaraderie like my brother, who was always a 'man's man', at home in the gentleman's clubs with his brandy and cigars and card games, or on a shooting weekend with old war chums. I have always found greater solace in my own company, much to the chagrin of my wife.

Old instinct kicked in and I stifled my tears. I did not want to make a fool of myself. What must that man think of me? I asked my host about the nature of this land I find myself in. His answers were shocking and disquieting, to say the least, and it is only now, in reflection, that I find myself coming to terms with them.

My fears were confirmed when Partholon told me I am in the land of the dead.

It chills me to write it. Yet this is not a universal Hades but the realm of my particular ancestors. *One* of the Afterlands, Merlin had called it. I have Welsh and Irish blood in me, so this is a very genealogical afterlife – that of my Celtic forefathers. Partholon tried to explain that this place is not in a collective past, but is 'ever-present' outside time. He could not explain this further. He only knows that the Celtic dead come here, that they have been coming here for millennia – and that their bones, the skeletons of the innumerable dead from the dawn of man, decayed and compacted, have created the chalk that lines the valley – as I had guessed, no natural downland. Hence the 'Bone Mountains'.

So, this is the land where the Celtic dead come to find final rest, although it is no Tir na nOg – they resume life at the age that they died, Partholon explained, and, unless killed in unnatural circumstances or through a desire to reincarnate, they will dwell for ever in this realm. Their status depends upon how they were buried and how they arrived. If they were buried in a fine tomb with many grave goods, as was the ancient custom, then they are rich in this world. A burial fit for a king will create a king in this world. But if someone was buried in a pauper's grave or, worse, killed unnaturally and left unburied – murdered or drowned – then they arrive here empty-handed. Yet when their murderers arrive, if they are of the same ancestry, then those murderers will be forced to work for them, to pay off their karmic debt, as the Indian sadhus would deem it. And others toil freely, having deferred a financial debt or other obligation until this life, so strong was the Celtic belief in the afterlife. So the 'serfs' I see have chosen this form of repayment in this world, unless they come rich enough to pay off their 'loan' outright. However, they are not slaves, for they have taken on this debt voluntarily and once it is paid off then they are free men and women once more. Some choose to pay off service in this world anyway, out of a sense of duty to their ancestors or elders. Those who wish to help the recently dead adjust to the transition of this world come to Caer Fintan to act as midwives for the dead. Souls often arrive disorientated, scared – especially the children. They are welcomed here, made to feel safe and given all the time they need to adjust. The House of Partholon is a true sanctuary. I am free to wander the enclosure and environs – sitting amongst the hazel groves, talking with other arrivals, or with the 'midwives', who are always on hand to offer advice or assistance. My favourite place is by the cataract of the Da'anu, which I have gazed at for hours, reflecting upon my life while scrutinising its glittering patterns.

A couple of days after my arrival, while I was writing up my journal on a smooth-curved bench in one of the sheltered alcoves overlooking the river, Merlin returned. He came to me and asked how I was getting on. He sounded almost concerned. I was a little annoyed with him for just vanishing like that and leaving me to it, but he only said, 'I come and go at no man's calling.'

I accepted his obtuseness with a benevolent tolerance. The time I've spent at Caer Fintan has made me accepting of my own faults, as well as others'. It is a place of harmony, not conflict. Any difficulties that arise are flowed around like water around rock, any anger embraced with love.

I have even started to grow fond of the old bird, but I stopped short of telling him so. I shared what I had learnt, and it helped to clarify things by articulating them in the clear light of day. The patterns of nature seemed to mirror this system of death and rebirth, of flow and growth, decay and transformation. Silvery salmon leapt up the cataract, striving to return to their spawning ground, wise with memory after their oceanic odysseys. And here, in this valley, I am in the place of my ancestors. I, too, have returned to my source ... It is a web of which we are all a part.

Merlin, eyeing the salmon with professional interest, said my arrival had already caused ripples. Before I could get him to elaborate, a boat arrived from downriver; a canoe paddled by two hawk-like warriors. Their passenger was an aquiline-faced man in a cloak ruffed with white eagle feathers. A golden eagle clutched his shoulder. Partholon greeted him and they embraced. Together, the two men looked down at me and seemed to be talking. They watched me with some interest as I conversed with the falcon. I waved back. Merlin flapped away, saying Eryr Eagle Lord had arrived and would be eager to talk with me.

I was summoned to the hall, where the two lords sat by the hearth. The Eagle Lord eyed me curiously. Partholon introduced Eryr, lord of Caer Ewilod. The tall, thin-faced man was bald and stern-looking. His blue eyes pierced into me as he went straight to the point: that I appeared to be a birdtalker. This is an advanced skill that anruths (his word for trainee windsmiths) are schooled in at Caer Ewilod. He was curious as to how I already had this ability. Windsmiths – when they reach a critical point in their training – are 'adopted' by a bird-ally. This will remain with them for life, as their guide – theirs and theirs alone, unless they transgress in some taboo way, breaking the rapport. A windsmith can have any bird as an ally. To have a falcon is deemed very special. Eryr's eagle sets him apart as a man of high status – the head of his tribe and guild.

I replied that I had not known I had this ability until I arrived in this land, that it was as much a surprise to me as to him. Eryr commented to Partholon that my fledgling birdtalking ability was a sign I had the makings of a windsmith.

Windsmith – the same word that Merlin had used, that I had heard in a story from long ago.

I asked Eryr what *he* meant by the term. He replied it was someone who had taken the 'way of awen' and had mastered the art of gramarye – of word-magic. A windsmith is a diviner, a summoner of winds, a soothsayer and a celebrant. In this valley the windsmiths' word was law and they were consulted on all things. They could bless or curse – their satires were feared, their praise sought. They were the guardians of lore, the remembrancers of their tribe. All the genealogies and histories were recorded in the stories and songs, englyns and triads they held in their vast memories.

In other words, they were bards.

It seemed my destiny was calling. Merlin had foreseen this ... What else had he glimpsed with those keen eyes?

The two chieftains agreed that this was a matter of great import. An extraordinary sign in extraordinary times ... I had to be taken to Caer Cernunnos, insisted Eryr. Bron, the Stag Chief, must be informed.

Partholon was concerned about this. The Stag tribe would not treat me so kindly, but Eryr was adamant. My presence could affect the fate of the Children of Anu, as they call themselves. I am not the first to fall from the sky, speaking a strange tongue.

Have they seen my pilot? Is Mallard still alive, as Merlin had implied? I asked after him, but they did not know his name. They only knew of a tyrant in the east, but they would not speak his name in Partholon's hall other than by kenning: Speaks-with-Thunder, they called him. The same title Merlin had used. Yet how can that be Harry? The last time I saw him, he had a bullet in his neck.

I was dismissed and left to mull on these mysteries alone. We are due to leave later today. Eryr and Partholon let me prepare for the next stage of my journey while they held private council.

So I sit here, writing down all I have experienced so far, from crossing the Void to this very moment in my beehive cell – a small but comfortable dwelling that looks out over the enclosure. I gaze up at the clouds, a battle of lead and silver – and I wonder … Do I have the makings of a windsmith as they say I have? What powers, then, do I possess? I can no more conjure 'gramarye' as make the dead dance. Merlin comes and goes as he chooses, not at my bidding. Any skills I have, of surveying and engineering, seem useless here.

Yet I feel as though all of my life I have been travelling to this place. A dream of it has sustained me through my life – and now I have arrived.

6

The Caer of Cernunnos

'Farewell, Isambard. May you find your source. Blessings of Fintan be upon you. Wisdom of the hazel guide you.'

Partholon stood at the gate of his caer as the sun straddled the heights of Mount Anu, the Bone Mountains' highest summit. Kerne wore about his shoulders a simple blue cloak, fastened by a silver salmon brooch and half covering his airman's overalls. Partholon nodded to one of his monks, who brought forward a hazel staff and presented it to the departing guest. A hole near the top, made by a witchknot, provided a perfect thumb rest. Kerne's hand fitted it well. It felt good to be holding such a stick again. The Y-shaped stang he had bought on his honeymoon on the Isle of Purbeck had been with him all of his married life. It was only when Maud allowed Archie to break it at Samhain that he had been finally released, as though his soul had been tied up in it in some way. Kerne thought of the Long Man with his staves. Was the figure entwined somehow with his destiny as a windsmith?

'Thank you for your hospitality and generosity, Partholon. Like the salmon, I will not forget where I came from.'

Partholon smiled and nodded. 'Let destiny take its course.'

'Come,' said the Eagle Lord sharply, 'we must get you to Caer Cernunnos before nightfall.' Eryr hurried Kerne along, the eagle upon his shoulder growing restless. Hawk warriors escorted them down to the tethered canoe.

Eryr stepped into it while the Hawks held it steady. After the Eagle Lord had taken his place, Kerne was gestured to join him, face to face on rich cushions.

The Hawk Warriors jumped in, the rope was untied and they pushed out into the fast-flowing current. The paddles dipped and plashed in the low winter sunlight, water dripping from them like quicksilver.

Kerne, sitting backwards, watched the Caer of Fintan recede, the tiny figures of the monks and nuns diminishing, until only the chalk figure of the salmon god was visible. Then even that was gone as they followed the windings of the river. Sheer cliffs towered above them once more, blocking out the sun.

Eryr looked hard at Kerne. 'Do not expect such pleasant treatment at the house of Bron. These are dangerous times.'

Kerne looked back at the stern visage of the Eagle Lord, wondering whether he detected a warning or a threat in his voice.

'I have come from a war, Eryr.'

'Let us hope you have not brought it with you.'

Silently, the cowled Hawk Warriors paddled on between the shadow-clad cliffs. High above the dying sun gilded the tree-lined edges, but a chill descended over the darkening valley. Kerne wrapped his cloak tighter about his shoulders.

They continued along the dark gorge in grim silence and Kerne was relieved when the cliffs widened out into green hills again and they passed beneath the chalk figure of an eagle.

'Caer Ewilod – impenetrable to all except anruths and windsmiths,' declaimed Eryr. Towering from lofty crags erupting from the grassy riverbank, the hill fort commanded a view of the valley. 'The birdless may not enter.'

Kerne wished Merlin would make an appearance, just to stop the talk of the Eagle Lord, who obviously distrusted him. But the falcon was nowhere to be seen. Some guide he turned out to be! Merlin did not seem like the bird allies Eryr talked of. The eagle on the Master of Ewilod's shoulder was not as opinionated for a start: it just looked at Kerne with a cold scorn.

The canoe came to halt at a rock jutting out into the river like a beak. More Hawks greeted their lord. Eryr alighted, and climbed up the rock-cut steps before turning.

'Farewell, skyman. May the Stag give you the welcome that you deserve.'

Eryr's eagle let out a piercing cry and took wing, flying up to the unscaleable buttress of Caer Ewilod. The Eagle Lord turned in his long grey robe and disappeared into the folds of the cliff-face.

And so, escorted by the taciturn Hawkmen, Kerne was taken further downriver towards the fortress of Cernunnos in the deepening gloom.

The words of Eryr preyed upon him as they journeyed swiftly along the windings of the Da'anu. Why was the Eagle Lord so hostile? Perhaps it was just in his nature and Kerne was reading too much into his contemptuous manner.

The current swept them quickly to their destination. Suddenly Caer Cernunnos came into view, its battlements lit by torches in the twilight. Carved out of the chalk, a giant antlered figure glared down from the heights – a horned man sitting cross-legged, holding a torc in one hand, a ram-headed serpent in the other. Kerne had seen that figure somewhere before, if only he could remember …

Stern-looking warriors guarded the landing area below the caer, dressed in leather armour and wearing horned helmets that covered their eyes, nose and cheekbones. They challenged the vessel and the Hawks replied, 'We have a special guest for the Stag Chief, sent by his brothers of the Salmon and Eagle.'

The Stag Warriors lowered their spears and allowed them to land. The canoe slid on to the gravel bank. The Hawks leapt out and pulled it ashore, bidding their passenger alight.

Kerne stepped out. He leant upon the smooth staff of hazel Partholon had given him. It gave him strength.

The Stag Warriors received the guest, and the Hawk Warriors pushed out into the river and headed back towards their caer, making haste to arrive before nightfall.

Kerne was escorted up the steep path, past the long gouged curves of the chalk figure, towards the hill fort silhouetted in the quickening dusk.

Ahead, between the pallisaded ramparts, were the gates of the hill fort – large, wooden and formidable. Torches blazed from the battlements where warriors kept sentinel, their long spears glinting in the sallow light. Crude banners flapped in the breeze that heralded night.

A challenge was bellowed out to Kerne. At first the tongue seemed incomprehensible, but as the question was repeated his ears adjusted to understand.

'What is your name, stranger, and your business at this fey hour?' barked a dark-eyed, broad-shouldered man in a wolf-fur cloak.

There was an awkward silence. What century was this? What world?

'Quickly, answer him! He is not one to be kept waiting!' hissed the guard to his right.

'I am Isambard Kerne, officer of the Royal Flying Corps, British Expeditionary Force of His Majesty's Government.' The words seemed incongruous as he spoke them, and Kerne felt faintly ridiculous in his bedraggled uniform. He tried to muster some dignity, but he was exhausted and aware of the ghosts at his back. He did not want to have to spend a night on those hills. 'I have … lost my pilot and aircraft.'

There was dumb-founded silence from the battlement. Torches gutted. Flags snapped in the breeze. Men pulled cloaks about them.

'Charioteer. Say "charioteer" and "chariot"!' whispered Merlin, the voice inside his head. Kerne looked up, but could not see the falcon in the dusk.

The warriors surely wondered why he turned his head to the side. Could they see a bird in the gloom? Did they think him mad?

'… my charioteer and chariot.'

'Who is your chief?'

Chief? Kerne had to think quickly.

'King George of Great Britain.'

'I do not know your tribe or chieftain. What business have you coming down the ghost road at night-break?'

Kerne needed no prompting this time. His body knew all too well what it needed. 'I request food and shelter for the night. As you can see, I am injured and need rest.' He leaned heavily on his staff, not exaggerating the throbbing pain, made worse by the cold. Whatever Partholon had put on his ankle was starting to wear off. 'The welcome I received at Caer Fintan was more hospitable.' Kerne jerked his head to the salmon-brooch, which glinted in the torchlight, and the guards recognised it.

The scaled wolf warrior grunted. Their laws of hospitality could not be denied. 'Open the gates,' he roared.

The heavy timbers were drawn back and the crude gates pulled open. Silhouetted in the doorway were three warriors, cloaked and hooded against the night chill. They wielded long leaf-shaped spears.

Kerne approached. 'Thank you! I thought you were never going to let me in.' He waved his staff at the wolf-cloaked guard above, but the gesture was misinterpreted and it was knocked out of his hands. Kerne exclaimed in surprise, but before he could explain another guard lashed out with his spear, knocking Kerne to the ground with a sharp blow to the head. Shadows engulfed his vision and he blacked out.

Kerne awoke in a dark place to find himself bound. His wrists and ankles were tied together with tough gut that bit into his skin. His vision was blurred at first, his head throbbing from the crack of the guard's spear against his skull. Tenderly he tested the place where it had struck. It was caked with blood but felt no worse than a bruise.

As his sight cleared, Kerne saw that he was in a round wattle-and-daub hut with a heavy door and a low thatched roof through which smoke was filtering. Before him a small fire flickered in a fire pit, where a wooden bowl of stew had been placed on a warm stone. By it was a clay beaker of water. His throat tasted of ashes and dust. Kerne reached for the beaker with a shaking hand and gulped greedily. Feeling a little more clear-headed, he sat up and huddled by the fire to wolf down the broth. A stinking fur had been thrown over him, but still the chill seeped into his bones. The stew – rabbit, he hoped – started to thaw him out as he licked the bowl empty. He shuddered uncontrollably as the warmth crept through his limbs.

Outside he could hear sounds of excited talk. Shadows passed the hut, visible through the cracks of the heavy door.

Was his fate being decided? What would they do to him? The airman checked his body – all of his belongings were gone, all of those attached to the Sam Browne belt at least. They'd even stripped off his boots, presumably to stop him escaping on the snow barefoot if he managed to force open the door. All that was left was the notebook and pencil in the breast pocket of his overalls. Kerne teased out the notebook with his fingertips and flicked it open. He scanned the strange sigils he had drawn in the cave. The crude marks flickered in the firelight, reminding him of his vision of them in the Void. He intuited that if only he could remember how they had sounded they might, somehow, be able to help him. Yet his head was dulled with pain and no sounds came.

Instead, he began reading what he had written describing his arrival in this strange world, from his time in limbo until his time at the House of Partholon, whose gentle sanctuary seemed so far away now. Its chief had expressed concern to Eryr about how he might be treated, and Eryr himself had warned him that his welcome would not be as warm, but he hadn't expected this ...

He took comfort in his journal. It was his touchstone. While he could continue to write in it he could somehow make sense of things. It would keep him sane. Yet it had a practical purpose also. Perhaps, he hoped, it could be used as evidence – if he ever made it home – against charges of desertion, punishable by court martial and execution. He was doomed in either world, it seemed, yet what this one was remained a mystery. Merlin had described it as a 'Shadow World'. And certainly his fate looked very dark indeed, right now. It seemed as though he had been captured by some primitive tribe, perhaps freedom fighters in the Balkans ... But who was he fooling?

When he cast an antiquarian eye around his immediate surroundings, remembering what he'd seen outside, it all looked like the dark ages of prehistory brought to life. There was no denying it. The barrows were certainly Bronze Age, but the hill fort could be from the Iron Age ... Yet Kerne was the most obvious anachronism. And what of his feathered guide? Where was Merlin now? Had he been a product of a concussed mind? Perhaps the whole of the last nine days had been brought on by the crash of the Breguet ... Maybe he was in a fever somewhere, hallucinating the whole thing. And yet ... his bonds seemed real enough, as did the throbbing pain in his leg.

His body ached from head to toe, but now an inexorable weariness came over him as his meal digested and the journey down the mountain caught up with him. The small fire burnt low until only the embers glowed. The effects of the stew, fatigue and his head injury made him fade into unconsciousness once more ...

The airman was awoken by a bucket of icy water thrown over him. It shocked him to try to stand, but he crumpled because he was still bound. The gut had made raw weals on his wrists and ankles. His head throbbed from where he had been struck. Two guards in fur cloaks stood in the hut, the open doorway behind them, the sharp daylight making him squint.

'Blast you!' Kerne cried, spitting into the fire pit, which was hissing from the deluge. With his tied hands he did his best to wipe the water and sleep from his face.

'Come,' one of the warriors grunted. The man had a scar down his left cheek and his face was painted with deep blue spirals. The other, a younger man, beardless, a white band of paint across his eyes, a wolf-teeth necklace about his neck, his cloak smelling of piss and campfires, helped Kerne to his feet and the two of them frogmarched him out into the stark light.

It was a clear winter's day, the sky a deep blue. From the snow-covered roofs of the roundhouses came tendrils of smoke. The compound of the hill fort was slowly coming to life – chickens clucking, thick-furred dogs chasing each other, red-cheeked raggedy children playing at warriors. Fierce-looking wild-haired women stood in the doorways of their huts, clutching babies to their bare breasts, staring at Kerne harshly, protecting their children from the stranger's glances. Bare-armed, dark-browed men, biceps spiralled with torcs or tattoos, busy mending weapons, fences, farming implements, stopped what they were doing and sized up the outsider in their midst. Their hands rested on the bronze swords or axes at their belts.

Kerne was half dragged through the snow, his legs still bound, and his feet bare, white with pain. The glare of the snow was blinding. His head swam in disorientation. Where was Merlin? Had the falcon brought him to his doom? Perhaps Eryr had been right. He was no windsmith. He was just out of his depth.

The two warriors led him to the largest roundhouse in the centre of the hill enclosure. Two more woaded warriors guarded the entrance with long spears. They opened the heavy doors and Kerne was dragged inside.

Along a short dark corridor they came to an open space centred with a large fire pit surrounded by fur-lined wooden benches. Figures reclined upon them in the shadows. Kerne was placed before them in the shaft of light coming down from the smoke hole. His escorts stood either side of him to make sure he did not stray. He fell to his knees as his ankle gave way. Was this to be a trial? His execution day?

There was an uncomfortable silence as Kerne was scrutinised by unseen eyes. In his airman's overalls, with his clipped hair and bare feet, he must have looked a strange sight.

'A fine welcome for a stranger in need,' Kerne commented.

'Silence, dog!' One of the warriors behind him, Scar-Face, butted him with the end of his spear in the small of his back. The breath went out of him and he fell to one side.

'Forgive our hospitality, stranger,' said a deep voice in the darkness. 'These are difficult times. We have to be careful.'

Out of the shadows, a mighty-framed man leaned forward, black beard plaited, bone-beaded and streaked with grey, neck encompassed by a thick golden torc tipped by stags facing one another. His eyes were steel grey and belied the mock politeness of his words. This was not a man to gainsay. Everything about him cried leader – his poise, his voice and the accoutrements of his office. A broadsword was balanced over his knees. At his feet two great wolfhounds panted, teeth bared at the stranger, growling low as he stroked their heads. To his left a woman sat, equally as regal – red-haired and magnificent, with cool eyes and cheekbones like a lioness. To his right, another warrior full of ire and vigour – and Isambard recognised him as the man at the gate. He was the spit and image of the chieftain, but half his age: only one plait in his jet beard, secured with an amber bead; a thinner torc about his muscled neck; a plaid of red half covered a glistening chest, becoming a kilt at his waist, where a bronze sword hung in its scabbard. Other relatives, aides and allies sat around the fire-circle – a hundred of them, Kerne estimated, but the shadows made it difficult to be accurate.

'He came from the ghost hills, father,' shouted the warrior to the chieftain's right. 'He is not to be trusted! We should kill him now!'

'Perhaps you are right, Brak, but first we should find out all we can. Can you not see he wears the brooch of Fintan? He has Partholon's blessing.'

A one-eyed man stepped out of the shadows, small but with a strange air of power. His ancient face shone in the firelight, his one eye gleaming with intelligence. Around his hunched shoulders was draped a cloak of many feathers, and he used a gem-studded club as a walking stick, striking the ground with it to emphasise a point. 'Whatever he knows may help us against Speaks-with-Thunder.'

At the mention of the kenning, there was a hiss of fear and hate among the council. Women spat over their shoulders and warriors loosened their swords in their scabbards.

The one-eyed man approached Kerne warily, but with fascination. Then he turned and gestured to the chieftain with his bejewelled club. 'This is Bron, mighty chief of the Stag tribe, battle reaver, ring-giver, oak of his people! You sit within his hall, within the Caer of Cernunnos. And I am Ogmios. Speak your name, stranger. Tell us your tribe, your ancestors and your passage.'

'I am Isambard Kerne, officer of the Royal Flying Corps, British Expeditionary Force. My ancestors were … Irish and Welsh. My passage … is to the Forbidden Kingdom.'

At this there was a collective gasp.

Brak stood up, brandishing his sword. 'I told you he was a demon!' He lunged forward, ready to administer the coup de grâce to the prone airman, but his father, rising with surprising swiftness, checked the blow. With a massive bear-like grip he held back his son's sword arm.

'There will be no murder of guests under my roof! Sheathe your sword, son. There will be plenty of time for Ravengiver to do its work.'

Brak relented, sheathed his black-hilted sword and, shrugging off his father's grip, sat back down, staring daggers at the outlander.

Bron towered over Kerne, a figure from another age. His hands rested on his broadsword gleaming in the half-light.

'Kerne … Kerne … Stranger, you have a lucky name. No harm will come to you if you are protected by the Antlered One.'

In the flickering light Brigantia eyed him with a Sphinx-like expression as the chief sat back in his throne.

Kerne tried to comprehend what Bron had meant, but the one-eyed man continued the questioning, more intrigued than ever: 'So, Blessed-of-Cernunnos, why do you seek the Forbidden Kingdom?'

Why indeed? Was he mad? Because of something a little bird told him? He had to think quickly.

'I have business with Taranis.'

There was a sharp silence and looks of dread and terror flickered across the faces of the gathered.

'Do not mention that cursed name here!' warned Ogmios, making a gesture of appeasement and muttering an incantation. 'Your breath gives him power. Is he your ally?'

'He was … once.'

'You see!' spat Brak, hands held wide in appeal.

'But now it seems he is my enemy. And it looks like it's up to me to deal with him.'

Brak and his warriors laughed at this. 'You? Deal with Speaks-with-Thunder? Pah! I've seen more strength in a suckling babe!'

'What makes you think you can deal with this tyrant who has afflicted our lands, harried our people, raided our cattle?' asked Ogmios.

'I came from the same place as him – the … sky.'

Ogmios went to a bronze chest and pulled out Kerne's Sam Browne belt. 'It is true he has the same weapons and talismans that we have seen upon Speaks-with-Thunder,' he said to the council. Carefully he passed them to the Stag Chief, who looked at them with curiosity. Bron didn't seem impressed by the workmanship of the belt and item-by-item he scattered the contents of it upon the floor before Kerne.

'Your talismans have no power here it seems, skyman,' observed Ogmios.

But then Bron managed to unbutton the revolver and slid it from its holster. He held it gingerly but with deep fascination. 'What manner of weapon is this? It has no edge to it.' The Stag Chief waved it about, holding it first by the barrel like an axe, then by the handle.

As he pointed it in Kerne's direction the airman panicked. 'Woah, woah! Careful where you point that, my lord!'

Bron was interested in the effect the weapon had on his captive. It seemed to terrify him. His finger slipped on to the trigger and before Kerne could stop him he had pulled it by accident. There was a click. Kerne shut his eyes and waited for the report. Silence. Kerne squinted. He was still alive, and he realised with a huge relief that the barrel was empty. He had not loaded it – what need had he on a surveillance mission? Kerne collapsed in nervous laughter.

Bron tossed the Webley at his feet. 'Your puny weapon has no power here, Kerne. How do you propose to defeat Speaks-with-Thunder when our best warriors have not done so? If it wasn't for the protection of these hills we would have fallen long ago. Every raiding season they reach a little further upriver. It is only a matter of time before they reach our caer – the Grey Raiders and Demon-riders.'

'Would you allow me to show you how, my lord?'

Bron looked at Ogmios, who frowned, then slowly nodded.

Kerne reached over slowly for the Webley and asked for the box of bullets. It wasn't easy with his wrists tied, but he shook open the carton and clicked open the breech, then he dropped one of the bullets in. With a flick of his wrist he shut the barrel, and then he held it at arm's length with both hands, bracing himself for the 'mulekick', as Mallard called it – the recoil had nearly dislocated his shoulder the first time he had fired a pistol in target practice. The barrel was pointed at Bron, who looked at it with fascination, making a point of showing no fear before his tribe. His son was not so complacent; he gritted his teeth and clenched his sword. Ogmios thumped his club on the ground and chanted.

As they all watched, Kerne raised the weapon to the smoke hole and fired. The deafening report echoed across the valley. Many in the hut cowered and dived for cover, expecting the sky to fall in. Bron stood up to defend his family, but even his eyes were wide with terror.

'*This*. This is how I am going to defeat Taranis. Fight thunder with thunder.' Kerne's hands were trembling. He lowered the smoking gun, a tang of cordite in the air.

The sound had been deafening and it took a moment for everyone's hearing to adjust.

Bron was the first to gather his wits.

'Kerne – you have more power than it would at first appear … Forgive me for misjudging you … If we have angered you, then let us make amends. Guards, release him from his bonds.'

The two warrior escorts cut Kerne's ties. He cried out when they slit the gut around his ankles. He was allowed to put his belt back on and collect up his belongings. His hands shook as he refilled the pouches on his belt, carefully replacing the cartridges in the box – he had nineteen left.

'You are wounded. Let my windsmith give you medicine' – Bron gestured to Ogmios – 'and all that you require. You shall not lack in my caer. No one leaves Bron's hall empty-bellied. Eat and drink your fill. Bring mead and boar-meat! You are our honoured guest. Stay with us until snowmelt, three moons from now. No one can travel the valley in the snow, and the raiding parties will not begin again until the spring thaw – Cernunnos protect us. You have time to recover and perhaps learn a little about us. My daughter, Bronwen, will see to your needs.'

From out of the shadows stepped a lissom, flame-haired beauty in a shapely woollen dress of blue. She was the first gentle face Kerne had beheld in this harsh land.

With Bronwen and Ogmios, Kerne was escorted from the hall to Ogmios's medicine lodge; a round dwelling like the one he had been imprisoned in, but filled with drying herbs and arcane artefacts. He was made comfortable upon a bed of moss while the one-eyed shaman tended to his head wound. He ordered Bronwen to fetch a jar of pungent ointment and then to clean the wound upon Kerne's leg with a cloth. The maiden was nervous in Kerne's presence at first and her hand shook. Kerne tried to reassure her, but when he spoke she flinched, nervous as a deer.

'That'll be all for now, Bronwen,' said the old windsmith.

With relief the chief's daughter got up to leave. She glanced back through her fiery tresses, and then was gone.

Kerne thought how unlike her brother she was, how fair – but compared with her mother she was as spring to summer, her beauty not yet in full bloom. His reverie was broken when Ogmios applied the unguent with quick dabs. Kerne gritted his teeth. At first it stung, then it soothed.

'Rest now, bard. We have much to talk about, you and I.'

7

The Stone Lodge

The Journal of Isambard Kerne
Valley of the Chalk Folk, Day 3

I sit in Ogmios's hut writing this by the guttering light of a rank-smelling tallow candle. It is evening now, and the sounds of the Stag tribe have dwindled with the encroaching night, as if darkness deserves respect. With nightfall much activity within the caer ceases. All the inhabitants can do is gather by the hearth fires in their huts and eat, drink, talk, sing or sleep. An occasional burst of laughter carries in the still night air, or the strains of a whistle; otherwise there is a deep blanket of peace over the hill fort, a peace unlike any I encountered in my former life. A peace that encourages reflection, contentment and dreams.

I lie upon a fur-covered bed, with my blue cloak about my shoulders; rested, fed, and clean. My host is out – his services needed elsewhere no doubt – so I take this opportunity to catch up with my journal and savour this strange place I find myself in.

The hut of the magician is dark until one's eyes grow accustomed to its perpetual twilight – then details begin to emerge. It is a roundhouse, typical of any from the Neolithic to the Iron Age period from the outside, with a cone-shaped thatched roof, low eaves, lime-washed wattle-and-daub walls, one entrance and no smoke hole. The smoke from the central fire pit rises through the thatching, leaving a constant thick atmosphere, so one learns to stay low where the air is fresher and the eyes sting less. Bunches of herbs hang side by side with unrecognisable carcasses curing in the smoke. Charms of feather, grass and bone are attached to the inside of the wooden lintel and in each section of the hut, which seems to be divided into eight directions: each with a significance I have yet to ascertain. It's as though Ogmios has recreated within his living space a map of the universe as he sees it, a vast wheel at whose hub the fire burns, the fire that must never be left to extinguish itself, so he has instructed me.

The doorway, covered by a hide flap, faces east, so that the morning sun floods in, illuminating the stone altar opposite. In the northern section is the crude couch upon which I lie. Opposite that is Ogmios's sleeping 'quarters' – another crude couch but with a hide drape to block out the light. Either side of the doorway are stores: shelves of jars with pungent contents, unlabelled – a primitive apothecary, which only Ogmios can use. Flanking the altar hang Ogmios's ritual regalia: the feathered mantle of office, his gem-studded club, special necklaces, talismans, a skin drum, a gourd-shaped rattle, fetishes – all glistening in the flickering light of candle and fire. Around the fire pit is a circle of stones – 'ancestor stones', my host calls them – which talk when they heat up and 'speak' to him. Guarding the central hearth and holding up the roof are four square pillars blackened with smoke. Their edges are rutted with deep grooves, as if someone has been practising sword fighting on them. Yet, somehow, I cannot believe that: this is a true sanctuary.

The only anomaly is my presence.

Hanging over this bunk is my Sam Browne belt with its laden holster. Next to it is my leather flying helmet, its goggles reflecting the flames. My torn overalls hang up drying, having been washed under Bronwen's instructions – bless her – and my officer boots lie neatly side by side, having been scraped clean of mud and smeared with a crude dubbing mixture I managed to procure of animal fat and charcoal. I feel surprisingly at home, which is just as well. While I have been convalescing I have hardly been out of the hut. It's a wonder I haven't developed cabin fever. There is a strange atmosphere in here – the very air seems alive. Ogmios's presence is dogged by flurries of wind wherever he goes …

He has a barn-owl bird-ally called Blodeuwedd, who sits in the corner of the hut on a perch, white-feathered, spectral, scrutinising me with unfathomable eyes.

I wonder what has happened to Merlin, and why he continually abandons me. Did he know of the reception I would receive at Caer Cernunnos? If so, why didn't he warn me? Some bird-ally he's turned out to be!

It has taken a week for my leg to recover and for me to regain my full strength after the nightmare of the abyss. My head and back are still bruised, but it is more the wound to my pride that has taken longer to heal. I was indignant from the way I had been treated upon my arrival at Caer Cernunnos – worlds apart from the welcome at Partholon's hall – but I am beginning to understand why this was.

The valley of the Chalk Folk is under threat from Taranis, he who Speaks-with-Thunder – my erstwhile pilot, apparently. How Mallard could have become such a notorious tyrant so quickly is difficult to believe or understand – though Mad Duck always had rather aggressive tendencies, it has to be said. He had looked forward to the start of the war as thought it was the Glorious Twelfth. Yet the Chalk Folk's fear seems real enough. Ogmios said they have been raided in previous years and fear more attacks are to come. 'Previous years' … Surely that rules out Mallard, since he only arrived nine days before me? I wish I could explain that to them. But in this state of terror I am effectively under house arrest. I am forbidden by Ogmios from leaving the hut, though I can sit in the doorway if I want some fresh air. It is not the most pleasant smelling of prisons, although it has a curious charm.

Over the last week I have been at the mercy of Ogmios 'Sun Face' – as I discovered his epithet to be, presumably because the sun has one eye, yet perhaps because this particular Nestor has a curious light gleaming in his one good eye, and a burning intelligence. His piercing blue orb is often fixed on me, as if he is trying to work out the puzzle I represent. He senses something 'other' about me. He's fascinated by my presence – and I with him, it has to be said. Although short in stature, Ogmios has an air of power that belies his years. But most impressive of all is his cranium, which is formed like that of a Greek philosopher, a high noble dome, weathered and prone to furrowing. When he's deep in thought, Ogmios absent-mindedly chews one of the three grey braids that emerge from the crown of his otherwise bald head and hang in tangled skeins to the small of his back.

As I gaze at the shadows cast by the perpetually burning fire upon the uneven walls of the hut, questions arise in my mind. What kind of place is this? Who are these people? Do they know they are dead? What does it feel like? Could they die a second time? Could I die here, and what would happen to me? I feel that if anyone knew, wise-eyed Ogmios would. He's an old man by Iron Age standards – at least seventy, I would say – but not so unusual here, it seems. So many questions, yet Ogmios remains tight-lipped. My questions made him furious, as if I talked of taboo things. First I had to answer his. Who was I? Where did I come from? Who were my blood-parents? My ancestors? What was my craft? Did I have a wife and children? The last question Bronwen was especially interested in – she came twice a day to cleanse and reapply the ointment on my leg and head. She feigned shyness, but I could tell she was curious. And she was a nurse not to be gainsaid. I had to comply with her instructions to the letter, or face her wrath. I had not to move or exert myself in any way. Therefore, I have happily convalesced, in a simple woollen tunic, on my wooden couch covered with furs.

Bronwen was as tender as Ogmios was abrasive. I watched her head of russet curls shining in the firelight as she performed her duties. She is young, with the translucent skin of youth, not weathered yet by wind or sun like so many of the other tribeswomen. I have tried to fathom her age. Perhaps turning twenty – only half my age. Too young for me, by far, but I appreciated a woman's touch. I miss Maud, and my heart sicken when I think of how I made her let me go. I thought I was dead before Merlin told me otherwise. 'Till death do us part' … Yet if I live on, even in the land of the dead, then does our marriage?

Who am I kidding? I had to let her go. There's no point clinging on to the past. We are worlds apart. I had to let her lead her own normal healthy life. She deserves to find happiness. And yet …

I long to return home, to hold her one more time. But the likelihood of that seems vastly remote. I am lost in another world, with no way back.

I asked Ogmios where we are, and, to my surprise, he drew a map of the world – but not the world I knew. He rendered a circle in the ash with his staff then quartered it diagonally. He approximated a landmass covering all four quarters. He then spoke the quarters' names, starting in the east with HyperEurus, then HyperNotus to the south, HyperZephyrus in the west, and to the north HyperBorea. I had heard of the last one, I told him excitedly. The Land Beyond the North Wind – what the ancients called Britain! Ogmios nodded, pointing again to HyperEurus, then gesturing around us. So, this was HyperEurus. I was in a land beyond the east wind ... No wonder it's so bloody cold! Were the mountains the Carpathians or the Urals? Ogmios shook his head. 'The Bone Mountains,' he stated. In the right-hand quarter he drew a jagged line of mountains. In the centre towered its summit, Mount Anu, or the 'White Mother', as it's also known as. From that mountain range snaked a wavy line – the river, which he called 'Da'anu'. Between its loops and folds he drew thirteen small circles. The one nearest to the mountains he told me was Caer Fintan: salmon. The next was Caer Ewilod, eagle, on the other side of the valley, high and mighty on its clifftop. Caer Cernunnos was third. Next in order, going downriver, were: bear, wolf, deer, hound, goat, rooster, bull, ram, horse and, finally, man. Thirteen tribes, each with its own totem carved into the hillside of its rath. At the end of the valley of the hill tribes the river emptied into a vast lake shaped like an almond – Lake Mandorla. When I asked where the Forbidden Kingdom was, Ogmios jabbed at its other shore, where he drew another line of hills. Beyond them he indicated a vast unknown region.

This is where Speaks-with-Thunder dwells – the one Merlin said I must confront. The enemy the Chalk Folk – or the 'Children of Anu', as Ogmios calls his people – are terrified of. Are these people the Tuatha De Danann of Irish legend, the Lordly Ones who retreated to the Hollow Hills? How could that be?

Where did our world end and theirs begin?

I asked if they believe their world ended at the edge of the horizon. I could not blame them for thinking the Earth flat, since their culture originated in an age before Columbus.

Ogmios thought for a moment, then did a remarkable thing: he drew circles adjoining the one representing the Earth he knew. Circle after circle, overlapping and linked to this world, in a chain. Was he suggesting more than one Earth?

He nodded.

Then he messed up the ash and drew another diagram. I was still reeling from what he had implied ... but Ogmios insisted I pay attention to the next lesson. He drew three circles, one on top of the other, overlapping again. He described an upper world, a middle world and a lower world. The upper world was the realm of the gods, elders and greater spirits. The lower world belonged to the animal spirits and the ancestors. The middle world was all around us, he gestured. Then on to it he added circle after circle. There were many other worlds, I think he was saying – but the upper and under worlds were common to all. They could be reached in certain threshold places like lakes, springs, caves, mountains or sacred trees. Or through ceremony and prayer. Ogmios showed me his altar, gesturing above and below, as if to say he could communicate with the upper and lower worlds here.

The altar is a simple stone slab, laid with offerings – feathers, fangs, a tallow candle, incense, a beaker of milk, oatcakes – to a stone head, glittering with quartz. Three spirals, with bright crystals in their centre, adorn its cheeks and brow. Ogmios mutters prayers to the head, and its response is channelled through him. Then he performs his prophecies for the tribe – elaborate narratives peppered with dance and chant.

When he performed a ceremony Ogmios wore a cloak of feathers called a tugen and wielded his gem-studded club; I noticed it contained plugs of different kinds of wood. The old windsmith is as lean and taut as a drum skin, and as strong as seasoned timber. Whether it is an act of will that keeps him so, or a healthy discipline of diet and exercise – for he still chops his own wood and fetches his own water from the well – it is hard to say. He was rigorous in his ministrations and reminded me of my father, who had his own rituals.

I can still see Da, at Rose Cottage in Blackwardine: bathing before the fire in the old tin tub, washed down by Mam with no shame before us, after a hard day's graft; then changing into a clean vest, cardigan and slippers to smoke his pipe in his favourite chair, or read the paper to us, as Archie and I played at his feet, nervous not to disturb him – for though his temper was fierce we were keen to be near him, to imbibe his masculine energy, so different from Mam's. She was the nurturer, always there with a snack or a smack out of tenderness or anxiety for us; earthy and straightforward. She would listen to Da's pontifications with a wry smile. Any thoughts or opinions of her own she kept to herself – her life lived in service to us, her men, as she deemed us all. If she embodied wisdom, Da was a man of wit; intensely thoughtful, with always an opinion ready about politics, the state of the nation, or the plight of the workers. He wanted us to do well. He wanted us to better the Kerne lot. We had come from the land, and we should never lose touch with it – but there was no denying our father's ambition for us.

How I miss him now. I wished I could have said goodbye to him, and my sweet mother. There *was* a sense of finality the last time I saw them, as I left for training, but we all hoped I would return safe and soon after 'seeing some action', as Archie had put it. Nobody then realised that it would become the 'Great War', as Merlin called it. If I did meet my fate in the skies above Mons, perhaps I have been given a second chance, a chance to rewrite my ending.

One day, Ogmios came in to discover me writing in this journal. I instinctively went to cover it up – some deep-seated need for privacy created by having a prying brother!

The windsmith was curious, the firelight glinting in his one good eye. He wanted to know what I was doing. I tried to explain, but it left him completely baffled. So I showed him. He watched with fascination as I wrote in the journal. I told him I was 'writing'. 'What is that? he asked. The word was unfamiliar to him. This is a pre-literate culture, akin to the Bronze Age or Early Iron Age. The oral tradition must be prevalent. The Celts preserved all of their knowledge by memory; none of it was written down. I tried to explain as best I could what I was doing – recording my thoughts on the page, recording things that have happened. A form of storytelling, I offered by way of an analogy. Whom was I telling the stories to? Myself, I answered, feeling a little self-conscious. Perhaps it is pointless keeping a journal here. No one else is going to be able to read it. But perhaps that's an advantage. It helps me to order my thoughts, reflect on events and express secret opinions. I have become so used to recording my research and observations in a journal over the years that I think I would go mad without it. Not to be able to write would be like having a scratch I could not itch.

I read out a paragraph at random, following the sentence with my finger.

Ogmios twigged immediately – the symbols on the paper

were meant to represent sound. He placed a finger against the side of his other hand and uttered a guttural sound that to my ears sounded like 'beeth'. Then he placed two fingers against his hand and uttered another word, sounding like 'loose'. Then three fingers and 'noon'. There were other 'woodwords', as he called them, which he would not divulge. He said this was the secret language of the windsmiths – the 'dark speech' – which only the initiated could understand and use. He showed me the notches on the pillars, and, looking closely at the blackened grain, I could that the marks resembled the signs Ogmios had been making with his hand. Yet they seemed to extend – up to five marks either on the left, right, crossing or going diagonally across a central stem. I found it difficult to make them out in the gloom of the lodge, yet they seemed to resemble something I had seen before ...

So, I realised with growing excitement, they do have a rudimentary alphabet – perhaps a mnemonic shorthand for key concepts linked by a runic symbol.

Then, in a flash, I remembered what I had seen in the Void. I flicked through my notebook to the pages where I had scrawled down the sigils while they were fresh in my mind. Excitedly, I showed them to Ogmios. He looked at them with deep curiosity, recognising many of them and pointing to where the same ones were notched on the post, yet there were five he did not recognise. Turning the notebook this way and that, he scratched his white stubble and chewed one of his grey braids. These sigils were more elaborate than the post glyphs: one was curled like a question mark or a fern shoot; the next was a small grid of nine squares; another a diamond lozenge; the other two being crosses like 'X's – one to the side of the central line, the other intersected by it.

Frustrated, Ogmios jabbed his finger at one and nodded to me to make its sound. I shook my head. Growing impatient, he told me to meditate upon them, to release their sound. On scraps of leaves they were useless, he said.

He knocked my notebook dismissively and it fell open at the page with the pale flower I had picked from the cave behind the waterfall. A little embarrassed, I went to close the book, but the windsmith stopped me.

'You have a flower of life,' he gasped.

'You know of these?' I asked.

'Yes – they grow in the White Mother's Womb, behind Anu's Veil.'

I realised he was referred to the waterfall. 'You have been there?'

'Once, when I was younger and more agile. It is part of the windsmith's initiation. The flowers are highly prized, for each can restore life to one person. It is the greatest medicine we have. Being greedy, I plucked more than one and lost my eye and nearly my life coming back. It was only Blodeuwedd who saved me: she appeared then and guided me back. Part of the rite of passage is to find one's bird-ally. It is taboo for any but windsmiths to pierce Anu's Veil. Many have died trying to plunder the riches of the White Mother's Womb. You are fortunate to have survived. Partholon was right, it seems. You *do* have the makings of a windsmith.'

I have plucked a flower of life from behind Anu's Veil, I have a bird-ally, of sorts, and I've had a vision of a secret alphabet … Perhaps it is my destiny to fulfil the potential of my name.

Ogmios told me to look after the flower, for there would be a day when its magic would be needed.

I asked him how it could restore a life, and he told me you simply place it upon the tongue of the fallen and close their mouth.

I asked him if he had used his, but he would say no more.

He blew out the candle I had been writing by, and bade me lie down in his 'abaton'. I was to meditate upon the sigils I had gleaned in the abyss.

I was uncomfortable lying on Ogmios's bed, not least because of the musty stench, but I complied. My host was as short-tempered as my father and was not to be questioned in his own home.

Grunting, Ogmios lifted up a round heavy stone that sat on top of another. It had a hole in the middle and a wooden handle attached, so I surmised it was a quernstone. He ordered me to lie still and carefully placed it on top of my chest. The weight of it took my breath away at first, and I thought the magician meant to suffocate me with it. He thumped the stone, winding me further, and smiled his gap-toothed smile. 'Lie here,' he commanded, 'and do not move until you have inspiration.' He bade me dwell upon the sigils and left me to it, casting back the hide curtain so I was plunged into complete darkness.

It was a strange position to be in, left in the dark with a stone slab on my chest, in a village from the past in the middle of nowhere. But I was not going anywhere, certainly if Ogmios had anything to do with it. And so I tried my best to focus on the elusive sigils.

For how long I could not say, I meditated upon the symbols, seeking to articulate their sound. Nothing came. Whenever I tried to focus on them the gaping abyss threatened to swallow me again and I would recoil in horror, heart beating fast, covered in sweat. The stone seemed to become heavier and heavier, until I could hardly breathe. It was like my incarceration in the crystal tower. A terror overwhelmed me. I did not want to be trapped there again! Those demonic beings of fire swirled at the edges of my consciousness, threatening to strike, like wolves in the dark.

I screamed and pushed the stone off and reached to pull back the hide.

At first, I was disorientated. It was now night outside the hut. I staggered to the doorway to gulp the night air.

Ogmios stood there, his long clay pipe glowing in the dark, and scowled at me with his one eye. 'Call yourself a bard?' he lambasted me. 'You are not worthy of the name!'

It was true. Who was I fooling? I could tell no stories, sing no songs, play no harp. I had no windlass to open doorways. So how could I be a windsmith?

Exhausted from my ordeal, I guzzled down a jar of water and then collapsed on to my own couch. I slept under a cloud, overwhelmed by the penumbra of my problem in the darkness of the lodge.

I tossed in a fever, and the sigils screamed before me, mocking. Whenever I thought of them I was drawn back to that hellish limbo and did not want to go further. Fear stopped me. I was unable to speak the words of the dead. I was terrified I would not get out of there again.

I lay in bed throughout the next day, unable to move – the bardic ordeal had taken its toll. I lay half awake, vaguely aware of Bronwen's attentions. I felt the coolness of a cloth on my brow, the trickle of cold water down my throat, a soft hand, but little else. There was conversation around me and movement, but I perceived it as if through a fog of the senses.

I slept on for two more nights, then, on the third day, I awoke, refreshed, clear-headed. It was morning. Ogmios looked at me from across the fire, sucking on his pipe, unsurprised by my waking, as if he had been watching me for some time.

'Decided to join us again in this world, eh?'

He gave me a bowl of broth. I broke my fast – ravenous.

Ogmios informed me how long I had been in the fever. 'We thought we had lost you to Annwn ... I am sorry for forcing you to go back there. Perhaps it is best if you leave the sigils alone. The way of the windsmith is not for everyone to walk.'

At first I was devastated. I wanted to protest, to tell Ogmios that it was my destiny, Merlin had said so – that he needed to give me time ...

But perhaps he was right. How could I be a bard when I had no songs, no special words of power?

Ogmios busied himself with chores, ignoring me, and I sensed my presence was no longer welcome in his lodge. Sadly, I rose, finally able to put weight on my ankle, though I had lost a couple of pounds, despite the fattening diet of meaty broth and black rye bread. It was still tender, and I used my hazel stick to hobble about. Wrapping my blue cloak about me, I silently left the stuffy confines of Ogmios's lodge at last. I was glad to be able to take the sharp winter air and I set about exploring the caer of the Stag tribe.

The stark winter sun was blinding after the gloom of Ogmios's medicine lodge. There were patches of grass amidst the slushy snow. Snowmelt had begun and snowdrops were beginning to poke up through the soil. I was glad to see so familiar a flower. It made me feel not so far from home. I was shooed away from them by a red-faced milkmaid carrying pails of milk.

Dogs barked at me; children cried. It was not a good start, but I was out in the clean air again and I didn't care. The menfolk eyed me warily but let me run my tether. They knew I wasn't going far, with my ankle, this far upriver. The snow still blocked the main pass and the foothills were impassable too. I contented myself with a perambulation of the rath. If it was my prison, it was not an unpleasant one.

The majority of the roundhouses were situated within the

lee of the rampart, as were stables and coops, workshops and storerooms. A leather-aproned, bare-chested, blacksmith toiled in one, giving me a dark stare. He radiated power, and I could see why such mystery had grown up around smiths, the first alchemists. In nearby buildings were a tinsmith, a tanner hanging up his stinking skins, a leather-worker bradawling at a hide, a carpenter bodging on a pole-lathe. Industrious men, each with their role, their responsibility.

What is mine? To be a bard, as my name suggests? Yet I have no gift of tongues, it seems. All I can do is observe and record in this notebook, although for whom I write I cannot say. Perhaps for my own sanity.

At a loose end, I wandered to the other end of the caer where the womenfolk dominated. A group of chattering mothers spun wool on simple spindles, wove it on looms, dyed and knitted it – like the Fates themselves, in control of threads of destiny. They sized me up, clicking their tongues. I must have looked quite a sight, stubbly and bleary-eyed, in my woollen robe and the rank fur gripping around my shoulders. Hardly a catch, by any stretch of the imagination. All I could do was smile and wave politely, which made them burst out laughing, showing their black teeth.

Other women made pots – beautiful vases decorated with braided cord. Smaller children played with the spare lumps of clay, filthy and happy. The beakers were stacked carefully in a roundhouse. I wanted to inspect but was ushered away by a cross young women with a child on her hip.

The faces of the tribesmen and women seemed familiar, the dark-haired ones reminding me of my Welsh mother, the red-haired ones of my Da's side. This is as it should be if these people are truly my ancestors, yet the idea that I am with them now is astonishing. Are my long-dead or long-lost relatives here? Or even more recent ones? I have not recognised anyone I actually remember, but perhaps it's only a matter of time.

Filled with an overwhelming sense of déjà vu, I continued my perambulations about the hill fort, so like the many I have explored in my field-trips, yet this one was brimming with life. I passed Highland breeds of cattle and sheep kept in pens, some backed on to roundhouses to share their warmth. Ewes were beginning to drop their lambs with the coming of the first signs of spring. This turning of the wheel was marked by a ceremony I was allowed to witness a couple of days later in the main hall.

Each villager held an unlit candle. For this ceremony Ogmios stepped aside; this rite was sacred to the females of the tribe and was led by the Three Mothers, hooded and masked. The one-eyed windsmith sat with Bron, Brak, Bronwen and Brigantia – and he gestured for me to join them. I felt honoured. Brak's eyes burnt into me in the twilight. I had put on my uniform and tried to make myself look decent, although I wouldn't pass muster back on the parade ground in Blighty. The white cliffs of Dover seemed a very long way away.

White-robed women kindled a sacred fire and on a bed of rushes offered gifts of milk and corn dollies to a goddess they called 'Breed', the Bright Mother (Brighid, I imagine, whose name appears across Britain in places like Bridport, St Bride's Bay, Long Bredy, Little Bredy and the countless Bridewell Lanes). Nervous lambs were brought in by young shepherdesses and blessed with water from the secret spring issuing from the flanks of the hill fort, jealously guarded by the women for their mysteries.

Bronwen caught my eye across the circle. She was one of the maiden priestesses and looked more beautiful than ever, with her hair spiralling like sheaves of wheat, her face whitened with ash. Yet it was her mother whom I thought looked most magnificent of all, crowned and resplendent as the embodiment of Brighid, bringer of fertility to her tribe. She was honoured that night, and Bron took a back seat, proud of his queen.

Then I was ushered forward, to my astonishment and embarrassment, and commanded to drink from the cauldron brought forth. A dark heady concoction swirled inside. Bronwen offered me a wooden chalice filled with the liquid. I hesitated, but she smiled, so I took a sip, fought back the urge to cough and swallowed hard. A cheer went up, and the music began – drums and reedy pipes, small harps and bone-clickers. My head swirled as the cup was passed around. To my relief, everyone drank from it, even the children took a sip, but not the babes. The celebration went on late into the night. The centre circle became a dance floor where nimble maidens and lively lads jumped and wheeled, trying to outdo one another leaping over the fire.

It seemed everyone was expected to perform something. Suddenly I found all eyes were upon me. There was a hushed sniggering as they waited. Breaking into a nervous sweat, I tried to clear my throat. I was tongue-tied, but the cauldron brew seemed to loosen my tongue and at the moment when the awkward silence became unbearable I found myself declaiming Tennyson's 'The Charge of the Light Brigade', a poem I had learnt by rote at grammar school:

Half a league, half a league,
Half a league onward,
All in the valley of Death
    Rode the six hundred.
'Forward, the Light Brigade!
'Charge for the guns!' he said:
Into the valley of Death
    Rode the six hundred.

After I finished the poem, there was silence, the flames crackled in the hearth, and then Bron clapped, followed by the rest of the tribe, not rapturously – but I felt I had won their respect. Bronwen's eyes shone at me.

The poem had tapped into something universal. As I recited it I could see the faces of the Cernunnos tribe shining with understanding. Womenfolk held tightly to their warrior-men; old veterans gazed into the flames wistfully; young boys sat rigid with attention; mothers looked proudly at their sons. Although some of the references were alien to them, the hopeless situation and courage against all odds they could easily relate to. A bardic account of a battle is something all too familiar to them. The greatest honour is to be immortalised in such a poem for one's valour or generosity.

Ogmios nodded his approval, striking his club on the ground. Since my failure to bring back the runes, he had grown impatient and dismissive of me, so his response was especially welcome. Bron was impressed and tossed me a silver ring. Brigantia asked about the 'cannons'. I said they were like my Webley, but a lot bigger – the size of one of the beams. They looked aghast at this, imagining the deafening report of a pistol amplified tenfold.

My recited verse gained me more respect than anything else

I could have done. The tribe have a deep respect for the spoken word and for bardic memory. I was showered with compliments and given flagon after flagon of ale to drink, and was invited to share the mead bench with many there.

For me, the poem has other associations. I thought of the folly and waste of the Boer War, to be tragically repeated in the so-called Great War. I am one of the many who have ridden 'Into the jaws of Death, Into the mouth of Hell'. And now, it seems, there is no going back and the cycle of violence continues, even in the Land of the Dead.

My head reeled and I made my excuses to leave, especially as the flirtatious glances of Bronwen and angry glares of Brak were making me feel uncomfortable.

As the feast roared on merrily into the night I clumsily made my exit, slurring goodnights to all. The slap of the cold air rapidly sobered me up. Unsteadily I stumbled back across the ice to Ogmios's lodge, gazing at the Milky Way above. This is not a bad place to be, I thought, even if it is an Afterland.

Afterland ... Where did that term come from? I slowed to a standstill under the stars. Had Merlin whispered it into my head? Was he out there somewhere in the night?

A rough arm checked my progress. It was Brak, breath heavy with the cauldron brew. For a moment he just glared at me, his breath freezing through clenched teeth. 'If ... if you lay one finger on my sister, outlander, you'll regret it.'

I shrugged him off, full of beer-fuelled bravado. I wanted to tell him she was too young for me, but I resented his tone – a pup, half my age, telling me what to do? I felt like cuffing some sense into him, but I thought better of it. He was resting a white-knuckled hand upon the hilt of his bronze sword, and I was sure he wouldn't hesitate to use it. He'd had it in for me since I arrived – Lord knows why.

'Goodnight, Brak – peace be with you,' I said cheerfully.

Yet despite Brak's belligerence, I felt the Stag tribe were beginning to warm to me. As the snow melted, their glances became less hard, their words not so cold. I have even been offered a cup of hot nettle tea or an oatcake here and there, and I'm beginning to learn the names of the different families and their pets. The children are less wary of me than the adults, who know I am not of their time. I suppose they are afraid of me and what mysteries I carry with me. They taste the otherworld on me – *my* world. The land of the living. Do they sense the life still in me? Does it make them envious? Perhaps these people are my ancestors, but I will never truly belong here, while I live ...

And just my presence here is a threat to their very existence. Is this how I repay my hosts? Every day here I feel more indebted to them; I am beginning to feel like the karmic serfs. How will I honour this debt? With my death, or with their destruction?

8

The Burning Valley

'Still your mind. Fix your eyes upon the rising sun. Let the light of awen pour into you. Feel protected by this sacred circle. Feel the balance of this day within yourself.'

Ogmios walked slowly in a circle, arrayed in his brightly feathered cloak, gem-studded club in hand, his three grey braids blowing in the wind like tentacles.

Dressed in a dun-coloured woollen shirt and blue chequered trousers, and simple moccasins soggy with mud, Kerne sat cross-legged on his cloak on the dew-laden grass in the centre of a stone circle. The Circle of the Old Ones overlooked the valley of the Chalk Folk from a commanding hilltop behind Caer Cernunnos. His mentor paced around him, speaking slowly and softly.

'Anruth, you see around you the twelve stones marking the great circle of the year. Between each pair is a gateway where we greet the Goddess in her changing guises. Name the months, as I walk the circle and point at the season-stone.'

Ogmios slowly paced the inside of the stone ring, using his club to point at each stone in turn, and the glyph carved upon it, highlighted in red.

Kerne called out the moon-month names he had learnt by heart in the last few weeks, starting with Summer's End: 'Samionos, seed fall; Dumannios, darkest depths; Riuros, cold time; Anagantios, stay home time; Ogronios, time of ice ...'

'Good, keep going.'

The image on the next stone was too abstract. Kerne could not read it. He licked his lips. He hadn't felt this nervous since sitting his eleven-plus. His mind seemed to go blank. 'Come on, come on!' he hissed to himself.

'Take your time. Find your centre. Feel where you are.'

The airman took a deep breath and closed his eyes. The drumming of his heart subsided, to be drowned out by the susurration of the wind. Suddenly, the answer came to him: 'Cutios, time of winds.'

Ogmios grunted approval and bid him continue.

Back in the flow again, Kerne finished the cycle. 'Giamonios, shoots show; Samivisionos, time of brightness; Equos, horse time; Elembiuos, claim time; Edrinios, arbitration time; Cantlos, song time.'

'Good. Now relax. Be fully present. Behold the new day: Cutios, the Eighth of the waxing Atenoux.'

Kerne had been patiently instructed by Ogmios in the lunar calendar of the Chalk Folk. The month of twenty-eight days was divided into two halves, or 'Atenoux', based on the waxing and waning of the moon. It was confusing and disorientating at first – for it could be the same date twice in a month as the fourteen-day period was repeated – until his body began to adjust to the natural cycle of growth and flow centred around the full moon in the middle of each month. The extra days were sacred days, outside time, dedicated to the festivals.

Kerne's head was buzzing, but he let it be soothed by the grandeur before him. It was the dawn of a bright spring day. The sun cleaved the Da'anu Valley hills like a sword. Clouds scudded across the sky as if on important business. Blodeuwedd, Ogmios's owl-guide, was perched on the tallest megalith, aloofly scanning the proceedings with yellow eyes, ear-tufts alert.

There was a change in the air, and it wasn't just the dawn breeze. The valleys were being released from their winter's ice: the streams were overflowing with the melt-waters; spring flowers were budding; the song of birds was returning to the hillsides; the birch forests that lined the valley were covered with a mist of yellow-green.

The one-eyed sorcerer, dressed in his wind-teased tugen, was checking the alignment of the sun on the horizon. It was a little further north every day, and now, Ogmios declared, they had come to the time of equal night and day – the equinox. This was not so important to the tribe as the fire festivals of Imbolc, Beltane, Lughnasadh and Samhain, but the old windsmith observed them with his own secret rites. The stones had been placed here by his ancestors of spirit, he said – generations ago, time out of mind.

If the Chalk Folk were equivalent to the late Bronze Age, then he must be referring to the Neolithic stone-raisers, Kerne surmised.

All of his life Kerne had been fascinated by the ancient stones and strange earthworks that littered the British landscape. Perhaps this *was* the realm of his ancestors and it had been in his blood all along. Maybe he was following the path of his forefathers. He wanted to ask Ogmios about this – was he in the past, or in the land of the dead, or were the two the same thing?

But Ogmios was intent on his apprentice practising the wind sigils. It had been three moons since he'd arrived and he had not made much progress ...

Fear still prevented Kerne from journeying deep into them. He did not want to have to return to that cold place, to Annwn, as Ogmios had called it – that no-man's-land of limbo. Yet here he was sitting in the centre of the stone circle, cross-legged on the hubstone, while Ogmios commanded him, club in hand. The windsmith had brought him here to practise within this sanctuary and under the eye of day, where night and enclosed spaces had failed.

'Focus on one woodword, bard. Visualise it in your mind's eye. Think of nothing else. Let it burn into your brain. Then release its sound. You do not have to discover it – it is there already. Dormant, like the life of a seed. Listen ...'

Kerne concentrated upon the silence. In the stone circle he felt a calmness, clarity and protection he had not in the Ogmios's abaton. Here, high up, it was possible to get perspective, and peace. Kerne felt rooted and elevated at the same time. From the depths of his mind came a murmur – he tried to ignore the screaming shadows that threatened to pull him down, back into limbo. With Ogmios he was safe. And a sound came ... He began to mouth it.

'Straiiiiiffff...'

From the depths of his mind a burning sigil emerged, shaped like a claw. Then out of the sky screamed a falcon. Kerne opened his eyes, his trance shattered, and blinked. It was Merlin! He had returned.

Blodeuwedd screeched and became restless at the arrival of a rival totem.

Kerne was beginning to think the falcon had only existed in his imagination. Yet here he was, swooping in to land on the tallest stone, aligned to the tallest peak of the mountain and the river below. Blodeuwedd was dislodged to a lower stone, her feathers ruffled, indignant.

'Merlin, you're back!'

Ogmios bowed before the bird. 'Hail, Master Windsmith.'

'He can see you!' cried Kerne. 'You *are* real!'

The falcon bristled his feathers, gripping the lichened standing stone with his talons. He shot a fierce glance at Kerne.

'There's no time, fool. You're all in serious danger! Taranis is sailing! His warband is attacking the Caer of Brighid. And they will not stop there.'

'Raiding party!' cursed Ogmios. 'I should have seen it coming.' He strode over to the edge of the circle and gazed down the river valley, still half sunk in shadow and mist. The sun was an angry eye rising in the east.

'Look, there! Beacon fire …' Ogmios pointed with his club, and Kerne strained to follow, to spot what the man's keen vision had singled out. In the blue hazy distance, at the far end of the valley where the foothills gave way to the great lake that stretched to the dark horizon, Kerne saw a flash of fire, like a flower of flame suddenly blooming. Moments later another fire lit up at the next hill fort upriver.

One by one the beacons were lit, warning each of the caers – thirteen in all. Below them the caer-fire of the Horned One was lit as a signal to any of their tribe out in the hills and to warn the Caers of Eryr and Partholon. Then Kerne remembered that Brak was away with a hunting party – some of the finest spear-throwers in the tribe.

'I've got a terrible feeling about this …' muttered Kerne.

They observed the panic catch like wildfire in the enclosure below. The villagers ran about, making what preparations they could. Thus far, the raiding parties had not reached them – but now they had to be ready. Cattle were hurriedly brought in from the fields. Workers left their seed-sowing.

Ogmios went pale, as if he'd suddenly recalled something dreadful.

'What is it?' asked Kerne.

'The women are at the spring!'

The secret spring where the women celebrated their mysteries was hidden in one of the wooded folds flanking the hill fort. Its stream emerged from the women's grove of hazel and flowed down to the river past banks of hawthorn and alder.

'They will not have seen the beacons …' Ogmios observed.

'Bronwen!'

'Yes – she is with them.'

'We must warn them!' Kerne pleaded.

But then a fearsome sight checked them – the beacon fires were growing. They were no longer solitary flames, but more like conflagrations. Smoke billowed from the first hill fort.

'Brighid is burning!' cried Ogmios.

Kerne knew that the caer at the river mouth was dedicated to the goddess Brighid; sacred to poets, blacksmiths and healers. It was governed by Tuan, the oldest chief of the Chalk Folk.

As he watched, the next beacon started to expand into an uncontrollable blaze.

'They are razing the forts!'

Suddenly they heard the blare of war trumpets and the deep pounding of drums echoing up the valley like rolling thunder.

Ogmios and Kerne stared at one another.

'This is not just a raiding party ...' said the old man.

Merlin cried out, 'I shall warn the womenfolk. You two should get back to the fort and do what you can to protect it!' The falcon flew off, swooping down into the valley, to the woods flanking the Caer of Cernunnos. The Stag Lord's effigy in chalk gazed out over the river. What protection he could give his people, Kerne did not know, but he found himself praying for it.

'Come, bard, we must do what we can. Defend or fall with your people!'

'My people?'

'*Your* ancestors, fool! Haven't you understood yet? And if *we* die, you will cease to be!'

The angry one-eyed windsmith and Kerne raced down the processional route – the old man striding ahead with surprising speed, feathered robes billowing behind him, club striking the ground like a bandmaster's baton. A brisk wind pushed them along.

As Kerne ran, glad to have the use of his legs back, a bead necklace rattled about his neck. A gift from Bronwen. The thought of innocent young Bronwen being in peril was almost too much for Kerne to bear.

He hoped Merlin had reached the women in their secret grove. Yet when he reached the gates of the caer and saw all the activity he wondered what he could do. Ogmios rushed off to Bron. The mighty chief was shouting orders in a clear, loud but calm voice. Everyone seemed well drilled. The tribal enclosure became a fort. The last of the cattle were being brought inside. The gates were being pulled to. Kerne rushed to them.

'The women are still out there!' he roared.

A warrior on the gate called down; 'They are coming now – we will not lock them out. Don't worry, skyman!'

Kerne scrambled up to the palisade and saw a group of women scurrying back up the hill, lifting their skirts clear from the ground, baskets under their arms. Behind them was a scene of devastation;

more of the hill forts were burning. And now long, low-slung ships, black sailed, glided around the river bend, blown by a biting easterly. Upon their prows were painted demonic faces. The banner of a black horse flapped from the stern. The shrill war trumpets blared out, and the drums pounded louder, quickening the pounding in Kerne's chest, the blood roaring in his ears.

As the first wide-bottomed boat reached the shallows at the foot of Cernunnos, a spear-wielding warrior on a small but powerful armoured horse leapt from the deck and splashed ashore, galloping up the path towards the women. Other warriors, clad in scale armour, faces obscured beneath round helmets with chain-mail veils and a hole on top for a tail of long black hair to spill out, erupted from the boat in his wake, unsheathing curved swords and letting out a piercing battle-cry.

'Grey Raiders!' someone cried out.

The rider was dressed in a long shirt of woven-metal armour and a pointed helmet trimmed with fur. His broad, cruel-eyed face was protected by leather side guards down to his shoulders. A short bow was slung over his shoulder and with the same arm he held the reins. In his other hand he wielded a spear. A quiver full of black-feathered arrows was strapped to his saddle. He ascended the steep path to the caer with ease, the horse an extension of himself. He lifted his spear arm to take aim.

The men on the battlements screamed at the women to make haste. They started to run. Among them Kerne saw Bronwen, in sacred white, brow garlanded with early spring flowers.

'Hurry!' Kerne yelled, feeling helpless. He remembered his revolver, but it was back in Ogmios's hut. By the time he could return with it, it would be too late.

Perhaps it already was.

The dark rider had caught up with the women. Two of them turned to defend the rest – Kerne recognised Modron and Maga, the tribe's midwives. They pulled out crescent-shaped daggers from their belts, normally used for cutting herbs and umbilical cords and in their secret ceremonies. The rider instantly threw his spear at one – Kerne couldn't tell which – and she fell, impaled through the stomach, her basket cascading its contents over the hillside. In one swift movement the rider loaded his bow and fired at the other, keeping perfect control of his horse. The arrow punched into her shoulder, knocking the dagger from her hand. The rider galloped his horse over the crumpled bodies of the two women. Yet their sacrifice had given the others time to nearly reach the gates – all except Bronwen. The rider was galloping after her. She was still fifty feet from the gates. The hill was steep and slippery from the snowmelt. Bronwen's foot slipped and she tumbled, her white dress smearing with mud. Her pursuer was upon her. He knocked her unconscious with the pommel of his sword, and then scooped her up, slung her over his saddle and rode back down the hill under a shower of stones.

'Stop! You'll hit Bronwen!' Kerne cried out.

The onlookers watched helplessly as the horseman rode back down the hill with her, past the Grey Raiders rushing towards the caer with swords drawn.

Kerne watched in stunned disbelief. They had taken her.

The surviving women stumbled inside, weeping. Some wanted to return to the fallen, but were held back, shrieking in anguish. A group of warriors ran out, enraged. They were met by the raiders swarming up the hillside like rats. Some wielded fire – which their archers used to light their arrows before firing them into the palisades.

The caer's brave warriors were desperately outnumbered, but their fury enabled them to reclaim the bodies of the two women. Some went into a battle-frenzy and whirled into the enemy naked except for arm-torcs and shield, covered with blue woad, brandishing sword or spear – fierce, unstoppable, until overwhelmed by sheer numbers. Of the twenty who had confronted the enemy, only nine returned in a fighting retreat, carrying the two women – the one with a spear wound limp and lifeless, the other writhing in agony.

Quickly, the gates were bolted shut with a massive beam, but already the palisade was on fire in many places. Grappling hooks were thrown over, too many to stop, and the fire-weakened fences were pulled down. The Grey Raiders burst through the walls of flame and were met instantly by spear and sword. Yet the tribe's weapons were no match for the invaders' – bronze was bent by iron, smashed out of hands, or cut in two.

Kerne was cut off from his hut – weaponless, useless. He saw Ogmios standing upon the exhumation platform in the centre of the caer, summoning to the sky, chanting. Blodeuwedd screeched around him. Grey Raiders who tried to approach the windsmith were knocked off their feet by some invisible force.

Not a time for prayer, thought Kerne. Yet perhaps that was all they had left.

Then Bron took to the field, wielding a massive broadsword, torc around his bulging neck, wearing his helmet of horns. Behind him his queen, Brigantia, stood fiercely in the doorway of the hall, guarding its entrance with spear and shield.

'Fall back, brothers!' he roared. 'Defend the hall! Women, children, old and sick – inside!'

The caer was consumed with panic: babies crying, women screaming, lowing cattle, dogs barking. The Grey Raiders ran amok among them, grim, unstoppable. Beneath their pointed helmets their flat-nosed faces were expressionless. All had long ponytails of sleek black hair and wielded their scimitars with ruthless efficiency.

The men of the tribe rallied around their leader, watching the walls burn around them. They were the last circle of defence against the raiders. Inside the hall were their loved ones, the future of the tribe. Inspired by Bron, they defended it with renewed courage.

'Fight for the Caer and may Cernunnos be with you!'

Where was Brak when you needed him? Kerne ran to avoid the burning buildings, the swinging sword arms. It seemed the fight was passing him by; but it was *his* fight too, whether he liked it or not. These people had given him hospitality, friendship. He had earned their trust; now he would not betray it. He crept to the hut where his gun waited. He had never fired it in battle, but it was the best chance they had.

Then a blood-splattered warrior extracted his scimitar from his latest kill and turned to face him. Kerne went to pull a spear from a fallen man and defend himself as best he could. It was nearly knocked out of his hand with the first blow. He was unused to hand-to-hand combat. He should have spent his time here training, not wasting it with Ogmios, trying to utter words of fire. What use where they now? And what good was Ogmios doing, up on his plinth? The gods had abandoned them, it seemed. Fuelled by the anger of seeing Bronwen captured, Kerne tried to fight back.

'You … will … not … kill … her. Do you hear?' he spat through gritted teeth. He parried the warrior's blows, more by luck than skill, but his adrenalin-fuelled ferocity was giving him strength.

All his life he had been a man of peace, but destiny had brought him to a time of war. As the Grey Raider fell backwards, tripping over a dead body, Kerne roared and lunged, impaling him with the spear. At the same time, a great cry went up. He turned as his opponent toppled, to see Bron stagger back, a grievous wound in his side from a spear. He roared defiantly and lunged forward like a wounded lion, cutting the head off the man who had dealt the blow. Two more came and he dispatched them, but his strength was flowing away. His warriors fought valiantly side by side, but one by one they fell before the onslaught. The roof of the hall was burning as burning arrows rained down upon it. Children screamed inside.

Kerne looked about at the horror – perhaps this was Hell after all. An eternity of fighting, of death and destruction … It was not so different from the Earth he knew.

Three Grey Raiders ran towards him, crescent swords raised like scythes. Kerne knew he had no chance. He would never reach the lodge; he would never see another dawn. The Caer of Cernunnos had fallen and all within it were doomed.

Then a wind stirred, building in strength, until it became a whirl-wind and stopped the raiders in their tracks. A gale suddenly howled about the hill fort, scattering anything loose – carts, corn, farm tools, washing – knocking men back.

Kerne looked up to the centre of this maelstrom. Ogmios had summoned the wind! It knocked warriors off their feet, blinded them with dust, struck them with flying detritus. Anything unsecured was whipped into its vortex.

Suddenly, familiar warriors cut down the dazed assailants from behind – mud-splattered leather armour making them lighter on foot then the iron-clad raiders. It was Brak and his hunting party! They had returned at last. With the wind at their backs they laid into the enemy and the minions of Taranis were cut down from two sides. Chaos and panic reigned as the supernatural gale howled about them.

The falcon and the owl screamed above, plucking out Grey Raid-er eyes.

The wind reached a climax, blowing out all of the fires on the caer, then ceased. On the platform, untouched by the devastation, Ogmios dropped to his knees, exhausted. Bloody-taloned, the owl flew to its master; and the falcon settled by Kerne, preening itself on the corpse of a raider.

The tide of battle had turned – the raiders were slain or pushed back. A horn sounded, and the rest retreated to their ships, some cut down as they ran. They severed their anchors and let the angry river carry them downstream. In one boat the horse reared up and Kerne remembered what treasure was held there. Bronwen!

And before the door of his hall the father of the tribe, mighty Bron lay dying, toppled like an oak, blood pouring from his many wounds. Brigantia cradled his broken body, heedless of the gore upon her.

Brak rushed to the fallen chief and fell to his knees. 'Father, I came as soon as I could. We were far from the caer. I should have been here. Together we would have beaten them!'

'Son.' Bron was ashen, his voice hoarse. 'Do not be ashamed – you saved your people ... Nothing more can be expected of you. The gods favoured you – they saved you to protect the tribe now – I have done my duty. Now it is yours – and your mother's.'

Brigantia sobbed silently, holding him to her breast.

'Wife, it is my time to go to the Hills of Peace ...'

'No. Nononono,' she wept.

Ogmios raced to his side, breathing heavily. All eyes were upon him as he fumbled in his craneskin bag for a bundle of moss to hold to the wounds.

'Kerne, quickly, fetch your flower! There is still time to save him.'

But Bron weakly held up his palm. 'No.'

His tribe looked on him in anguish. He had a chance for life. Why didn't he take it?

'I do not want to live on as a lame man. I have lost my sword arm, and more blood than I should have. What use am I now? You understand this, Ogmios. The Chief and his Land are one. If I am damaged in any way, so will the land be. I am unfit to rule now, but I would rather die as a chief than as a useless old man. Give me my dignity. Give me my death. To die defending the hall of the forefathers and the lives of my loved ones – there is no nobler way to the Halls of the Blessed.'

Kerne wavered, waiting for the decision from Ogmios. The old windsmith sighed, and shook his head at Kerne.

'You have served me well, Ogmios. As you served my father. Remember how you restored him to life once – but he was never the same after that. He told me he would have rather died in battle. He never forgave you, but I do. Let me go.'

Ogmios nodded sadly and stood back.

The Stag Chief's body shuddered in agony. 'Aargh, Cernunnos! Make me strong in crossing ...'

The windsmith held his club over the Stag Chief's chest and uttered a spell of Passing to smooth his journey into the next world: 'Feithim saire ...'

'Remember, Ogmios, how you instructed me at my torc-giving: "Let him who is chief be a bridge." Now it is my time to cross over ...'

Brigantia held her husband's hand tightly, kissing it. She washed the blood from his face with her tears, wiped the filth of battle away with her hair.

'Dear Bri', do not weep,' he whispered. 'My life has been a good one,' he said louder, the ghost of a smile on his face, a look of pride in his eyes as he gazed on his family. 'I have had the love of a wise and beautiful wife, a lovely daughter, and a strong son to be proud of. What more can a man want?'

The ragged survivors of the caer had gathered about their chief – injured, weary, bruised and dirty. Bron cast his eyes upon them, the light in his gaze dimming. 'Tribe of the Horned One! It has been an honour to lead you! Rebuild this caer, keep it safe and remember the dead. Guard the way to the Hills of Peace – and one day you shall rest with me in the Halls of the Blessed.'

Kerne stepped forward. 'My lord, they ... they took your daughter ...'

Brigantia went white, staring at the airman with wide eyes of horror. Brak leapt at him, grabbed his throat. 'If she has a single bruise on her body, you are a dead man.'

The chief reared up, coughing blood. 'Bronwen? In the name of Cernunnos, no!' He looked about in despair, and for the first time he looked beaten, the fire dying in his eyes. 'Get her back for me, get her back ...'

Brak dropped Kerne as his father shuddered in agony. 'Father!' He fell to his knees, weeping, helpless. 'You cannot die, you cannot!'

Bron gripped his son's arm and gazed at him with eyes that flared like the dying rays of the sun. 'Be strong for me,' he whispered raggedly through gritted teeth, 'for your mo-therrr ...' He exhaled, and slumped backwards, his battered helmet falling off into the hands of his son. Brak held it in disbelief, his body trembling.

Brigantia crumpled over the body of her husband, kissing him with fierce intensity, then arched backwards, letting out a terrible keening that her kinswomen took up, holding her as she pulled at her hair, scratched her face, tore at her robes.

The elder-women, gnarled like old roots, started to sing a low and chilling dirge over the fallen chief's body. Ogmios knelt wearily, using his club as prop, and lowered his lord's eyelids, touched him upon the brow and heart, intoning his incantations of Passing into the chasm.

Stray fires spluttered out as a bitter drizzle blew in, and in the mud the bodies of Chalk Folk and Grey Raider cooled, lifeblood draining into the spring soil.

Kerne stood uselessly by, still shaking with adrenalin, holding his crimson spear – hot rivulets running down its shaft, mingling with the cold rain.

9

The Hills of Peace

Dawn, cold-eyed and pitiless, breached the eastern horizon, slowly revealing the aftermath of the raid on the hill forts of the Chalk Folk. Caers smouldered along the valley of the Da'anu. And on the barrow hills the tribe of Cernunnos had gathered, garbed in sombre cloaks, subdued by the morning mist and by their mourning hearts.

In front of the empty hexagonal grave lined with timber and resinous yew branches Ogmios stood draped in his feathered tugen, leaning heavily on his glittering club, still exhausted from his wind-summoning. Along with the people of Bron stood Partholon and Eryr, their caers untouched by the raids, but not their hearts.

Other chiefs had sent emissaries to pay their respects in their place after word had been brought by Ogmios's owl, Blodeuwedd, via the network of windsmiths. These chieftains had suffered their own losses and damage, and there was much clearing up and recovering to do. The emissaries carried their tributes under their arms and kept their heads bowed.

Kerne noticed the bronze brooch insignias they wore upon their cloaks depicting each tribal totem – like the salmon upon his own. It was good to see the watery-eyed Chief of Caer Fintan again, he thought, though he had not been able to go over to speak to him. A slow nod was all he got when he made eye contact. Even aloof Eryr looked shaken by the unforeseen devastation, his eagle still and silent, though it cast its imperious gaze over the proceedings. When Eryr saw Kerne he cast him a bitter look.

His own bird-ally, if Merlin could be called such, had left with the raiders, tracking Bronwen. Ogmios said the bird would return with word of her whereabouts. The waiting was frustrating, but there was little they could do at this stage. Nothing would have been gained by immediate pursuit except more lives lost. The Chalk Folk's bronze swords were no match for the Grey Raiders' iron. Other tactics would be needed to achieve Bronwen's rescue.

The damp morning air was heavy with grief. Glad to be wearing his fleece-lined airman's uniform once more, Kerne stood to one side, outside the circle, feeling awkward at this intimate time, but sharing in their grief.

Aneurin the tribe's bard, a dark-bearded young man with piercing blue eyes, dressed in a cloak of deep green fastened by a silver brooch, sang over the armoured body of Bron lying upon a bier. The bard plucked at the strings of a small harp. The chill notes hung in the air. In a clear mellifluous voice resonating in every heart he sang a lament for his lord, praising his generosity and valour, his wisdom and strength.

When the song finished, feather-cloaked Ogmios stepped forward, his one eye shining from his white face, and spoke: 'Bron, may the Undying Ones bless his name, was the best of torc-bearers, the most generous of ring-givers. He was an oak to his people, sheltering and protecting. And he has been toppled in his prime ... But he died defending his father's hall, sword in hand, and many he took with him for the Eater of the Dead to feast upon. It was a noble death befitting a noble man. His strong spirit will remain inviolate. It will find its way back to the source, or, if he chooses, to life once more, where his mighty spirit will benefit mankind. The gods know how humanity needs good leaders to guide us. The world we all once breathed in is blighted by men who rule without wisdom, who are everything Bron was not. I have seen this in the Eye of the Moon ... May Cernunnos protect his mound, and may the blessed spirits guide him on his way.'

Lowered on the bier by four of his sword-brothers, Bron was laid in the hexagonal pit. He wore his full bronze scale armour and regalia as chieftain of the tribe – horned helmet, a thick torc about his neck. His battle-damaged broadsword was placed along the length of his body, hilt towards his heart. Leaf-shaped spears were placed at his side. Over his chest a many-tined pair of antlers were placed in his hands. One of his faithful hounds was laid gently by him, sacrificed to guard him in the next world. The other wolfhound pined by Brigantia's feet, looking sadly up at his mistress.

Around Bron were piled rich vessels, shields, grave goods – prized gifts from each member of the tribe. One by one they had come forward and placed their offering, and then the emissaries did the same. And now they all stood silent in a circle around the pit. At its head Brigantia and Brak stood, grim-faced and dark cloaked. At the other end, Ogmios performed the funerary rites, intoning a dirge to guide the spirit of Bron on its way, his gaunt face lit by tallow flares flickering in the chill March wind.

The wind always blew from the east in HyperEurus, from the endless plains beyond the Red Hills – whence the raiders came, bringing death. It was a bitter wind, with the taste of desolation, merciless in its deathly touch.

The cold sun rose, piercing the stark shadows of the Bone Mountains. From the mist around them rose the mounds of the fallen, like islands. And the tribe seemed like the ragged remnants of some catastrophe – the only survivors of a deluge, washed up on a distant shore, bereft of all certainty, their axis mundi toppled.

Brak took off his twisted gold arm ring and cast it into the pit. His face was red as he fought back the rage and grief.

'I will avenge you, father, or die trying!' he shouted to the mountains, defying the gods.

His mother, took a sharp knife from her belt and, stiff-lipped, cut off her long red hair and gently laid the thick braided lock on her husband's heart. Her face was streaked by tears from a night of keening with her women. She looked hollow and gaunt. Piece by piece she took off her jewellery and placed it around the body of Bron; then, finally, she placed her bright embroidered cloak over her husband, replacing it with a black unadorned one offered to her by her white-faced handmaidens. All the tribe had daubed their faces with chalk-paste, and it was these cracked masks that looked to their queen now.

'He was a good man. He was my husband. He was your chief.' Her voice nearly broke with grief, but she steeled herself and Kerne was reminded of Maud. 'Raise a mound worthy of such a great man!' she commanded, and she walked away, supported by her women.

Brak raised his sword and roared, 'To Bron!'

'To Bron!' echoed the tribe, the cry reverberating around the foothills until fading into silence.

Ogmios finished his incantations, scattering in a pungent dust of herbs and incense only he knew the meaning of, and then stepped back as the soil began to be cast over the body. All day long the soil was piled on top of the fallen leader, cut from the surrounding circle with antler picks and ox shoulder blades. The chalk was packed into place by every member of the tribe, and by dusk a great new mound rose from the Hills of Peace, aligned with the barrows of the chieftains and the Halls of the Blessed beyond.

Kerne cast an uneasy glance at the treeline, remembering what dwelt there in the shadows. He pulled his fur-lined collar closer about his neck and blew into his hands, the fingerless gloves not giving much protection from the numbing chill.

The mourners were now offered a simple funeral meal of rye bread, beer and warming pottage. The steaming bowls were passed around and gratefully received.

While he sipped his broth with a wooden ladle, Kerne pondered the pyres lighting the darkening sky. Along the valley the other hill forts smouldered, in ruins. They too would be burning their dead – bringing them upriver on black boats to raise mounds on the Hills of Peace.

They had stood alone and fallen alone. Surely they had to cooperate if they were to survive another attack, Kerne thought. The raiders would not come again until next year, to give the Chalk Folk time to replenish their wealth. Could they afford another reaving?

A meeting of the tribes had been arranged for the next full moon, Ogmios had explained, at Drunemetom upon Moot Holm – an island in the river, halfway down the valley where a sacred oak grove grew.

Kerne wandered over to the windsmith – who had been conducting the burial rites all day, stern, strong, but brittle. Pure will alone seemed to be keeping his bones from moving. He was as gnarled and tough as a blackthorn stick. Kerne wanted to tell the old man to take it easy. Instead he offered some of his broth and bread.

'Even you need to eat.'

The windsmith grunted, absentmindedly accepting the bowl. They chewed in silence; Ogmios squatting like a carrion crow, his ragged cloak of feathers flapping in the morning breeze.

'I will somehow make this right,' Kerne surprised himself by saying. Ogmios looked at him quizzically with his one eye. 'If somehow I caused this calamity, then I will find some way to make amends.'

'You cannot blame yourself, skyman. It is the will of the gods. Who can tell the river where to flow? The fish does not regret swimming its course …'

'So, we have no choice, then, is that it?'

Ogmios placed a gnarled hand upon Kerne's shoulder. 'We can choose how we die, if we take destiny by the sword-hilt.'

Caer Cernunnos was in ruins, but anything that could be salvaged was. The palisades would need much effort to repair. Kerne thought of improvements, but he didn't know if it was his place to suggest them. As he watched the raising of the mound, an idea came to him that would improve the defences. It came from his memory of

Maiden Castle's labyrinthine henges in impossibly faraway Dorset. At the moment, only one ditch surrounded the Caer of Cernunnos, but there was no time to do it now. Bronwen had to be rescued; they had no time to waste. Yet there was the protocol of mourning and the business of the living to attend to before anything further could be done.

It was a time of excess drinking, dancing and sexual abandonment when normal taboos were suspended. In the wake that followed, a licentious orgy ensued between the young men and women of different tribes – who were exempt from the taboo placed between fellow tribesfolk, Ogmios explained – to release the ghosts of death, to cancel out the slaughter with the dance of life.

Kerne tried not to be embarrassed or appalled watching the promiscuous behaviour, the maidens rolling about with the warriors in the straw, or on furs in corners. He could not apply the etiquette or standards of Edwardian England here. This was a more honest approach to life, not based upon a façade of respectability.

Kerne thought back to the last time he had made love to Maud, just before his departure to war, when he had uttered, 'Thanatos … Eros.' It was all too true that the taste of one's own mortality kicked in a primal urge to procreate, to pass on one's genes. Yet Maud had been childless. He had told her it did not matter.

But it had mattered to her.

Kerne learnt from Ogmios that relationships within the same tribe were usually strictly forbidden, for everyone within a caer was directly related. Thus, marriages between caers were encouraged. This still made Kerne uneasy, for surely *everyone* in the valley was related in some way. Even the idea of a kissing cousin made him feel uneasy. The prospect of being intimate with a direct ancestor made him feel nauseous. No wonder he had felt so on edge around Bronwen and Brigantia …

As he watched the couples frolic in the firelight he marvelled at that such apparent incest, distant or not, did not lead to inbreeding; but Ogmios assured him that no one could conceive in the Afterland. 'The dead are barren,' was his blunt reply.

'What of the children?' Kerne asked. There certainly seemed no shortage of them. Many of them still were play among the tables, ignoring the adult debauchery, or mimicking it in giggled hysterics.

'Life can be fatal to the young as well. We care for whoever appears at the gates of Partholon. Every day the borders of Wight Wood are searched for lost children. Most are found in time.'

The very thought of those haunted woods made Kerne shudder, horrified by the prospect of children and babies wandering or abandoned, lost in a grim fairy tale come true. How many had become fodder for its inhabitants? It was the stuff of nightmares.

Three days later, after the 'funeral games' had finished, the whole tribe gathered in the hall for the inauguration of their new leader.

'A tribe without a chief is like a body without a head,' said Ogmios, resplendent in his tugen. 'We must choose who will lead us, the Caer of Cernunnos.'

Many expected Brak to be chosen, as indeed he did himself. His men muscled their way to the front, and he strutted about, oiled and ornamented.

Ogmios presided over the coronation. He explained the situation and presented the torc of chieftainship not to Brak but to Brigantia.

Brak was furious.

'Am I not the strongest here? Fight me if you think otherwise!'

No one stepped forward. All watched him in silence. They were used to his fits of fury. 'Surely, windsmith, it is wisdom for the strongest to lead the tribe.'

Ogmios sized him up. Only he was able to stand up to the brash bully. He had done so since Brak had been a little boy. He was used to handling his tantrums. 'You are right, Brak. That is why I have chosen Brigantia, for she is stronger in spirit. Only a mother knows the strength it takes to bear a child, to raise it and to bear losing it. Mighty Bron, peace to his spirit, turned to Brigantia for advice in all tribal matters. Strength of arms failed us. We need wisdom now to save us.'

There was a murmur of assent from the crowd. Some of Brak's followers barked them down. An argument ensued, until someone cried, 'Let Brigantia speak!'

Brigantia had remained quiet throughout, but now stood up. She looked formidable in her black cloak, red hair short and spiky, and face death white.

'My son, your strength is needed now more than ever – as our tribe's champion. We need you to lead our men in battle. Will you not rise to your destiny and do what the gods have gifted you to do – and make your father proud?'

This appeased Brak. 'I will!' he shouted, thrusting his spear into the soil.

A great cheer went up.

'Then I choose you to be the champion of our tribe,' declared Brigantia.

This time the cheer shook the roof.

'I accept this role with honour and will defend Caer Cernunnos to my dying breath. Let the gods hear my vow!' Now Brak glared at Kerne. 'And as your protector I say this stranger is ill-omened. He has brought this doom upon our tribe and he should die!'

Everyone turned their attention to the airman. It was true, they knew, he had come at a time of great calamity. The death of the chieftain and the abduction of the daughter were a disaster, a rupture in the vital continuity of the tribe.

'Speaks-with-Thunder fell from the sky and brought terror with him,' Brak explained, 'and now this stranger appears, bringing death.'

There were murmurs of assent. Kerne felt their eyes burn into him. He felt guilt. It was true that he, in part, had brought the virus of warfare to their Hills of Peace. He could not deny Brak's accusations. They needed a scapegoat, and he fitted the bill.

Brak suggested offering the stranger as a sacrifice. His head impaled above their gates should make any attacker think twice. An argument ensued, with Ogmios defending Kerne.

Kerne stepped forward and offered to set things right. 'If I have begun this, then I shall end it! I will go to the Iron King and sort it out.'

There were bursts of derisive laughter from Brak's followers.

'It is true we are connected, like … brothers.'

'What did I tell you? They are demons from the same hell!'

'Not demons – men. It does not take a devil to make war, to slay a fellow human being. We are men, like yourselves, made of flesh and blood and we can die like you. This man, who you call Speaks-with-Thunder, was once my friend. We flew together, not by magic but on a "sky-horse". I don't know what has happened to him, to turn him into this tyrant, but I might be able to persuade him to stop.'

Brak laughed at him. The bard against the warlord? Not a chance!

Then Kerne reminded him about the gun. He pulled it out of his holster, and everyone flinched, remembering the thunder it spoke, everyone except Brak that is, who strode up to Kerne and stood so the gun was against his chest, challenging him. Kerne could feel his rage, but also see the grief in his face. This young man felt that he had let down the tribe as well, by being away. He wanted to avenge his father – or die.

'Stop this foolishness!' commanded Brigantia, knocking the

weapon aside. 'You both have honour to repay. You shall go together!'

The men looked at one another with horror and disgust. Kerne shook his head; he wanted to insist that this was *his* quest. He knew that Brigantia would not be gainsaid, yet the thought of sharing this heavy responsibility with a hothead half his age galled him.

Brak spat back, 'It's *my* father we are avenging! *My* sister we are rescuing! And you obviously cannot fight! I did not see you where the fighting was hardest. Your spear arm is weak. Do you intend to walk into the Forbidden Kingdom and the Caer of Taranis unchallenged?'

Kerne hesitated. He had no plan. He was no warrior. Who was he trying to fool? He looked at the young warrior bristling with anger, with weapons, with strength.

'Very well,' he agreed. 'Let's do this – together.'

Brak bared his teeth back at Kerne, 'Yes – let us finish this.'

Brigantia presented the mead horn. 'Then drink your bond, bind your oaths – and let no man break them.'

'The mead horn is said to shatter if an untruth is spoken over it,' decreed Ogmios, looking at both of them sternly.

Reluctantly Brak accepted the horn from his mother. 'May the gods grant us success,' he bellowed and he took a deep draught. Reluctantly he passed it to Kerne.

'May the gods grant us success,' Kerne oathed, watching Brak the whole time. The mead slid down his throat, sweet poison.

Later that night, at the back of the hall behind a tapestry, as the carousing continued, Kerne and Brak discussed their plans; Ogmios keeping the peace between them, reminding them of their horn-oath. They would travel together along the river to Lake Mandorla, to the edge of the Forbidden Kingdom. Brak had ventured there before, famously venturing into Wolf Forest, as the woods lining the eastern lakeshore were called, and spying on the Red Hills, the borders of Taranis's realm. He was confident that he could get them that close – within sight of the Caer where, no doubt, the enemy had taken Bronwen.

'What do we do then?' asked Kerne testily.

Brak was uncertain; he was a man of action, not words. He would find a solution on his feet, he spat, not over the gwyddbwyll board.

It was clear to Kerne that the champion was no strategist. Kerne's hope was to negotiate a safe passage to the hall of Speaks-with-

Thunder, using his friendship with Mallard as leverage – if, indeed, the pilot lived.

'More like we'd be captured!' snarled Brak.

'Well, then at least we'd get a free escort.'

In the morning they set off, well furnished with supplies and weapons, though little use the latter were to Kerne. He had his Webley, but he wanted to use his words.

Ogmios talked to Kerne, gave him what advice he could. 'Only words can defeat him. There is so much to teach you, but no time. You must find the windsmith within yourself.'

The wind howled down the valley. In grim silence they departed down to the slim vessel waiting for them – a canoe painted with signs of the stag. They packed in their supplies and pushed off, Brak at the front, determined not to lay eyes upon the airman.

It didn't promise to be a pleasant journey.

Sighing, Kerne settled down to the paddling as the current carried the canoe swiftly downriver.

'Bonaventure,' he uttered, but it fell on deaf ears.

As the craft left the aegis of the caer, Kerne thought he saw a falcon: Merlin! The bird swooped down and landed on the prow of the boat.

'Merlin, you're back!'

'Why do you always state the obvious, Kerne?'

Brak did not seem to hear and went to shoo the falcon away with his paddle.

Kerne grabbed the oar as the warrior went to lunge.

'Remove your hand, skyman – unless you want to lose it!' Brak hissed over his shoulder, breath reeking of meat.

'I wouldn't touch that bird if you want to know where your sister is.'

Brak shrugged the paddle free, looked suspiciously at the falcon and then carried on paddling.

'He is my bird-ally.'

'Hmph!' Merlin ruffled his feathers.

'I do not trust you windsmiths,' Brak muttered through gritted teeth. 'You could not save my father.'

'But we can still save Bronwen, if you listen for once.'

'What need do I have for words? Your stick speech was not strong enough to defend the caer! The time for words is over. Swords and deeds are what my sister needs now. I am not interested in any other kind of talk.'

Merlin flew to the stern of the boat.

'Looks like you've found someone at your level at last!' the falcon mocked.

Brak did not seem to hear.

Kerne sighed. 'Looks like this is going to be a great trip!' he breathed to himself. 'What better travelling companions could a man want? A brute and an offensive bird.'

'Less prattling and more paddle-talk, skyman!' growled Brak.

As they negotiated the first bend, the protective presence of Cernunnos receded from view. The fast river, swollen by the snowmelt, carried them inexorably to their fate.

Book Two

The Iron King

10

The Lake of Silence

The Journal of Isambard Kerne
Cutios 12th, Waxing Atenoux

We passed the burnt-out shells of hill forts in grim silence. Brak kept his muscled back turned to me the whole time, applying himself with tireless effort to the business at hand. The pace he maintained was relentless and exhausting, my shoulders ached, and blisters were already beginning to form on my hands. The only time the Champion of Cernunnos deigned to acknowledge my presence was whenever my clumsy paddling went askew; then he would bark something in contempt. His hatred of me was palpable and only mitigated by the circumstances that demanded our uneasy alliance. It seemed his fuse would only last as long as it took us to achieve our task – if that indeed be feasible. The rescue of Bronwen from the clutches of Taranis seems an impossible endeavour. Do we expect to just stroll into the Forbidden Kingdom and walk out with her? It seems that, whatever strategy we take, the accomplishment of the feat is wildly optimistic. Yet my hope is that my old friendship with Mallard will give me some leverage.

I still cannot imagine how he can have turned so seemingly tyrannical and 'legendary' in such a short space of time, if indeed it is him. Speaks-with-Thunder, Taranis, the Iron King – can these epithets really belong to my erstwhile pilot? He seems to have a habit of picking up names. Has Mad Duck finally gone completely bosky? His short fuse was well known in the squadron, and he was ribbed for it, but it was tolerated, like so many of his fellow pilots' ticks and peccadilloes, because he was one of the best flyers in the RFC. Mallard had a wild genius for flying; he was truly in his element up in the windstream. A true maverick of the air. But this time has he gone too far?

I hope I will be able to bring him down to earth, to help

him see sense – if sense can be found in this weird world I'm in. It'll be a relief to be able to talk with a fellow Englishman of the twentieth century about all this 'Puck of Pook's Hill' stuff. In fact, I've started to look forward to seeing him.

Thus I tried to keep my spirits up, perhaps naively. But Merlin was always ready to wither my optimism. He seemed to take pleasure in detailing what we were up against.

'I followed the Grey Raiders for two days. Bronwen was kept bound and blindfolded the whole time, but was untouched. They transferred her to a cage on a cart and took her to Caer Taranis – an impregnable fort at the head of Ironwound Pass, the only way through the Red Hills. The pass is guarded by watchtowers. You'll not even make it past the first one, facing the lake. The only way to get close is through the woods that line the Red Hills.'

I described what Merlin had told me to Brak. Windsmiths can understand the bird-allies of their fellows, according to Ogmios, but the falcon's harsh account had fallen on the deaf ears of a warrior, both thick-headed and deliberately ignoring me. His ears pricked up at the mention of the woods.

'Wolf Forest … I have ventured there before, under the noses of the enemy. Much of what you say I have seen with my own eyes. Don't worry, skyman, I will get us close enough to spit in the face of Speaks-with-Thunder.'

That I did not doubt, but how we are going to persuade Taranis to let his lovely captive go is another matter. Brak is not one for thinking too far ahead, or worrying about such details. He trusts his sword arm and quick reflexes. He claims to be able to think on his feet, but I'm not convinced. Worrying about what may or may not happen is 'woman's talk' to him. Yet I yearned for that as we struck silently east, towards the cold glare of the early spring sun.

As we passed each caer, Merlin explained whom they represented: the bear of Caer Andarta; the wolf of Caer Blaidd; the Caer of the White Doe; Caer Cynon of the hound; the boar of Caer Henwen; the raven of Caer Vran; the white bull of Caer Findbhennach; the ram of Caer Minas; the horse of Caer Epona; and, finally, at the river mouth, the goddess effigy of Caer Brighid.

Halfway down the valley, just past Caer Blaidd, the river forked around a steep-sided island covered with mossy boulders and cypresses: Moot Holm. Merlin said it was the most sacred site of the Chalk Folk. On its summit was the Drunemetom – the sacred oak sanctuary of the windsmiths. Sounds of chanting drifted down from the bird-thick branches. White-cloaked Sanctuary Guards watched us sternly from the crags. I was lured towards it by a strange magnetism. I sensed the power of the place – it seemed to be the heart of the whole valley, its omphalos.

On the riverbanks surrounding it were various ramshackle workshops. Noises of metalwork emanated from them and the raucous sounds of bartering, drinking and rough laughter. Traders came and went in small canoes. They looked unlike the Chalk Folk I had seen so far: the tall, pale and thin; the short, stocky and swarthy; the flaxen haired and long-nosed; the dour and mighty. These were the Metenaidd, Merlin said – the metal-smiths of the higher valleys. They came from the tributaries we passed along the river – the silver, copper, tin and lead streams feeding into the Da'anu of the Bronze People.

Looking up at the wooded slopes we passed, burgeoning with early spring growth, I sensed the hard eyes that stared down at us from the ramparts of the hill forts, victims of the recent raids.

We passed the great hill figures, mute and massive, each one proud and defiant. However, a shock awaited us when, at mid-morning, we reached the end of the valley, where white pinnacles of chalk stood like broken teeth in the mouth of the river. We gasped as one when we saw the last chalk figure – the goddess Brighid. She had been desecrated by the raiders, her simple elegant curves carved up, the turf scattered over the hillside.

Brak cursed the raiders very colourfully. Such vandalism was the ultimate insult to the Chalk Folk, their totems being so entwined with their identity. Yet, seeing the despoiled icon filled me with foreboding as I contemplated the treatment gentle Bronwen would receive at the hands of Taranis.

We passed beyond the protection of the white cliffs stretching either side of us as the river Da'anu flowed out into the wide stretch of water known as Lake Mandorla. The lake glimmered in the changeable spring light, a cauldron of quicksilver and lead. Our path lay across it, to the dark ridge of hills beyond: Wolf Forest.

Beyond this dangerous threshold, Merlin imparted cheerfully, lay endless steppe swarming with brutal Horse Nomads – the Forbidden Kingdom of HyperEurus, where the east wind ruled.

Our task seemed hopeless, but we could not turn back. The fast current of the Da'anu swept us into the lake and far out into the wind-stirred water. Ejected from the relative safety of the Valley of the Chalk Folk, we were now exposed to the whims of fate.

Behind us loomed the foothills of the Bone Mountains, rising in ascending ridges towards the misty heights far to the west. From them tumbled and snaked three rivers feeding the massive body of water, the lake draining to the south – to waters uncharted by the landlocked Chalk Folk, who seemed to be almost part of the valley they lived in.

I wanted to ask Merlin what lay beyond the southern edge of the lake, but the falcon took wing, saying he had matters to attend to. He would 'keep an eye on our progress' and was gone before I could ask him more.

Brak seemed pleased he was gone, breaking wind noisily to show his relief.

Ahead, the watery film shimmered and rippled with wind, a mirror of light and shadow. The dark corona of wooded hills lay beyond, a sinister sentinel over the lake.

The eye of the sun, now at its zenith, exposed us to all, for miles in every direction. I estimated the lake to be fifteen miles across, the same again north and south. It would take us all day to cross it, and already it was midday. I broached the subject with Brak, but he grunted back that I should put more effort into using the paddle instead of my tongue. He seemed to have something in mind – at least, I hope he did! My arms were aching, my hands blistered, and I was longing for a break. We had been paddling for four hours at least. My gaze was hypnotised by the bunching and flexing of Brak's spiral tattoos. His taciturn frame filled my immediate vision. There was not much else to look at as the visibility reduced.

A veil of grey drifted across the lake from the east, and I knew we were in for a drenching. I watched it come, the water hissed around us with raindrops, but still we paddled on – until I had to turn my attentions to bailing. Brak seemed furious with me – as if it was my fault – but threw me a wooden bowl to use, while he continued paddling. A gust of wind made it difficult to make headway with one manning the oars.

In disgust Brak cast down his paddle and rummaged about for something. To my delight he produced a wineskin and some provisions, wrapped in an oilskin. He took his ample share and tossed me the rest. Gratefully, I descended upon this, but was prevented from wolfing down the dried meat by its toughness. The bread rapidly became soggy and I was completely soaked, but I didn't mind. I smiled at Brak. and rolled my eyes at the rain. 'April showers – just like the Welsh Borders,' I joked, but he just spat out some gristle, chewing in silence, looking at me with hooded eyes.

Yet the repast had put new energy into my limbs and I was happy when we pushed on. While we paddled, our differences weren't so obvious – at least we were working towards a common goal.

The shower passed at last. It had washed away the sweat and the accumulated grime of the last few days. Refreshed, we pushed on across the lake in silence.

It was then I noticed we were no longer alone.

Across the restless water I began to notice other craft that looked like fishing junks. More and more appeared. Silent and staring, their Asiatic-looking crews watched us pass, holding nets, or baskets of fish, pausing in their work. With little sails, they scooted around the lake with seeming effortless ease, while we struggled against its hidden currents. Whose ancestors were these?

Indifferent to them as much as me, Brak paddled on, head down, but I could finally see where we were heading: a floating village in the middle of the lake. It was partly hidden by an outcrop of rock shaped like a sword thrust out of the water and covered with elongate trees. It seemed to be some kind of sanctuary. It had an ornate doorway on the east and west sides, and stone steps carved into the rock to its pinnacle, lined by prayer flags. At the summit were giant wind chimes under a pagoda of ebony and gold. Occasionally, the wind would cause a ripple of sound from these. On the tower was a weathervane, forged like an eye with an arrow through it, which would swing in the direction of the sudden gust – predominantly from the east. The breath of Eurus: the God of the East Wind.

The village moored around the sword-shaped sanctuary was

a far more makeshift affair. It seemed so flimsy – as if a sudden gust would blow it all away. On a series of platforms constructed by large wooden tubes, rather like bamboo, lashed together and covered with planks, was a collection of simple dwellings with bark walls and roofed with reeds. The place made me think of how I imagined the Iron Age lake village, discovered near Meare on the Somerset Levels, but there were distinct differences in the details. Moored to a kind of floating harbour was a clutter of junks. Around the quays Fisher Folk hauled their catch ashore, haggled and bartered, mended nets, smoked long clay pipes. There was a serenity about them – everything was done with grace, and with hardly any speaking. Apart from the creaking of the timbers, the slap of the paddles, the constant restlessness of the water, the only sound was that of the wind whistling through the buildings, slowly turning the village this way or that – and the wind chimes' deep ripples of sound. The soughing was eerie, but strangely soothing and a welcome relief from Brak's belligerent silence.

We took the canoe into one of the quays, and Brak threw the rope to a fisherman, who begrudgingly pulled us in. Brak leapt out as soon as he could and secured our vessel. A group of Fisher Folk gathered around us; enigmatic faces difficult to read, clothes of a simple light material of various soft tones. Their faces squinted in the afternoon sun, flat-nosed, long-eyed, with olive skin. They reminded me of Tibetans I'd seen in Royal Geographical Society photographs. They sucked on pipes that gave off a pungent smell of iodine. Was their tobacco some kind of seaweed? We were a long way from the sea. But these were traders, as I discovered.

Brak produced an oilskin package and unwrapped it before them. It contained a white crystalline substance. He licked his finger and dipped it in, tasting it, then gestured to the Fisher Folk to do the same. An older man sampled it and nodded. A deal was struck. We were allowed to stay and rest. Later I found out Brak had paid for our safe passage with salt – a valuable commodity to the Fisher Folk, so they can store their fish.

We unloaded the boat and, with the help of porters, took our supplies to a small, spartan room with two flat straw mattresses by way of furnishing. This was to be our lodgings for the night and I was grateful for it, flopping on to the bed after the exhausting row. Here I took a siesta – and later woke refreshed. I splashed my face in the lake but was pulled up and cuffed aside by one of the Fisher Folk. Suddenly there was a commotion – faces leered at me, furious, voices I did not understand. I was surrounded, disorientated, confused. Then Brak was there, explaining, even apologising in his gruff way. He made out I was a simpleton, ignorant of their ways. I meant no insult. He pushed me into our chamber and insisted I stay there. It took some pacifying and another one of our packages to calm down the mob, but eventually they left us in peace – if that is possible with one so belligerent as Brak. But I was impressed by his diplomacy for once.

He was not impressed by my actions, however.

'Tell me what I have done, then I won't do it again! Remember, I am a stranger here. I know nothing of their ways.'

Brak took a deep breath, and explained: the Fisher Folk believe the lake to be sacred and under their jurisdiction. Only they have the right, by ancient lineage, to fish in it or to take its water. Their god dwells within it – the King in the Lake – and has to be appeased at all cost. Their very existence depends upon a harmonious relationship with their lake god. Hence the numerous offerings and rituals. In the same way, any traveller on the lake has to appease the Fisher Folk by paying for safe passage. The Fisher Folk are master sailors and can catch anyone who dares to cross without doing so. Brak told me to watch myself and not to get into any trouble. The Chalk Folk have a longstanding trading relationship with the Lake People, exchanging salt, wood and wool for fish.

I explored the floating village very carefully that evening before dinner. By this fish-oil lamp I will record my observations of this curious tribe.

The Lake People, or Mandorlans, as they call themselves, live their lives in balance, not only on their floating village, blown by the wind across the surface of their lake, but in the way they have to contend with different tribes, trade with all. This they only achieve through their neutrality – though some would say amorality. But they are in a difficult position, and cannot take a strong stance without jeopardising their very existence. This ambivalence is seen in their seeming nonchalance. They appear emotionless to the outsider, but it is because they have mastered their emotions, not because they lack passion. They are the exact opposite of Brak – and how they tolerate his tantrums I don't know. Yet worse must be the growing threat of the Grey Raiders – the raiding party must have passed this way, pausing at this convenient stop perhaps. How did the lake people cope with their thuggishness? Probably with the same grace they cope with all the vicissitudes of life. They have found a secret, an inner equilibrium. Maybe it comes from living their life afloat. It is said, Brak tells me, that they never step foot on land. When they die, their bodies are excarnated – picked clean by carrion birds on the rock of the Windeye – before the bones are cast into the sacred lake.

That night I discovered why Mandorlans are renowned stargazers – it's their favourite night-time occupation. Over the centuries they have developed a deep understanding of the stars and their cycles and given their own names to the constellations: the Boat, the Fisherman, the Heron, the Snake, the Shell and others. I was told that a great astrological event was due to occur at the next midwinter solstice – the alignment of the Salmon and the Sword.

I visited the rock-cut citadel of the King in the Lake which I had noticed as we arrived. In an alcove shone a sword and a silver suit of armour scaled like a fish. It once belonged to a great king, so a walnut-faced, wispy-bearded monk informed me, eagerly telling me the legend in a hushed voice that resonated within the dark echoes, his reverent tone punctuated by the dripping of stalactites:

'Once there was a king called Ollav Fola who was wise and kind. He ruled all the lands about the lake, a vast kingdom that made him wealthy and powerful. But he was so appalled by the world and its ways that he put aside his sword, renounced violence and offered himself to the lake as a sacrifice if it would bring an end to suffering and strife. We Mandorlans used to live around the shores of the lake, but we constantly fought over fishing rights and territory, until we nearly destroyed ourselves through civil war. I know it is hard to believe now. You think of us as peaceful, but that is the result of centuries of work. Once we were angry, hot-headed. Arguments often ended in murder. Brother fought brother. Families were torn apart. Ollav Fola, blessed be his name, pleaded with us to stop but we would not listen. And so he took off his armour, put down his sword and offered himself to the waters. This selfless action shocked us into submission. An era of peace began as we humbled ourselves through selfless action. Our ancestors vowed never to take up arms again. They made floating homes in order to live upon the lake, casting off all attachment and claim to worldly things. Yet this has made us perhaps a little aloof and amoral. We trade with anyone but will commit to no cause. We will not help our neighbours for fear of upsetting the others. We rejected the world and turned our gaze inward, worshipping the King in the Lake – yet not giving up hope that he will one day forgive us and return. It is believed the King took the form of a giant salmon, for the lake has many magical properties; some say it is a gateway between worlds. As the guardian of it, he watches over us, making sure we do not exploit its riches. Our floating homes prevent us from owning more than we need. Our only treasure is the armour of Ollav Fola, kept within this citadel in perfect condition. Any who touch it in anger are taken by the lake. Many have tried and many have failed. It awaits the King, as do we all. The centuries have passed yet still we have not given up hope.'

I thanked the monk for the fascinating tale and, with my imagination ablaze, I returned to our hut as the sun dropped low in the west, turning the Bone Mountains pink. I noticed Brak look longingly at them, like a hound waiting for the return of its master. What lies beyond them? None of his tribe has ever passed beyond their fastness. Does Merlin know and will he tell?

Yet my gaze was drawn to the east, where the dying sun caught the pine trees on the ridge of hills stretching the length of the shore – a row of flames. Beyond this threshold lies the Forbidden Kingdom, the land of the Iron King, and our destination. The dark line of the trees there contrasted with the white cliffs of the west, yet it was the shadows of the Bone Mountains that now stretched east, while the sun still clung to the slopes of Wolf Forest – light in darkness, darkness in light.

And as the moon rose in the west I saw why the lake is sometimes known by another name – Mirrormoon – not merely because it reflects the moon's light in the indigo water, but because its shores echo the moon's two halves – the crescent and shadow of maiden and crone. The moon is in its fullness now, a lamp over the lake. And I recalled something I once mentioned to my darling Maud in another life, another world: 'earthshine' – the maiden in the arms of the crone.

Bron's daughter is now in the clutches of death and we have to get her back. The task seems as insurmountable as the Bone Mountains themselves.

Lost in this conundrum, I gazed at the moon and its rippling reflection. The silver path it created was as insubstantial as our hope. Yet still we have to push on.

We shared in silence a meal of fish and rice, washed down with a pungent grainy brew, a kind of rice wine. Afterwards, the conversation began and Brak exchanged news in a guttural dialect, gleaning that the raiders had passed that way with their captive, who wasn't allowed off their longboat.

I wish I could have joined in the conversation. It had been a long day of silence. Yet I was mute in this place, nothing more than a dumb animal, a simpleton. And so I share my thoughts on the page instead. I am glad of its companionship.

At least music is universal. A woman began to sing, accompanied by a simple lute, and her voice seemed to echo the suffering of her sex, the notes rising into the night. In the darkness the world had no edges. Village, villagers, lake, shore and sky – all blurred into one. I had to be careful where I stepped, unsteady on my feet from the constant rocking of the floor. The rice wine had not helped matters and I staggered back to our hut. Lord knows what they would do if I fell into the lake!

That night, as I drifted asleep to the strains of the eerie singing, I dreamt of a Kraken-like monster waiting to devour me. I bolted awake, breathing heavily. Brak was snoring nearby. My fatigue eventually overcame my night-terrors.

In the morning, the first rays of the sun illuminated the western shore of the lake, revealing the white cliffs in all their glory, reminding me so much of the south coast of dear old Blighty. I am so far from there, perhaps too far to return.

As we turned away from my adopted home – the Valley of the Chalk Folk – and pushed our craft out towards the dark eastern shore I could not but feel a sense of foreboding. The dark line of forest looked even darker in the shadow of the new day. A point of no return if ever I saw one. Our path lies there. If we are to avoid the eyes of Ironwound we must risk the uncertainties of Wolf Forest to reach the Forbidden Kingdom.

And there I hope to find Mallard. But what kind of man has he become?

11

Wolf Forest

The forest watched them. Kerne felt it had been watching them all morning as they approached the long dark ridge of pine forest that stretched along the eastern shore of the lake as far as the eye could see. Their canoe was a needle in a forest of needles, slipping towards the tangled shore, hoping not to be noticed ... but how could they not be? As the mist had burnt off, the two travellers had become visible to anything that cared to cast a glance over this water the colour of molten metal.

Kerne groggily watched the dew on Brak's wolf fur cloak slowly evaporate. After the soothing respite of the floating village, it was back to the cold-shoulder regime. At least they had a purpose they could apply themselves to, a common goal, though a seemingly hopeless one.

Somewhere in that vast wilderness was Bronwen. The thought turned Kerne's stomach. If he had been a true windsmith he could have saved her, could have prevented her father from dying perhaps. But he had been useless and what good was he now? A passenger? Just ballast, in Brak's mind, he was sure. Kerne had to remember it was *his* friendship they were relying on – if they got close enough to talk to Taranis. Yet it seemed chancy that they would even get that far: it was punishable by death to step foot in the Forbidden Kingdom, so Brak informed Kerne as they pushed the canoe towards the willow thicket that lined the shore.

Brak scanned the tangled fastness, looking for something only he knew – some landmark he recognised, Kerne could only surmise – and he steered the craft towards the wall of trees. It looked like they were going to crash into the mesh of trees, but at the last moment the branches parted, revealing a narrow inlet, hidden by the willows. Brak carefully guided the canoe into the stream that ran between the palisades of trunks. The atmosphere immediately changed; the brackish smell of stagnant water, the resinous smell of pine needles, the damp shade of the branches and the overwhelming silence of the endless forest demanded the attention of their senses. They certainly felt like they were trespassing in the Forbidden Kingdom now.

Branches snapped, or whipped back against the canoe's hull like drum snares. Kerne hoped their approach was unnoticed. They had a long way to go yet.

As quietly as they could they paddled upstream. Brak pushed branches aside, taking care not to let them break but letting them whip back in Kerne's face. If Kerne complained he hushed by his angry companion.

They followed the stream inland for a couple of miles until their progress was checked by a small waterfall and rapids beyond. The stream widened out into a pool flooded with light by the break in the canopy.

Brak leapt out and waded ashore, pulling the craft after him. He commanded Kerne to throw him the supplies. They lashed the boat to a root, and Kerne disembarked as Brak sorted through the supplies, deciding what needed to be taken. They loaded their leather packs with the salted fish they had traded from the Lake People, the flatbread, water skins, cloaks to sleep in, flint and tinder, fishing hook, sling, spears and daggers. Brak took a bulky bundle and placed it in his pack, but he gave no clue as to what it contained.

Kerne checked his Sam Browne belt with its assortment of standard issue equipment. His rations were long gone, traded for various favours or goodwill, but he still had sulphur matches, shaving mirror, pocket knife, hip flask, notebook and pencil. He had brought his water-stained officer's papers, in case he needed to prove his identity to Mallard. The tin cantina swung at his hip, leaking a little on to his overalls. The box compass was proving reliable again, its needle swinging north. His Webley was secure in its holster, and he hoped to God it would stay there.

Compared with Brak, he felt ill prepared. When he had set off that morning with Mallard in the Breguet biplane he did not expect to end up in another world. A 'morning's photography' had turned into a journey into the unknown.

Brak's gruff voice reminded him they weren't here to daydream. They had to reach the ridge before nightfall. The warrior would not say why.

Untethering the craft, they lifted the boat out of the water, tipped it up and placed it on top of their stored supplies to protect them. Then they covered the craft with moss, ferns and branches until it blended into the forest. Satisfied, Brak picked up his pack and weapons, bid Kerne do the same, and, without any ceremony, they set off into Wolf Forest.

As they ascended the silent wood the sun sank with a sickening inevitability. The jagged tree shadows lengthened, the sun's light penetrating the thick canopy at almost an acute angle as they climbed. They scrambled up the slope, holding on to roots, their feet slipping on the deep mulch of pine needles, exposing the reddish soil beneath. They were lashed on either side by the low branches, until their bodies were lacerated by countless scratches, leaving behind a thin trail of blood like yew-berries on the bright green fronds.

Reaching an outcrop of ochre rock, they stopped to get their bearings and to eat something. They were about halfway up the slope of the hills and the sun was low in the west. It was clear that they were not going to make the ridge by nightfall. The way only got steeper and more treacherous. And at night the forest became far more dangerous, warned Brak. The Grey Raiders were the least of their worries.

Below, they saw the gorge that split the ridge: Ironwound Pass – the only way through the Red Hills. It was narrow and steep sided, and lined with crude watchtowers made from stripped pine trunks sharpened into stakes.

They kept close to the outcrop so as not to reveal their profiles. Even if it would be difficult to hunt them down in the forest, they did not want to announce their arrival to the enemy too soon.

'So what now?' gasped Kerne, pausing for breath. The young warrior had barely raised a sweat.

Brak smiled sadistically. 'We carry on … all night. We do not want to stop here, believe me.' He jumped down from the outcrop and started weaving rapidly between the branches.

'Wait! How will we see where we're going?'

'The moon will be our eye.' Brak gestured to the east. He was right: the moon was already rising, slowly – a pale orb glimpsed through the trees in the deepening indigo. 'Hurry or the wolves will eat you!'

Sighing, Kerne shouldered his pack and tried to catch up with his agile guide – half his age, a hunter who had grown up using his body. Kerne wished he'd looked after his better. He was beginning to feel the strain, a stitch in his side. But he would not let the arrogant youth win the day. Brak may have speed, but as a mature man Kerne had learnt stamina.

'The hunt is on, my friend,' he growled under his breath, running into the undergrowth after Brak.

They ran as the shadows lengthened through the trackless forest, climbing, always climbing, scrambling, grabbing roots, brushing branches aside, until they could no longer see where they were going, no longer even see their own hands in front of their faces.

Kerne stumbled.

Brak shouted back, 'Get up!'

The airman staggered to his feet, wiping the mud from his cheek, and continued. Then he slipped and fell again, nearly twisting his ankle – the one that had taken so long to mend. He cursed in pain.

'This is ridiculous! I can't go on! I can't see a bloody thing.'

Brak panted, a silhouette, eyes gleaming. It was true – the forest was pitch black. 'Pah! What a hunter you would make! Walking-Falls-Over I shall call you.'

Kerne was glad Brak could not see the expression he had pulled, but suddenly the forest was flooded with light. They both turned to see the moon breach the dark ridge, full and huge.

'There is our torch! Now even you can see, skyman.'

The forest was transformed into a web of black and white. Everything took on a strange two-dimensional quality.

'Ah, good. A little light on the subject ...' murmured Kerne.

Suddenly, a howl pierced the night. A primal howl. Followed by another, then another, then a feral chorus. Some ancient instinct in him recognised the chilling sound. *Wolves.*

'Great – now we have company!'

'I suggest you keep up!' hissed Brak as he ran ahead.

Now it was easier – at least Kerne could see where he was going – but the thought of wolves in the forest unnerved him. He jumped at every shadow and gripped the dagger at his belt tighter. He was glad of the spear in his other hand, and not just for support, though it did prove a useful aid to climbing.

After a frantic flight through the light and dark they came to a little clearing created by a tree fall. Moonlight flooded in and the map of heaven was revealed; configurations unfamiliar to Kerne, though he gave them little attention. He was more intent on getting his breath back.

Brak stopped in the grove. Wolves howled closer. 'I will raise help here. Stand back – but within the circle.'

Kerne wasn't sure what Brak had in mind, but the young hunter ignored him, slid off his pack and pulled out the mysterious bundle he carried. He unrolled it gently on top of the fallen stump. In the moonlight Kerne could just make out a pair of antlers, a gourd rattle and incense.

'Help me light a fire – quickly!' ordered Brak.

'A fire? But surely it will give away our presence for miles in every direction.'

'Don't argue – no one walks Wolf Forest at night! And in the morning we will be gone. If the gods let us survive. Firewood, now!' Brak stripped down to his breechclout and applied himself to his occult task.

Wondering why no one ventured into the forest at night, not even the fearsome Grey Raiders, Kerne scanned the edge of the clearing for suitable fuel, jumping at any sound.

While Kerne hurriedly collected bundles of dead branches, Brak concentrated upon lighting the tinder from his grandfather's fire box, vigorously gyrating the wand of wood in its niche with a small bow, until a spark was created from the coupling. He knocked this carefully into the bed of tinder and gently gathered it up in his palms. Kerne marvelled at this tender and skilful act from one so brutish. Brak blew on the tinder ball until a glow illuminated his face. Then he allowed himself a satisfied smile. 'Is the fire ready?' he barked.

'Yes.' Kerne had been working flat out to create the small stack. Much of the wood was damp but resinous, although he had managed to find some dead twigs from a half-fallen tree that were dry enough for kindling.

Brak placed the ball of smoking tinder in the centre of the bed of pine twigs and bracken prepared by Kerne, and then he carefully placed the kindling over it, blowing on it gently until the kindling caught. Brak chanted all the time, murmuring ancient cantrips into the bones of the fire, bringing it alive with his breath. Suddenly a flame leapt. Brak uttered a prayer in thanks and sat back on his haunches. 'Keep this going. Whatever you do, don't let it go out!'

As the flames grew, tended by Kerne – he was used to lighting the morning fire in his mother's house back in Blackwardine – Brak lit a bundle of incense and offered it to the gods. Then he took up the rattle and began shaking it into the night, moving in a clockwise direction, casting a circle about them. The rattlesnake rhythm and the crackling of the flames began to take their effect on Kerne, who slipped into a light trance as he fed the fire. The awareness of imminent danger around him receded as an ancient part of his brain responded to the primal protection of the fire.

Suddenly the hairs on the back of his neck stood up and Kerne was aware they were no longer alone. Outside the circle, he glimpsed the lambent eyes of wolves. The airman slowly placed his left hand on his holster and loosened the Webley, cold against his hip. For once he was glad of its heavy reality.

If Brak was aware of their presence, he ignored them. He shook his bone rattle over the antlers, kissed the skull, placed the skull down between them, then picked up the tines, one in each hand. Then he began to dance with them, like a hunter, like the hunted, moving like the stag. It reminded Kerne of the famous cave painting from the Trois-Fréres in southern France – the so-called Sorcerer.

The wolves paced the perimeter of the fire circle, unable or unwilling to draw closer. Kerne saw their fangs flashing, tongues lolling.

Brak worked himself up into a frenzy, head shaking, hair smeared over face, eyes feral, teeth bared, saliva spitting, guttural animal sounds coming from his curled lips. His tattoos gleamed with sweat, illuminated by fire and moon. Then he stopped, raised the antlers above his head and cried out, 'Lord of the Animals, Cernunnos! Come to me! Protect us tonight. Give me the tongue. Let me speak with my brothers and sisters, the four-legged ones, the Older Ones. Let us pass through this forest in peace. Spirit of the Trees, grant us safe passage. Let us find my sister and bring her back to the fort of my father, the hearth of my mother, her skin still soft, her heart beating strong. Cernunnos, make this so!'

Kerne was impressed. He had never heard Brak speak so much, but all of this light and noise seemed designed to announce their presence to the night. Surely the whole forest must be aware of them by now!

Then a ripple at the forest's edge, branches crashed aside, something massive moved towards them. The wolf pack grew nervous, tails lowered, slinking low to the ground. This time Kerne reached for a flaming brand – some instinct telling him only fire would protect them now.

Into the clearing strode a mighty stag, a red deer. He stood before them, massive, flanks steaming, eyes wise with time and ancient mystery. The moon shone from between his many-tined antlers as if caught there.

Brak bowed before him. 'My lord.' He spoke to the animal in a strange tongue. The stag seemed to listen, to understand, nodding.

Then quickly, neatly, Brak placed the antlers on the cloth, rolled up the ritual bundle and put it back in his pack. He plucked a brand from the fire and began banking down the flames, throwing damp ferns over the dying glow.

'Quickly, we must go!'

'What about the wolves?'

'Cernunnos protects, Cernunnos leads!'

The stag knelt before them. Brak mounted, and commanded Kerne to do the same. The mighty beast rose, bellowed and began to lumber off with surprising speed, unimpeded by his burden. He pushed aside the trees with ease. Brak and Kerne held on tight, awkward in the intimacy that the situation dictated. The wolves let them depart, giving the stag a wide berth. But to Kerne's surprise they now ran with them, flanking them, like an armed escort. Together, the strange group made their way up to the heights.

Although they had left the protection of the circle, Kerne felt safe within the aegis of the stag – Cernunnos. And he felt something of the beast's massive power within himself. He was *Kerne* after all ... Did he not also speak to animals? Where was Merlin in all this? Where were his own skills? His own power? He was being led by a youth half his age.

The strange company made its way through the moon-striped forest. The stag seemed to know the secret paths and with determined force found his way easily up the tangled slopes. They had to hold tight lest they lose their balance and fall off on to the rocks below. Kerne tried not to look down at the jagged slopes plummeting down. Yet they were making headway ... So this was Wolf Forest. What threatened to be their obstacle proved to be their ally. Brak had hidden gifts, though he hid them well.

Kerne wondered when Brak would stop, when he would mourn. His father had been dead for only six days. For all the hate directed at Kerne it seemed that Brak was really blaming himself. Brigantia had been wise to send him on this quest so he could find the redemption he needed. Somehow, the rescue of his sister would balance things, even if the blood-price he had to pay was his own. In his eyes the fort had fallen, his father had died, because he had not been there, because he had been hunting. Would he ever forgive himself? Only through action – through continual acts of bravery proving to the ghost of his father what he would have done had he been there.

Despite his rudeness, Kerne felt for the lad and wanted to offer some crumb of comfort, but he knew it would be refused. Kerne had to redeem himself in Brak's eyes as well. To the proud youth, ruled by a hunter's and warrior's instinct, Kerne was the root cause of the entire calamity that had befallen his people since Speaks-with-Thunder came. To Brak, the skyman was responsible and it was up to him to rectify it – or die trying.

Riding the stag, feeling his mighty sinews beneath one's legs, being carried by his strong back, reminded one of one's father. How long had it been since either of them had been carried like that? For Brak, ten years? For Kerne, three times as long. And now Brak, becoming a man, had to learn to carry himself, to shoulder his own burden. From now on he would be the protector of his tribe. He had responsibilities – he could no longer think just for himself, act selfishly and go off hunting whenever he chose. He had others to think of, the tribe, his ancestors, the spirit of the land, ghosts that needed appeasing.

The rhythm of the journey on the stag's back was trance-inducing. The flickering shards of moonlight hypnotised Kerne, made him fall into a trance – between the worlds ... His mind tasted the void he had been trapped in. The sigils flashed before him, then the screaming demons trying to pull him back into the abyss, tear his soul apart. They were hungry. They wanted their payment for his crossing. Someone had to pay ... He felt himself lurch, as though falling, and snapped out of his trance to stop himself slipping from the stag's back just in time.

The cold night air slapped him in the face. He was acutely aware of the vast night around him once more, the countless eyes of stars, the endless ranks of trees standing to attention in their uniform of black, green and silver. Among them the wolves still loped, wild eyes shining. Then he noticed the pack freeze, sniff the air, growl.

Suddenly, Kerne became aware of other eyes watching them. Between the negative spaces of the trees, in the dark pools where the moonbeams failed to reach, either side of the deer path, they loomed, two pairs of eyes, flickering with fire. Rows of fangs like pinnacles of ice. From their jaws issued tendrils of steam. Behind leopardine heads massive shoulders bristled, night dark and glistening with stars. The wolves howled and whimpered, running back and forth, hindquarters low – they knew these beasts were not of their world. These creatures, whatever they were, were strangers to the forest. If the wolves were worried, Kerne knew they were in trouble.

The stag stopped, snorting.

'What in the name of Andraste are they?' Brak brandished his spear.

Kerne slid out the Webley from its holster. He did not want to have to use it if he could help it. The report would echo for miles around. If they had not announced their presence already, then such an alien noise would surely warn Taranis of a threat at his border.

Brak began whispering in animal tongue; the spirit of the Lord of Animals was still burning in him. He tried all the tongues he knew, but the chimeras just glared.

They had no choice – the demons of Annwn were blocking the only way forward.

'Be prepared to fight or flee,' Brak warned as he kicked the stag into life.

Warily the stag approached the narrow defile guarded by the sphinx-like cats. The wolves were going mad with fear; some defecated or cowered, but were nipped back into rank by the alpha. They had a job to do like Kerne and Brak. They formed the vanguard as the stag and his riders neared the narrowest point of the ravine. Then the chimeras leapt, streaking like meteors across Kerne's vision. The firecats ploughed into the front wolves, picking one up in a massive maw, clubbing another aside with raking claws. Other wolves tore at their flanks, leapt on top of them, trying all the time to reach their throats.

'Go!' Brak roared, and the stag pushed through the melee. The chimeras tried to reach them, but were held back – at terrible cost – by the wolves. With spears, Brak and Kerne forced the demonic beasts back as best they could. And then they were past. The stag galloped on. The passengers had to hold on for their lives as the gradient increased and speed lessened. Glancing back, Kerne saw the wolf pack being decimated. Then there was silence, followed by a roar that reminded Kerne of the abyss. The chimeras bounded out of the darkness – meteors of vengeance. The stag could run no more; the rocks were too steep. He turned to face his pursuers.

'Off!' shouted Brak. 'Climb!'

'But what of the stag?'

'He knows what he must do. Go!'

Without hesitation, Kerne began to scramble up the slope, using his spear for leverage and grip. The cliff-face was stark in the moonlight but depth of field was deceptive and he had to grope around for holds. For the next few moments he felt awfully vulnerable, his back to the beast. He could hear the fight down below. The stag was keeping them busy, performing his grim duty.

Halfway up the cliff, they hauled themselves up on to a ledge. Breathing heavily, they turned to see the situation below. The chimeras were slowly wearing down the stag, which was bravely fending them off with his massive crown of antlers. Yet as he swept one aside, the other would lunge at the noble beast, raking his neck with needle-like claws. He was losing a lot of blood and swayed groggily. Then he sank to his knees. Seeing its chance, a chimera leapt – but with a final effort the stag impaled it on his tines. The chimera let out a terrible wail and flared up suddenly, exploding with light. The other did not mourn its fellow but struck with renewed savagery, sinking fangs into the stag's ruined neck. The mighty beast collapsed on to the rock with a bellow and the chimera finished him off in a frenzy. It did not feed as such, but sucked up the stag's life-force, leaving a withered husk, an empty skin shrivelled like an autumn leaf.

Seething with stolen life and dripping with gore, the chimera turned its attention to the men, beginning to climb with feline agility.

They cast down rocks at it, but the chimera just shrugged them off.

'Climb!' implored Kerne.

'No,' said Brak. 'We must stand and fight.'

'We don't have a chance!'

'We have our honour. I do not want to die without that. I could not face my father. Cernunnos is still with us.'

Kerne could see the fire in the young hunter's eyes.

'Very well.'

The hunter and the airman stood side by side – Brak with his spear, Kerne with his Webley. As they waited for the coup de grâce on the shelf of rock they looked out over Lake Mandorla and remembered its tranquillity. Beyond lay the Valley of the Chalk Folk and the safety of the hearth. Kerne longed to be back there; it was the only home he had now. He wondered if they would ever see it again.

Over the edge of the lip of rock the chimera came, paws like grappling hooks. Its eyes burnt like the furnaces of Hell. It reminded Kerne of something he had tried to forget.

'Where has this demon come from?'

'I don't know, but it's going back there!'

They looked at each other with grim resolve and then charged forward while the chimera was vulnerable. Brak cast his spear at it, and the point lodged in its shoulder. Irritated, as if by a splinter, the creature scraped it off on the rock ledge and leapt.

Kerne pointed his pistol, braced himself and pulled the trigger. The recoil of the revolver shocked his arm into its shoulder joint. The impact stopped the beast in mid-flight, flipping it round with a feral cry. It imploded with a flash like a camera's, rendering everything in negative momentarily, before the shockwave knocked them back. The crack of the Webley echoed about the forest, thunder in the night. If the enemy had not known they were there, they did now. They might as well have gone up to Taranis's door and knocked. But it did not matter, for the moment. They were breathing. They were alive.

Kerne gripped his shoulder. It hurt like hell.

Brak looked pale in the moonlight, eyes wide at the smoking barrel. Breathing heavily, wiping his brow with his forearm, he retrieved his spear and jerked his head at the pistol. 'You – you have a strong weapon,' he said in wonder.

'Taranis is not the only one who can speak with thunder,' said Kerne bitterly. What had he done? What had he become?

Brak held out his hand. 'I – I misjudged you. Perhaps you have a warrior's spirit after all.'

Breathing heavily, the men gripped each other's forearms, a look of mutual respect on their faces.

'Cernunnos, thank you for guiding and guarding us tonight. Mighty One, go in peace. May the spirits of our wolf and stag brothers find good hunting in the sky.'

The night sky was brightening in the east. They were high up, near the highest point of the ridge. A nimbus of grey light silhouetted them and Kerne was glad to see the ridge, even if it represented the threshold of the Forbidden Kingdom.

'Come, it is nearly dawn.'

Together Brak and Kerne, weary but relieved to be alive, made their way towards the reddening ridge.

12

The Red Hills

The stag warrior and the skyman ascended towards the ridge, towards the promise of light. Brak and Kerne were exhausted from their ordeal in the forest, but they had to keep going. They knew they would only be safe once they reached the heights, out of the shadow of that haunted forest. Who knew what other strange beasts lurked there?

Brak had been shocked by the chimeras. He had not recognised them, had not been able to converse with them in the tongue of Cernunnos, Lord of the Animals. It still troubled him. He was sullen and silent – even more so than usual – but something had changed between the two men, a begrudging but growing respect. As they approached the twilight of dawn they glanced at each other uneasily, seeing one another in a new light: battered, bruised, scratched and muddy, but with determination in their eyes – a resolve that drove them both on, despite their hunger and fatigue. They would rest awhile when they reached the ridge.

The growing light, red with the blood of a new day, pulled them towards the ridge's zenith. They used it as a focus, an incentive, despite the ridge being the true threshold of the Forbidden Kingdom. The dawn represented some kind of hope at a primal level, no matter how unfounded, how frail that hope was.

But an unexpected silhouette greeted them as the breached the brow of the hill.

Kerne staggered back, gasping.

It looked at first like a crude crucifix – an iron cross against the ruddy sky. A strange symbol in a pagan land.

Brak slunk close to the ground. This was new to him as well. Some instinct told him to be wary of it, whatever it represented.

Kerne, a man under its spell, was drawn to it with morbid fascination.

'Beware, skyman!'

He ignored the warrior's warning and staggered towards it. A sinking feeling in the pit of his stomach told him he recognised it, recognised the inverted cross, a wingspan across.

In the burgeoning light Kerne began to discern the details. On each crumpled wing a thick red circle with a black dot in its white centre looked out like an eye. It was a biplane, a Breguet from the Royal Flying Corps – the one he had crossed over in with Mallard.

Stunned, Kerne staggered around it in a daze, gazing at its reality – an object from another world. *His world.* He inspected the passenger seat where he had sat before being flung out in the turbulence of the Angel Gate. That was when he had been separated from his pilot, Mad Duck, whose battle frenzy – fuelled by his vision of Saint George – had taken them into the mysterious vortex.

The pilot's seat was empty but uncrushed. He must have tipped and cracked it, thought Kerne, imagining what must have happened: the biplane striking the ridge, ploughing into the red soil, wheels buckling underneath, and then the machine tipping nose up, casting the pilot out on to the ground as it came to a standstill. And there it remained, tail up, a curious icon, like a totem warning them they were crossing into the Forbidden Kingdom of Speaks-with-Thunder.

What had happened to Mallard, though, to turn him into a tyrant?

Brak approached when he saw the object was safe. He sniffed it warily, giving it a wide berth. He prodded it with his spear and when there was no reaction he kicked it, buckling a panel on the fuselage. 'Sky dung.'

Kerne nervously touched the fuselage. It felt icy cold and hard. Yes, it was real. He ran his fingers over its rust-riveted, buckled, dust-scoured surface, blasted by the constant wind that rolled up from the Steppe. It looked like it had been there for decades. Its canvas wings were as threadbare as leaves in autumn.

Gathering his wits, he checked the cockpit. It had been thoroughly scavenged. Mallard must have survived the crash and taken what he could with him. Unless others had been here ... The passenger seat was similarly empty, except for shards of photographic plates. Among them Kerne spotted the sturdy box camera. He pulled it out and inspected it: still intact, but useless without plates. Shame, it would have been good to have taken some souvenir shots of the spectacular landscape. Yet who would ever see them? The Ordnance Survey map of Mons had been taken from the glass panel; perhaps Mallard had hoped he could use it to get his bearings. But they were a long way from France or Belgium.

Holding the empty camera, Kerne slumped against the upper

wing, now parallel with the ground. The propeller was bent over like tyre irons, the engine a burnt-out shell.

The hills spread out below them; red in the dawn light, they stretched from north to south in a vast crescent, or claw, reaching west. Far away to the east, across the trackless Steppe that the hills led down into, the sun breached the horizon, amber and bloated. The grasslands were slowly revealed as the shroud of mist began to burn off. The Forbidden Kingdom. No Chalklander had ever laid eyes upon it and lived – 'except Brak!' boasted the young warrior, thumping his chest.

Kerne scanned it with his surveyor eyes. Somewhere down there, in Taranis's clutches, Bronwen was being held captive.

While he and Brak huddled there against a wing of the biplane, catching their breath after their climb and combat, wishing the sun would warm their limbs, Kerne recalled Windover Hill, where the Long Man of Wilmington strode with his staves. Holding the camera triggered memories and they flicked before him like a photographic album. Often had he walked up there with Nubi, sometimes with Maud as well, striking out from Eastbourne. It was always refreshing, but one day in March he remembered it having been particularly windy up on Windover, so much so that he lost his hat over the hillside and had trouble even standing up. Only in the lee of the barrows had he found some respite; otherwise only his stang gave him some stability as he traversed the downs, like Dru the Windsmith, the diviner of winds and surveyor of windmills, who was said to be the inspiration for the Long Man. If Kerne recollected his story correctly, told to him and Maud by the Reverend Burrows at Wilmington vicarage over tea, Dru could not only dowse the wind but *summon* it. Kerne had to learn the windsmith's secret – the key that unlocks the gates between the worlds – if he ever was to get back home.

Kerne listened to the ceaseless, mournful sound of the wind rolling up from the trackless Steppe. It filled him with a sense of desolation. Once he had held the key in his hand, but he had let go of it like a fool. He had discovered his windlass too late. Maud had the power of song to open the way between the worlds and with it she had managed to release him from the no-man's-land of limbo. He had *made* her let him go for her own good as well – she needed her life back, she needed to move on and find new love. Kerne was glad for her. Yet now he was alone and without her song. And he was no singer himself, that was for sure. Yet he had seen the sigils. If he could turn them into sounds then he would be able to use them to raise power, though it was chancy business: Ogmios had warned him one had to be careful what power was invoked – and banished.

Restless and ill at ease, Brak did not want to linger by the strange craft. 'It is cursed,' he brooded. He was not used to contemplation or inaction, so he was glad when they got moving again.

The wind scoured the hills, blasting the trespassers back as they breached the leeward ridge. Kerne had felt its icy touch before on Mount Anu, but now they experienced its full force. 'The breath of Eurus', the Chalk Folk called it: the God of the East Wind. The wind he had to master if he was to master his own destiny and not be blown about like a weathervane by the vicissitudes of fate. Somehow, he had to become a windsmith, a lord of the air, of gramarye.

At dawn, on a hostile hillside, it seemed an elusive goal. How was he ever going to make the wind bend to his will? Was he just grasping at castles in the air?

A sudden blaring of horns from below broke his reverie and made them dive for cover.

Scanning in the direction of the sound, they saw – unveiled as the dawn mist thinned – a massive hill fort guarding the head of the pass between the bare red hills. From the gates issued riders who were turning their steeds up the hillsides in a cloud of dust.

'We've got company. A search party – for us,' spat Brak.

'I knew I shouldn't have fired my weapon,' Kerne sighed.

The young hunter placed his hand on the shoulder of his companion. 'You had no choice – it was either us or … it.' Brak shuddered as he thought of the chimera. 'That was no usual denizen of the forest. My animal tongue had no effect on it. Even Cernunnos did not know it.'

'It was nothing of this earth. Only my Webley killed it …' The airman looked haunted. 'That was the first thing I have ever killed in my life. I am no hunter like my brother.'

'Get used to it. It is a fact of life around here … Come, we must keep on the move. We have Grey Raiders on our tail.'

The two men braced themselves against the wind and began to pick their way down the rock-strewn slope. The hunt was on. They were hungry and tired, but fear gave them new strength.

Silently and swiftly, Brak and Kerne wove between the boulders. The red dust clung to their cloaks, smudged their faces, as their feet kicked up clouds of it which was whipped by the wind into swirls and eddies.

They had to make their way to the hill fort, for they were sure that was where Bronwen was being kept. But that was the place most heavily guarded, the place from where their pursuers had emerged.

The report of the Webley had alerted Taranis to their presence, and not just to their presence but to the existence of another one who spoke with thunder. This was not the way Kerne wished to 'speak'; he would rather speak with whispers, with the power of the windsmith. Yet there was no time to learn the art. Events had accelerated. He was caught in them now, as surely as his descent down the red hills was unstoppable. He had to run with the current, or fall.

They came on horseback, like riders of the apocalypse, but twelve of them, wreathed in red, helmets pointed and fur-trimmed, slits for eyes, ring mail rattling, spears in hand. Their steeds sweated beneath their burdens, muscles bunching as they galloped up the diagonal path into the hills. The trespassers had been spotted on the bare hillside, and the riders raced to intercept them.

The two intruders slid down the slope, casting up a pall of red dust. They would never outrun the horses. Finally within range, the first rider aimed and hurled his spear. It thudded into the ground just in front of Kerne's leg.

'He was just getting his range – the next one will hit!' shouted Brak, who scooped up a stone, loaded his swing and cast the missile. It cracked against the helmet of the warrior, stunning him enough to make him lose aim. The spear went wide.

Other riders were within spear range now.

'Use your thunder-arrow!' Brak implored, diving to get out of range again.

'No, I can't kill a human being!' gasped Kerne, his chest burning from the pursuit.

'Then we are doomed!'

Their descent was checked by a steeper slope, leading to what looked like a cliff, which they couldn't see over. The pursuers knew they had them, and reined in their horses, cutting off the intruders' only escape route.

'Give yourselves up!' barked the leader in a thick accent. 'Taranis demands your presence!'

Brak showed them what he thought of the tyrant's demands by making a squatting gesture, then turning his back on them.

The Grey Raiders took aim and threw a brace of spears. As the spears whistled towards them Brak pushed them both over the edge of the escarpment. The two men half ran, half stumbled, sliding uncontrollably down the steep slope.

At first they thought their end had come. They found themselves sliding down a shaft, a bit like a blowhole or air vent. Hot stale air blasted their faces. The sides were narrow enough for them to slow their descent a little by putting their arms and legs out, but still they bounced down the hole in a painful manner, till they landed in a heap at the bottom on a pile of chippings, groaning but alive.

When they had recovered from their fall and checked no bones were broken, their eyes began to adjust to the gloom. They were in a cave – a system of caves. And they could hear the echo of tools and the murmur of people.

'Wait a moment,' Kerne whispered. He needed to get his breath back. He pulled out his cantina, offered it to Brak. The warrior smiled and accepted. Quietly they shared the water and washed a little of the dust from their faces. Then they chewed on some biscuits.

'What a way to wake up!' joked Kerne grimly.

Having recovered a little, they began to explore, creeping to where the sound came from ... They edged to a ledge, where they looked down on a scene from Hell.

Kerne could not believe his eyes.

Figures moved in the murk, illuminated by lamps reeking of animal fat. It was an ore mine worked by slaves: a mixture of ethnicities, including some of Brak's people, starving in rags, bent double, carrying huge baskets of rock on their backs by means of a head strap. Antlike columns of them were climbing the rickety ladders with their loads, depositing them with great relief into carts which were pulled away by more slaves. Then they would descend another ladder and start all over again, collecting their load from where it was brought up in leather baskets by a great iron wheel from a deeper shaft below. Among them were women and children, weak with hunger and fatigue. They saw a young man collapse. His fellow workers tried to pick him up, but armoured guards approached and barked at him to get up. He didn't respond, so they lashed him with a whip. He was dragged off to some evil fate, to the laments and keening of the slaves, until they were forced once more into silence.

'I know of silver, lead and copper mines, but nothing like this,' whispered Brak, 'What are they mining in this hellhole?'

'Misery, by the looks of things ... Perhaps iron – that would make

116

sense – for armour and weapons. Like the ones they used to sack your valley.'

'A stronger metal than bronze?'

'Yes, and easier to work. You don't need to mix it with other metals. Just need extremely hot temperatures.' Kerne held a rock in his hand. He had an engineer's knowledge of materials. The GWR had been built on Brunel's iron. Kerne knew the hills' redness had been caused by air reacting with the ore. Even in this Otherworld some basic physical laws were the same, he was relieved to notice.

Unfortunately, other things were similar too, including man's ability to treat his fellow man so cruelly and to exploit the resources of the planet. This was more like the afterlife of the Greeks – the shades of Hades, trapped in an underworld of suffering and regret. Here were a thousand Sisyphi pushing their burden upwards in endless toil and torment. Here was the tyranny of Taranis.

Did they have more to rescue besides Bronwen? How could they ignore the plight of these people?

Kerne tried to persuade Brak of this, but he would not accept responsibility. Everyone creates their own doom, the hunter whispered. They had no obligation to help – they would be honour bound to those they freed for changing their fate. Their duty was to Bronwen.

The two men argued on the ledge, becoming more animated, though keeping their voices low, until one of them chanced to dislodge a rock. They watched in horror as it clattered down, to the feet of a guard in his demonic helmet. He looked up and spotted them and then barked to the others. Guards started to climb the ladders towards them.

'Great – out of the frying pan, into the fire!' Kerne exclaimed.

Once more they stood side by side, preparing to fight.

Suddenly, there was uproar behind the guards. Miners and guards were scrambling out of the lower pit, screaming. The iron wheel buckled and collapsed – no, was pulled into the pit, knocking some of them back.

The world seemed to bend, then out of the pit erupted a ram-headed serpent, scales rippling white and red with fire. Just like the firecats, thought Kerne in a moment of fear-frozen lucidity. The monster illuminated the cavern, casting a glance over the humans. The mine was filled with terrified screaming. Guards were sent running towards the monster, poleaxes raised. The serpent picked them up in mouthfuls and tore them apart. Others it knocked into the pit with a swipe of its horned head.

The guards climbing the ladders had lost interest in the intruders now. They were more intent on escaping. But the serpent saw them and plucked them off, one at a time, as they screamed. The guards' weapons bounced off its thick hide. Nothing could stop it.

What had released the monster? Kerne had a sick feeling in his stomach. He couldn't explain it, but he felt it was up to him to stop the beast.

They could run away in the confusion – as Brak insisted they did – but, Kerne pleaded, they couldn't leave the slaves at the mercy of the monster. *They* would not be able to escape.

'Come on – let's get out of here! Whatever that thing is, it's a good diversion.'

'No, Brak!' shouted Kerne over the chaos. 'We can't leave those people. Some of them are Chalk Folk! We have to do something!'

'With what, this?' Brak jabbed his spear.

Kerne pulled his Webley from its holster. 'Let's hope this has the same affect as it did on these firecats!'

Kerne waited for the serpent to rear up. He fired, but missed. The pistol's thunder echoed around the cavern, maddening the serpent. It lunged at the ledge and butted the rock face, dislodging rubble. The airman was knocked back, and his right arm was trapped by a boulder, the Webley still in his hand. The serpent reared to strike again. Kerne was now helpless. This time Brak stepped in and tried to ward it off with his spear. The monster snapped the weapon in its mouth and spat out the fragments contemptuously. The young hunter braced himself for the coup de grâce, unsheathing his knife and roaring at the serpent, 'May Cernunnos protect me!'

At the last moment, screaming in pain, Kerne managed to pull the revolver free and fire it at the serpent's head. In a flash of fire that knocked them both back the monster exploded and disappeared.

As they lay there stunned, the riders who had pursued them over the Red Hills appeared at the cave mouth. The mine guards pointed to the ledge and the Grey Raiders quickly ascended. Before the intruders could recover they were apprehended.

'You are coming with us now,' said their captors' leader. 'As guests of Taranis.'

13

Crossed Paths

The cage rattled and creaked along, the iron-rimmed wheels striking the rutted, rubble-strewn track, sending vibrations shuddering up to the two chained prisoners. Brak and Kerne sat manacled to the bars at the front of the cart. It was pulled by a great black war horse led by a Grey Raider. Other warriors flanked them on horseback, watching their every move from beneath their pointed helmets, eyes squinting in the harsh light, spears in hand ready to prod the prisoners if they began to speak. Brak had already received a couple of gashes for his insolence.

Kerne resigned himself to their fate. They were getting a ride to where their duty led them, after all. This must be the kind of cart Bronwen was taken in to Caer Taranis, he mused grimly, remembering what Merlin had told him. He hoped she was being treated better than they were.

The captives' bodies were bruised and aching from their ordeal: the flight through Wolf Forest, the pursuit across the Red Hills, the fall into the mines and the fight with the serpent. They'd had no sleep and little food. Their packs had been taken, and they had been stripped of any weapons, including the Webley. In torn garments they shivered in the light of a new day. A constant breeze blew in from across the vast Steppe. The grass plains stretched as far as the eye could see. The world looked different in the east. They were in the Forbidden Kingdom now – a place few outsiders had seen and from where none had returned.

Black smoke billowed from massive stone ovens where cartloads of iron ore were deposited and smelted by soot-smeared workers. The entourage passed low buildings of dun wattle and daub, round-shouldered against the wind. Sounds of clanging came from these open-fronted workshops where green flames flared. Kerne spotted blacksmiths in leather aprons hobbling about in their smithies, their sweat-streaked torsos momentarily illuminated by spark showers, their faces furrowed in intense concentration, eyes protected with thick glass goggles reminiscent of Kerne's flying pair. Before he could make sense of this strange juxtaposition the cart trundled on.

The prisoners were taken through a shanty town that had excreted itself on to the flanks of the fort, reeking of animal and human refuse, its central track guttered with sewage. Here Kerne spotted more slaves – painfully thin, threadbare and broken. Only the very old, ill or young remained during shift hours. The horse warriors patrolled constantly, clad in fur against the biting wind, proud and cruel. Yet the Horse Nomads were of no one distinct race. Within the small contingent that escorted them to the fort there was a mixture of Eurasian ethnicities: features as distinct as a Scotsman from a Cymro, a Cornishman from a son of Ireland to a native inhabitant of the Steppe, no doubt, but difficult for Kerne to distinguish and place. They were indiscriminate in their treatment of the slaves – striking down young or old, male or female without hesitation. Some wielded the cat-o'-nine-tails, which they used on horse or human alike, though their love of horses was obviously greater.

If the Da'anu Valley was the realm of Kerne's ancestors, whose was this? There was no time to unravel the enigma. They were nearing the dark silhouette of the fort. Its massive buttresses guarded the pass through the Red Hills, a gorge lined with pine trees. Four roads intersected here: west from the lake, east from the Steppe and north and south along the length of the Red Hills. Before each of its heavily timbered gates the road was straddled by what looked like gigantic wicker figures. As the captives passed under the legs of one they could see the charred remains of humans and animals.

Kerne observed that these giants were made not of wicker but of metal – iron strips threaded and welded together. This metalwork was tinted red, oxidising in the cold stream of air from the east, and covered with congealing black globules of fat. Kerne thought he saw bones and teeth trapped in the concrescence, but he could not be sure.

The cart was hauled up the steep track to the gate. The palisade of sharpened pine trunks was topped by severed heads in varying states of decomposition, some no more than bleached skulls with wisps of hair. The black-cloaked guards on the battlements shouted the customary challenges despite recognising the riders as their own. A guttural password was barked, the gates creaked open, and the prisoners passed into the fort. The heavy gates were quickly shut behind them and the massive bolt lowered into place.

They were not going to be leaving here in a hurry.

In contrast to the ramshackle slave town below, the fort was well made and run with ruthless efficiency. Across the flat-topped hill the low-slung dwellings were laid out with military symmetry. It reminded Kerne of the British Expeditionary Force camp in Calais. Workshops and storehouses backed against the high walls. A wide timbered track ran through the middle of dwellings bustling with activity. Kerne imagined no one was allowed to be idle in such a place.

In the centre of the hill fort towered the main hall, constructed of overlapping timbers like bony fingers crossed. Goliath red-cloaked guards stood in front of doors carved with horses and humans and inlaid with gilt.

The prisoners were untied, pulled out of the cage and frogmarched by the Grey Raiders into the hall.

As his eyes adjusted to the dark interior Kerne gained an impression of massive beams, ornate pillars, long mead benches lining crude tables, a packed-earth floor strewn with straw, shields and weapons hanging from each pillar or cross-timber, all lit by the slits of light that shone through the narrow windows high in the roof, pointing down like spotlights.

And on the other side of a large fire pit, upon a dais, on a throne of iron covered in furs, sat gold-torced Taranis: steel-eyed, blond-maned, brown beard red in the firelight – a powerfully built man in a richly embroidered tunic, bear-fur cloak wrapped around his shoulders, a silver goblet in one hand; his other, ringed, holding the symbol of his office over the armrest of the throne, a Webley revolver.

'Mallard, is that you?' Kerne was incredulous. The difference in years refuted the reality of what he saw, those familiar Viking eyes.

The air strained around them – the same thing he had felt before the chimera had appeared, Kerne realised. The chthonic carvings seemed to writhe in the firelight. The very hall itself *throbbed*, the beams like the ribs of a monster that had devoured them.

What new monsters would appear in this world of madness?

The Royal Guard gripped their weapons, their spearheads and helmets gleaming in the flickering firelight.

The prisoners were cast before the King.

'Isambard Kerne, I presume,' the King said with ragged mirth.

The young Chalklander leaped to his feet like a feral cat. 'Murderer!' he spat. 'Give me back my sister. Give me back my father's life!' Brak lunged for the King with his bare hands but was struck down by a guard. He lay stunned, blood oozing from a wound in his brow.

Kerne rushed forward to aid him but was knocked back by the swift butt of a shield-boss that knocked the air from his lungs. The guards coolly restrained him with barbed spears at his throat.

'Bronwen, step forward. Your brother wants to see you.' The King spoke with a voice hoarse and harsh.

From behind the tapestries that hung behind the King stepped Bron's daughter, veiled and dressed like a courtesan: midriff and cleavage exposed, coin-waisted, narrow ankles braceleted as though shackled, jangling bangles, smelling like a rosebush after the rain.

Brak looked up and couldn't believe his eyes. 'Sister, what have they done to you? Has – has he made you his whore?'

'Silence!' commanded the King, and a guard struck Brak on the back of the head, knocking him out.

'Brak!' Bronwen stepped forward but was held back by the guards.

The woman wept, until through her tears she saw Kerne. She looked at him fleetingly, then turned her bruised glance away. It had been six days since Bronwen's capture – to them. How long had it been for her?

'Unhand the prisoner.'

Kerne felt the eyes of the King burn into him and he recognised their fervent gleam. Beneath a jagged iron crown, the heavy jowls, the tawny beard of many winters' growth, there gazed the steel blue eyes of Mallard. They showed no sign of surprise or warmth.

'So – you've finally come at last. We're certainly on the Dead Side now, hey, mapman?' The King gestured flamboyantly with his pistol. 'Welcome to my kingdom.' His voice was ragged, his Yorkshire accent barely discernible. Kerne noticed the scar at his throat between the ends of his ram-headed gold torc. He recalled his pilot receiving a bullet in the neck. He had survived, but his voice box hadn't.

'Mallard. It *is* you! I hoped it wouldn't be.' Kerne gazed at his fellow airman. 'Harry, what have you become?'

A dark shadow passed across the pilot's brow. 'It's Madoc now – King Madoc!' His voice strained; his face reddened. He took a deep breath and spoke with a ragged whisper. 'Or Speaks-with-Thunder, as I'm known affectionately. In the local tongue: Taranis. I let this do the talking for me these days ...' He waved his pistol in the air. 'I have come a long way since we flew in the skies above Mons.'

Kerne looked aghast at his old pilot. He was older and different. He'd always thought the man had a gung-ho streak in him – he seemed to love the 'Game of War' as he called it – but now he had become a tyrant.

'What, aren't you impressed? Why do you look at me like that?'

'You've changed. You look older, a lot older.'

'Whereas you look hardly different from the last time I saw you, except for the state of your uniform. But then neither of us would pass muster, hey, old bean?' He smiled with thin lips. 'How long have you been in this world, Kerne?'

Kerne thought back to his arrival last winter. It seemed a lifetime ago. 'Six months perhaps – it's hard to keep proper track of time.'

'It's even harder here …' Madoc waved at the guards. 'Release him. Please, sit. Forgive my manners … Let us have a drink for old times' sake, hey? Bronwen, don't you want to pour our guest a drink? He is very thirsty.' Madoc gestured to the guard holding her and he released her. She hesitated, then picked up the copper pitcher on the table and went to pour Kerne a drink, her hands shaking. He noticed again the bruises the veil obscured. Her eyes were full of terror and urgency.

'See what you think of this particular vintage, one of the many things plundered by my raiders from the tribes of the south. Not quite a pint of mild, but I've got used to it, even fond, you could say. As you may recall, I like my tipple …' He sighed, swilling the wine around in its goblet. 'Where does all the time go, hey?' Slowly he looked up at Kerne. 'I've been here twenty-five years.'

The words slammed home like a prison sentence. Kerne shook his head in disbelief. 'How can that be? We only crossed over half a year ago?' But as soon as he'd said that, Kerne remembered how long it had been for Maud since his disappearance. Nine years. It seemed the same time anomaly occurred the deeper into HyperEurus you went. Time ran differently in different zones. He recalled Merlin saying as much. Who could know how much time had passed back in the Bone Mountains since they had left?

'To old times?' Madoc raised his glass.

Kerne declined to join in the toast. 'Let Brak and Bronwen go.'

Madoc sighed and shrugged, taking a draught of his wine. 'Down the hatch, old boy.' He wiped his beard with the back of his pistol hand, giving Kerne a mocking look. 'As straight-laced as ever, aren't you! I remember, in the barracks, you'd never join in the gambling. In France, you wouldn't go whoring with the men.'

'Let the brother and sister go.'

'I'm afraid I can't do that, old boy.'

'Why not?'

Madoc plucked a hunk of goat meat and chewed on it absent-mindedly, spitting the gristle into the fire. 'Because Bronwen …

keeps me company. And it's best not to sleep with one's ancestors. I'd rather avoid the possibility, however remote … The women here are … supple, but not so pretty. It's never a good idea, breeding with the natives, eh, even if they are all barren. Got to keep one's standards up. We *are* ambassadors for the Empire, after all.' Madoc made a mock toast and emptied his goblet, wiping a trickle of wine from his lips. 'And as for the Chalklander prince, he'll make a useful hostage, or sacrifice.'

'You can't do that – that's barbaric!'

'You're in the land of the barbarians now, in case you haven't noticed. It's not the Home Counties any more, old bean.' Madoc leaned forward, a dangerous gleam in his eye. Voice lowered, he continued, 'I don't know how we came to be here, but if this is the world of the dead, and we died that day at Mons, then we can't die again! Our bodies have survived. Maybe even our souls …' He raised his arms and his voice. 'We're immortal! And if the people here are dead then it doesn't matter if I kill them, does it? How can a ghost feel pain?'

'You have become inhuman! What happened to the cause? We went to fight for right – at least we thought we did – and now you have become worse than our enemy.'

'Perhaps we are more like them than we care to imagine. I had Viking ancestors. Perhaps it's in my blood … You know, I've been thinking a lot about that. It's seems I have more in common with these Huns than I realised at first. I get a feeling my Viking forefather slept with a Hun bitch. You know, in those days, when an army marched it took everyone with them, blacksmiths, prostitutes, the whole shooting match. You know Attila's hordes reached as far as Gaul? There was the famously bloody Battle of Châlons in 451, so I'm told by some of the people who fought in it, can you imagine? Perhaps my forefathers fought in that as well, as a hired mercenary – who knows? – and enjoyed the spoils of war afterwards … I'm just carrying on the family business, as it were.' Madoc laughed with his broken voice.

He took another swig, emptying his goblet. He banged it on the armrest of the throne, bidding Bronwen to refill it. He ogled her as she poured the wine, running the pistol barrel down her cheek, her neck. 'My father ran a foundry. I used to love to watching the smelt-fires.' His eyes were ablaze. 'The way a man of strength can bend anything to his will.' The barrel came to rest between her breasts. Bronwen whimpered with fear, spilling wine. 'Iron is in my blood,' he breathed at her, trying to making her reach for his trews. She screamed and dropped the pitcher. Madoc cursed and struck her across the face with the back of his hand. She fell to the floor, stunned.

'You're inhuman!' Kerne lunged and was struck down also. He writhed on the floor in pain beside the stirring figure of Brak.

Bronwen sobbed, holding herself and rocking. Her hair fell over her face, matted with blood and tears.

'Guards, take the Chalklander away.'

Madoc glared contemptuously down at Bronwen. 'You can go too. You're a mess and you're beginning to bore me … This one can stay' – he said pointed at Kerne – 'until I've taught him some table manners …'

The guards dragged Brak away, and handmaidens helped Bronwen into the shadows. A servant quickly cleared up the broken pitcher and spilled wine.

Madoc clapped his hands. 'Bring more wine, and food!' he roared. A flurry of servants set to work bringing in pitchers and dishes of food. Soon a feast was laid before them.

The Iron King seemed to relax a little. 'Sit, eat – I insist. Brak's safety depends on your behaviour. Relax.' Madoc cast a glance at the guards as they lifted Kerne up and forced him into a seat. A tray with a platter of meat, bread, fruit and sweetmeats was placed before him. Kerne had not eaten properly for a two days and found it difficult to resist. Though he detested the treatment of the captives and slaves, he found himself devouring what was in front of him. It felt like dining with the Devil.

'That's more like it. It's been a long time since I've seen a familiar face. It is good to see you, mapman; it really is! It's been lonely, though I'm seldom alone. You must understand a man's need for company.' A lecherous smile came over his face. 'Bronwen is rather charming, isn't she?'

Kerne gave him a hard stare. 'She also is a human being who has the right to choose her own life.'

'Did we have a choice, my friend, when we were taken into Saint George's Gate?'

'The Angel Gate, as I think of it, is a mystery, that's for certain.' Kerne eyed Madoc warily. 'The events on that day in August were beyond our control. We were sucked into the vortex of war along with everybody else, but since then, since crossing over, to wherever this place is, the choices have been our own.'

'Have they? Did we have any choice where we ended up? By some strange turn of fate, you ended up with the Chalk Folk, and I ended up here with the Horse Nomads.'

'Yes, but I haven't become a warlord. Whereas you, you have become a tyrant.'

'Really? You don't know what I have to deal with here. That's the only language these savages understand. You should have seen the place when I first arrived. It was like the Dark Ages. I am bringing the enlightenment of civilisation to their lives.' Firelight flared in Madoc's eyes.

'It doesn't look like civilisation to me out there ...'

'It's progress! Victorian England wasn't exactly easy on most of the population. I remember what it was like growing up then. Every day I would see those awful slums, the workhouses and the smog – but look where it got us, the greatest nation on Earth! Machines! Speed! Efficiency! That is what I am bringing to them. This could be a new colony of the Empire! I am merely doing the King's duty. So a corner of this Otherworld will be for ever England. Where's your patriotism, dear boy? This is no more than Clive did in India.'

'This is not patriotism; it is despotism. It is not noble. Don't try and dignify it. You're just consumed by your own lust for power. It has corrupted you, turned you crazy. You think you're doing good, and you use that to justify all of these atrocities in the name of saving these people from themselves. Who chose you to be their redeemer?'

The fire flared up as a log dislodged itself, sending sparks into the shadows.

Madoc looked coolly at Kerne. 'Destiny. I had no choice.' His voice was steady. 'And you better hold your tongue – if you want to keep it!' He held Kerne's gaze until the latter lowered his eyes.

Madoc took a gulp of wine. 'Let me tell you how I came to be here, and then perhaps you'll understand. Just hear me out. Not that you have any right to judge me.' Madoc gripped his pistol, an angry gleam in his eye.

Kerne wasn't going to argue with him. He sat and listened, hoping his presence would placate his erstwhile pilot. No amount of reasoning with him would work, he knew that. Mad Duck had always had it in him, but now his psychosis was fully formed. Given free rein it had run amok.

Madoc stared into the flames and remembered. 'That morning above Mons ... above the battle ... I saw Saint George and felt filled with courage. I took the old bird down for a bombing run ... That's

126

when I got a bullet in the neck. Fortunately, its trajectory through the fuselage and cockpit had taken out most of its edge, but it was enough to damage my voice, as you can hear. No more singing in the barracks for me, hey? It took months to heal and has never fully recovered.' Madoc drank to ease his throat – it obviously hurt him to talk so much. But he continued with fervour, letting the memory play itself out. 'I thought my time was up. Then we hit the cloud of fire and everything went barmy. The plane spun around like a child's toy – I suppose that's when you were thrown out.'

Kerne nodded. This was interesting to hear. He had wondered what had befallen his pilot and he was finally finding out. Perhaps it would help him understand.

Fired up by his story, Madoc continued: 'I was losing a lot of blood, my vision was blurred red and my hands were slippery, but I managed to grab hold of the controls and straighten her out. I'd flown in some bad storms before, but that was the worst. I thought I heard screaming, thought I saw demons tearing at the wings, but I suppose it was some atmospheric phenomenon or the battle below.'

Kerne kept silent. His friend's lack of imagination had been his best defence in limbo – while Kerne's imagination had nearly torn him apart.

'Then the clouds cleared and I was flying above white mountains. They reminded me of the Alps, but how could that be? The Alps would be too far south. I didn't have time to ponder such things; the old bird was in bad shape. She had taken a hit in the engine and smoke was billowing out. I had to get to somewhere safe to land. I passed over some foothills, the forts, a river valley lined with figures like that horny fellow in Dorset. Then I was over the lake, but I didn't want to ditch her there – I'm a useless swimmer. Fortunately, I still had some altitude, and managed to take her over the water and, with the last of her juice, above the treeline of that cursed forest, until I hit the ridge of the Red Hills. It wasn't a pretty landing. I cracked her up, but was thrown clear before she blew. Must have made quite a bang. Certainly announced my arrival to the world. And that's where she stayed, nose down, tail up, like a diving whale.'

'I know; I saw her – it. Thought it was a cross at first ...'

'Did you? Well, I see it as a hammer – like Thor's. Left it there as a bit of a statement, a kind of "Keep Bloody Out!" sign.' He chuckled to himself, but Kerne did not feel amused. Madoc ripped off a piece of roasted flesh and began to tear at it absent-mindedly. 'Y'know I've got into my ancestry since I've been here. Don't know why. I suppose it's like living in the past. My ancestors were Vikings who settled in the north of England after they had got tired of raping and pillaging. Even marauders like to settle down in the end, I suppose. You could say I'm getting back in touch with that side of things. If I'm a natural warrior, it's because it's in the blood ... After I crashed I was out for the count and in a bad mess, weak with loss of blood, and a couple of broken bones. I awoke to see three men standing over me speaking a strange language – sounded like Kraut to me at first. Luckily I had my Webley still with me – loaded as usual – and without thinking I fired, killing two. The third fell to his knees. He was some kind of medicine man. A shaman, as they call them around here: Crow-Walker, who later became my court magician. I had killed their chief and champion, by speaking with thunder. I couldn't say anything else at first, other than croaking 'Mad Duck' over and over like a lunatic. I admit I was in a bad way, perhaps a little hysterical. I just kept repeating my nickname. Mad Duck, Mad Duck ... It was all I could do to keep sane. I seemed to forget my real one, even my memories. I was in danger of losing myself ...'

Kerne recalled how he had felt when he had first arrived on Mount Anu, anonymous and voiceless.

'So I became known as Madoc, their king. It's kind of funny when you think of it. The medicine man, shaman, took me back to his people and said I had fallen from the sky and spoke with thunder ... The simple savages believed it and fell to their knees to worship me. Suddenly I found myself their king. The medicine man healed my wounds, covered them, and me, in animal fat and fur and fed me honeymilk until I healed. I took over running their tribe. Strangely, my ears became attuned to their tongue, as if I remembered it from long ago. And now it just sounds like English to me, though hearing you speak reminds me what real English sounds like, the King's English. Still, I couldn't complain – I had landed on my feet, so to speak. If I was behind enemy lines I had to ascertain my position and secure it. But that seemed impossible. It feels like we're somewhere in Eastern Europe – like Austria – but the plains seem more like the Steppe further east. Geography is weird here – like time. It seems to stretch and shrink ...' He looked in confusion at Kerne. 'Am I making sense?' There was a tinge of desperation in his voice.

Kerne nodded, and the Iron King breathed with relief, sitting back and swigging from his goblet.

'So, Madoc, how did you become their warlord?'

Madoc emptied his goblet and lowered it slowly. 'Their king, you mean?' he corrected, with a little gesture of the pistol.

Kerne could not risk it being loaded, but he wondered whether after all of those years it had any bullets left. How many people had Madoc killed to maintain his rule?

Oblivious, the King was continuing. 'Well, when I had recovered I began to assess my strengths. And any local threats. We were surrounded by warlike tribes. The villages were always being raided. They lived with a constant threat of terror. And so I decided to take the initiative. Pre-emptive strikes. I managed to knock out their champions with my trusty Webley. Each tribe we conquered increased the strength of my army, until we had control of the region. Speaks-with-Thunder ruled!'

'And now you are turning your attentions west. Why?'

Madoc picked at a bowl of fruit, holding, squeezing, sampling the different exotic varieties. 'There are valuable resources in those valleys: tin, copper, silver. And women, beautiful women ...' He settled on a golden, soft-furred fruit and took a deep bite, the juice oozing down his beard.

'You are raping the land and its daughters! You have become worse than the enemy we were supposed to be fighting!'

'No, Kerne. I am no philosopher. I am a realist. My strengths are practical. Lord knows where or when we are. I don't understand it. But what I do know is that someone needs to take charge. To sort this mess out. I think it's my destiny. I was born to do this! And think what we could achieve together ...'

Kerne went cold. 'What do you mean?'

'You and me, Kerne – well, how about it? Two Englishmen could conquer this world. We could rule the east and west between us. You could be my duke in west, overseeing operations there.'

Kerne stood up. 'No! I will not be sucked into your pit of hate. I will not become like you.'

'You would do well to think on it, Kerne.' Madoc's raw voice was low, controlled. 'For if you refuse I will have to consign you to the fires of Gogmagog. I give my metal giants that name after the giant porters consumed in the Great Fire of London. A touch of nostalgia, perhaps. Guards, take him to a cell and let him sleep on his fate!'

The Royal Guards grabbed Kerne and began dragging him away.

'You have until dawn, old chum. Join me or die! And if you don't die then Brak will. The gods are angry and must be appeased. The Red Hills echoed with thunder. I must reassure my people that there is only one who speaks withhunder! Tomorrow, the giant must be fed!'

The Pit of Stars

The Journal of Isambard Kerne
Cutios 1st, Waning Atenoux

I have been thrown into a prison-pit next to Brak's. I sit at the bottom of a ten-foot-square shaft. Above, all I can see is a square of clouds and blue sky beyond the heavy iron grill. I crouch in the stink and squalor of this pit while I write this. The guards did not take the journal from me, or the little slim pencil slipped into its binding. They probably had no idea what it was – certainly no weapon that they would understand.

I spotted Brak as I was dragged across to my cell in a corner of the fort. He was placed in a similar cell, but I recognised his angry rantings. He was cursing with admirable thoroughness and colour. I was thrown down into the pit. After I had recovered from the fall, and waited for the guards to leave – though I think they are not too far away – I began to talk to Brak. We could just about hear one another, our voices muffled by the shafts and the noise of the fort. What enraged Brak more than anything was seeing his sister 'dressed like a whore'. I tried to pacify him, saying she had no choice. She was trapped like us, but in another way. We had to be strong for her. I couldn't bring myself to tell him his fate was in my hands. That if I lived he died, or vice versa ...

Kill or be killed. Is that the only way to survive here? Yet am I prepared to die for my beliefs? And would my death be in vain? Didn't Merlin say it is up to me to rid this world of the iron poison that threatens to destroy it? Madoc came here with me – perhaps one of us must die 'to heal the rift'. Otherwise, it may tear this land apart ...

Guards soon came over and ordered us to be silent. They urinated into the pit to make us stop. Barbarians, indeed! And so I began to write in this journal. It's the only thing keeping me sane. Perhaps this is the last entry I shall write ... Who knows?

I ponder the brutality of man. Is the behaviour of Madoc (the name by which I now think of him) at all surprising? Isn't it in men's nature to be warlike and cruel? Isn't the whole history of humanity tainted with bloodshed? They say nature is red in tooth and claw, but isn't man also? Are we nothing more than animals? Bloodthirsty Madoc seems proof of that. Yet Brak's aggressiveness can be channelled positively, perhaps has a place – as defender of his tribe. How much violence is justified, if any, when defending oneself? Do we have to fight war with war? Doesn't that just continue the cycle of violence?

Madoc's particular road to Hell is paved with good intentions, about 'civilising' people, making them toe the line, play by the rules – our rules: the imperialist rhetoric drummed into us all by the 'glories' of the British Empire, the propaganda of the press and the military, Kitchener's call to arms to 'do the right thing' or face the spurious shame of the white feather.

Yet did I not enlist in the Royal Flying Corps to fight for King and Country? Well, I had little choice in the matter – it was only a matter a time, and it was better to volunteer. My brother wouldn't let me do otherwise. He is the hawk in the family. But isn't he part of me? Am I not of the same flesh and blood? Perhaps, and the thought is abhorrent, there's a part of me that is warlike too? After all, was not my ancestor, the first Kerne, a light-armed Irish foot soldier?

Yet, I am no warrior ... unless it is with words and not the sword. Could I not fight with the power of gramarye? I would, if I could master it. But my uselessness allowed Bron to die and Bronwen to be captured. And now I am captured and face death unless I am prepared to have blood on my hands.

I cannot see a way out of this impasse. What am I to do? I am lost. Madoc will conquer this world. His iron virus will spread. War will consume this Shadow World. And where will the soul find peace when the world of the dead is on fire?

Yet it would appear that Madoc and myself are the only 'sky people' in this world. Why is that? Surely many of my contemporaries have Celtic ancestors. Do they each have their own Afterland, their own 'Land of the Forefathers and Mothers'?

Too many questions. I am literally in the dark. The sun has moved across the sky, the shadows lengthen, and the further west it goes the nearer I am to death. I know I cannot let Brak die on my account. I must die, the ferryman will be paid and then this world will perhaps find peace.

I wish there was more light. I look up, gazing at clouds, imagining myself flying amongst them; free as bird ... Just now I noticed one soaring overhead, a bird of prey. A carrion-eater? Is it waiting for me? Can it sense my doom? It is coming closer ... It's a falcon!

I have just spoken with Merlin. He has found me! But before we could exchange plans the guards shooed him away. He told me not to give up hope. To meditate upon the oak rune. 'Duir!' he cried – and before he was driven away he dropped something in the stinking mud before me.

I picked it up, wiped it clean on my trouser leg. It was an acorn. Such a familiar, earthly thing was a comfort to me, whatever it portended. I rolled the small brown nut in my hand, drawing strength from it. I tried to chant, '*Duir*,' but nothing came at first. I settled down in the shadows, sitting cross-legged with my back against the damp wall, relaxing my body, slowing my breathing as I had been taught, and then I tried again. This time a glimmer of the sigil came to mind. I could visualise the two bands pointing left. The sigil swirled in my head as I chanted it over and over again, for hours. I called to the dryad of the oak and he finally appeared faintly before me – or at least in my mind's eye. He was a stout, strong-looking fellow, massive-limbed and deep-browed. I sensed his strength, his power, and drew sustenance from it. Memories of my father came to mind, how he had always been there for us, supporting the family with the strength of his body, working those long, gruelling shifts on the railway so food could be on our table, so Archie and I could have an education. He was not good at showing his feelings like Mother, but he loved us in his gruff way. In his company I felt safe, as though nothing could harm me.

I opened my eyes and looked up. The square was full of stars, like the roofless tower of Glastonbury Tor at night. The dryad was nowhere to be seen, if indeed he had ever been there at all, but I no longer felt trapped. I could hardly see the bars. It felt as though I could float up and be free, but when I tried to lift myself up I slid back into the pit. I was still earthbound, but felt as though I'd accessed the power of duir, the oak sigil representing doorways and strength.

My vitality had returned. Though it had been twelve hours or more since I had last eaten, I had found inner nourishment from some deep reserves of the spirit. I felt awake, alert.

I called out to Brak, and on the second attempt he responded, wearily, spirits low. Our whispers carried further in the stillness and silence of the night. We hoped the guards were nodding off somewhere and would not punish our communications. None came.

And so there, in the dead of night, we talked, talked about memories, about people and places we have known. I had never heard Brak talk so much. I could tell by the strain in his voice that he was worried about our fate, but he covered this with bravado.

I could imagine him clearly. The meditation had sharpened my senses, and perhaps opened other ones as well. I tried to reassure the young hunter that he would live. Life was strong in him; he had far to journey. He was young. One day he would have a family. I said that my one regret was never having a son, but that if I'd had one I would have been proud if he had been like Brak.

Then I heard a low sobbing from Brak's pit. I called out to ask if the young warrior was alright. He responded with a primal cry of despair which brought the guards running. They tried to make him shut up, but he howled back at them like a caged animal. All the anger, all the sadness of his father's death poured out of him like molten lava. He taunted them to come down into the pit so he could tear them apart. They responded by throwing a bucket of cold water over him, which shocked him into silence. The guards departed after warning him they did not want their watch disturbed again. Next time it would be boiling oil.

I asked again if my fellow inmate was alright. Brak responded with a disturbing sound – he was laughing quietly to himself. The exorcism of his grief seemed to have put him in good humour. It had broken the carapace over his heart, and we were able to talk very freely, for we had nothing left to lose.

We gazed up at the stars while we talked. I had never been colder in my life, or more painfully alive. If this was to be my last night on Earth, then I wanted to savour every minute of it.

I tried to point out to Brak the constellation of Orion, with his three-starred belt, and Canis Major, his faithful hound, at his feet. Brak called them Andraste and her Hare but seemed to find strength in my likening Orion to him. He showed me what I think of as Leo – he said this was the Great Stag, which carries the dead across the sky on his back, along the White Road that leads to the Halls of the Blessed. I gently asked if Bron was there now. Brak replied, 'Yes, he is looking down on us.' I could tell Brak wanted his father's forgiveness. I tried to ease his sense of having failed him by saying that surely mighty Bron would be proud of what he had done, how far he had come. His bravery has never been found lacking. He is a true hunter and fit to join his father in the 'sky-hunt', as Brak calls it.

'Thank you, skyman. I know I have not been open in my heart to you but I see you walk with dignity and do the best you can. That is all any of us can do. I am glad to have run with you, brother. Perhaps I will see you in the sky.'

Brak believed that if he were to die here in enemy lands, unhonoured, unburied, he would become a wight, doomed to haunt the woods of the twice-dead. He held on to the illusion of the sky-hunt and I gladly affirmed the comfort it gave.

'Not for a long time I hope!'

We grew silent, taking our own counsel, making peace with the past while we could. And in the pale twilight I write down this account of the night.

With dread inevitability the sky begins to pale and then slowly flood with colour like a corpse's. Where will my soul go if I die today? Will I return to the Earth I know as a corpse on a hillside? Will my bones rot here and my soul wander for eternity? Or, worse, will my spirit be trapped in Annwn? The prospect of that nightmarish limbo terrifies me more than anything. But I cannot let another die in my place.

I must face my destiny.

There was the sound of guards above, stirred into action by a horn-blast, yawning and grumbling as they approached. Shadows blocked out the pale morning light. Kerne's solitude was shattered by the sickening drawing back of a bolt. The grill clanged back on the semi-frozen ground. Kerne quickly gulped down the acorn.

'King Madoc wants to know your answer,' shouted a grizzled guard. 'Speak!'

The airman stood up, clearing his throat. 'I will not join him!'
'Then you will burn!'

15

The Burning Man

It was a clear cold spring morning, a slight breeze sending thin tendrils of cloud scudding across the bleached sky. It might have been beautiful if not for the fate awaiting Kerne. The east gates were opened and he was led towards the metal giant. A pyre was being prepared underneath it; logs stacked high so they would roast whoever was unfortunate enough to be inside the cage of the giant's belly. A ragged, rancid shaman, who Kerne presumed must be Crow-Walker, blessed the fire with his painted, carved rattle. Casting herbs into the wind-tossed flames, he 'blessed' the sacrifice as well.

When all was in readiness a large aurochs horn was sounded, the blast resonating across the wind-buffered battlements. The dark gates of Caer Taranis swung open and King Madoc approached on a smoke-coloured warhorse, accompanied in a carriage-cum-cage by a slender veiled figure wreathed in coin-embroidered black. The entourage was surrounded by the grim and silent Royal Guard, sentinels of steel, their eyes slits of hate. They made the milling crowds flinch back as they passed, though Grey Raiders lined the way to keep the excited hordes in check. It seemed the whole ragged population of Iron Town had come out to watch the burning and were either forced to show enthusiasm or actually enjoying the spectacle, for the atmosphere was buzzing with anticipation.

Kerne felt like the condemned man waiting his turn on a London gallows.

Madoc rode to the pyre, his black bear cloak draped over the flanks of his steed, the iron crown upon his head echoed by the spikes of the giant's head. He stopped his horse in front of the prisoner, turning side-on to look imperiously down.

'So, Kerne, you have chosen to die to save the savage. How noble. And how predictable of you. Ever the prig, mapman. You always had old-fashioned ideas about how the world works … Ah, but it's a pity it had to end this way. We could have ruled this land together … Perhaps it's for the best. I was never very good at sharing.'

'You and your kind destroy what you desire,' seethed Kerne. 'That's why the world's in the state it's in. Ruined by the greed and arrogance of men like you.'

Madoc dismounted and approached. Kerne half expected to be struck, but to his surprise the King embraced him in a bear hug. He felt something being thrust into his belt – something hard wrapped in a bundle of cloth.

Madoc whispered into his ear: 'Here, take this. Use it when it gets too much. It will help you on your way.' He pulled away, whispering, 'Goodbye, old friend.' Then, more loudly: 'It is men like me who build empires and fools like you who pay the price. Gogmagog will appreciate your sacrifice. Guards, feed him to the giant!'

Grey Raiders pulled Kerne away as Madoc climbed back on to his horse and rode to a safe distance.

Kerne was forced at spearpoint up the ladder and into the belly of the structure via a small iron door. He was thrust inside what looked like a giant iron ribcage, open to the elements. Beneath his feet he could see the pyre being prepared. Two guards squeezed in after him. While one held a spear to his throat the other roughly tied his wrists to the giant's spine. The airman gazed coolly at the guard. Beneath his fur-trimmed helmet the man looked no more than eighteen. He looked mockingly at the outsider, his face split by a cruel grin. The guards left, clanging the door shut and drawing the bolt. They descended the ladder and pulled it away. Then the horn was blown again and Madoc took a torch handed to him and addressed his people. Some looked down from the hill fort; many others were gathered below – the slaves, allowed a brief holiday to watch the burning.

In his hoarse voice Madoc called out to them, 'Who is it but I who speaks with thunder?'

'Taranis!' shouted the crowd, used to this call and response.

'Who is an angry god, a jealous god?'

'Taranis!'

'Who protects you with his strong sword arm, his keen-edged blade?'

'Taranis!'

'Who has brought you the horseshoe and the wheel?'

'Taranis!'

'Who has brought you victory over your enemies? Who has given you the helmet and the shield to make you invincible?'

'Taranis!'

'Who demands this sacrifice to appease the ancestors, the spirits of this land, to keep the peace?'

'Taranis! Taranis! Taranis!'

Madoc cast the torch into the pyre and the oil-soaked logs caught quickly, whipped by a sudden gust. Crow-Walker began to drum rapidly.

In the carriage-cage Bronwen sobbed behind her veil.

Panicking, Kerne pulled at his bounds. Little good it did him. He struggled with the gut binding around his wrists, rubbing it against the massive metal vertebrae. Sweat dripped into his eyes as he looked out through the iron ribs of the giant at the hundreds of people watching him.

So was this how he was to end his days? As an offering to Gog-magog? He could feel the warmth from the flames licking his feet, and he lifted them alternately off the grill – all that separated him from the pyre. Soon the flames would by high enough to reach through. Smoke began to make him cough and splutter. He spotted Madoc looking at him through the sparks with grim satisfaction. His anger flared up, and the heat-dried cord snapped, releasing his hands. He rubbed the weals on his wrists, and then remembered the package Madoc had thrust into his belt. He pulled out the small heavy bundle and unwrapped it. His Webley! He checked the barrel: there was one bullet inside.

Kerne realised what Madoc had done – he had given him a chance to end his life quickly. A last-minute pang of conscience, perhaps. Maybe a shred of mess-room camaraderie had remained. Kerne tried to catch the look on Madoc's face. Perhaps he was play-ing the brutal king to his audience. Who knew what turmoil raged inside?

Whether he was hearing the shaman's drumming or the pounding of his heart, Kerne could not tell. The heat made his vision swim, cooked his brain. The grill beneath was getting too hot to stand on. Even through his boots he could feel it. Kerne thrust the gun back in his belt and climbed the ribs. He could only get so far in the gi-ant's cavity. He could still see Madoc through the smoke and the thought occurred to him that he could shoot him from here and make an end of his tyranny. The notion crossed his mind like a dark cloud. He could give the bastard a taste of his own medicine! Crammed into the highest part of the chamber he could reach, Kerne felt the gun pressing in his side like a spear. He could end the pain now ... Madoc must have known Kerne would never bring himself to shoot another human being – especially someone he knew, someone who had shown him this shred of mercy. No doubt Madoc had to be seen reasserting his control, since his authority as Speaks-with-Thunder had been challenged. What better way to make a sacrifice? He could claim the 'thunder' of that final shot as his own. Taranis would be shown to be all powerful.

The thick smoke was making Kerne choke. His lungs were burning. Rasping for breath through the gaps in the giant's ribcage, he gulped down what fresh air he could. He was grateful now for the breeze that blew in from the east.

'Merlin, where are you?' he breathed.

The east wind sighed over the endless expanse, catspawing the grassland. The world was empty of hope. He was doomed. The blackness edged closer.

Then, through the smoke, he saw a bird of prey circling above. As it flew closer, Kerne could see it was a falcon.

'Merlin …' croaked Kerne, reaching through the iron ribs, gasping for air.

The winged magician swooped as close to the pyre as he could without scorching his feathers.

'Use the sigil! Open a door!' the bird screeched.

Kerne remembered the woodword he had chanted the previous night – how it had made the bars seem to melt away, made him stronger. With the last of his strength he began chanted it, visualising the sigil till it glowed in his mind's eye: *'Ddduuuuuuiiiiiiiiiiiirrrrrrrr.'*

The smoke made him break the chant, but he gulped down more air and tried again, tried to ignore the heat and the smoke that stung his eyes. He felt the acorn growing in his belly. The sigil awoke it, and it give his limbs strength as the oak-dryad possessed him, helped him to hang on to the sides longer, though the heated cage blistered his hands. The bolt began to strain and shift across the door. He was moving it!

Yet even if he were to escape out of the Gogmagog he was still surrounded by guards. He would just be captured again and thrown back to his doom.

'Merlin!' Kerne uttered one last time before the smoke engulfed him.

The falcon circled the burning man, screeching. The magician was intent on his own business. The wind whipped up, the cold east wind, fanning the flames higher, but then increasing in power until it made the guards stagger sideways, the horses rear up, wild-eyed and whickering. Flags and shields were stripped away, knocking people over or unconscious.

Crow-Walker stopped his frenzied drumming and stared in terror. 'Eurus!' he screamed as he was blown into the pyre by a punch of wind. In shrieking torment he was consumed in the flames, a twitching Guy.

An almighty gust blew out the pyre entirely, as though an even greater giant had snuffed it out like a candle. The Gogmagog creaked and swayed in the wind. Kerne was shaken inside it, eyes streaming, retching, but still alive. Beyond the scorching skeleton was chaos, as though the world was splitting apart. At first the airman thought the hellish sound was the howling of the wind, but then it took on a keener edge, reminding him of the firecats.

Out of the sky swooped fiery griffin-like creatures with the bodies of lions and the heads and wings of eagles. Yet these were far more hellish than heraldic griffins. They seemed more like Valkyries gathering the dead. They plucked up Grey Raiders and Royal Guards alike, crushing them in their talons, biting off their heads with beaks of gold and casting the decapitated bodies down on to their comrades.

For the first time, Kerne was glad he was inside the now cooling cage ... But then he saw Bronwen's carriage suddenly blown over by wild wind. A chimera was plucking at its door as she screamed inside.

With fresh impetus Kerne chanted the sigil, while the wind bent the flame-shrouded colossus over, its legs softened by the heat death of the fire. As the Gogmagog tipped towards the ground, Kerne hung on and braced himself for the impact. The goliath did not topple completely, only hung over at an angle, slowing to a juddering stop. Kerne shouted the sigil one last time, filled with its strength, and the iron door burst open before him. He dropped from the cage on to the floor, unseen amid the confusion.

The Valkyries swooped and snatched guards around him, the men's weapons useless against the onslaught. Madoc had been knocked off his horse and was cowering in cover ... Kerne saw his chance and leapt on to the cloud-flanked horse.

His brother had been fond of horses and occasionally they had ridden out together before Archie had gone to the Boer War. Kerne grabbed the reins and dug his boots into the animal's sides. The horse bucked at first, but was keener to escape the chaos than lose its new rider. He held tight and tried to stop it bolting. He had to rescue Bronwen. The chimera had ripped open the carriage door and was about to grab her. Kerne had one bullet, one chance – but before he could take aim there was a sudden crack and the chimera exploded as the firecat and serpent had done. Kerne traced the source of the sound. Madoc was using his Webley. When he saw the effect his iron bullet had on the demon, he began firing into the sky. One by one he picked them off as though it was a pheasant shoot. Kerne realised Madoc must be using the ammo taken from his belt-pouch. He had given Taranis fresh thunderbolts.

Kerne made the most of the gunshots and explosions to ride quickly to the overturned carriage.

'Get on!'

Bronwen looked terrified, but when Kerne offered his hand she took it. He helped her on to the back of the horse, then he dug in his heels and the steed raced out of the madness.

The gates of the fort had been blown off their hinges and most of the soldiers were occupied in stopping everything from blowing away. Kerne and Bronwen rode through to the cells, where Brak waved at them through the bars. Jumping off the horse, holding its reins, Kerne shouted to Brak to get down. The hunter dropped to the ground as Kerne kicked back the bolt. A rope was dropped down and Brak was pulled up, filthy but grinning.

Brother and sister embraced, reunited at last.

'Quickly – we have no time for this! Use the horse. Escape while you can!'

Brak leapt on to the horse. 'What about you?'

'I will create a diversion,' Kerne shouted against the keening wind. 'Go! Get her home, Brak!'

Brak gripped Kerne's forearm. 'A hero's welcome will await you in Caer Cernunnos. Make it back, by Elen!'

Bronwen gave Kerne a haunting look, yet she could not speak.

Grey Raiders had seen them and were approaching. The Chalk Folk champion needed no further prompting. He rode off through the gale-burst west gate.

Kerne turned to see a guard take aim at the back of Bronwen with a spear. The man was just about to cast it when the falcon flew from the sky and plucked out his eyes with his talons. The other guards turned to fight it, but it was like fighting the wind.

Brak and Bronwen rode under the legs of the fallen Gogmagog and sped away towards the gorge.

Kerne seized the moment to release the whickering, dark-maned horses from their corral. Grabbing one for himself as they bolted, he mounted it with a leap, filled with the last of the dryad's might. It took him at speed towards the east gate, swept along with the rest. The guards who tried to stop them were run down in the stampede.

The horses poured out of Caer Taranis like an angry river that has burst its banks. Nothing could stand in their way. Keeping low, hidden among them, Kerne made good his escape. The horses raced out on to the vast expanse of the Steppe. Once in their native element, they were unstoppable, untameable – the steeds of Eurus.

The east wind itself seemed to be carrying Kerne along. He gulped down its clean air, felt its soothing coldness on his burnt feet, his blistered hands. His whole body still vibrated from the woodword he had invoked. He had summoned a dryad with its sigil; he had used the gramarye of the windsmith! He had saved them; he had survived. He was alive. He was free.

16

Windwalker

The Journal of Isambard Kerne
Cutios, Waning Atenoux, day unknown

I write this in the wilderness, the tabula rasa of the Steppe – my journal battered, pages few, pencil blunt. When the pages run out I do not know what I'll do. I feel run out as well – batteries flat, broken, silent and still. My stolen horse is in not much better shape either, though it seems happy enough, munching on the short dew-soaked grass, its flanks slightly steaming in the chill of the dawn.

I sit in the lee of the incessant wind as I write this, back against a standing stone I stumbled across in the darkness of the long freezing night. At first I was just grateful for the shelter it affords me from the wind on this exposed plain. With the slow light of the dawn my saviour is revealed: a crude mother figure, wide-hipped, heavy-breasted, round-faced, made of ironstone, so she is red flaked and lichen dappled like a rusting icon of industry, a Queen Victoria of the Steppe. I follow her blind gaze, looking west across its vast expanse – a green-gold ocean splashed with millions of flowers, soaked with dew, which soaks me too – and wonder how I am to get home. On the horizon is the dark smudge of the Red Hills. It is strange to see the barrier to the Forbidden Kingdom from the other side. I cannot run the gauntlet of the Ironwound Pass without risk of capture or death. I must find another way to get home. Home – strange to think of the Valley of the Chalk Folk in that way, but I have come to think of it as such, and indeed, as the home of my ancestors, it is the source of the Kerne stream.

I just pray Brak and Bronwen have made their way back to the boat and across Lake Mandorla in safety, so that all has not been in vain.

My limbs ache from days on my stolen steed, my clothes are

rags, I stink, and I'm famished and thirsty. Lord knows when I last ate. Only the springs I have found occasionally have kept me going, but I am exhausted. The use of the oak sigil has taken it out of me. Merlin did not warn me of that.

For days I have wandered the wilderness of grass in a feverish haze. Unable to stop and rest, I gave this strange stubby horse its head and fortunately it did not return to Caer Taranis. I watch it chew contentedly on some grass – black-maned and stout-limbed, with a steady gait ideal for riding long distances, like the horses ridden by Chaucer's pilgrims. Earlier it placed its head in my hand, wanting company, it seemed, some human kindness. Perhaps it has been mistreated. Horses are used for pulling the ore carts and for general toil. 'Tarpan' I heard the Horse Nomads call them. Mine seemed to like this taste of freedom, which perhaps reminded it of the times it ran the plains unimpeded. After we escaped from the fort it galloped east for many hours until it had run out its fear. It had been terrified by the creatures in the air. And what the hell were they? They seemed *wrong*, even in this strange world. They were of a similar ilk to the firecats and the ram-headed serpent.

What monsters am I unleashing? Not the least, Madoc. I feel partly responsible for bringing him here, for unleashing his iron virus upon the world. And now he will be mad at the escape of not only his hostage and his sacrifice, but his captive 'bride'. He will not let her go so easily. I remember how he loved to chase and conquer local girls back at the airbase. He wouldn't give up until he had won them over, then he would drop them and break their hearts. It was for 'the thrill of the chase' as he called it, as if that justified it. His rapacious instinct has run amok here; without any of the normal constraints of civilisation it has grown unchecked. He has become the tyrant of his own kingdom, but it would appear he does not want to stop there. He has turned his gaze west. I must get back somehow to the Chalk Folk and warn them. I fear a war is coming. The juggernaut of Taranis will move soon and this time they will not be satisfied with raids. Madoc wants the riches of the river valleys; his war machine needs their metal. It seems the madness of Europe has spread here – a war across worlds.

And it is up to me to stop it.

Although … looking out over the Steppe, so vast, and I so

insignificant, I realise how hopeless this is. One might as well try to carve the wind. But as I look up into the sky, the fiery pageant of sunrise, I see a bird of prey circle overhead and swoop down towards me. I have seen other birds of prey – the steppe eagle and buzzard – and mistaken them for my feathered mentor, but this time it *is* him. My heart lifts. Merlin is here!

I watch him fly gracefully down and land on the rocky outcrop, fluttering his wings like a shopper shaking their umbrella as they come in out of the rain.

'Merlin, it is so good to see you! Where have you been?'

'Why must I always answer your imbecile questions? Isn't it obvious: I have been following Brak and Bronwen.'

After days of desolation and silence, it was good to hear a 'human' voice, thought Kerne, even if it was in his head. At that point even Merlin's mocking Scots was welcome.

'How are they? Did they escape?'

'Yes, they made it back to the boat. Brak is a tracker of great skill, I'll grant him that. And they launched on to the lake before the Grey Raiders had managed to capture the bolted horses to give pursuit. They were well on their way across Mandorla when I left them.'

Kerne breathed a sigh of relief. 'Well, that's some good news anyway.'

'You took some finding – and you look in a terrible state.'

'I let the horse go where it will. God only knows how long I have been wandering.'

'Three days.'

'*Three days?*' Kerne was aware of the susurration of the wind, whispering to him. He scanned the uncertain horizon. 'Out there, in the Steppe, alone, hungry, listening to the song of the wind, the rhythm of the horse sent me into a trance.' The airman tried to articulate what he had experienced, but it slipped through his fingers the more he tried to grasp it. 'Eurus spoke to me … I sensed him in the wilderness. I heard his song, his voice.'

'Go on. What else?' probed Merlin.

'The sigils came to me. I saw them rise in my mind's eye. I could see them and hear them. The wind, the ceaseless east wind, whispered them to me, but one most of all stood out. Again and again, I saw the spindle and heard the "oir" chant. It seemed to permeate the very substance of the Steppe. Somehow, I was hearing its vibration. I sensed the presence of Eurus so close, powerful, overwhelming – the one you summoned, the mighty Sky God whom the Horse Nomads worship. He had noticed me, the interloper in his kingdom. He asked me who was I to trespass in his kingdom, in a voice full of whispers. At first I could not answer. My sense of self was drowned out by the voice of the wind. I felt obliterated by it, stripped bare, back to my soul. My spirit burnt low, as frail as a candle flame. Eurus could easily have extinguished me. Frozen in time, I watched a storm roll in, darkening the heavens. Lightning like sigils split the sky. And that's when I beheld the "oir" sigil most clearly, the back-to-back triangles and a word, deafening, terrifying, punctuated by the lightning bolts: "Tharan! Tharan!" He was angry with Taranis, with the iron curse he had brought with him. But he showed mercy – he let me live.'

'You are fortunate indeed to meet a god and live. He has revealed to you his secret name. You have the power now to summon him.'

Kerne shuddered at the thought, remembering how drained he was by the 'duir' summoning, and how devastating was Eurus's might. In Caer Cernunnos and Caer Taranis he had seen what it could do.

'I sense your trepidation. Good. We do not summon gods lightly … What else did Eurus tell you?'

Kerne cocked his ear to the haunting wind, trying to decode its enigma, trying to recall its secrets. 'He told me the secrets of the sacred breath, its power and purpose. How we are the exhalation of the Creator, and how the Great Outbreath of All Creation, what the Christians call Genesis, will be followed by an Inbreath, Armageddon. What the universe has given can be taken away. Civilisations are like outbreaths of humanity – they rise and fall in cycles, each one thinking it is the greatest. Species, too, reach their zeniths, followed by extinctions. At this moment, the universe is expanding – but one day God will breathe in. And each one of us is a microcosm of that – we are breathed out into life, filled with awen, burning brightly, and then the breath withdraws. Some are snuffed out too soon. Each breath we take is sacred. We should never waste it: we should always speak with honour and humility, taking responsibility for the words we speak, for they have power and impact. When we let the awen flow, we speak in harmony with the universe. Spirit expresses itself through *us*.'

'What of the sigils?' queried Merlin, like a professor in a tutorial.

Kerne was used to these colloquies now, having endured several with Ogmios. 'The sigils act as filters and channels, focusing the energy into different forms, expressing its nuances – but ultimately it all comes from the one source. And we would do well to remember that, whatever name we give them. Letters and language become Babel-like, dividing what once was one. Yet without the specificity of each alphabet the current cannot be grounded. Each letter acts as a conduit. It fixes the form, that particularly energy … I practised each sigil and noticed its effect on my surroundings. Even in the wilderness the effects were frightening. I probably didn't do the flora and fauna any good with my testing. The power is double-edged and has to be used carefully.'

'Good, you are learning caution. That is a start. Such technologies can turn on their master …' Merlin grew thoughtful. 'You used one of them to escape. Perhaps you are not as useless as I first thought! There may be hope for you and this world yet, for you need to hone your skill as a windsmith to defeat Taranis. You can summon the east wind, but you must master it to defeat him. I fear there is not enough time.'

Kerne thought back to his escape from the Gogmagog, and the deadly Valkyries. 'What *were* those monsters, Merlin?'

The falcon immediately knew of what he spoke and sighed. 'They are caused by *you* being here with Madoc. Whenever you two draw close, the rift in the continuum caused by your initial arrival is widened. You are *not* meant to be here – it's as simple as that.'

The words hammered home like a Gatling gun. Kerne's mind reeled. *He* was the cause of them? And now he realised where he had seen them before – in the Void. They had threatened to tear his soul apart, until he was saved by Maud's song – and now they threatened the whole of Shadow World. *He* had brought them through with Mallard!

'You are alive in the world of the dead. One of you must die, or this world will be torn apart …'

'I feared as much,' said Kerne wearily. 'So, it's either him or me.'
'Yes.'

Kerne sighed with despair, head in hands, as if crushed by the sky. The wind moaned around them, insistent and restless.

'Remember, Isambard,' said Merlin, 'we create our own choices, but they are shaped by our destiny. Follow your alignment to the end.'

Taking a deep breath, the airman finally stood up to face the task ahead. 'To the end, then,' he said with determination. 'I must get back and warn the Chalk Folk – help them prepare for the war. Do you know of a route?'

'Of course – there are many gateways and roads across the worlds, if you know how to open them. Although this one will not be an easy path for you. Come, I will take you.'

Kerne mounted his tarpan, which was somewhat restored after its rest and repast. Being back on the horse made his legs ache again, and there was a dull throb in the small of his back.

Merlin led the airman west across the emptiness of the Steppe. For a while Kerne brooded in his own thoughts, thinking of the repercussions of his presence. It threatened the very existence of this Afterland – the realm of his ancestors. It was an awful burden, but he had to accept it. This was his doom, and his alone. Everyone must own the shadows they cast.

Suddenly, Kerne felt thunder beneath the horse's hooves and feared Madoc's Horse Nomads were drawing close. There was nowhere to hide in that bleak treeless land. As they climbed the next rise he feared the worse, but Merlin insisted they carry on. Kerne acquiesced. He was resolved to confront his fate.

As they breached the brow of the hill, what was making the noise was revealed to him: a massive herd – of what it was hard to tell at first, owing to the huge cloud of dust their passing created. Through the dust, Kerne caught fleeting glimpses of a creature smaller than a horse, more the size of a goat. It seemed to be some kind of antelope, but it was a type Kerne had never seen before. In profile they had strange trumpet-like noses. The vast herd stretched as far as the eye could see and was moving south at high speed along some ancient migratory route.

'What are they?' asked Kerne.

'Saiga,' called out Merlin.

Kerne looked more closely as they passed. Some had long twisted lyre-shaped horns. He had heard reports in *The Times* of this animal's slaughter and imminent extinction.

'Their numbers have increased here rapidly,' Merlin observed.

Kerne had an awful feeling that fact was directly connected to their decimation in his world. Then he remembered Nubi, his lurcher. As an animal whose spirit was earthbound, the loyal hound had not been able to join his master. So what were animals doing here in the Afterlands? Perhaps the ancestors of animals dwelt here, or ones that had become extinct. The more species were wiped out on Earth, the more they would appear here, repopulating Eden. It was a sobering thought.

148

The herd slowly passed, the thunder eventually subsided, leaving a ringing vacuum. As the dust settled, a wide corridor of grassland was revealed, trampled down and churned up. The tarpan and the falcon traversed this dung-strewn wake and they continued in silence.

In the distance Kerne could make out the western ridge of the Red Hills catching the morning sun, a signature of fire written on the night-washed plain. They headed towards it, Kerne's spirits lifting with the rising sun. He was light-headed with hunger, shivering and weary, but the shimmering vision gave him hope. After days of featureless void, to have a landmark by which to gauge distance and progress was a sight for sore eyes.

Slowly but steadily the hills grew before them, until the flat land started to rise. The grass grew shorter and was replaced by heathland dotted with furze. The tarpan protested, unused to anything but flatness, and growing weak. Kerne reluctantly slid off and, half slumped over its back, walked beside it. They were both in a bad way. 'How much further?' he croaked.

'We are here,' replied the falcon.

Kerne raised his head and rubbed his eyes. The bleak land, battered by the wind rolling off the Steppe, was littered with small mounds.

'Round barrows?'

'They are known as "kurgans" by the natives, but they are identical in function to your British Bronze Age counterparts.'

After days in the wilderness, it was reassuring to see some sign of human activity, even if it was a graveyard.

Kerne led his horse silently through the graves – they reminded him of the hills of peace on the sides of the Bone Mountains. Whatever their differences, the peoples of this world were united in death – *if the dead could really die*. Kerne remembered the barrow wights with a shudder and hurried along. The tarpan perhaps sensed them too, for it grew skittish. He smoothed its flanks and whispered into its ear to reassure it.

At the far end of the burial land they came to an avenue of spiral-carved stones leading towards a weathered lichen-dappled cromlech half buried in the hill side. The chamber was shallow and ended with a massive stone. Darkness clung to the walls. The structure reminded Kerne of a long barrow, but its purpose was unclear.

'If you want to return to the lake, you must open this.'

Kerne was nonplussed. 'Me? How?'

'In the same way you opened the cage. In the same way you passed through the Angel Gate.'

'Using the woodword? So could I use the sigil to get home? Back to England?'

'No – it will require greater magic than that. Traversing one world through these portals is one thing. Walking between the worlds is in a different league entirely. You must master the four winds to be able to navigate your way home.'

The wind keened around them as the impact of what Merlin had said sunk in. Kerne gulped, tried to moisten his tongue. 'So, are you saying this is just the beginning ... From HyperEurus, I must travel to other Afterlands, to master the winds in each corner of Shadow World?'

Merlin paused, deciding whether to answer, then breathed, 'Yes.'

Kerne sank wearily down. 'I have not the strength to pass through.'

'We must find you food to restore your strength, and the wood you need to pass this place – an underworld tree. I shall search for the right wood. As for food, you may find help from the guardian of the place.'

Merlin drew Kerne's attention to a low dwelling apart from the barrows. The dun-coloured roundhouse blended in with the rock behind. It was set back from the track that followed the edge of the Red Hills from north to south, fading into the distance in both directions. It was a lonely place to live. Who would dwell in such a place?

'I have observed this man for some time. I sense he is sympathetic. He chooses to live among the kurgans to be at peace with his ancestors. The Horse Nomads let him be, as long as he shoes their horses when they pass on the Border Road. Treat him with respect and he may help. Bear in mind that Steppe-dwellers like to trade. Good luck. I shall return!'

And Merlin flew off as a man emerged from the hut, stocky and surly-browed, an arrow notched to his bow.

Kerne was too exhausted to do anything other than stare. For a dilated moment the two strangers observed one another. Kerne reckoned the man to be in his mid-thirties. He had walked with a limp, holding his left leg out straight as he had emerged from the roundhouse. He wore a simple grey tunic that reached down to his bare knees, with a deerhide cloak attached by a long bone pin over his left shoulder, a quiver of gold-feathered arrows over the other. At his chest a knife was sheathed in a leather pouch and around his waist was a jute belt secured with a shale belt ring. A slate wrist-guard protected his pulling arm as he held the bowstring tight, the small flint arrowhead pointing straight at Kerne. The weathered biceps stood out, bunched, out of proportion to the rest of his body. His legs seemed almost withered in comparison, ending in hide moccasins. The face was smooth and broad, the eyes dark and fierce, the black hair pulled back in a ponytail. Despite being shorter than Kerne, he exuded a steady power.

Kerne knew this man meant business. He had to treat to situation very carefully. As slowly as possible, he dropped the reins of the tarpan and lifted his hands into the air, showing them to be empty.

The Steppe-dweller warily approached, keeping his arrow pointed at Kerne, until he stood by the side of the horse. With a quick side-glance he checked over the animal. 'The horse is in a bad way.'

The accent was thick but Kerne's ears adjusted to it, like a radio tuning into a stronger signal. Had his Celtic ancestors heard and understood this tongue? Was this man an ancient neighbour?

'You have ridden far on it.' Whether the words of the Steppe-dweller were an observation or a judgement it was hard to tell.

Kerne found himself smiling, suddenly thinking how they were like two strangers in a municipal park walking their dogs, discussing their pets' merits and foibles because these offered a neutral subject.

Yet the man cast a professional eye over the tarpan. He put down his bow and began running his hands over the animal, whispering to it. He lifted up a front leg and checked the hoof, shaking his head. Then he did the same with the back.

'She needs new shoes, and rest, or she'll go lame. You have run her into the ground.'

Kerne was starting to feel guilty. He felt the man's sharp remarks were meant as criticisms. 'I ... was in a hurry.' Kerne sensed it would not be to his advantage to be indirect with this man. He did not look like someone who would take kindly to being deceived. 'Look, I have been travelling for three days without food or rest. I don't suppose there's any chance of a meal and a place to lie down for a bit ...' Kerne remembered what Merlin had suggested: the natives liked bartering. He had hardly any possessions upon him except his Webley, which was too valuable to give up, even if he didn't really want it, and his boots, which he did need and probably wouldn't fit the man anyway, even if they had been of use, for he was plainly lame. There was only one thing he could give him.

'You can have the horse in exchange.'

This caught the man's attention. He seemed genuinely overwhelmed by the offer. 'You would trade your horse for a meal and a bed?'

'Yes.' At that point in time the prospect of food and shelter was worth more than anything in the world. If he did not get sustenance soon he would blow away.

'A horse of my own ...' The man shook his head in disbelief. 'It is forbidden for men like me to own a horse. The Horse Lords would punish us both.'

The man hobbled around the horse, sizing it up, admiring it, and looking at it in a new light.

Kerne realised what such a gift would mean to a lame man.

The man turned to him, beaming with broken teeth, offering him a forearm scarred with burns. 'My name is Baramis.'

Kerne reached out and they locked forearms: Baramis had a grip like iron and rough callused hands. 'Kerne, Isambard Kerne.'

'Please, come to my house, Bard-Kerne. It is not much but I will offer you what little I can.'

Baramis tethered the tarpan outside and led Kerne into his simple dwelling. It was dark and musty, simply furnished with a bed, a low table and a stool, which he offered to his guest. From a clay pitcher by the central hearth Baramis offered him a beaker of white pungent liquid, which Kerne gingerly accepted. His nose wrinkled at the smell: sour milk.

'Koumiss – fermented mare's milk. Drink.'

Kerne felt obliged by his thirst more than a willingness not to offend his host. He took a sip and at first his stomach revolted, but he persisted. It tasted like alcoholic yoghurt – strange at first, but soothing after a while. It slid down his gullet in globules and lined his ravenous stomach.

Next, his host offered him a platter of what looked like black twigs. Eager to take away the cloying taste of the koumiss, Kerne plucked one of the black twigs and bit into it. His palate was surprised: it was sweet and tasted exactly like ... 'Liquorice?'

His host nodded.

Delighted, Kerne helped himself to a half-dozen more of the sticks until his hunger had abated.

All the while, Baramis intently watched the stranger in his house.

It was only after they had finished eating that Baramis attempted conversation, but it was plain to Kerne he was not used to company. His words were direct, although Kerne did not feel he was being

152

blunt out of rudeness.

'Where do you come from?'

'From the Valley of the Chalk Folk.'

'You do not sound like a Chalklander, but you have their look about you.'

Kerne scratched the beard developing on his chin. This was always going to be difficult to explain.

'I come from an island far from here, but I am related to the Chalk Folk. They are ... my distant kin, my clan.' Saying it seemed to affirm it. Despite the reservations of some of the tribe, he *was* connected to them. He didn't sound like a Celt, but he was one at heart. It was in his blood, his soul.

This answer seemed to satisfy Baramis, whose gaze darkened as he reflected upon his own: 'My family was slaughtered in raids by the Xiongnu,' he said simply and sadly.

'*Xiongnu?*' Kerne attempted to repeat the word.

'The devils on horses.'

Kerne realised he was talking of the Horse Nomads, and the word he had used had sounded similar to 'Hun'. Kerne noticed that Baramis looked slightly different from the Asiatic Horse Nomads. He asked where his village had been.

'In Scythia,' Baramis explained. 'The horse-devils stretch their terror far. I was kidnapped, like all the older boys and younger women, and brought here to slave for the horsemasters. I was one of the lucky ones. Because my father had been a blacksmith, instead of being thrown into the iron mines I was made to work in the forges. Yet there was a price. The Xiongnu cripple all of their blacksmiths to make sure they don't run away.'

Kerne recalled the smithies in Iron Town, where the blacksmiths hobbled.

In the half-light of the hut Baramis showed Kerne his left knee – what was left of it. 'They remove your left kneecap.'

Kerne did not want to imagine the pain of that. But the fact was that the cruelty of the Huns had not crushed the Scythian's spirit. He lived an independent life, taking pride in his trade. He had chosen this remote posting to be closer to the spirits. Blacksmiths were stationed at regular intervals all the way along the north–south road, the Scythian explained, but only Baramis dared to live near the dead.

A blacksmith who lives by a long barrow ... Kerne remembered the legend of Wayland's Smithy on the Ridgeway. Was Baramis an ancient echo of that: the first blacksmith, crippled like the Greek

Hephaestus, drawing to him fear and superstition, an initiate of arcane mysteries … In other cultures such a man as Baramis would have been respected and wealthy. Here, he was one of the slaves of Taranis.

Baramis led him into an antechamber, lifting up a blackened leather flap, and proudly showed him his forge.

Kerne's eyes passed over the small anvil, the rock-lined furnace, the tools hanging from nails in the smoke-blackened posts, to a stack of iron swords. The Scythian picked one up and spun it around in his hand with a flourish like a master swordsman. He tossed it to Kerne, who was relieved to catch it by the handle. It was a simple, unadorned but well-made, well-balanced blade.

'King Madoc has ordered a huge number of these,' Baramis said gruffly.

Kerne had a pretty good suspicion why that was.

'I do not like making weapons for my enemy, but as long as I keep myself useful I am left in peace.'

Kerne respected his craftsmanship. The blacksmith obviously took pride in his work. He seemed keen to show the interested stranger his trade and began building up the heat in the furnace with bellows. Asking Kerne to keep operating them, he took a tang that he'd been tempering in a pail of rusty looking water and thrust it into the forge, letting it heat up while they talked. When it was white hot he took it out with a thick leather mitten and placed it on the anvil, hammering it, bending it to his will.

The coals of the furnace glowed, blown by eddies of wind. Yet the flap of the forge was closed to the constant wind outside. The blacksmith looked at the smouldering coals with fascination, flames reflected in his widening eyes. He looked up at Kerne, who shook his head in bewilderment. Did he think *he* was doing it?

Unsettled, Baramis quenched the blade in a genie of hissing steam, hung up his tools and showed his guest back to the lodge, where he gestured to the fur-lined bed. 'Rest, Bard-Kerne, and I will find us some meat.'

Kerne protested but was grateful for the chance to recover from his ordeal in the wilderness. His journey was not over yet. He still had a long, long way to go.

Overcome with fatigue, he found himself falling asleep almost instantaneously. Something about the blacksmith made him trust him. He was a solid, reliable friend, and that was priceless for someone in Kerne'ss position. Of course, Baramis could have gone out to alert the Huns, but somehow Kerne doubted the Scythian would inform on him to his hated overlords even if he could have reached them from so remote a place. Nevertheless, the blacksmith had seemed eager to leave, as though he'd suddenly found Kerne's presence unsettling ... What had caused the furnace to glow by itself, as if operated by invisible bellows? Kerne was too tired to think of an answer, but it preyed on his mind as he slipped into unconsciousness.

Kerne was awoken from his exhausted slumber by a soft thud upon his chest. He opened his eyes to be confronted with the still-warm corpse of some kind of podgy mammal impaled on an arrow.

'Boboc,' the Scythian beamed, showing an abscess. It took Kerne a moment to realise 'boboc' was the name of this rodent-type creature. Baramis threw Kerne a knife, which landed with a dull thud on the ground next to his leg. 'Prepare the meat, and I'll prepare the fire.' Baramis seemed eager to divide the chores in this way. Perhaps after the incident at the furnace he did not trust the stranger with the flames.

Kerne was glad he had paid attention to his Da, who had been adept at skinning rabbits, though it had disgusted him at the time, since he was more squeamish than his bloodthirsty brother. He took the knife Baramis had given him, took a deep breath and slit open the animal's guts, letting them slide out on to the grass, reeking with hot fumes. On a large flat stone he skinned and gutted the bobac and laid it on a rock. Meanwhile Baramis prepared a small fire of pine cones. He did this as discreetly as possible, no doubt aware of how the smoke might travel and alert the Horse Nomads to their presence, but by the time they got here Kerne hoped he would be long gone. Not that it was an unpleasant stopover. In fact, it was turning into one of the very best. The legends of the Steppe People's custom of hospitality were true.

As the fire cooked supper on a spit they talked over a jar of koumiss, to which Kerne had become quickly immune. It no longer made him nauseous, just numb. They talked of their families. Kerne found himself describing Maud and their house in Eastbourne.

'How many children?' asked Baramis.

This was a moot point. 'None. I had to go to war.' He thought of his unexpected paternal urge back in Caer Taranis with the young, fatherless warrior. How death makes us think of such things, he brooded. A species survival urge kicking in, perhaps. Yet in the case of his marriage, biology had had other plans. He did not elaborate on his wife's barrenness. He had never held it against her. He'd had his research to occupy him. It filled up his spare time, growing into an obsession … until it bled the life from their marriage. If anyone was to blame it was him. Selfish to the last.

Baramis was lost in his own reverie. He had lit a black cheroot and took a long slow draught of its pungent aroma. 'Ah, war deprives families of many fathers.' He blew out the smoke thoughtfully. It had always been his regret that he'd never had a wife and family, he explained, but who in their right mind would live out here in the land of the dead with him? There had been a girl back in his village, he sighed, but that was 'a long walk into the past'. He had been taken from there so long ago. What had happened to his family he did not know – even whether they were still alive All he remembered of the day the Grey Raiders came, when he was 'no higher than a tarpan foal', was the yurt suddenly on fire, screams, people running, being killed or raped. His mother had thrust an effigy in his hands before he was dragged away from her and thrown in a cart. That was the last he saw of her or his brothers and sisters. He was sent to the ore mines with captured Scythians of different tribes: mainly young fit men. One of them had been the son of a blacksmith, who had been learning his father's craft. They became friends, learning to survive the rigours of the ore mine together, all the while Baramis learning about smithcraft from the blacksmith's boy, until his friend died of exhaustion and malnutrition. But Baramis survived; he had to – for now he had three lives to live: the father's, the son's and his own. He vowed not to let their deaths be in vain. He started to show a knack for metalwork whenever an opportunity arose, mending a tool here, spotting good ore there, and was transferred to the smithies, where he consolidated his apprenticeship – at the price of a kneecap.

Kerne sensed the blacksmith appreciated his company. It was as though the Scythian had been waiting a long while to pour out his burning past, like molten metal into a cast.

'This is all I have from the time over the horizon.' From an altar hidden behind a pile of smelly clothes, he shyly showed Kerne a small statue similar to one he had seen on the plain. He called her 'Tabiti', fumigating the statuette in his cheroot smoke and pouring some of his koumiss into a sticky stone dish in front of her.

Kerne mentioned he had seen a larger version in the wilderness. Baramis said 'she' was Api, the Great Mother. Tabiti was the goddess of the hearth. Kerne asked about Eurus. Baramis seemed nonplussed, so Kerne waved his arms wide and made the sound of the wind hissing through the grass.

'Ah, the Sky God ... Papaeus, we Scythians call him ... He is angry with the Steppe People. I cannot talk with him. Only the Great Mother will listen to my prayers.'

Baramis showed Baramis the small vegetable patch behind his hut. The black soil was very fertile, he explained, allowing him to grow a few simple crops – enough to stop him starving, although the Steppe could feed everybody, he protested, if the horse-devils would let it. 'But they don't like crops getting in the way of their horses, so they trample any down they find.'

Kerne thought it was a cruel land to live in, but Baramis seemed to like its bleak grandeur. The wind whistled outside the hut.

Kerne described the verdant Da'anu Valley, extolling the virtues of his adopted home.

'We are told they eat their children ...'

Kerne disabused him of that notion, explaining the different forts, the clan system, the karmic serfs, the chalk figures, the freedom.

'So, when your slaves have paid back their debt, they are set free?' Baramis said in disbelief.

'Yes, and nobody gets crippled or clapped in irons either. They are repaying debts of honour they have deferred for one reason or another until this life.'

The last comment seemed to go over the head of the Scythian, who was preoccupied with the vision Kerne had conjured for him. 'The Valley of the Chalk Folk ...' he said with new wonder.

Kerne tried to draw a map in the dirt, depicting the almond of the lake, and the mouth of the Da'anu opposite Iron Wound Pass.

'Find it and ask for Kerne and you'll be most honoured and made welcome,' he promised.

Baramis pointed to the place where Caer Taranis was located. Word of the skirmish and escape had reached him along the grapevine of the North Road. He mentioned this with a strange strangled chuckle. It seemed to please him that King Madoc had been humiliated.

'So, you knew I was a fugitive all along?'

'Yes, and any enemy of Madoc's is a friend of mine. I will do all I can to help.'

The smell of the roasting flesh was making Kerne's mouth water. Baramis took it from the spit and carved it up on the stone, placing half upon a wooden platter with a hunk of black bread.

The bobac's flesh was stringy but surprisingly tasty, especially washed down with more koumiss. The two men sat in the porch of the lodge as they ate, gazing out over the vast Steppe. They were content to sit there in companionable silence for some time.

Their reverie was broken by a shriek in the dusk sky.

Kerne looked up and was relieved to recognise the familiar profile. Merlin swooped down, clutching a small yew branch, which he dropped into his lap. 'There is a yew wood to the north where the archers get timber for their bows.'

Baramis watched Kerne talk with the falcon with interest. 'You are a windwalker! You talk with Skyhunter?' Baramis asked, gesturing to the falcon.

'Windwalker?'

Baramis explained that this was a kind of medicine man. His mother had been one, a 'shamanka' he called her. She had communed with Papaeus and the other gods, but he had not learnt her songs. His sister had been called by the spirits instead, after a near-fatal illness. She had started to walk her mother's path.

Kerne realised these Scythian shamanka were the equivalent of the windsmiths. He described the latter to the archer and he nodded at the similarities.

Baramis looked upon Kerne with new respect. 'I will guard you while you work.'

'Trust him, fool!' Merlin chided. 'I will check on the whereabouts of your search party. I have seen much movement up and down the North Road.'

Kerne reluctantly set to work, crouching within the cromlech, meditating upon the yew.

It soon became freezing. The temperature plummeted on the exposed plain, but Baramis kept a fire going in front of the cromlech all night.

Kerne tried to block out the freezing cold and focus on the yew sigil … It was not an easy task, shivering and doubt-ridden as he was. Who was he fooling? No success; nothing moved. It reminded him of having the stone on his chest in Ogmios's abaton. There were many times that night when Kerne felt like giving up, as though he was just banging his head against a brick wall. But Baramis's support encouraged him to continue. Whenever he flagged he saw the stocky Scythian willing him on from the other side of the flames. Kerne sensed he was escaping for him too. Baramis needed to believe in him, needed him to be genuine, like the legend of Ollav Fola. Yet Kerne felt unable to summon the gramarye – and he felt he let his friend down too.

At first light Kerne awoke bleary-eyed. His whole body ached, cramped into a foetal position and covered with a deerskin – Baramis's. He must have nodded off, though it felt like he'd had no sleep at all. Crying out in pain, he extricated himself from his tomb, his body unwilling to oblige. It simply did not seem to function any more. Shakily, he stood up, and promptly fell over.

'Like a newly dropped foal!' roared Baramis, who was squatting by the smouldering fire.

Stiffly Kerne joined the Scythian, who was brewing some hot liquid over the fire he had kept going all night.

'Any luck, windwalker?'

'No – it is hopeless. I … I cannot do it.' Kerne's voice was raw from the night of chanting.

The blacksmith handed Kerne a beaker of hot barley drink, which he gratefully cradled in his hands.

'We shall see.' Baramis smiled his ragged smile. 'There's more to you than meets the eye, Bard-Kerne.'

The fire suddenly flared into life. A wind seemed to be picking up. Yet it was still the predawn stillness. There was no dawn chorus to herald a new day on the Steppe. The vast silence was disquieting.

Baramis ducked into the forge, scrabbled about and re-emerged with a bundle. He gave Kerne an iron sword.

'You'll need this where you are going.'

Kerne was speechless. He knew what Baramis meant by this gift, though his pride stopped him speaking: *Free my people.*

Baramis also gave him a suede satchel of basic provisions: dried meat, flatbread, nuts, dates, water.

'I will see you again, my friend.'

'Thank you, Baramis. I'll not forget the help you gave me – the risks you have taken. Come to the Valley of the Chalk Folk and you will be richly rewarded.'

'I hope to make it there … one day. I have heard whispers of a secret path around the lake which is many days' ride. Now I have a chance of making it, thanks to your princely gift.'

They gripped one another's forearm.

'Now go!' Baramis insisted. 'The horse-devils approach!'

Kerne felt the ground rumble with the thunder of approaching riders. The Scythian had sensed it, being attuned to the subtle equilibrium of the Steppe. At any moment, Kerne's presence would be discovered. There was no time left.

Merlin appeared. 'Horse Nomads are coming! Quickly, sunrise is the most auspicious time! Back to the cromlech!'

'Why didn't you tell me that earlier?' said Kerne through gritted teeth, resentful at having had to struggle all night.

'You needed to prepare yourself. Now your hard work will pay off. But there is no time to lose!'

'Now go! Quickly!' pleaded Baramis. 'I will distract them. I know how to deal with them.'

'Do as he says!' screeched Merlin.

'What about you?'

'I cannot follow there – I will see you on the other side. Stay on the path and don't look back! Use the awen to light your way!'

Taking up his gifts, thrusting the sword into his Sam Browne belt opposite his Webley and slinging the satchel over his shoulder, Kerne ran back to the cromlech and picked up the yew branch from where he had left it.

As he resumed his summoning position, standing on one leg, with one eye covered with a hand, the other holding the yew branch, Kerne's body protested. He felt in no fit state to do this now, but if he failed, it would jeopardise the lives of both him and Baramis.

'Focus on the yew! See it as a gateway!' Merlin called.

Standing before the gateway Kerne chanted the yew sigil. He strained and nothing came. Merlin told him to relax, to let the awen flow through him, not to block it out with mental will.

Kerne imagined the three rays of light just as dawn happened: the sun breached the horizon, striking the distant Earth Mother statue he had rested against, its beam shooting across the hazy enshadowed grassland, down the avenue of stones and straight into the heart of the cromlech – like a sword into a scabbard.

The stones bathed in the warm light and seemed to soften and yield … The doorway began to open. The hoof beats of the approaching riders combined with the beating of his own heart. He heard harsh greetings, Baramis's supplicant reply. A horse whinnied. He dared not look around, dared not stop …

There was a blast of wind and the passage opened before him. A chasm gaped, rank with the stench of the underworld. The darkness did not look inviting, but Kerne had no choice. The riders were at the Scythian's hut.

Casting one last glance at Baramis and Merlin, silhouetted in the dawn glare, Kerne stepped into the darkness and the rock rolled back behind him with a sickening finality, blocking out the light, plunging him into pitch black, a black so palpable he could feel it clinging to his skin.

Kerne felt the grave-breathed shadows rise around him, wanting to drag him down – like in the Void … He tried not to let the fear overwhelm him. 'Use the awen!' Merlin had said. Kerne began to chant it, as he had been taught by Ogmios – visualising the three rays of light emanating from the source. The awen echoed down the endless depths of the tunnel. The yew branch seemed to glow in his hand, but light actually emanated from his brow. He stepped forward into the abyss.

17

Eater of the Dead

Kerne walked slowly along the tunnel, yew branch in hand. His forehead glowed with the chanting of the awen and offered the only light in the stygian gloom. There were no walls or ceiling he could see, but he felt oppressed, as if the darkness itself was matter, crushing down on him. He tried to keep his nerve, maintaining the chant, walking in as straight a line as possible. Exactly *what* he walked upon was hard to say, but he dared not look down. It felt like bones cracking under his feet. He had never been afraid of the dark, but here in Annwn there were real terrors of which to be mindful.

Memories of his incarceration in the Void flashed into his mind, but he tried to subdue them – the fiery chimera trying to tear him apart, the vast crushing emptiness. He had spent nine days in that no-man's-land and he had no wish to return there, but return he must, every time he used the woodwords, those portals to spirit. He had to reach into the abyss to summon the sigil. Each sigil acted as a doorway. He had to ensure nothing came through except what he intended. The yew branch gave him passage through the underworld – for it was the long-living tree of the graveyard, with its lethal berries and its roots said to grow through the mouths of the dead – but not necessarily a guaranteed safe passage.

Who knows what monsters dwell in the depths of the world? The chimera had come from somewhere ... Was it from *here*, this realm of deeper shadows, through the rifts being created by the continued presence of two living interlopers in the land of the dead?

Kerne tried to walk as fast as he could. His heartbeat tapped out a military tattoo. The pounding in his ears became louder, became the pounding of howitzers. A flash blinded him, splitting the Void.

Suddenly the hellish sights and sounds of no-man's-land were around him – the shrill whistle of shells, the sound-sucking explosions, the scattering of shrapnel and bodies, the screams of the dying – yet here the dead did not lie still, they continued to thrash about in the mud, pulling themselves up on their broken limbs, propped up by rifles and fellow cadavers. Trailing entrails, leaving half their faces and limbs behind, they approached Kerne's bone-path, which now seemed like splintered duckboards over the bomb-cratered quagmire. *Zombies* … Kerne had heard of such creatures from his brother, who had claimed to have glimpsed them at a voodoo ceremony while serving in Africa during the Boer War. Kerne had assumed they'd been more creatures of his imagination, designed to impress – as many of Archie's war stories were.

Yet here he was, faced with the ugly truth. The undead pressed around him, their rotting flesh making his stomach turn. A skeletal digit pointed at him; hollow eyes stared accusingly. The soldiers lumbered inexorably forward, reaching out arms of bone and sinew. Kerne tried to push through them, brush them off like leprous beggars in a Bombay ghetto, but they clung to him. Now he could see they were both British and German infantrymen.

United in their hatred for the living airman, the soldiers tore at him with skeletal claws, an angry mob bent on *revenge* – the vengeance of the dead upon those who mock them with life.

In the press of mangled bodies, the breath of the dead upon him, the hungry shattered souls pulling him down, Kerne found it difficult to maintain his focus on the yew, to continue chanting – but whenever he stopped, the light faded from his brow and the darkness was unbearable. The War Dead tried to pull Kerne from the duckboards, down into the stinking mud, into a river of blood bubbling up, filling the trenches, the bomb craters and sniper pits. It rose up to his knees, and kept on rising, chilling him to the soul as he heard inside his skull the screams of the victims whose blood had been shed.

Suddenly the pounding of the guns, the surging blood, the endless screams were drowned out by another sound – a demonic howl. The War Dead turned to see a massive shadow move across no-man's-land like mustard gas, sucking in the fallen and *eating* them. The monster of darkness devoured the soldiers in swathes, guzzled them down into its bottomless belly. It scooped up the zombies in handfuls at a time and sucked the glowing soul-light out of them.

Then only Kerne was left, and it towered over him – a wrathful wall of shadow. The glow of the windsmith's brow was a tiny candle flame in a storm. The creature of darkness seemed drawn to this; it seemed greedy for his soul-light. It opened wide its massive maw, which gaped into infinity, a tunnel to oblivion. From it came the foetid reek of death.

The airman closed his eyes and prepared for the inevitable. The Void closed around him and he was consumed by utter darkness and icy cold …

But nothing happened.

The shadow spat him out in disgust.

'Not dead!' it roared. Turning, it oozed on through no-man's-land – the spectre of death itself, seeking more suitable fodder.

Kerne was left in the strangely peaceful aftermath – the eerie silence after a battle. The hellish scenes of conflict and devastation melted away. He was alone once more. His assailants had been dealt with and he had survived.

Unpalatable to the Eater of the Dead.

Shaking uncontrollably, he had to sit for a moment to compose himself. But the endless darkness pressed down on him and he was compelled to continue. He did not want to be left in the Void again.

He resumed his chant. The light of awen returned, faintly at first, then stronger as he fed it with his breath. Clutching the shaking yew bough as though his life depended on it, which it probably did, the airman staggered along the path before him.

Ahead, he saw a light, faint, but with the promise of escape. He made his way towards it, his steps heavy with guilt. Until that moment he had not thought of the battle he had left behind, his brothers in arms dying on his behalf – for whatever foolish reason. He had escaped the horrors of that war, along with Madoc, but he could not escape its consequences. Its impact even reached the bowels of the Shadow World. He recalled what Merlin had said: what occurred in the upper world was echoed here and vice versa. The devastation of those years of war – Maud had told him it had raged for four years – was still having repercussions in both worlds. Death on such a vast scale had shattered the natural cycle – 'overloaded the system', as he had coldly put it to Maud. Kerne and Madoc could not escape the aftermath of that; indeed, they had brought the disease of war with them. And now it threatened to destroy both worlds.

Wearily Kerne made his way towards the promise of light, feeling as though he was dragging the shadow of death with him.

18

The King in the Lake

Kerne staggered into the light of a new day, gulping down the fresh air with relief. The air was scented with the pine forest, deep and rich around him in the fold of the hill where he emerged. The trees were still awakening with life, birdsong filled the glade, and it was sweet to his ears. He collapsed on to the ground and breathed in the dew-laden grass of the clearing, washing his face in it, washing the murk of the underworld from him. The horror of that hellish place still made him reel and retch. He recalled the walking corpses of the soldiers, how they had grabbed him and tried to pull him down into their hell. Their accusatory eyes haunted him. Did he really have their blood on his hands? He had not been responsible for the madness of that war. He had tried to do his bit and had perished in the first battle. Yet he had not died, he had crossed over, and the reaction of that creature, the Eater of the Dead, proved it once and for all. *Not dead*, it had said in disgust. He was a man alive in the world of the dead. His presence, along with Madoc's, was disrupting its equilibrium – the balance between life and death – causing a rift between the worlds, out of which issued the creatures of chaos, the chimeras. It *was* his responsibility to stop the destruction. He got up, brushed off the pine needles and girded his loins. He had a job to do.

Looking back at the exit from the underworld, Kerne saw only a shallow moss-draped cleft in a rock face. The way had shut; there was no going back, only forward. Slowly, stiffly, he made his way down the slope through the reviving forest.

How different it had seemed at night when they had been pursued by the firecats! Now, it appeared a lush sanctuary in stark contrast to the bleak Red Hills and austere Steppe of the Forbidden Kingdom. Ahead, between the trunks of pines, he saw the glittering waters of Lake Mandorla, a sight for sore eyes if ever there was one.

Kerne stepped out on to the shore and blinked in the reflected light of a new day. As his eyes adjusted he took in the vast panorama of the lake, which stretched into haze in both directions. Catching the first rays from the east, the white cliffs of Chalkland shone on the far shore. They pulled him like dear old Blighty. He longed to be back in the Caer of the Stag, with the tribe he had begun to think of as his own. He hoped Brak and Bronwen were back there safe, enjoying a warm hearth and a hearty breakfast. His stomach growled. He couldn't remember the last time he had eaten. No wonder he felt so light-headed and weak! If Wolf Forest offered any sustenance, he was not able to locate it. How could he tell the poisonous from the palatable? The waters of Mandorla offered the possibility of fish, but he had no line, hook or bait.

Then a screech overhead made Kerne look up. He recognised the silhouette of Merlin immediately. The falcon swooped out of the sky and called out, 'Catch!'

Kerne held out his hands as from the bird's claws dropped tiny objects. He caught most of them: hazelnuts!

'Breakfast! Thank you, Merlin!' He began devouring them.

'Don't eat all of them, fool! They are to pay for your crossing.' Merlin settled on a branch of needles next to him.

'How's Baramis?'

Ever since Kerne had left the Steppe he had worried about the blacksmith. He prayed the Scythian had not been punished for helping him, that the tarpan he'd given him hadn't been discovered.

'He's fine. He dealt with the Horse Nomads and when they departed he packed supplies and set off north on his new steed. He's making his way around the edge of the lake as we speak.'

Kerne was relieved and pleased by this news. 'You mentioned a crossing. Do I need to find a ferryman?'

'Of sorts … The King in the Lake.'

'The one worshipped by the lake people?'

'Yes. You must summon him with a hazel sigil. It is Llyr's favourite food.'

'Llyr?'

Merlin sighed. 'Must I always spell things out? The King in the Lake is called Llyr. He's currently in the form of a giant salmon.'

'What?' Kerne grew incredulous. 'Are you telling me I must summon a giant fish and ride on its back?'

'Have you not fought with monsters? Have you not just walked the path of the dead?'

Kerne shook his head. If he hadn't experienced what he had over the last six months he would have found the thought of this new wonder hard to swallow. But this life was proving stranger than the one he had known before.

'Now focus; there is no time to waste. Call the hazel spirit to you. Ask for its help, its wisdom. Chant the "coll" sigil.'

Kerne was weary, but the hazelnuts had given him a new burst of energy. He settled down on the edge of the lake and held the hazelnut tightly in his hand, concentrating on its dryad, as Ogmios had taught him. He had always struggled with this leap of faith, that trees had a living spirit that could be contacted and communicated with, but perhaps the experiences of the last few weeks had persuaded him anything was possible. He relaxed his body, slowed his breathing to the rhythm of the lake's inhalations and exhalations and called out to the hazel dryad, chanting its kenning in a deep monotone: '*Cara bloisc …*'

Whether she appeared before him, or in his mind's eye, Kerne could not say, but suddenly there she was: slender, hazel-eyed and naked except for the tendrils of long brown hair that wrapped around her glimmering body. She looked at him with wise eyes and he knew she understood what he wanted of her. She nodded, a sprightly smile upon her lips, and dived into the water.

Softly Kerne chanted the 'coll' sigil over and over, visualising its shape in his mind's eye, the four branches pointing left from a central stem, projecting it on to the surface of the lake. The gentle lapping of the water, the glittering reflection of the morning sun, the susurration of the east wind through the firs lulled him into a trance. How long he remained in his reverie he could not gauge, but after an endless moment the smooth surface of the lake erupted as the hazel dryad shot out in a graceful arc, scattering water droplets in a rainbow, before winking and slipping back into the hazelnut in his hand.

The water settled. Birds sang louder. A gentle wind catspawed the quicksilver Mandorla. Then the lake's surface bulged and boiled, and from its rose a giant rainbow-scaled salmon. Llyr! He gazed at Kerne with fathomless, world-weary eyes.

Kerne bowed before the King in the Lake. 'Hail Llyr!'

'Why do you summon me, mortal? Why does your dryad disturb my slumber?'

'I need to cross your kingdom, to return to the Chalk Valley, to Caer Cernunnos. The very survival of the worlds depends upon it!'

'The worlds, eh? So you have knowledge of more than one, do you? Who but I can cross the worlds' oceans?' Llyr ruminated, smacking his thick lips. His eyes bore into Kerne. 'Ah, but I see you have a strange look about you. You are out of your own water …

167

And I smell the reek of cythrawl about you. Are you a demon escaped from Annwn?'

'No, I am a man.'

'Are you indeed? And why should I believe you are what you seem, eh?'

Merlin alighted by the head of the salmon. 'Old friend, he is what he claims. Not everyone has been shape-shifted.'

'Hmph. Very well, for old Sharpclaw's sake I'll do this. What do you offer for this passage?'

'These.' Kerne held out a handful of hazelnuts.

Llyr seemed pleased with this offering. He allowed Kerne to place them in his mouth. 'Mmm. Nearly as good as the nuts from the Well of the Nine Sisters … So, I better take you across, though it hurts my dignity.'

'A king must always carry his people,' said Merlin.

'Mm, you're right, Sharpclaw. Your words strike to the heart, as ever … Step aboard, then, and don't let go!'

Kerne waded into the water and clambered aboard the giant salmon by gripping his rainbow scales. He hauled himself up and straddled the back of the fish, holding on to his scales as the salmon turned around and set off, rising and falling in a hypnotic way. It was like a dream, except for the spray in his face and the chafing of the scales beneath his legs. It was like riding a slippery rhinoceros.

Kerne thought of Baramis the Scythian and hoped the blacksmith would manage to escape the regime of the Forbidden Kingdom and reach the Valley of the Chalk Folk … He would like to be able to repay his kindness, his friendship.

Merlin escorting them overhead, the mighty salmon sped out into the deep lake and Kerne was aware that at any moment Llyr could plunge down and drown him. But the giant fish kept just enough above water to keep most of him dry, although his legs were soaked.

Flurries of wind teased the waves around them like a flock of storm petrels chivvying the waters. It was a breezy, exhilarating day to be out on the lake, but this wasn't any kind of sailing Kerne had experienced before. In his youth his Da had taken them out on the Severn in the blue dinghy he had saved up for all of his life: *Kingfisher*, a retirement gift to himself.

'There's a good breeze at your back,' observed Llyr.

They passed fishing boats and the fishermen stared in, first, astonishment, then awe and reverence, bowing low, hailing their god.

The salmon cruised past the floating village and the pinnacle of

Sword Rock, with its Windeye, where Kerne had first heard the legend. So much had happened since then. And now he was riding the King in the Lake. Life had become more magical and more dangerous. The world he knew was no longer stable.

They continued towards the white cliffs. The crossing took a fraction of the time it had taken Brak and Kerne. So much had happened between them since then. They had found mutual respect and friendship. They had both been tested. Brak had returned with his sister and with a new respect for the stranger, while Kerne had found within himself the power of the windsmith – and the cost of that mantle and his presence here in Shadow World.

Kerne decided to ask Llyr some questions to sound his knowledge. The mighty salmon god was renowned for his deep wisdom, according to the Fisher Folk.

'Llyr?'

'Mm?' The salmon's voice bubbled up not from below, but from inside Kerne's mind. He spoke to him like Merlin, but his voice was slower and sadder.

'Where does this lake flow to?'

'To the sea.'

'Which sea?'

'The Wyndark Sea. I have swum in it many times. I have crossed the oceans of this world. Never have I become lost. I know the subterranean roads. I can sense the earth dragons in my blood.'

Earth dragons. This idea intrigued Kerne, who had spent his life trying to chart the 'Shining Roads', as he had called them. He had tracked them across England, even to Brittany, but the war had curtailed his research before he had been able to draw any conclusions. He had instinctively felt they were more than navigational aids, that they somehow connected with one's life path; and that such alignments can run through time as well as space and perhaps even through people. Were they connected to names? If, as Merlin suggested, a name contained the destiny of the named, were words themselves a kind of road, and would knowing the right words, in the right order, get him home? Certainly, it seemed the windsmith's gramarye provided keys and the tree sigils acted as doorways.

Kerne as if he was imbibing Llyr's wisdom just by being on his back. But he tried to articulate his questions once more, wanting to find the words that would help orientate him in this strange world and perhaps identify his destiny.

'What lies to the south?'

'The lands of fire and dust. HyperNotus.'

'What lies to the west?'

'The Blessed Isles of HyperZephyrus.'

'What lies to the north?'

'HyperBorea, the Land Beyond the North Wind.'

'Is that Great Britain?'

'Prydain, Brutus's Isle, Clas Myrddin ... There are many names for that place. Your Logres is but one of many Englands.'

Logres! It was only his Ma's name for England, but it called him from deep inside like a mother's call to her young.

'How can I get home?'

'Home?' Llyr boomed.

'To my source – to the place I was born?'

For a moment the Salmon King ruminated, then his answer surfaced: 'You must learn and master the four winds, then you will be able to navigate your way home – but do not expect it to be the same as when you left.'

'But I am not meant to be here! I am alive in the land of the dead.' Kerne shuddered as he remembered the Eater of the Dead. 'What happens when people die here?'

'Their souls are trapped in Annwn. They become wights if they die violently, or return to Gwynvedd if they make peace with their souls and are ready to move on.'

'Gwynvedd?'

'I am using names from your mother tongue but these realms of existence are known by many. Gwynedd is the realm of purity, of perfection. Some call it Heaven. There is a realm beyond that, called Ceugant, but only the Creator can exist within that, although everything exists within the Creator. Ceugant is a circle that has no centre, its edges everywhere, but it is the source of everything, the pulse at the heart of the universe. It is the spawning ground of all light, all goodness.'

'So is Gwynvedd our ultimate destination?'

'No. Some choose to return to Abred to continue their lessons.'

'What is Abred?'

'It is the middle world, the world you came from.'

'And what is Annwn?'

'It is the underworld you passed through under the Red Hills.'

'You know of that?'

'Every action creates ripples, nowhere more so than in this Shadow World, where the effects are amplified. They are like ripples caused by a rock thrown into the water. Ceugant is the first impact, the primal source, the next ripple is Abred, and the last is Annwn, where the impulse of life is at its weakest.'

'What happens if I die here?'

'That I cannot answer – it has never happened before. All I know is that *one* of you must die – you know of whom I speak – or the rift will continue to widen in the barrier between the worlds: the dead will walk with the living, and the living will be claimed by the dead lands. Your presences are creating too many ripples. They are giving birth to monsters of cythrawl.'

'"Cythrawl" – you mentioned that word before. What does it mean?'

'The forces of darkness and destruction that constantly threaten to overwhelm the worlds. Only the power of the Godhead can keep them in check.'

'Are you not a god?'

Llyr brooded on this. 'I am a splinter of the Godhead perhaps, as are we all, but not the source. A god? No … I only know I've been alive for centuries. I do not know of any other creature who is older than me. Even Merlin does not have a longer memory. I never forget the paths of the oceans I have swum, all the wonders and terrors I have seen. But sometimes such a memory is a curse; sometimes I wish I could forget. It is only in my sleep that I find respite. In blessed sleep …'

The Salmon King began to snooze and started to submerge. The icy water came over Kerne's legs.

'Llyr!'

'What? Oh! Sorry, slipping off there! Now quiet – let me concentrate. We are approaching narrow waters.'

They were nearing the mouth of the Da'anu and the Valley of the Chalk Folk. And a surprise awaited Kerne. The defaced effigy of the Goddess Brighid had been recreated as a phallic giant wielding a club: a defiant gesture to Taranis and his raiders. It reminded Kerne of the chalk giant of Cerne Abbas, and he had a strange feeling of déjà vu as they entered the steep-sided valley.

And something else was amiss … The trees were shedding their leaves already. Brak and Kerne had left on the rescue mission in early spring, possibly March. And now, to judge by the colour of the leaves and the chill in the air, it looked like autumn. Yet he couldn't have been away for more than a week. Kerne was too tired to work it out. It had been an exhausting ordeal and he was just glad to see the valley again. It was the nearest thing he had to home now.

Chalklander sentinels on stout stone watchtowers spotted them, and horns were blown, echoing along the hills, from fort to fort. Villagers stared in awe and wonder, until someone cried out, 'It is the Lord of the Animals! It is Cernunnos! He has returned!'

The cry was taken up along the valley as more and more Chalklanders spotted the man riding the giant salmon accompanied by a falcon.

'Cernunnos! Cernunnos!'

As Llyr wound his way upriver – as though returning to his spawning ground – Kerne looked with relief at the Chalklanders' effigies standing proud on the hillside; at the rebuilt defences of the caers; at the lines of Chalk Folk watching and waving, calling out the name of his destiny; and truly felt he was coming home.

'I have … enjoyed our conversation. It is lonely in the deep and it has been a long time since I have talked to anyone. I hear the prayers and wishes of the Mandorlans, but it is not a dialogue. Any who see me bow down in awe and terror. It is not easy being worshipped, you know. Sometimes, it is quite tiresome. Your company has been … refreshing. It has reminded me … of a dream I sometimes have of a king who was so disgusted with the world and its ways, with the violence his people inflicted on one another, that he relinquished his crown, forsook his sword and went into a deep sleep … and then I always awake at that point. Strange … It disturbs me …'

The Salmon King's dream reminded Kerne of something he couldn't quite put his finger on. Before he could pin it down, the effigy of the Stag Lord was in sight.

'Ah, here we are. Forgive my ramblings. I swam up here many a time to talk with Partholon. He alone talked with me in the past.'

They approached the chalk giant of the horned god. Above it stood the proud walls of Caer Cernunnos. The salmon allowed his passenger to disembark in the shallows.

'Good fortune, Isambard Kerne. You have a mighty task ahead of you. Choose wisely. We must all be responsible for the ripples we make. Farewell!'

Kerne watched as the salmon turned and vanished beneath the dark waters of the Da'anu. He was aware of warriors and women running down the slope to greet him. He went to step ashore and stumbled, his legs weak. It had been a long journey home.

Book Three

The Cauldron of War

19

Wind Dogs

The Journal of Isambard Kerne
Cantos 5th, Waxing Atenoux

There is something in the air, a restless energy, a quickening. The pages of my journal turn over of their own accord. The firepit in the centre flickers and flares, drying herbs sway in the beams, jars and beakers rattle on their shelves, the skins hanging about the walls fail to keep out a draught.

Yet outside it is a still day, not a breath of wind in the sky.

I sit upon soft, musty furs in Ogmios's hut while I write this with the stub of my pencil. I'm awake again after a long sleep: washed, wearing a clean tunic, and with several helpings of broth and bread inside me. I awoke refreshed this morning after last night's celebration in the hall, from which I departed early. After what I had witnessed on my journey back through the bowels of Annwn I was in no mood for celebration …

Exhausted from my ordeal, I had collapsed upon my arrival, despite the joyous reception I received and intense interest in my exploits. I was too fatigued to share anything at that point – all I could do was accept the embrace of Brak, my brother in arms, and the warm blessing of Brigantia. She commanded me to be carried to Ogmios's quarters and be allowed to sleep. And sleep I did.

I didn't get much rest the following day amidst the excitement of my return. I was welcomed into every hut, but it was in Brigantia's hall that I was made guest of honour and encouraged to share my adventure. Haltingly, I did, but Brak, unable to contain himself, took over, saying I was almost as bad at storytelling as I was at canoeing. This got a laugh from the audience. He winked at me, then took off, quite literally making a song and dance of it – turning our mission into a performance that he danced for those gathered, miming the different creatures we encountered, the ordeals we endured, the canoe journey, Wolf Forest, the Red Hills, the iron mines, Madoc, the prison and the escape.

I wanted to add about the blacksmith who had saved me, but it did not seem the right time to broach the subject of Baramis. Besides, Brak was in full flow, dominating the hall with his presence. He exaggerated greatly, in the custom of their speechmakers, proud to boast about our success. The young warrior came alive in the firelight as he swayed and jumped, his tattooed skin aglow, mimicking the chimera attacking or the burning giant, to the gasps of awe and admiration from the audience.

As Brak finished his version of events, paddling Bronwen back across the Mandorla, to rapturous applause, anyone would think he had achieved the rescue single-handed, but, to his credit, he called me up and let me share in the glory.

The hall fell quiet. I was encouraged to add my version, but I had not the stomach to boast about my tyrannical pilot or the Eater of the Dead. My mouth went dry as I stumbled to select the right details. All I could muster was a few muttered words: 'It was a hard journey. Brak does it more justice than I can. There is little I can add.'

Folk wanted to know about how I escaped from the Forbidden Kingdom, how I crossed the lake on the back of Llyr, but Brigantia seemed to understand. She clapped her hands at the growing chatter and the revellers fell silent. She looked more beautiful than I remembered her – her shapely body wreathed in a deep blue material, silver coiled about her bare arms, an amber necklace at her neck, cropped coppery locks framing her pale proud features. Were it not for the flattering fire glow the lines of sorrow and care would have been visible on her face, but she wore her maturity with dignity and it made her all the more comely.

'After the tale-telling comes the gift-giving. We must reward our heroes.'

This I had not anticipated.

First Brak was given a splendid bronze shield – its boss inlaid with gems – and was called 'shield of his people' by Brigantia. Then a helmet with short horns, like a roebuck's, was brought forth and placed upon his head.

The young warrior stood proud in the glow of the fire,

gleaming with bronze, glistening with sweat.

'Hail to the Champion of Cernunnos!' Ogmios declared and we echoed, the cheer raising the roof.

Then I was called up before the circle by the chief. How differently I was regarded now compared with the first time I stood before Bron.

Brigantia called me forward and gazed upon me with her electrifying eyes. 'Isambard Kerne, when first you came here we mistrusted you, but you have proved your worth. You are no ally of Speaks-with-Thunder as we feared. Brak has told us how you fought bravely and risked your own life to allow my children to escape. You have a warrior's heart, though you may use other ways of fighting, so Ogmios tells me. No treasure could fully repay your returning my precious daughter to me, but this gift is a sign of how much what you have accomplished means to me.'

There was a collective gasp as Brigantia ordered her hand-maidens to pass her a fabulous golden breastplate. It was diamond-shaped, about a foot across, and decorated with parallel lines and zigzags.

'Behold, the Lorica of Bron!' declaimed Ogmios. 'It is imbued with protective charms. Whosoever wears it will be protected by his mighty spirit.'

Brigantia presented it to me. I was overwhelmed. It is, indeed, a gift fit for a king. I bowed low and went to step out of the fire circle, but the gift-giving was not over.

Bronwen, in her turn, gave me a gold brooch of similar shape. When first I beheld her after my return I was shocked – her maiden hair was shorn, a harder look was in her eye, the soft smile that once graced her face was now faded like a spring flower. Garbed in a leather jerkin and breeches, a black cloak about her bare shoulders and pinned with the brooch of a raven, a bone-hilted copper dagger at her hip, she looked more like a warrior than a princess. Shadows lingered under her eyes, and she avoided my sympathetic gaze. Since her return she has trained with the Morrigan, the warrior women, who teach the arts of death at Caer Vran under the strict rule of Nemain. These fierce women wear warriors' garb, blacken their hair and decorate themselves with raven feathers, painting their faces white with a black band across the eyes. They are terrifying to behold and in battle, I am told, implacable and unstoppable. Their banshee screech strikes terror into the hearts of their enemies. Once Bronwen combed her hair every night; now, so they whisper, she sharpens her sword with a whetstone. I sense she will not be helpless again, but I could not help but mourn her transformation. She seems edgy about me and men in general. I only hope that time will ease that.

And finally Brak stepped forward. To my surprise, he gave me a fine belt with a gold buckle like a smaller version of the lorica. He too appreciated what I had done, especially the sacrifice I had made to allow them to escape. He put his firm sword hand on my shoulder and smiled his big ferocious smile. 'Sword-brother,' he simply said. Then he made me empty a mead horn with him.

I downed the dregs, spluttering, but I was more choked by emotion, unable to say anything gracious except express my deepest thanks.

These three gifts have had a profound effect on me, and it's not just because of their generosity or the heightened status they give me in the tribe ... I run my fingers over them now, along the fine grooves, the grids and zigzags. I have seen these somewhere before, but I cannot remember where. I am hoping it will come back to me.

And now as I rest in a corner of Ogmios's hut, staring into the firepit, its flickering light gleaming on my gifts hanging on a post, I reflect upon the changes wrought upon myself, this tribe and this land since we left on our quest.

Since the successful rescue of Bronwen I am thought of differently and the means of my mysterious escape from the Forbidden Kingdom and my dramatic arrival have caused great wonder. The mighty salmon kept good his word. Llyr brought me to the foot of the fort. I have learnt from him much wisdom, beyond even that of Ogmios – what lies to the south and the sea beyond; the fabled island kingdoms to the west and to the north, a place that could be my Britain ...

Will I ever be able to truly return home? Am I not in the land of the dead? A return to the world of the living does not seem possible. So where do I belong? At the moment it seems as though I belong *here*. I have been accepted into the tribe now that I have proved myself.

After our adventure together Brak looks upon me as a

brother. He has changed his tune considerably since first we met. He does not stop singing my praises, literally! Everyone is impressed, except Bronwen. She is grateful, but edgy around me. The only man she seems comfortable around is her brother. What happened to her in Caer Taranis, I dread to think. She has grown distant from me, as if she associates me with Madoc. Brigantia looks upon her with deep concern but understands what she is changing herself into. She too has altered; she has come into her power as matriarch of the tribe, yet she no longer wears the mourning garb. Her tawny hair has grown again and she wears colours once more, though more sombre ones than before. I notice her watching me with her piercing eyes, the colour of shadows on Mount Anu. I am unnerved by her, for she is a formidable woman. I do not deny her beauty, or that I find her attractive. Yet is she not my ancestor? Would not love with her be incest?

Even if that were not so, I still feel the loss of Maud. When I finally *could* appreciate her fully, and she could finally understand me, we were sundered. We were married 'till death do us part' – and if I am not dead, then am I not still married to her? Yet I made her let me go. I have no claim upon her now, so does she have no claim upon me? I suppose death has separated us – it seems it is an unbridgeable divide. But it is too soon to think of romance, and circumstances will not allow it. War is looming. I have warned the Chalk Folk to expect retribution. Madoc will not stop until he has exacted his revenge for the escape of his bride, for the chaos at the burning giant and for my escape.

There is to be a council of war at the Drunemetom on Moot Holm. All the chiefs of the Chalk Folk will be there. I have been asked to attend. They want to hear my plans. Since my return upon Llyr I have been looked upon as a man of magic. Flurries of wind seem to follow me everywhere.

As I write this Ogmios's lodge seems beset with its own wind devils. They seem to want to make a mess of things, scattering my possessions across the floor. I shall go to pick them up for the umpteenth time, trying to recall where I had first acquired my own gremlins ...

Ogmios came back in at that point from an errand and surveyed the chaos, laughing. This seemed an odd reaction from someone whose home had been trashed. But then his expression became severe and his tone of voice harsh and with a series of quick clear gestures and sounds he stopped the disruption.

After we had cleared up the mess, Ogmios sat down with a beaker of nettle tea and explained: I am attracting 'wind dogs' – air elementals – as I become a windsmith. This is the surest sign that the power of the awen is awakening in me. The wind dogs are drawn to it, like water spirits to a stream or a dryad to a tree. Such elementals can be useful allies, but if they are not acknowledged and indulged they can become a nuisance, even dangerous. To illustrate, Ogmios clicked his fingers and threw his club across the room. To my astonishment it was caught in mid-air, brought back and dropped at his feet. Immediately, Ogmios picked up a piece of bread from the platter and cast it into the air. Before my eyes it was snatched and consumed, vanishing without a trace. Then Ogmios threw the club again. Once more it was dropped in his lap. But this time the old windsmith began chewing on a piece of bread. Within a minute a beaker was knocked over, spilling milk. This was licked up by invisible tongues in the blink of an eye.

The moral, summarised the old windsmith, is always to honour the 'folk of the air', as he calls them: never talk disrespectfully about them and always leave an offering. Otherwise they will take their own toll. But Ogmios advised never to test 'the crew that never rest'.

He asked me then when I had first noticed them. The disturbances had become so common I had grown accustomed to them, an affliction I was always accursed with, but then I remembered.

The forge of Baramis.

So I explained to Ogmios about the blacksmith archer. It was good to finally talk about him, to honour the remarkable man who had helped me in the wilderness: a friend in a hostile country.

Ogmios liked the sound of the fellow and looked forward to meeting him one day if he made it out of the Forbidden Kingdom. But that wasn't our concern at present. Why did the wind dogs first show themselves there? questioned Ogmios.

I thought back to my time in the wilderness of the Steppe when I had communed with Eurus and understood the woodwords. Had they followed me from the Steppe? I postulated this to Ogmios. He said they could come from any-where; it is whether we are ready for them that matters. I had attuned to the wind in the Forbidden Kingdom and they had been drawn to me. I did not walk through Hell alone after all.

They do not always show themselves, Ogmios added. Perhaps this explains why I had been unaware of my mentor's own wind dogs until now – he does not like to flaunt them. It is best to ask for their help only when you need it, he advised in earnest, but even then it is best not to rely on them or expect your wishes to be followed precisely. The wind dogs are, by their very nature, light-hearted, playful and capricious. Yet they can be a windsmith's best friend.

Ogmios is impressed, in his gruff way, with my progress. He questioned me endlessly about the King in the Lake. All of his life he has wanted to behold and talk with him. He hears that Llyr talks with Partholon, but how and when the Chief of Caer Fintan keeps to himself. Then I come along, offer him a few hazelnuts and jump on his back! The windsmith's laughter melted away any bitterness. He said I have a stronger awen than even him. I spoke to him at length about my experiences with the woodwords: how I used the oak sigil to escape from the burning giant; how I heard the sound sigils in the wilderness; how I communed with the east wind and spoke with Eurus, learning his sigil of summoning – one of the five new woodwords I had brought back from the Void. Ogmios had his own way of invoking Eurus – he said every windsmith must find his own means of dialogue with the Divine. Gramarye must come from the heart to have any power; it must be wrought by the painful lessons and particularity of personal experience. Only then can a main artery be opened to the infinite.

The old windsmith was silent for a while, gazing into the fire, as he reflected on all I had told him. Then he said I must be careful with my new-found powers. What I had done was foolish and dangerous – though he admits I had little choice. But the sigils I used could have just as easily blown apart my mind as the 'duir' woodword did my prison door. Before I use them again, he warned, I must study them carefully: focus upon each of their effects, the nuances of their vibrations. He said they present a spectrum of power – filters for the awen, affecting how it manifests. These prisms are essential; the pure force of the awen would destroy my mind. And so I must train, practising a sigil every day. Ogmios recommends eating a small cake each day marked with the sigil I wish to master. 'But there is not much time!' he lamented.

I was away for only seven days, yet seven months have passed here. Brak and I left in the height of spring and it is now late autumn. Time runs slower in the east, which means Madoc has had more time to prepare for war.

I shudder at the thought, having tasted Annwn's horrors so recently. Ogmios sensed I was holding something back, some unspeakable memory. He coaxed it out of me like a septic splinter. It turned out he had heard of my underworld passage from Merlin, who had kept him informed of my progress via Blodeuwedd; yet he waited until I was ready to speak of it. I told him how I had meditated upon the yew sigil and how I had managed to open the cromlech – one of the many entrances to Annwn. I faltered in describing the shocking vision of no-man's-land, a battle scene from another world, another time. Ogmios assured me that each traveller in that country of nightmare confronts his own worst fear. He too has been there, as all windsmiths have to as part of their initiation, and he narrowly escaped being devoured by the Eater of the Dead. The trauma of it made him grow pale. Reassured that he could empathise with my experience, I continued my account. When I had finished, though I trembled I felt lighter, unburdened. I still carry a lot of guilt about the war, tied up with Madoc, so my shrewd mentor gauged, his words like a surgeon's blade. It is true that I feel greatly responsible for the devastation we are bringing to this world, the monsters we are unleashing, the apocalypse we herald.

Sooner or later I will have to confront this doom.

And it seems I will not have to wait long.

There are only two weeks until the moon is full, when we suspect Madoc will strike. We must prepare. This time, like Bronwen, the tribe will not be defenceless.

20

Drunemetom

The birds came from out of the night – barn owl, eagle, wren, robin, dove, hawk, raven, swan, songthrush, heron, kingfisher and merlin – converging on Moot Holm in the heart of the Valley of the Chalk Folk. The steep outcrop of rock stood dark-shouldered and proud in the middle of the silver-threaded Da'anu. The thin new moon glimmered frail as a candle flame in the dusky sky above the sacred oak grove. On the summit of mossy boulders and tangled, cliff-perched trees, thirteen oaks grew tall in a circle like a wooden crown: the Drunemetom, sacred to the Goddess of Groves, Nemetona. No edged weapons were allowed into her sanctuary; no hard words spoken. Anyone who entered had to bow to the earth and walk barefoot. The birds settled in the oak trees, one to each, except for the merlin and the owl.

Garbed in his blue cloak, and wearing his golden gifts of breastplate, belt and brooch with pride, Kerne entered the sacred grove in solemn procession behind the other windsmiths, pacing sunwise around the circle. The carved faces of oak were lit up by the light of the bonfire in the centre around which the tribal chieftains were gathered, facing inwards, their backs guarded by their broadshouldered champions. Kerne could see that each tree was carved with a tribal totem: stag, bear, salmon, eagle, wolf, deer, hound, boar, raven, bull, ram, horse and human.

The windsmiths formed an outer circle behind the champions and the tribal chiefs on their ornately carved wooden thrones, torcs glinting in the firelight.

The chiefs each spoke their name in turn, flame-haired Brigantia wielding the antlers of her office; thick-bearded, heavy-jowled Arthus, chief of the bear tribe, in a bear-fur cloak; wise, watery-eyed Partholon in his rainbow-scaled skull cap of salmon skin; sharp-eyed, beak-nosed Eryr with his white ruff of eagle feathers; wolf-cowled Cormac, restless, alert, salt-and-pepper-maned; graceful Saar, slender and upright in her deerhide dress; grizzled and surly Setanta with his spiked collar and mantle of dog-tails; portly Tawrk, bald but for ginger mutton chops handlebar moustache and a boar-tusk necklace; Nemain garbed in black raven feathers, thin-lipped and dark-browed; the massive Donn with his bullhorns on his broad shoulders, large forehead shining with sweat; hard-nosed Cyndyn with ram's horns in his hands; elegant golden-haired Macha, beautiful in white, wielding her horse-whip; and ancient Tuan, beard long and white, leaning on his gnarled staff.

Then one by one the windsmiths called their names: Ogmios; Urswick, the Bear Priest; Finegas, the Salmon Priest; Uscias, the Eagle Priest and chief of the windsmiths; Gwyllt, the Wolf Priestess; Esias, the Deer Priestess; Morann, the Hound Priest; Bladud, the Boar Priest; Morfessa, Nemain's dark priestess; Senach, the Bull Priest; Ruadan, the Ram Priest; Gwydion, the Horse Priestess; and Simias, the priest of the Tuan – figures pale in their robes, faces in shadow but eyes gleaming, still as the lichened megaliths.

The champions did not speak but their silent muscular presences were impossible to ignore.

The airman himself was the honoured guest, Ogmios had informed him, but he stood outside the secondary circle, waiting his turn to be invited in to speak. He felt the power of the thirteen tribes, their collective strength knitting together like the web of branches above through which sparks spiralled, turning into stars. There was a gust of wind and an acorn fell at Kerne's feet. He stooped and picked it up, sensing the champions watch his every move, hands on weapons. He cradled the acorn in his hand and felt it give him strength. He would need it tonight.

Ogmios stepped forward, brandishing his crystal-studded club. He bowed and addressed the chieftains. 'Let each chief speak, as is the custom, only while holding the speaking stick. We proceed in the order of the sacred river that links us all. Let no man gainsay another until all have spoken. This is a grove of peace and respect. Here our forefathers and mothers have come since first we settled in this valley. No weapon may be wielded except words. To break the taboo is to suffer death. Let the Drunemetom begin!'

The one-eyed windsmith passed the gem-studded club to graceful, watery-eyed Partholon. 'Noble chieftains of Da'anu, these are troubled times – times that will test the strength of our tribes, of our warriors and of our beliefs. I suggest we need to proceed with caution and with wisdom. Let no man act in haste, but when the time comes we must all follow our calling. Larger forces are at work here, guiding us to our destiny. I have dreamed by the Blessed Da'anu and I sense the time ahead will define us or destroy us. Everything has been flowing to this point, and we must work together to survive it.'

The Salmon Chief passed the speaking stick to his eagle neighbour and sat down. Eryr looked harshly at his peers from beneath beneath the skullcap gleaming in the firelight.

'My salmon-brother speaks wisely as ever. Yet I disagree about his tactics. I have seen far also. My winged agents have reported the mustering of a large war-host at Ironwound Pass – they prepare to march west, to make war on the People of Da'anu. We must strike swiftly. Time is against us.'

This announcement caused a stir of alarm.

'We must defend ourselves! It is a doom brought upon us by the stranger! The Sky Gods are angry. They spat him out. His presence offends them and brings their ill will upon our valley.' Eryr pointed at Kerne with the club, his voice rising to a shrill hiss. 'I say he must be made sacrifice!'

Eryr passed the club to Brigantia. She snatched it from him in anger. The firelight gleamed on her bronze breastplate. With fierce green eyes she scanned her peers. Kerne knew her well enough by now to know that when her blood was up no one could gainsay her. 'Kerne is under my protection. See, he wears the Lorica of Bron. If any touch him they will have the Stag tribe to answer to!' Her challenge was met with awkward silence. Brigantia glared at Eryr until he turned his gaze, rolling his scornful eyes. 'Taranis has struck already. His Grey Raiders have exacted a terrible toll. Mighty Bron, the great chief of the Stag tribe and my husband, is dead. Others have been murdered. My daughter was abducted and only the bravery of my firstborn, Brak, and the skyman, Kerne, saved her.'

Everyone cast their eyes over the stranger, who stood to attention in his washed and repaired Royal Flying Corps uniform. The golden breastplate, brooch and belt-buckle gleamed in the firelight, strange on top of the fleece-lined overalls, but Kerne was glad to be wearing them. He sensed the chieftains' suspicions ease.

Brigantia resumed her appraisal: 'Most of our forts were damaged and it has taken us all summer to repair them. We know the Grey Raiders will strike again; our grain vats are full, yet it is not merely the wealth of our fields they want. I am informed that Speaks-with-Thunder desires the riches *below* ground also: the metal ore he craves – the silver, lead, copper and zinc that these lands are blessed with. His greed knows no bounds. He will not stop until he has what he wants, until he has plundered and desecrated all that we hold dear. So we must work together to defend ourselves. We must be prepared for him and his army of iron demons when they next attack. Everyone must help, or no one will survive. I have spoken.'

Brigantia passed Ogmios's club to thick-browed Arthus and sat down. Arthus looked uncomfortably at the club, turning it over in his massive hands, his deep-set eyes glinting. Then he spoke in a gruff voice, simple, powerful, direct. 'The noble Brigantia speaks with a bear's heart. We must join forces to face this common foe, or one by one we shall fall. I, Arthus, commit my tribe to this cause. For once, the bear will not sleep in his cave while winter rages.'

Arthus passed the club to grizzle-maned Cormac: 'Noble chieftains, you know why we have gathered here under our tribal oaks. Our very existence is threatened. We are at war.' He bared his teeth. 'It is a war not of our own choosing, but we will not shy from battle!'

Murmurs of agreement rippled through the grove.

Slender Saar accepted the club next, as graceful as Cormac was fierce, her voice like water against rock. 'I am not eager for bloodshed. All life is sacred. But if war is to come then let us protect the vulnerable and may the Goddess spare those who go to battle.'

Setanta plucked the speaking stick from Saar's slender hands, eager to speak: 'Let them come! My Wardogs will be waiting!'

Heavy-jowled Tawrk took the club from the shaven-headed youth. 'Not everyone is as eager as you for sword-talk, Hound of Battle. Many of us would like to enjoy our old age and indulgences, but if war comes to our gate then let them try to rout a boar in its den!'

Like a panther poised to strike, raven-haired Nemain spoke next. She took the speaking stick from the Boar Chief with a curt nod, gripping it like a mace. 'We should not wait until the enemy is at our gates, Chief of Henwen. We should strike first and strike swift! My Morrigan will gladly initiate them into the mysteries of death. No man alive can defeat us on the battlefield. The Goddess gives life and can take it. That is her right!'

Next, the Bull Chief, Donn Cooley, accepted the club. It looked like a chicken leg in his massive hands. 'Well said, Mistress of the Raven, and my Bullmen will fight by your side. We will not shirk from the slaughter. War is ugly, but not as ugly as cowardice. We must fight with honour or die in shame. If war is what they want, then let them know that the gods of the Da'anu will be eager for their sacrifice.'

'War is expensive!' finely dressed Cyndyn protested, taking up the speaking stick next. 'Have you thought of the cost?' There were howls of derision, but hard-headed Cyndyn ignored them. 'We must make provision. Ensure we have plentiful supplies. If we are to raise our own war-host then they'll need equipping, feeding. Families who lose warriors will need compensating ...'

Macha took the club and struck it against her thigh like a riding crop. She paced up and down in her long riding boots, tossing her mane of tawny-gold hair. 'Let us not count the cost of defending the land of our ancestors. We must do all we can to stop the enemy desecrating her.'

Finally, ancient Tuan took the club. His voice was like sand. 'The Goddess has already been insulted. Now we need the might of the Dagda. Stand proud before your enemy. Show them no fear. Together we will fight, or together we must fall!' The old man sat down, weary.

Ogmios accepted his club back. 'The Chieftains of Da'anu have spoken. Now let the skyman speak.'

There was consternation at this. Kerne heard mutterings about him not having the rank allowing him to speak in the Drunemetom, but Brigantia stood by him, and Ogmios at his other shoulder.

Kerne took the club and stepped forward. 'I am honoured to be allowed to speak here. I arrived in your valley a stranger, but have been made welcome in Caer Cernunnos. Some of you may not trust me' – Kerne looked pointedly at Eryr – 'but I have proved my loyalty by rescuing Bronwen with Brak, whom I am proud to call my sword-brother. I alone know our enemy. He was once my friend' – gasps of surprise and suspicion rippled around the circle – 'but no longer. He too fell from the sky, but something happened to him and now he is a tyrant. His cruelty knows no measure. He will stop at nothing until he gets what he wants, mark my words. I feel responsible for his presence. I will deal with him ... but I need your help to deal with his army. This is not a battle I will win alone, nor will any of us, individually.' Kerne cast about for inspiration. 'You are like this grove; one tree standing alone is weaker than many together. Your combined strengths are like the branches of these trees, weaving together a knot. You are outnumbered. You have inferior weapons ...' There were sounds of outrage at this. 'Hear me! The enemy fights with iron, not bronze. Iron can snap your finest swords in two. But you have one advantage, and it is a good one. You are defending family and hearth. This will make your warriors braver, their sword arm stronger, their aim truer. Taranis's army consists mainly of hired mercenaries, fighting for a fee, or for their freedom. But they will not die easily. There will be much slaughter on both sides. The river will run red with blood before this is over.'

For a moment, the vision of the river of blood in Annwn flashed before him. The War Dead still haunted him. He had to wash the guilt from him with action. 'I will do what I must. We must each play our part. *Together* we are stronger. *Together* we will win.'

There were some murmurs of agreement, but not all of the chiefs shared Kerne's conviction.

The Donn took the club again. 'There are not enough of us by ourselves. Taranis's army may consist of thousands. We have, what, thirteen hundred at the most? We need more!'

Suddenly, all the chiefs were speaking at once.

Partholon asked for the mace and waited until there was silence, his steady gaze and silent centredness drawing the chiefs in. 'There are the Ore Tribes.'

'Pah! When have they ever thought of anything but themselves?' spat Setanta.

Ogmios raised his hand. 'Setanta, you do not wield the mace. You cannot speak!'

Kerne remembered Ogmios telling him about the Ore Tribes – the Metenaidd. They lived along one of the five tributaries that fed into the Da'anu. Each had its mineral wealth. Ogmios had drawn a serpentine wiggly line in the ash to represent the Da'anu Valley, with five lines joining it. He called this image the Tree of Life. The elfish Arianedds mined and worked silver, the dwarf-like Copors worked copper, the dour Plwms lead, the long-faced Tuns tin and the Morrigan themselves mined zinc. Each traded with the other at Moot Holm and the ores combined created the best bronze. Weaponsmiths lined the banks at this trading post, where the sound of hammering usually echoed across the valley.

Partholon shrugged. 'Setanta is right, the Metenaidd keep to themselves, but this time there is a difference. If Taranis conquers our valley, and may Llyr prevent it, then their valleys will be next. Speaks-with-Thunder will use this valley as a bridgehead to stage his invasion of the rest of HyperEurus. We must send runners to each of the ore valleys and ask for their help.'

The Donn took back the mace. 'Yes … with the combined strength of the Metenaidd we may have a fighting chance.'

'We do not know their strength in arms,' growled Cormac.

Ogmios gave him a hard stare.

'True enough, brother,' replied the Donn, 'but we have no choice. We need all the sword arms we can.'

Cyndyn requested the mace. 'If the Metenaidd help us, they may want a trade agreement, we may have to reduce our river tax. We will lose profit.'

Everyone looked at him with scorn.

'Now is not the time to worry about such things, Cyndyn!' said Eryr. 'What price is our survival?'

'But what of our children's bellies if we let the Metenaidd fleece us?' Tawrk grunted.

An argument broke out, until Saar calmed everyone down with her gentle presence and soothing voice.

Nemain snatched the mace and stood up, tall and imposing, bristling with fury. 'We will win no war if we bicker like serf-brats! We need leadership; we need someone who will remain clear-headed and be decisive. We need to choose a war chief.'

Setanta mocked, 'And I suppose you think you're the best choice?'

Nemain glared at him, but Setanta just leant back and picked his teeth with a splinter of wood.

'It is true that I am skilled above all in the arts of war. If any gainsay me then let them meet me in combat!' The men looked at their boots, avoiding her stare. 'But I do not presume to be the obvious choice. Search your hearts and choose wisely for our lives depend on it.' Nemain placed the mace back in the central stone and sat down with a rustle of feathers. The mace stood upright, gleaming in the firelight, challenging them.

Who was it to be? Arthus was strong but perhaps too slow in decision-making; Partholon was wise but no warrior; Eryr too intellectual and aloof; Cormac was a good fighter but too wild and self-willed to lead others; Saar too gentle; Setanta too angry; Tawrk too selfish; Cyndyn too petty; and Tuan too old. Brigantia stood rigidly alone from the candidates, her sword in its sheath. That left three: Macha, Nemain and the Donn.

Ogmios stepped forward and gestured to the solid stone ring around the firepit. 'The Moot Stone is the sacred heart of our valley. It is prophesied that it will cry out when a true leader stands upon it. Whosoever wishes to be considered for the position of war chief step forward on to the stone and speak your name. If you are the one, you will feel no pain. If you are not, then it will be you who cries out.'

'That stone's red hot!' spat Setanta. And it was true, the stone had been heated by the bonfire all evening. The idea of being the war chief was suddenly less appealing. Any with doubts in their hearts knew it was not worth the risk. Only Macha, Nemain and the Donn stepped forward.

Macha stepped on to the stone and shouted her name. She screamed in pain and leapt back on to the cool grass, nursing her feet.

Nemain stepped up and called out her name. Her face contorted in pain, but she refused to scream. Awkwardly, she stepped down.

Finally, the Donn stepped up and stated his name. The stone let out a loud hiss as if doused in cold water. The Donn remained on the stone.

Ogmios declared, 'The Moot Stone has spoken. The Donn has been chosen as your war chief.'

One by one the chieftains knelt before the Bull Chief. The Donn accepted their allegiance.

'Hail to the Donn!'

'Hail to the Donn!' they all cried out except one – Macha.

'I will not be ruled by any man!'

'Fear not, noble Macha. I will not rule you like a tyrant. I am here to command our army. I will listen to the advice of you all before making any final decision. I am not here to give orders to you, Macha, or any chieftain. As caer chiefs of Da'anu we are still equals and will continue to sit in a circle for council. No one is above another. We all must do our best. We all have special skills and resources that no one else will govern.'

Macha was appeased by this. 'Very well. Hail to the Donn, our chief-in-war!'

'We have work to do. Each of you speak in turn. What can you offer to the war chest?'

The Donn passed the club around.

Arthus spoke first: 'We can protect the children, sick and elderly in our caves.'

Arthus passed the club to Eryr and sat down.

'We shall provide sentinels to watch the lake, and send swift messengers to the Metenaidd.'

Cormac spoke next: 'My wolf pack shall hunt down the enemy. Others will guard the lair.'

Saar took the club. 'We shall use our swiftest runners to deliver messages and our healing skills to aid those in need.'

'We shall provide soldiers strong in arm,' offered Setanta.

Tawrk held the speaking stick. 'We shall coordinate provisions and the feeding of the army.'

'My Morrigan will fly into battle and tear out their hearts,' boasted Nemain and no one doubted her.

'We shall trade with the other valleys to ensure we have all the supplies we need,' declaimed Cyndyn.

'My charioteers shall lead the assault and my Whisperers will make their horses bolt and cast off their riders,' declared Macha.

Finally, Tuan offered his support: 'We shall provide the headquarters for our leaders and house the warriors while the war lasts.'

Ogmios stepped forward. 'And we windsmiths shall lend our strength. I hear from Kerne that Taranis has lost his chief magician, Crow-Walker, yet our valley has thirteen. Speaks-with-Thunder may have strength of arms, but we have the magical advantage. I shall consult with my circle and we shall prepare a suitable welcome for his army.'

Kerne asked if he could speak again. 'I offer to design and oversee the construction of new defences. I need manpower and materials: wood, earth and stone.'

The Donn looked at Cyndyn, who replied, 'You shall have all you need.'

Then the Donn spoke: 'My men shall help building defences. And you, skyman, shall guide their hands. Bring forth the Mace of the Maker!'

Ogmios produced an ornate stone mace from a skin bundle. The handle had a black-and-white zigzag inlay that shone in the fireglow.

'Step forward, skyman, and kneel.'

Kerne did as he was bid.

The Donn held the mace over Kerne's head. 'It is no longer a time of words, but one of deeds. Each knows what he or she must do. Skyman, take this mace and use it to supervise the work you must do. With this symbol of authority the Chalk Folk will do as you command. When your work is done you must return it here.'

Kerne reached up and accepted the mace. It felt heavy. The head was dark, smooth limestone. The bone zigzag inlay caught in the firelight. He had not expected such a prestigious gift. A strong feeling of déjà vu overcame him and Kerne shook his head.

'I cannot take this ...'

'You must, Kerne. The Donn commands it!' Ogmios insisted.

Kerne bowed, beads of perspiration running down his brow. His body trembled; his hands felt clammy. The mace felt as heavy as the

190

huge responsibility upon his shoulders. The trust they had bestowed upon him was humbling. And there was something else, a feeling he couldn't shake off, a presentiment. A ghost of a feeling, of a memory … But the immediate circumstances prevented him from gauging it. He felt the stares of the council burn into him.

'I vow to do all I can to help you bring peace to this valley.'

'Good, then let us do our duties. May the Great God and Goddess bless us all!'

Nemain added, 'And may Andraste bring us victory!'

'Victory!' the chieftains shouted, their voices echoing into the night from the grove, a tiny circle of light against the darkness.

21

Blood Line

The Journal of Isambard Kerne
Samionos 4th, Waxing Atenoux

I have become my ancestor. This shocking and puzzling realisation has come to me as I rest here out of the biting east wind
that rolls off Lake Mandorla, in the shelter of a beech tree
overlooking the downlands of the valley of the chalk giants.
The revelation weighs heavily as I roll in my hand the ceremonial mace with its hypnotic zigzag inlay, the mace of 'Bush Barrow Man' – another item of his grave goods to land in my lap.
Only that strange milk-white stone of his is lacking to complete the set. Yet, I feel typecast by fate already, wearing 'his'
breastplate, brooch and belt-buckle, constructing earthworks
as he would have done, the so-called builder of Stonehenge.
How far away that mighty monument seems, on mist-
shrouded Salisbury Plain, though the memory of it is a close as
yesterday.

I recall vividly that fateful midsummer dawn by the Giant's
Dance with Maud, when I was overwhelmed by a feeling of déjà
vu while exploring the barrows of Normanton Down, where
that so-called 'Bush Barrow Man' was found by Cunnington
and Colt-Hoare. I had a powerful sense that *I had been that person*. Maud had mocked me then and lost her temper. After my
forgetting our wedding anniversary it had been the final straw.

And I lost my temper too, at having my beliefs mocked.
That is why I kept them to myself for so long.

Yet here I sit, in treasures identical to those found on Normanton Down, gifts from Brigantia, Brak and Bronwen, certainly, but it seems I am not the only thing to cross over into
Shadow World. Vindicated perhaps, but it is a pyrrhic victory,
trapped here on the other side of death.

It is a chill late autumn day. Late October by my reckoning.

The month of Seed-Fall, Samionos, by the stone calendar of Ogmios. The great fire festival of Samhain – Summer's End – is only days away, at the time of the Death Moon. It's a week and a half until the moon is full and we fear the Iron Army will attack then, when the night will be brightest for ill-doings and the blood will be up.

Below me, overlooking the mouth of the river Da'anu, is Caer Dagda, home of Tuan, where I have been overseeing the strengthening of palisades, the deepening of the ramparts and the adding of further ditches to create a mazelike killing alley for any would-be attacker. I remember seeing such at Maiden Castle in dear old Dorset on a cold wet day. These rolling chalk downlands that stretch out along the western edge of the lake remind me so much of that green and pleasant land … I was so impressed by the huge system of defensive earthworks I saw that day that I drew them from memory when I returned home, marvelling at the manpower and ingenuity they must have required. And now here I am, with a thousand men at my disposal, creating my own earthworks. I see them working below me: some on the caer, others on the track leading to the next hill fort – a line of white carved from the hillside. The men work there in file with crude antler-tine pickaxes and the shoulder blades of oxen for shovels – all bronze being reserved for weapons. I hear them singing rough working songs to keep the momentum going and their spirits up. The melodies have an Irish air to them. They remind me of navvies working on a railway or road, and I think of my grandfather, my father's da: what a hard life he must have had, breaking his back digging those canals for the coal barges so he could provide for his family.

I feel guilty watching them while they work for me, but this is a rare chance for a break. I have hardly stopped for days. I must go down and thank them personally, make sure they have sufficient refreshment and shelter. These are the menfolk of all caers, volunteers, not just serfs. All have put their backs into preparing for the inevitable attack. For the first time the men of separate tribes work together enhancing each other's defences. The work begun here is being replicated up and down the valley. I visit the other sites as much as possible but I have trained twelve other budding engineers to supervise the construction in their respective caers once I have shown them the design and method applied to Caer Dagda. The priority was this one, the home of Tuan, nearest the mouth of the river and the most vulnerable. Yet now the proud figure of Cerne Abbas stands defiantly guarding the entrance, like a Celtic Colossus of Rhodes.

And I, Kerne, feel like I have come home to myself. This is where the alignment of my life has been leading me all along.

Yet how can this be so? How can I inhabit my own past? The only answer I can think of is that here time runs differently, it does strange things. There seem to be alternating zones of fast and slow time, but the edges seem to blur, circles within circles. And if time runs in a circle, may it not also run in a spiral?

If I wear the accoutrements of a high-status burial known in my world, on the Earth I know, then am I just down amongst the dead men, with all the deposits of history, or is it my destiny to end up under that barrow?

Perhaps that's the only solution. One of us must die. And if I cannot bring myself to kill Madoc, then it must be me … Under my Stonehenge regalia I wear my other symbol of office – my officer's pistol.

One bullet left; meant for me, or Madoc?

The sounds of activity rise from the valley on the incessant wind. The clang-clanging of the weaponsmiths, the roar of the bronze furnaces, the banter of bartering as stores and supplies are traded. And I can see a long line of Chalk Folk: carts full of possessions, families, screaming babies, elders – refugees of war, heading upriver for the safety of the higher caers along the road I have surveyed.

With great pleasure I found myself with sighting poles like the Long Man, surveying the most level and safe passage along the valley. To act as an escape route primarily, but also improving communications and trade between the caers. It was just like surveying a route for the railway. The track was cleared and cut out of the hillside in a week. It is crude – nothing more than a stone-lined path, but Saar's runners can traverse the length of the valley in a morning and be back by evening.

Yet I enjoy no feeling of pride as I watch the refugees wind their way up the narrow track. I never thought I would see such a sight here. It looks all too familiar. If the Great War raged for four years, as Maud informed me, then such upheaval must have have been all too common in Europe.

Now the shadow of war has reached these lands ... It seems there is to be no peace, even in the land of the dead.

Only I can stop it. I could stop it now, with a bullet to the head. But that is no solution. It may well stop the worlds being torn apart, but who is to say that it would halt Madoc? At least if I am here I could make a difference. And I dread to think what would happen to my soul if I committed suicide here. Would I become a wight, or something worse? Would I be taken into cythrawl? There would be no barrow for a coward. I must summon courage and fight for these good people. If they are my ancestors then I have a great obligation to them. This is my chance to give something back.

I will not let them down.

I must descend and reassure the refugees, speak to the workers. I must do what I can. I feel implicated in all of this – perhaps I seek forgiveness in their eyes.

I have had a tremendous shock and need to sit down and gather my thoughts. There was I, thinking I had become one of my ancestors, when it seems I am surrounded by them! I went down to help the refugees in any way I could. A heavily laden cart was stuck in the new track and I lent a hand. A mother with two young children clutching her dress hem watched from the front of the cart. I couldn't bring myself to look at them. I could feel their eyes burning into me. Pressing down on me I felt a responsibility for the whole turmoil and upheaval they were suffering – their displacement; their fear; the absence of their father and husband, who has probably been conscripted into the defence force; even the fact that their cart was stuck. Perhaps I was taking on too much of the burden, too much of the blame, but my strength failed me, their cart would not budge. Many others were stuck on the track behind it; tempers were rising, nerves fraying.

Then I felt my burden ease as the menfolk who had been lining the track with stones lent their muscle to the cart and it began to budge. The wheel lifted out of the rut and the horses whinnied, able to pull their load forward again. There was a weary cheer and the line of refugees continued on their way, the mother and children looking back at me. One of them waved, the youngest, a little girl, and I waved back, wiping my brow with the back of my RFC overalls sleeve.

The men who had helped waited for the carts to pass, waving goodbye to their own loved ones. No one knew when they would see one another again.

I wanted to thank them, so I went over to the main gang and tried to get their attention, but the men, covered in sweat and chalk dust, were preoccupied with the departing caravan.

Then a firm hand gripped my shoulder, nails battered and dirty, skin calloused. It was a grip of iron. I half expected to be struck in the face as I turned around, but still I turned, prepared to accept whatever I deserved.

And I was nearly knocked sideways by what I saw.

It was my father.

He stood there gnarled and tough like an old tree, older than I remembered him, yet his furrowed face was unmistakable. His features were my own seen through the lens of time. He had been sixty the last day I had seen him, the day I set off to RFC training. The man before me was at least seventy, but it was unmistakably him. I saw the Kerne in his eyes, of which I was a gleam. He was covered with the colours of his trade as if he had just come home from a day working on the railways. He had never been ashamed of his dirty overalls, his oil-stained hands, his muddy boots. 'Nothing shameful about an honest day's graft, lad,' he would say when my nose wrinkled at the smell of his toil. His return to our warm home, which always smelt of freshly baked bread, or a cake in the oven, or spring flowers on the kitchen table, everything scrubbed and scoured, was the intrusion of another world into our comfortable, mother-dominated life; the only life I knew before I won a place at grammar school in Hereford.

And here he was before me again. I did not know what to say. I blurted out, 'Da, you're here!'

We embraced and he gave me his customary bear hug. I pressed into his broad chest. I had not been able to say goodbye. War had taken me away and I had not returned. Then it dawned on me and I felt my stomach sink. I pulled away and looked at my father, his proud dark-browed features that I so adored. He had aged a decade since last I saw him, but he was still strong in limb. All his life he had worked with his hands and his strength had not left him yet. But I knew … He had been nearing retirement the last time I saw him and wasn't looking forward to a life of leisure. The prospect of long hours of inactivity had worried him. How much allotment-digging can you do when you've got all the time in the world? The prospect of being under Mam's feet, day in, day out, didn't appeal to him. 'You'll have to get yourself a hobby,' she would have said.

'Da, you're here …' Then I said it. 'You died, didn't you?' The words stuck in my throat. I could never imagine my father dying. He had seemed immortal.

'It happens to us all, son … Straight after the war, I caught that Spanish flu, like so many others. Millions copped it that year. The Devil had his due after what the world had done to itself. Christ, what a bloody retirement gift! But here you are! It's so good to see you! You haven't aged! You look such a … man!'

Da looked me over approvingly. 'It's good to see some soil under your fingernails, lad. But you always were the grafter, in your own way, not like Archie – though I love him too … Is he here?'

I hadn't thought of that. The prospect appalled me somehow, as if Archie's presence would make a mockery of this personal paradise. Yet Archie was the firstborn and was always foremost in Da's thoughts. If ten years on earth have passed since my departure, who knows what may have happened? When I try to understand all this warped chronology my head spins.

As the refugee caravan passed us by, we sat on a couple of tree stumps and stared at each other.

'I should have realised I'd meet you here, Sam. When you went AWOL at Mons I *knew* that you'd passed over, though Martha and Maud never gave up, silly as each other, the pair of them. Though, I must admit, I never wanted to either. By 1919 it was obvious that you weren't coming back. But here you are, at last!' He clapped both hands upon my shoulders, eyes wet with tears. 'Ten years is a long time to hope. It seems like I have met everyone I ever dreamed of here, lost aunties and uncles, missing brothers, my great-grandfather – everybody, except the one person I wanted to see most of all.'

There was I, completely stunned by this meeting, whereas he seemed to have been half expecting it. He stuffed some tobacco into a clay pipe and lit it with a burning twig from the fire the men had burning to thaw out their wind-numbed limbs. He looked at me proudly, seeming to take pleasure just in the sight of me. 'I always knew you'd turn out well, Sam.'

He was the only one in the family who ever called me that, and it always made my heart glow.

'You were good at your studies. I knew you'd go far. The day you became a surveyor for GWR was the proudest of my life.' He sucked on his pipe and then exhaled a strand of blue smoke. 'To think we started out as navvies ... But then, your Grand-da always said the Kernes would go places. And here we are, eh? This is about as far as you can go, eh, lad?'

Tears smeared my vision. I shook and the just held my father's rough hand.

'I can't wait to tell Grand-da you're here. He'll be over the moon.'

'Grand-da's here?' My mind whirled. I hadn't seen him since a boy.

'Sure, they all are – Grandma, Aunt Molly, Uncle Seamus, the whole clan. It's like a family reunion. There's family here I didn't even know I had! I bump into another relative every day! Remembering all of their names, though, that's a different matter ...'

I wanted to ask my Da so many questions but all I could do was sob with joy. He held me again, then got up and called over his gang-mates. 'Look, here's my boy!' he shouted proudly. 'He's an important fella now, so mind your manners.' They were a rough lot but they shook my hand warmly and slapped me on the back. They were aware of my breastplate and mace, but no one mentioned it. I managed to ask them if they were getting enough rations, if there working conditions were okay. They seemed happy enough, doing their bit 'for the cause'. I thanked them all for the excellent job they were doing and promised them double rations that night, with a barrel of ale thrown in. This met with a cheer and they merrily went back to work, laying the cobblestones that would stop the track churning into impassable sludge.

My Da thanked me also and said he should get back to work. I didn't want to let him go at first, but he said we could have a beer together later, at the end of his shift. It was hard to let him go after only just seeing him again, but it must have been harder for him. What had been ten months for me had been ten years for him.

I waved goodbye and returned to the caer, where matters required my urgent attention. I walked in a daze, glancing back to check he was still there, was real. I could see him, bent to his task despite his years. He seemed pleased to be doing useful work. All of his life he had paved the way for others, as had his father before him – first the canals, then the railways. It seemed fitting he should continue to do so here, for, as I have found, the road does not end.

After I had seen to business in the caer and made sure everything was in order, I retired to the hut set aside for me and wrote up this encounter. Writing this has helped me to come to terms with it, although I am still trying to grasp its implications.

It was only with the unexpected arrival of Merlin that things were clarified. He arrived in his useful aloof way, as if he'd walked to the shops and come back three years later with no explanation.

I told him what had happened, and he did not seem surprised at all.

'This is the valley of your ancestors – what do you expect?'

Merlin has a way of making everything sound obvious and the person he is speaking to a fool. He paced awkwardly on the table I had constructed, upon which various parchments, weighed down with stones, depicted the designs of my defences and the route of the Sky Road, as it's become known; made by the skyman.

'Haven't you understood yet?' The falcon looked at me with his imperious eyes. 'Everyone here is related to you in some way. These people are *all* your ancestors, from the very first seed of your family tree.'

I sat down heavily in the wicker chair. This revelation confirmed what I had felt so often since arriving, the feeling of déjà vu that had not gone away. It explained why everyone here looked so familiar. Now it all made sense. And it made the effectiveness of my defences even more crucial. The fate of my ancestors was in my hands. If I got their blood on my hands it would be *my* blood.

I prayed these defences would hold and that I wouldn't lose my kin a second time. There is so much I wish to ask, but now is the time not for words, but for deeds.

I will not let them down.

Merlin broke me from my reverie with an announcement.

'Ahem, when you've finished daydreaming you may want to look outside.'

Puzzled, I looked at the falcon, but he just hopped out of the tent. Sighing, I got up and blindly followed. I had long stopped questioning my 'ally's' demands.

There was a flurry of activity at the battlements. I ran across the enclosure and climbed up a ladder to take a closer look. Guards were pointing down at a flat-bottomed ferry crossing the river mouth, pulled by Eponan guards, distinctive with horse-hair crests on their helmets. With them were a man and a black-maned horse. My heart leapt as I recognised them both.

'Your friend from the Forbidden Kingdom has arrived, although a hard time he's had of it. I've been tracking his progress. He's a remarkably stubborn fellow, despite, or maybe because of, his injury.'

If I could I'd have kissed the falcon. 'Baramis – he escaped!'

I ran down the slopes of Caer Cernunnos to greet the man who had saved my life on the merciless Steppe.

After the hubbub of excitement caused by the Steppe-dweller's arrival I finally have chance to complete this summary of recent events. Baramis's appearance was first greeted by suspicion by Eponan scouts patrolling the downs north of the Da'anu Valley. At first they took him for a spy of Taranis, for no one walked the grim North Road; at least no one had in 'living memory', if I can apply that phrase here. But when he cried out the name of Kerne they checked their spear arms. Scouts had been briefed to expect the blacksmith-archer after Brigantia had heard the account of my meeting him. Baramis had the tarpan with him and the Eponans were curious, for they had not seen such a horse before, being used to taller Arabian breeds. They had escorted him to Caer Epona, where Macha welcomed him. She was keen to learn all she could from her guest from the Forbidden Kingdom, but remembered her obligations and sent him across the river.

I was so glad to see him, and no doubt he was glad to see me also. He had taken a great risk in not only escaping from the Horse Nomads, but travelling to what was effectively the enemy camp with only my word to go on. It was good to repay his hospitality. He was exhausted after the long tense ride around the northern edge of the lake. At any moment he'd expected Horse Lords to run him down, but he had got away. He thought that this was because they were all too busy preparing for war to bother with small fry like him. Yet he has been a real boon to us, for he has come not only with knowledge of the Iron Army's plans but also with iron weapons: on his horse were packed a dozen or so swords. He has offered these to our war effort – a kingly gift, which has won him many friends. The caer chiefs accepted the swords and gave them to their champions to use in the coming battle, so at least one warrior in each tribe has the edge. I know that Brak, for one, will cherish the sword gift. There is a delightful irony in using the enemy's weapon against them. Yet even more priceless: Baramis brings with him the secrets of iron itself. This makes him a most valuable asset to the Bronze Age Valley of the Chalk Folk. Alas, there is no time now to smelt the two baskets of green ore Baramis also brought with him and forge more weapons. We will need other weapons to defeat the horde that he says is amassing.

After our brief reunion, Baramis was summoned to a war council to brief the chieftains. I hope to see my friend again soon, but who knows what fate will have in store when the tide of war engulfs us?

22

Eye of the Moon

It was a clear cold night when Kerne approached Moot Holm in a canoe paddled by a silent Chalklander warrior. The bronze-spiral shield slung on his back was illuminated by the single torch the passenger carried. The flame-glow caught the details of Kerne's own apparel. The airman was dressed in a red woollen tunic held in place by the Sam Browne belt and holster, with the Webley pistol and ceremonial mace tucked into it; a grey cloak fastened at his left shoulder by Bronwen's brooch; plaid breeches held up with Brak's belt; officer's boots held together with thongs; and Brigantia's lozenge-shaped breastplate held in place by four straps tied around his back. His black-grey hair was shoulder length and straggly. He scratched his full salt-and-pepper beard. It was the first time he had let himself grow a beard. The shaving facilities around here left a lot to be desired. He still had his well-travelled shaving kit – the badger-hair brush that slotted neatly into its own silver tube, the tin soap dish and box of razors – but the last few weeks had given him little chance to keep up appearances, especially the last frantic fortnight when he'd been working night and day. Besides, he was getting to like not standing out like a sore thumb any more. And he felt strangely comfortable like this, as though he fitted into himself at last.

Flares flickered on the craggy shore of the small island. Spears glinted in the sallow light. There was a glimpse of torsos covered in blue spirals. All the warriors had covered their bodies with woad dye in preparation for the battle. The serpent patterns writhed, greenish in the torchlight.

Kerne's craft was hailed and halted. The password was given by the paddler, and Kerne was allowed to step ashore. It was a matter of routine, for his gold breastplate was instantly recognisable to all. The Drunemetom guards bowed as he alighted. The canoeist pushed off; no one was allowed to step foot on the island unless invited.

Kerne had received the call from Ogmios from a runner. He had been overseeing the construction of the last of the defences. His men had been working flat out, and by some minor miracle they had completed the raising of the ramparts. All non-fighting Chalk Folk had been removed to the safest caer, upriver. Supplies were stored; weapons were sharpened, oiled and ready. Even now, the final players were moving into position; boats bristling with warriors were moving silently down to the river's mouth.

The valley of the chalk giants waited, dark and still.

Kerne climbed the steep rock-hewn steps, his circle of light briefly highlighting the moss-covered boulders that littered the way, the cliff-face tangled with roots, overhanging trees, and ogreish faces. He was glad of the torch he carried. The Moot Holm was a haunted place – every rock seemed sentient, every shadow watchful.

Breathless, he reached the brow of the hill. More guards demanded the password, and then he was in the sacred enclosure. He walked across the uneven exposed ground towards the oak grove, marvelling at the above that dwarfed his own frail light. Was it the chill in the air that made him shiver? The air seemed alive.

In the centre of the grove burned a small fire, teased by the restless flurries of wind. By it sat Ogmios in a blue cloak, leaning on his gem-studded club, staring into the flames. Without looking up he said, 'Welcome, Kerne. I am glad you came.'

Ogmios always unnerved him when he did that. It was as if he had eyes in the back of that shining head with its three grey strands. Then Kerne noticed the windsmith's white owl, Blodeuwedd, sitting in a branch of one of the oaks. Her wide eyes sucked in the light and gleamed opalescent and fathomless. Her head swivelled back. She always seemed deeply bored by him.

Kerne stepped forward and wondered how he was related to Ogmios. After the recent revelation of Merlin's, he looked at the windsmith in a new light.

Ogmios turned around and smiled. His bald weathered face was as gnarled and tough as his club. And now Kerne saw what had stared him in the face all along. There, in the windsmith's one eye, was the gleam of a family likeness.

Kerne had grown close to the old man, as if he had been the grandfather he had never known, who had died before Isambard was born … Tales of 'Old Man Kerne', told by his Da with great relish, had made his Irish grandfather loom larger than life. His Welsh 'Tad-cu', as Mam called *her* father, had been a dour Chapel man from the Valleys, always slightly disapproving of a grandson who spoke no Welsh. 'There's no coal in his soul,' he would say, sucking on his pipe and exhaling foul fumes, much to the eternal vexation of 'Mam-gu', his small fierce wife, Kerne's Welsh grandmother. Kerne had always wished he had met his Da's da. Now there was a strong chance he *would* meet him here, in this valley of his ancestors.

Kerne was still getting over meeting *his* old man. They had been catching up over a few mugs of grainy brew each day after the shift had finished. He was still nursing the hangover from last night, yet it had been worth it. The tangled skein of Kerne family lore had been unpicked in a week of boozy sessions with his Da and his workmates – many cousins and uncles, as it turned out – though sometimes it had been hard to decipher truth from fiction in the raucous anec-dotes.

The Irish side of his family had always fascinated him, but the facts were confusing, the figures elusive. Old Man Kerne was the real link to the past, straddling the centuries: he had seen the glory of the canals come and go, and the rise of the railways. He had crossed over from famine-ravished Ireland to Victorian Britain, forced into exile, looking for labouring work. He had found it on the canals as a navvy. Kerne had always wondered what he had experienced, for his Da was tight-lipped about the brutal truth and had filled in the gaps with his imagination, until Old Man Kerne had become a family leg-end. Maud's parents had never been close, and Nan Kerne, the Old Man's wife, had lost her wits – whether from poteen or a life devas-tated by the potato famine, Isambard had never been able to discov-er. He had missed out on a whole generation's wisdom, until now. To sit with the elders and listen to their knowledge was something he had wanted to do all of his life. Ogmios was not his grandfather, he knew that in his bones, but this was the nearest he'd had ever come to really knowing one.

'Sit and warm yourself, my friend.'

Kerne was glad to join him by the fire, but felt a little awkward sitting in the sacred grove like this, so casually. He let the fire thaw out his stiff limbs. He had pushed himself these last few days. His body ached, but it was a satisfying fatigue.

'You have worked well. The defences are looking impressive.'

'There is still much that could be done ...'

'The thousand imperfections ... Each one reminds us that we are not the Creator.'

Kerne sighed. 'Yes, I am only a man and can do only so much.'

'You have done your best. That is all we can do.'

Kerne looked into the skein of flames and slowly nodded. The activity of the last fortnight had been frantic. At times he had thought he was going mad. The work had reached a fever pitch. They had been carried along by the energy of it. Now there seemed to be only stillness, but with a palpable tension. His head felt *stretched*. He rubbed his temples.

'Ah, you feel it, can you? She is coming, look.' Ogmios pointed with his club to the west. Beyond the web of trees, on the far side of the valley, above Mount Anu there was a nimbus of light, bright in the darkness. Ogmios slowly stood up and, leaning on his club, walked stiffly to the edge of the grove. 'Come, we should greet her properly.'

In silence they walked to the edge of the Drunemetom. Below, the cliffs plunged to the black river. On a promontory of rock shaped like a finger they stood and watched as the moon breached the mountain line, large and magnificent, flooding the valley with her soft light.

Ogmios produced a small flask from his medicine bag, and two clay beakers.

'Here, drink this.' The old man poured him a pungent drink from the flask.

Kerne took the beaker. 'What's this?'

'It will help you to see more clearly.'

Ogmios filled both their cups and toasted the moon, bidding Kerne do the same. 'Hail, majestic queen. Your children awake to honour you.'

They drank the liquid in one. It tasted like pond water and contained slimy stalks.

'Urgh! What is it?'

'A little concoction of mine – a seeing potion.'

Ogmios gestured around them, and Kerne gasped. Each of the chalk figures glowed in the moonlight: eagle, wolf, deer, hound, boar, bull. The others were hidden by the twists of the valley. The economical and elegant symbols shone luminously from their respective hillsides as if designed to be seen in the moonlight. And from each hilltop echoed an eerie ululation.

'The womenfolk greet the Great Mother.'

'It's beautiful,' said Kerne, suddenly savouring this frail Afterland.

Ogmios reached into the folds of his cloak. From a leather bag he produced a round object rolled in silk. In a flourish he revealed a milky round stone. 'Behold: the Eye of the Moon.'

Kerne gazed into its depths. As it caught the moonlight it glowed and its trapped clouds swirled. He couldn't believe his eyes. He had heard Ogmios mention it before. Not only that: *he had seen it before*! This was the last treasure of Bush Barrow on Normanton Down!

'Take it. Hold it with care and respect.' Ogmios handed it to him.

It felt like an icy skull.

'What do you see?'

Kerne was hypnotised. It was like holding the moon. His mind reeled. He thought of all the artefacts he now had upon his person. Now he held the last piece of the puzzle. *He* was the Bush Barrow Man!

'Clear your mind. Concentrate upon what you see in the stone. Do not expect to see anything. Just look. Look with all of your body, not just your eyes.'

Kerne focused. The milky clouds swam before him.

'Don't push away what you see with a hard stare. Soften your gaze. Let it in.'

This time Kerne stopped trying. He just let the moonstone play upon his mind. And that's when the clouds in the stone parted and he saw strange visions flitting across it.

'Tell me what you see.'

Kerne rocked and chanted in a sing-song voice. 'I see … boats like crabs on a beach. Two armies clashing: one grey, one red. The dead rising from a cauldron. A cauldron that moves on wheels of iron. Ravens picking the bones of the fallen. I see many barrows being raised. A bull being slaughtered. A great feast for one. A king rising from the ice. A boat sailed by invisible hands. Then wave upon wave to the edge of the world …'

Exhausted, he slumped. Ogmios deftly plucked the stone from his hands, covered it carefully and slipped it back into his bag.

'Come, you have visioned well. Let us return to the fire …'

But the airman felt as though he was on fire. His body coiled and he suddenly leapt to his feet. In a fever he staggered along the finger of rock.

'I can see! I can see everything!'

'Get back from there!'

Kerne stood on the furthest point. Five hundred feet below, the river Da'anu flowed inexorably.

'I can see the tide of blood! Here it comes, down the valley!'

Kerne saw war canoes slide along in the centre of the current. In each dark splinter of hull sat woaded warriors. He saw every tattoo, every spearhead; the murderous gleam in their eyes. Leading them were the Morrigan – the women warriors in black, raven-feathered, white-faced. Among them he spotted Bronwen – even behind her war paint he could recognise her. Her face shone like a death mask in the moonlight. Once she had been a beautiful maiden with a warm smile for a stranger.

But he was no stranger; he was her descendant. To think he had looked at her with desire! That she had given him love-tokens! He still wore the shell necklace she had shyly gifted him.

Suddenly, Kerne's stomach lurched and, falling to his knees, he vomited over the cliff. His head pounded with the implications. *They could have slept together!* It would have been like sleeping with his great-grandmother. His stomach retched until it was empty. Shaking, he clung to the rock, his eyes streaming.

The war canoes sailed silently towards the river mouth, to death or destiny. He counted a hundred of them, ten warriors in each. He sensed the Chalk Folk watching them go by from every battlement. His ancestors, *all* his kith and kin. They knew their fate was in the hands of the warriors below. The very survival of the Chalk Folk would be decided in this battle.

'Not enough!' Kerne screamed, wracked by another surge of hallucination. 'There's too many! Too many!' Whenever he closed his eyes he saw them – the horsemen, the slave army and … the legions of the dead. War dead in tattered uniforms, limbs hanging off, bodies broken but relentless. Rising, rising, again and again. Unkillable, unstoppable. 'They are coming. They are coming!'

Kerne could see more canoes approaching the Drunemetom, sliding out of the tributaries, manned by strangers. Was this some kind of ambush? Had Taranis tricked them? Was the attack coming from upriver? Kerne was on the verge of hysteria?

In one cluster he saw long-faced warriors clad in silver and black armour, white-haired, almond-eyed.

In another flotilla, stout bearded warriors in red armour.

Another carried flaxen-haired warriors with beaked noses, sharpening sickles.

And the fourth brought large warriors in grey and plaid, wielding long swords.

Ogmios spotted them too and recognised them. 'The Metenaidd! Our valley allies are coming in our hour of need!'

And it was true. The war-host Kerne had seen had come to help the Chalk Folk: the Arianedds, the Copors, the Tuns and the Plwms. Lending their strength to the cause, as well as the metals they mined and worked, would make an Army of Bronze to be reckoned with. The Iron Horde would not find their conquest easy.

His vision telescoping, Kerne could see all the way to the end of the river, to glimmering Lake Mandorla. Hundreds of war canoes crossed in silence, oars glittering in the moonlight like crabs' legs.

'The enemy is here!'

His eyes on fire, Kerne staggered, slipped and tumbled from the precipice. It seemed like he fell for an aeon, over and over, towards certain death on the rocks below.

Above, the silhouette of Ogmios receded. He seemed to be chanting something, Kerne noticed abstractly. He felt strangely at peace. Perhaps this was meant to be. His death would end the conflict. Would heal the widening rift between the worlds.

Then there was a sudden gust of wind and Kerne's body was swept into a tree halfway down the cliff.

The last thing he noticed was a falcon looking at him crossly from a branch.

23

Dawn of Battle

Kerne awoke with a start, head pounding. Bullhorns echoed along the Valley of the Chalk Folk. It was the warning signal they had all dreaded.

The Iron Horde was approaching.

The war trumpets seemed to echo in Kerne' skull. He groaned, rubbed his temples and blearily looked about him. It was nearly dawn; the grey sky was filled with ragged racing clouds. A wind had whipped up overnight, bringing with it rainclouds and the threat of storm. Kerne's body ached, but nothing seemed broken. The previous night seemed a feverish blur now, but he recalled being tangled in a tree. He realised he had slept at its base, wrapped in a dew-damp blanket. The remains of a fire still gave off warmth.

Ogmios sat opposite, pouring something steaming into a beaker.

'Ah, you're awake. Good. There's not a moment to lose. Here, drink this. Then we must go.'

Kerne sat up and took the beaker, sniffing it suspiciously.

'Don't worry; this one will lessen the after-effects of the vision potion. It gives you quite a headache, doesn't it?'

Kerne smiled thinly at the old man, but sipped the liquid, which tasted of astringent herbs. It warmed his bones, making him shudder.

'Why didn't you warn me, Ogmios?'

'I ... I did not know it would have that effect upon you. You must have the seer's gift in your blood. Some people don't see anything of note.'

'Well, lucky me – I nearly died!'

'It was most ... fortuitous that Merlin was close by. His wind-summoning softened your fall.'

'Where is the old bird? I would like to shake his, um, wing.' Kerne noticed Ogmios's owl was not to be seen either.

'Merlin flew at first light, once he knew you were alright. He sensed the Iron Army was approaching. He's on watchout with Blodeuwedd and the other bird allies, keeping the windsmiths and their chieftains informed of the enemy's movements.'

'Then my vision is coming true …' Kerne shut his eyes and the disturbing images flashed before him. 'I saw a nightmare …'

'I heard, but now's not the time to interpret your moondream. Drink up. We'll break our fast in the boat.' Ogmios stood up and banked down the fire. 'Get moving, Kerne, or you'll slip back into the visions.'

Even now, he could feel the sickening tentacles of the potion within him, making the edges of his vision swim. He rubbed his eyes and got up. At first his body resisted, aching, but he was warmer at least.

Ogmios was hurrying down the stone steps with his club. As Kerne hurried to catch up, he quickly checked his person: Webley, mace, belt, brooch and breastplate. Nothing lost then, except perhaps his mind.

They were greeted by white-cloaked Sanctuary Guards stamping their feet to keep warm. There was a tumult of activity. War canoes were streaming down the river in the growing light. The banks were alive with tense voices and dogs barking. Horses whickered, sensing the coming storm.

The two windsmiths jumped into a boat going downriver and were swept along in the current. The river mist clung to them like shrouds. Through it the dark shapes of warriors eager to get to the front could be glimpsed, and Kerne blinked. They could be from almost any century, any war …

In the distance, the sound of war drums could be heard – a dull throb at first, quickening the heart. The pounding reverberated around the walls of the valley, growing louder as they raced towards the river mouth. The sound of doom, thought Kerne. Then his stomach rumbled and he forced a grim laugh.

'Eat something,' Ogmios insisted, thrusting an oat cake at him. 'You will need your strength today.'

Up ahead, the mouth of the river gaped, flanked by the fragile white cliffs, the chalk pinnacles like stalagmites, or elegant chess piece. In the east, over the Red Hills, the sun rose like a gigantic egg of blood, revealing upon the mist-enshrouded surface hundreds of war boats.

'The Army of Taranis! May the gods protect us.' Ogmios shielded his eyes from the glare.

They pulled up the boat on the lowest shore, below Caer Dagda: a gravel beach at the river mouth known as Dagda's Cauldron. Here would be the main slaughter-ground. Spikes of ash had been driven into the clay, and the Army of Bronze gathered in readiness, preparing battle harnesses, shield straps, helmets. They lined up in rows along the riverbank, ordered into ranks by fierce commanders. There were some shivering – whether from chill or fear – wild-eyed skin-turners, naked except for their woad and weapons. Some were not much more than boys, their balls just dropped. They stood awkwardly self-conscious next to proud scarred veterans who were smoothing their long moustaches, strutting like roosters, shouting insults at the war-host, whipping themselves up into a war rage.

To one side was a dark circle of black: the Morrigan, performing their own secret incantations. Others performed their own rituals of propitiation or invocation, calling to the sky, the water, the rock, drawing upon the strength of the land in order to defend the land. The valley seemed to lean closer, to come alive with the sounds of the raising.

Wild-haired Macha galloped in with her horse warriors, right into the river, up to the kneebones of her stallion. 'Let them come! Epona is ready for their offering!' She let out an ululation, which was taken up by her mounted Rhianna. Her roan reared up, thrashing its legs in defiance, then turned and churned up the water as it galloped back on to the shore.

The Donn appeared in full battledress, bronze glinting in the sun, standing upon the hill at the foot of the Horned Dagda, the Good God, cocksure and defiant, surrounded by his personal guard of thick-necked Bullmen. Below him bald Senach, his windsmith, held a tethered white calf, a sickle glinting in his other hand.

'Chalk Folk!' the Donn roared. 'This is the day of our reckoning. The gods will not find us turning from the fight. We are ready to defend our families. We are ready to protect our sacred land. We are ready to crush the invader. We are ready to fight to the death! By the gods and totems of this valley let victory be ours today!'

A cheer was raised that shook the valley walls.

'You know your duties. Fight with stout hearts. Fight without fear. Let each man and woman do their appointed task and fulfil their destiny.'

The Donn's windsmith slit the throat of the white calf, which fell gurgling into the sand with a plaintive low. 'We offer this sacrifice to the mighty Da'anu to bring us victory today.' The heart was cut out and given to the War Chief, who held it aloft, blood dripping down his thick forearms and on to his face.

'To victory!'

'To victory!' the Chalk Folk echoed back in a cry that resonated between the steep buttresses of the valley.

The Donn cast the calf's heart into the river mouth and its blood flowed into the lake, straight into the path of the Iron Army.

The drumming was now deafening as it resounded off the bone-white cliffs. Kerne watched the fleet of boats appear out of the mist. They were barrel shaped and heavy in the water. The long oars bristling from each side made them look crablike – the rowers being covered by a semicircular shell. As they entered the mouth of the river a signal was sent to the Eponans on the far cliff, and they let rip with large wooden catapults camouflaged by foliage. The ballistae tossed large rocks into the approaching host as it was forced into the bottleneck of the river mouth. Some struck the water, sending up spumes of spray and creating big waves. The ones that hit home should have had a devastating effect, shattering the invasion craft to pieces, but the rocks bounced off them.

Kerne looked closer and gasped. 'Madoc has forged boats of iron!'

The invasion fleet ran the gauntlet of the ballistae, shrugging off the hail of rubble. The iron crabs drew inexorably closer to the shore and now Kerne could see that each one had a ramp at the front. As soon as they ran into the gravel of the shallows these dropped and, from out of the vanguard, warriors poured on horses, bounding ashore amid a chaos of water. The invaders were now too close to the Bronze Army for the ballistae.

It was up to them.

The fierce-eyed horse warriors – the same Huns who had hunted Kerne and Brak– trampled the first who came to fend them off. The Horse Nomads thrust down with their barbed, tasselled spears, keeping the defenders at bay, or impaling those who came too close. Any who got past the spears were hacked down by a slash of scimitars wielded in the other hand, the Horse Nomads not needing to hold the reins of their steeds. Horse and man fought as one unit, with one mind. They were the nightmare of every Chalklander child and, that day, of every warrior too. From each landing craft came six horses and their riders, plus a dozen foot soldiers. Between them they established a beachhead and hacked their way inshore.

Macha and her Rhianna were ready for them. They charged into battle between the ranks of the Chalklander spear-carriers.

'Eponaaaaaa!!!'

The Rhianna ploughed into the Horse Nomads to a deafening

clash of bronze and iron, whinnying steeds and thrashing water. The battle had begun in earnest.

The Morrigan elders were shrieking, sending fear into the hearts of the foot soldiers, while the young spun Greek fire, tossing fireballs into the landing craft, knocking off Horse Nomads, who were then descended upon by warrior-women – bodies painted black, leather armoured, wreathed in raven feathers, skull-faced and deadly. They moved among the invaders with deadly grace, fatal shadows, whose swift touch caused instant death. Among them was Bronwen, eager for revenge. Kerne saw her slitting throats with a pirouette and a slash of the metal spikes gripped in each hand. Lighter and more agile than the iron-clad invaders, the Morrigan danced their deadly dance among them; the cuts they suffered, red gashes in the leather, only increased their wrath.

From the ramparts of Caer Dagda the windsmiths rained down terrible curses upon the enemy, making their faces burst into red blisters, or sending them mad, foaming at the mouth.

It seemed the invasion was being thwarted ... It was all too easy, brooded Kerne. The vision from the Drunemetom haunted him – the dead rising and fighting. *Madoc, what's your secret weapon? What are you holding back?*

The Donn roared, 'Is this all you can do? Bring me more battle-meat – my axe is hungry!'

All the while the iron boats poured into the river. With the vanguard keeping the defenders busy, dozens more rowed past upriver. The Donn had accounted for this; more of his army waited around the next bend, on the flanks of Caer Epona. The Chalk Folk had wanted the first taste of battle – the glory. Some had boasted they would vanquish the enemy beneath the Dagda's prick. But the War Chief had contingency plans in place. Armed and ready, the Metenaidd waited silently in the mouths of their respective streams in small swift craft, poised to strike.

Yet it was obvious to all that the defenders were outnumbered five to one. Their bronze weapons could not last long against the iron swords. Many bent upon impact or became blunted with each blow. Frantically, Chalklander swordsmen tried to straighten their weapons in the midst of battle, and were cut down, caught off guard. Only the champions had swords to match the enemy – the blades of Baramis – and the skill to defeat them. But, Kerne despaired, they were too few – thirteen against a horde – and each champion defended his or her caer, so their strength was spread thin.

At least, as the airman had said in the Drunemetom, at least they had morale on their side, they were defending their homes. They would fight to the death. *And they may have to*, thought Kerne. But what could he do? What woodword could stop this? He had helped start this madness – he had to end it.

Kerne knew he had only one good weapon: the Webley. And only one bullet.

The air elementals around him seemed agitated, perhaps sensing the slaughter. Kerne felt the charged atmosphere tingle his fingertips, his spine. Standing on a ledge overlooking the melee, above the din of battle, he closed his eyes and quietened his mind as Ogmios had taught him. He slowed his breathing, taking deeper breaths, feeling the air within and without. The wind dogs caressed his cheek, the back of his hand.

'Walk with me,' he whispered. A whirlwind of white dust rose around the airman. ellowing, 'For my ancestors!' he leapt from the rock and ran into the fray.

24

The War Dead

Birds flew before the storm – raven, eagle, hawk, heron, owl – the Feathered Ones of the windsmiths, conducting surveillance and communicating battle movements and strategies to the caer chiefs.

The darkness gathered in the Valley of the Chalk Folk. The skies were heavy with it, yet the clouds seemed laden with more than rain. The very air itself seemed tinged with shadows. Kerne felt it on the back of his neck – the breath of Annwn. With a shudder he remembered Llyr's word for it: cythrawl, the dark energy of chaos.

As he had plunged into battle, expecting to be cut down in the melee, the enemy had momentarily retreated, like a wave sucked back before a breaker. The Chalklanders drove back the invaders into the churning waters of the Da'anu. The river ran red with the blood of Grey Raiders, but the foot soldiers had served their purpose, buying time with their lives for the next wave to run the gauntlet and penetrate further upriver.

'The enemy is getting through!' someone cried, yet there was little the land troops could do to stop their progress of the crab craft upriver.

On an outcrop of rock above the Da'anu, Ogmios stood on one leg, raised one arm, covered his bad eye and uttered his war curses: '*Banadh gnuisi!*' he screamed. One-eyed, one-legged and one-armed, the sorcerer with his club struck terror into the enemy. Those left on the riverbank fled with white faces and drowned in their armour.

Grey Raiders blew on aurochs horns to rally their troops, drawing back for the next onslaught, the next phase of battle. The pale sun rose implacably over the ragged defenders, its light piercing the steep sided valley like a keen-edged sword. For a moment there seemed to be an eerie lull, almost blissful after the clamour, but it was tainted with the cries of injured, of the dying. The riverbank was littered with bodies from both sides. A wounded horse flailed in the water, churning it red, until Macha, grim-faced, dispatched it with a spear. Its body floated out into the lake and sank into the depths.

A wind skirled the battle smoke, and a weird light flickered over the ruddy waters. Kerne and Ogmios sensed it at the same time: a new, deadlier presence was arriving on the field of battle.

And then they saw it – twice as large as the other raider craft, decorated with sigils of death and victory, a floating tank, and Kerne knew in his guts what it what: the Royal War Barge, Madoc's vessel. It was shielded by an escort of crab craft, which pushed into the river mouth and beached beneath Caer Dagda. The landing ramp dropped with a sickening thud on top of the high tide of bodies, and from it emerged spike-collared slaves, shadow-ribbed, breechclouted and shaven-headed, chained to their burden. This they hauled on to the beach in time to a relentless drum – a giant cauldron on wheels.

Kerne looked closer: it seemed to radiate a dark energy. He blinked. There, on the beaten metal plates was the roundel of the Royal Flying Corps. Kerne realised, with a sickening horror, that the cauldron had been made with metal from the Breguet, Madoc's bi-plane!

Then the pilot himself stepped out of his barge, draped in his fur cloak and war gear, iron crowned and wielding his Webley. He surveyed the carnage and he seemed pleased.

One of Cormac's wolf warriors broke through the Royal Guard and went to cut him down – only to be stopped dead by a bullet in the chest. The report echoed about the valley.

'Speak-with-Thunder is here!' cried the Chalk Folk watching in terror from the battlements of Caer Dagda. Among them was old Tuan – he had stubbornly stayed on, refusing to leave his caer.

Madoc's ragged voice ordered slaves to collect the bodies of the fallen. Gaunt-eyed ghouls, they carried back the fresh corpses and at the Iron King's command cast them into the cauldron.

Kerne looked at the cauldron with mounting horror – he had seen this in his vision ...

There was a rumble and a flash of darkness: then out of the cauldron climbed soldiers from the Great War – gaunt, hollow-eyed, uniforms covered in mud and blood, limbs twisted, flesh ripped, skin mustard yellow. Kerne recoiled in horror. He had met these war zombies before – in the no-man's-land of Annwn. Somehow Madoc had managed to bring them into this world!

'What new evil is this?' gasped Ogmios, and he spat over his shoulder. He cast a glance at Kerne, as if he knew that the airman had knowledge of this latest horror.

These men should be allowed to die in dignity. Instead, they had been resurrected – German and British, Tommy and Hun – united in death against a common foe. The zombies staggered relentlessly towards the Chalk Folk. Panic spread among the foot soldiers like wildfire. This was something alien to them. Unnatural. Only Kerne saw the irony – *they were dead too*, the ancient ancestors facing the War Dead. Yet the Chalk Folk had been given proper burials in their own time and had found their way to this Otherworld, whereas the zombies had been massacred on the killing fields of Flanders. Kerne and Madoc should have died too, but they had passed over. And their presence in the land of the dead was creating a rift – and now through it poured the nameless dead, the unknown soldiers.

A Morrigan warrioress, fierce and brave, intercepted the first zombie's path and hacked it down with a flying salmon leap. But the zombie slowly got up, its head hanging off, and lunged towards the stunned Morrigan – grabbed her throat. She collapsed on to her knees before him as the air expired in her lungs. The Donn's Bull-men ploughed in, knocking the zombie back, leaving the warrioress gasping for breath. But more of them had risen from the cauldron. For each of the fallen cast in, an unknown soldier would emerge: a corpse for a corpse. And the undead onslaught swarmed over the Bullmen and tore them apart with their bare hands.

A light rain began to fall. Kerne looked up but could see only the broiling clouds. He was sure they were no normal rainclouds.

Then movement above caught his eye. A falcon screeched out of the sky and landed by the airman.

'Merlin! Where have you been?'

'I have been fighting with the cythrawl that is being released into this world! The darkness you see around you is an outward sign of it. It is evil manifest. As you and Madoc draw closer the rift grows wider! Your pilot friend has constructed a portal from his skycraft. It crossed over intact, and so he is using it to bring dead from no-man's-land ... though how he found the dark wisdom to do this I know not!'

The undead staggered towards the defenders, who were forced to fall back before them or risk being torn apart by the inexorable tide. Spearmen tried their best to hold them back, but the zombies just impaled themselves on the leaf-shaped points and slid along the shafts to throttle the wielder.

Macha mustered her Rhianna and, with a piercing battle-cry, they rode down into the encroaching undead hordes. The horses trampled down the first line, but the broken figures only staggered to their feet again and carried on towards the defenders, lumbering but unstoppable. Seeing their efforts were in vain, the Rhianna rode in an arc back towards the crumbling bronze shield-wall.

Nemain and the Morrigan fought like banshees, but even their fury was of no avail against the undead. It was like trying to stop the sea with sticks.

The Donn ordered a fighting retreat. 'To the caer!'

In the frenzied scramble up the flanks of the Dagda, Kerne was separated from Ogmios and found himself weaponless and faced by three zombies: a German officer with a hole in his chest and two Tommies, one with his face missing. They lunged towards him as he slipped on the slope made muddy and slippery by the drizzle and the boots of the fleeing. Kerne reached out to a tree to check his fall. He recognised it as an alder and suddenly remembered its sigil of protection. He made the sign of 'fearn' with his fingers and projected the sound at the approaching zombies. '*Comet lachta*,' he chanted, visualising its kenning, the 'guarding of milk'.

As the zombies came within grabbing distance, suddenly a massive phantom warrior filled their path. His semi-opaque back was to Kerne, half blocking out the zombies, but real enough to them It was the dryad of the alder, Bran the Blessed himself, shield of his people. He crushed the undead in his hands, then faded.

Kerne, momentarily stunned by his summoning, gathered himself and turned to continue his ascent. Above him Ogmios offered his club as a grip and he pulled himself gratefully up, out of reach of the undead.

'Quickly! To the gates!'

The survivors were forced back towards Caer Dagda. They beat a fighting retreat on the flanks of the Horned God. They could feel his power give them strength. Yet it was not enough.

The zombies swarmed relentlessly up the hillside, pulling to pieces anything in their path. Macha and the Rhianna rode down as many as they could, but the War Dead would rise again while they had a leg to stand on. No weapon could stop them. Only Ogmios's wind dogs seemed to have any effect – blowing the undead back down the slope. The windsmith had a bag of meat scraps, which he cast into the air each time another zombie was dispatched.

Kerne tried to think quickly. His staff had been shattered from the blow of a Grey Warrior, yet still he clung on to it. He broke it over his knee and threw the sticks towards the undead. With grim humour he shouted, 'Fetch!' A gust of wind brushed past him as the elementals swept down the slope, knocking over everything in their path. Swiftly, the wind dogs returned with the sticks and dropped them at his feet. The airman laughed raggedly. 'Like old Nubi!' He threw the sticks again and the wind dogs blew the war zombies off their feet, yet another wave of them took their place.

'There's too many of them!' cried Ogmios, his scraps running out.

Some of the undead had already reached the ramparts of the caer and were pulling them down with supernatural strength. By Kerne's side, Ogmios held off the undead with his club, one of the only weapons effective against them – able to smash the decayed corpses to pieces. He was surprised to see the old windsmith so powerful and so adept at fighting. He was chanting the holly sigil – 'tinne' – and his gem-spiked weapon served as an effective holly club. From the corner of his vision, Kerne thought he glimpsed a green spiky giant shadowing Ogmios's actions.

The scene telescoped and time slowed as Kerne saw himself in the midst of the nightmare: overwhelmed by the War Dead, by a river of blood – it was the scene from the no-man's-land of Annwn replaying itself. The horror threatened to overwhelm him.

Then he heard a strange sound. Ogmios was humming a melody, a familiar melody, one his Da used to like to sing … 'Sir John Barleycorn'! Whether Ogmios knew the same song, or whether the tune just happened to be a very old one, mattered not. It was a lifeline. Kerne began to hum it too, then the words started to come to him: '… *sent men in with holly clubs to beat the flesh from bones*'. The song gave rhythm to his blows, kept his morale up, stopped him going mad. He sang it with gusto, lost in the surreal hysteria. '*To beat the flesh from bones! To beat the flesh from bones!*' he howled. He had never tasted the sharp edge of war before; he had only flown above it, aloof from the action. Now he was among the mud, misery and gore. All around him Chalk Folk were dying, killed by the rotting hands of the zombies. He tried not to look into the corpse-light glowing in the eyes of the undead. Any second he would be sucked into their vortex, into Annwn.

25

Battle of the Damned

In his mind Kerne heard the damned of Annwn calling him, taunting him – *You will join us soon, down amongst the dead men, where you belong.* He swayed, feeling the pull of their angry hunger. The eyes of the undead burned like tallow flames as they staggered towards him.

Suddenly he felt a firm grip on his arm. Ogmios pulled him around. 'Skyman, hurry up!'

The older windsmith must have seen the fey look in his eyes and sensed his unwillingness to move. Looking around, Ogmios spotted a broken spear shaft on the track, cast down, now useless in battle – but not to a windsmith. The shaft was made of ash. Ogmios chanted over it to summon its dryad – a slender and swift Venus.

'*Bag ban!*' he commanded, directing the cantrip at Kerne. 'Run like a woman's mind! To Caer Minas – go!'

Kerne snapped out of his death trance and found himself running towards the hill fort of Cyndyn, along with the rest of the routed party, who fled half in panic, half in fighting retreat. Tuan's surviving household carried what they could, Macha and her Rhianna guarding the flanks, Nemain and the Morrigan protecting the elder-women, while Ogmios fought alongside his fellow windsmith, masterless Simias of Caer Dagda. The woad-limbed Bullmen of the Donn provided the rearguard, their sheer brutal strength managing to hold off the encroaching undead who led the advance. Behind this relentless infantry the Grey Raiders picked off any who fled in terror. They were ill at ease with their undead allies but had no choice but to fight by their side.

Finishing off any survivors among the piles of twisted bodies were Madoc's red-cloaked Royal Guard escorting the war cauldron pulled by slaves. The fallen were picked up as they passed and tossed into the metal womb of rebirth, each paying the way for one to be released from no-man's-land. A deadly trade, thought Kerne, watching the sickening exchange. Either Madoc or he still needed to pay the price, or the airmen's' presence would tear this world apart.

How Madoc had conceived or created the cauldron still remained a mystery. He had had no shaman since Eurus had blasted him into the pyre meant for Kerne. There was no time to wonder: survival was all.

'Fall back! Fall back to the next caer!' roared the Donn as he led a fighting retreat. It was too late for Caer Dagda – the undead were surging into it. What fate had befallen its chief, Tuan, was unknown.

Routed and in disarray, the first wall of Chalk Folk defenders retreated along the Sky Road to Caer Minas, the dûn of Cyndyn the trader. As Kerne hurried along the track recently cut and laid by his own flesh and blood, he thought of his father most of all and hoped he was safe and far from danger. Yet as he looked back towards Caer Dagda, silhouetted against the glittering haze of Lake Mandorla, black smoke pouring from its broken ramparts, the cries of the dying mingling with the pounding war drums and blaring bullhorns, he felt sick in his very soul. They were *his* relatives dying in there, distant cousins he had never met and now never would, and he could not save them. Every life lost was unbearable agony to him, as though he was stabbed by invisible daggers. Even the destruction of the undead enemy left him guilt-ridden. Some of those men had been on the same side as him. They too had met their fate in no-man's-land, and because of him and Madoc they had found no rest and dignity even in death. They had been spared obliteration at the hands of the Eater of the Dead, to be exchanged with a fresh corpse from this battlefield – for what? – to die a second time here?

The Grey Raiders still came in their crab craft – wave after wave, an iron storm pouring into the valley, sweeping upriver, leaving destruction in their wake. The Morrigan and Macha's Rhianna did what they could to stem the tide, but it was unstoppable.

Merlin and the other Feathered Ones flew back and forth along the valley, shrieking reports of the tide of battle to the windsmiths below. Tuan had fallen with his caer. The Dagda was down. How many more would follow, Kerne wondered? Was this the flood Kerne had seen in his moondream? It seemed the Chalk Folk were doomed, unless he could stop Madoc.

The clamour of battle was deafening: the clash of bronze against iron, the battle cries of the victorious, the screams of the dying, the throbbing war drums and the blaring bullhorns. And the stench – of blood, of rotting flesh, of fear, of the emptying of bowels in terror – was unbearable.

War is not a pretty thing, thought Kerne, trying to catch his breath, sweat pouring from him. Others fell, sobbed by the roadside, unable to go on, until dragged, implored by others. Where was the glory promised in the recruitment posters? Where was the gleam of war trophies or medals? Where the boasting of the mead hall or officers' club? Fathers and brothers, nephews and sons, comrades and commanders were strewn in the mire. They had not sought this war – it had come to them. They were dying defending their homeland, their loved ones, their families sheltering in the Caer of Arthus. They were protecting their future, though they belonged in the past, for they were his ancestors. And the appalling thought came to him: if they died too soon, where would that leave *him*? Would a man without ancestors cease to exist? Whatever the twisted causality, he felt honour bound to them. These were *his* people. He would die for them if he had to.

And what of Madoc? ruminated Kerne, reluctantly starting to run again, swept along in the tide of kith and kin. It seemed *his* ancestors were the Horse Nomads, the Huns … Was Madoc not also honouring his past, being true to his nature? It was in his blood also, he would argue. Were they both playing out ancient roles, typecast by ancestors, forced to re-enact karmic enmities, bound by alignments of fate?

Kerne was jolted from his own thoughts when Macha let out a howl of anguish. On the other side of the river Caer Epona was burning above the effigy of the white horse. The flanks were overrun with undead and Grey Raiders. Kerne had blinked every time he saw that chalk figure, for it reminded him of Uffington so much and a sharp pang of hiraeth pulled at him, for the peace and solitude of the Ridgeway. Yet that was another world away … The track they made their way along now had been surveyed with his own sighting poles. He had made his road, quite literally, and now he had to walk it.

Finally, weary and bloodied, the company made it to Cyndyn's enclosure – fighting their way back through the maze of earthworks, their retreat covered by Cyndyn's ram-helmeted warriors from the banks. They held off the pursuers with long spears, slings and burning oil. The narrow way through the ramparts prevented the legions from approaching more than a half dozen at a time. This allowed the survivors to reach the compound.

The gates were barred behind them, and with the sound of the great timber beam sliding into place the survivors collapsed in exhaustion. It was roughly a mile between caers, over rolling hills. A light but steady rain had made the ground slippery underfoot and the going harder.

The survivors from the battle of Caer Dagda were covered in mud, cuts and bruises – and they were the better-off ones. Those who had received worse wounds were tended to immediately by Saar's green-robed healers. It was the ones left behind that Kerne feared for the worse: a swift death would be welcome compared with the fate that awaited the fallen – thrown into the cauldron, into Annwn, to be devoured by the Eater of the Dead.

A young healer maiden with a plain, practical manner offered Kerne a cup of water and asked if he was alright. He felt almost guilty for not sporting any battle wounds. He had not been courageous in the fight. He was no warrior. And he hardly was a magician. He was dead weight.

Ogmios leant heavily on his club next to him, catching his breath. Despite his age he was still a brawny man with thick arms and thighs. He had much life spirit left in him. Another healer wiped the blood from his wounds, 'scratches' he called them; he hardly winced as the gentle maiden applied a poultice of herbs to the cuts.

'This is not looking good,' he spat. 'Speaks-with-Thunder wields an even deadlier weapon now. That Cauldron of the Dead will be the undoing of us.' He looked hard at Kerne.

There was a crashing blow at the gates, sending men to its defence. 'Battering ram!' someone cried.

'Kerne, let's see what strength your fortifications have now,' Cyndyn shouted from the battlements with a scornful look. 'If they do not hold we are doomed!'

The pounding increased, threatening to buckle the gates. Cyndyn ordered timber beams to be braced against them. Then carts, wicker hurdles, barrels – anything lying around – was piled up before the gates to create a barricade.

The Donn lined his spearmen up ready to repel any who came through. All they could do was wait for the inevitable.

An emergency council of the chieftains present was held in Cyndyn's hall: Macha, Nemain, Donn Cooley, Cyndyn plus Kerne and Ogmios.

The riches of the trader adorned the hall. The caer chiefs looked awkward sitting on fine silk cushions in their muddy or bloodied war gear, handed sweetmeats and fine wine by anxious-looking karma-serfs, while the battle raged outside. In the great pit the fire flickered among them, lighting up their angry faces.

'We cannot stay here!' bellowed the Donn, knocking aside a tray of dainties. 'We must move on – leave through the rear gate and make for the next caer.'

'Yes!' asserted Nemain. 'We will be able to muster in Caer Morrigan. No man has ever stepped foot in there without my permission. The Goddess is strong there and will protect us.'

'What? And leave my caer to the Army of Taranis?' complained Cyndyn. 'It will be ransacked. I will be ruined!'

'This is not the time to worry about your damn possessions, Cyndyn!' said the Donn.

Cyndyn glared at him, but could not stand up to the surly War Chief. He was stubborn but not foolish. Unable to take on the Donn, Cyndyn vented his anger on Kerne. 'If the skyman's defences held like they should, then we would not have to consider further retreat.'

'No one is stopping you from staying,' mocked Nemain.

Cyndyn glared back. 'And end up like Tuan?'

There was a sorrowful silence as the chieftains remembered their fallen.

'I should have been with my people ...' said Macha sadly, a haunted look in her eyes.

'Nothing you could have done would have helped. And your death would have only added to the tragedy. We need you and your Rhianna here,' said the Donn.

'The defences were never designed to withstand the undead,' declared Ogmios, striking down his club. 'It is to Kerne's credit they have held this long.'

'The gate will not last the morning, and then the fort will be overrun,' stated Nemain, and no one gainsaid her cool appraisal.

'Very well ...' Cyndyn sighed, 'but I expect compensation from the other tribes for my losses.'

'If we survive this, we shall all be needing help to rebuild our lives,' said the Donn. 'I do not like to retreat. The very word sticks in my throat. It is not in my nature. But if we can get across to the other side of the Zync stream then we may have more of an advantage. Nemain's fort is well defended on its high crag.'

'And if that falls,' hissed Macha, 'what then?'

The council was silent. The flames in the firepit crackled. Macha looked into it, her eyes ablaze as her fort had been. 'We cannot run for ever. How can we stop the undead? No weapon seems to work on them. They are not warriors we can meet equally on the field of battle. They are of a different breed.' She spat into the flames, making them hiss.

'Spawn of Annwn – my Morrigan will send them back to the shadow place,' boasted the Morrigan chief. 'They will wish they had never risen from the dead.'

'They had no choice, Nemain – don't you see!'

All eyes turned to Kerne. A log dislodged and sent up a flurry of sparks.

'The fallen are thrown into the cauldron as an offering to the Eater of the Dead. In exchange a fallen warrior from no-man's-land is released. These are my brothers-in-arms we're fighting! *I* should have died with them on the battle field. Instead, I crossed over in the same metal that *they* now use to cross over, the Cauldron of the Dead. Yet they have no choice. They cannot find the peace they deserve. Even in death they must still fight. I have seen this in the Eye of the Moon.'

Ogmios nodded to the others, confirming Kerne's words. 'When will the slaughter stop?'

'We must fight, or die.' The Donn laid his broadsword heavily on the mead bench. 'It's as simple as that. A king who brings the dead alive to fight his battles is beyond contempt. Speaks-with-Thunder will pay dearly for it before the day is out. But now we must think of our people. The gates will not hold long. We must buy them time to escape to the next caer. Who will stay and fight with me?'

'My Morrigan will pluck out their hearts!' declared Nemain, thrusting her dagger into the knotted wood.

Macha cast down her riding crop. 'My Rhianna will lend you their horses. When the enemy break through, we shall run them down and then take you on our backs to escape.'

Cyndyn looked nervously about. 'I am no fighter – I am a trader ...'

'Then lead the survivors,' commanded the Donn. 'And what of the windsmiths?'

Ogmios scratched his beard. 'I feel Kerne has a role to play in this which could turn the tide of battle. We cannot risk losing him at this stage. And I need to return to the Drunemetom – there I will raise a storm with my fellow windsmiths to blast the enemy out of our valley.'

'Very well. Take the skyman with you. You could pick up a canoe at the Zync stream.'

The pounding at the gates grew louder.

'It is time to go. May the gods be with you!'

The council stood and crossed arms over the fire, as a sign of their accord, then hurried to their duties.

Cyndyn cast a sad look over the glorious hall. 'May the fathers of Minas forgive me.'

26

Tin Soldiers

Kerne and Ogmios fled with Cyndyn and his entourage and other survivors from the Caer of the Ram. Carts were loaded down with treasure and goods – Cyndyn's precious belongings -- and hauled with difficulty by bulls along the heavily rutted tracks. The rain persisted, making the soft chalk soil churn up easily. Carts became stuck and some had to be left, their goods transferred, or they toppled over, casting their riches into the mud. Dark-browed Cyndyn shouted at everyone. The tinge of terror in his voice did not make anything easier.

'That fool will win the battle for them!' cursed Ogmios, his three grey strands plastered to his bald head, his blue robe lank about his strong limbs.

Ogmios pointed the gem-studded cudgel and chanted the rowan woodword over the procession – '*Cara ceathra*' – calming for a while the rising tide of panic. 'My club contains the woods of all the grove,' Kerne remembered him saying once.

The darkness hung like a pall over the valley. Below, Kerne could discern the crab craft pouring upriver. The caers of the Dagda and Epona were burning. On the other side of the river, the tribe of Caer Findbhennach, its white bull of chalk shining below the ramparts, was defending valiantly, but the forces that assailed it were overwhelming.

At least they do not have to fend off the undead as well, thought Kerne.

Behind them, the legions of the dead attacked Cyndyn's caer. The Donn, Macha and Nemain held them off as long as they could to buy the evacuees time. They needed an hour to cross the long mile to Caer Morrigan. With the mud and the steepness of the road the procession was painfully slow. About two hundred ragged refugees, a dozen carts and one unit of Bronze Warriors – Cyndyn's personal guard. Everyone there knew how vulnerable they were should the legions break through the rearguard.

After a concerted slog through the hardening drizzle, eased a little by Ogmios's chanting of calm, the column breached the brow of the hill and started to descend into the next fold of the valley. Below, the Zync stream slithered down to join the Da'anu. Where the Sky Road intersected it there was a ford. Downstream, small boats were tethered to a bank lined with alder trees.

Black-robed Morrigan guards watched the crossing, hailing Cyndyn's host as they approached.

While the procession started to negotiate the ford across the swollen stream, Kerne and Ogmios commandeered a canoe. To enter the Da'anu at this time, when it was aswarm with the enemy, seemed like madness but the Morrigan guards let them go with a shake of their black-cowled heads. They had enough to worry about.

The canoe was made of a single piece of black timber and was sleek if unstable, sitting low in the water. Ogmios steered from the rear as the two of them wielded the light but strong paddles. They bade farewell and good fortune to the refugees. Some, who had crossed the ford, were already making their way up the steep approach to Caer Vran – gaunt and dark on its clifftop, the place of training for young warriors. Its battlements bristled with spears. Silhouetted against the grey sky, it looked like a gigantic raven's nest. Hooded figures watched them push off into the metallic-hued stream.

The canoe rushed down to join the sinewy, fast-flowing Da'anu. The valley echoed with the din of war. A flotilla of iron boats stubbornly pushed upriver, shrugging off the attentions of catapults on the cliffs. The tiny craft shot out into their path. The two magicians had to row hard to resist the current, which wanted to pull them towards the approaching enemy.

'Put your back into it, skyman!' shouted Ogmios. 'They've seen us.'

Almost immediately, there was a whistle of arrows striking the water behind them. They were still out of range, just, but not for long. Each crab craft had a dozen strong-armed rowers, and slits for the archers in its plate metal. They would soon catch up if the windsmiths didn't make haste.

For the next few minutes all their world consisted of was paddling. Ogmios chanted the alder sigil using the wood of the paddles. *'Fearn ...'* Instantly, Kerne felt protected; mighty Bran was again shielding them.

Suddenly, from the ramparts of Caer Vran a hail of missiles soared over the heads of the magicians to pummel the iron crabs.

'The Morrigan's wrath!' shouted Ogmios, laughing with relief.

The hail of arrows from the battlements of Nemain's fortress drew the fire of the enemy and enabled the canoe to put some distance between them.

The iron-carapaced craft shrugged off the hail of arrows and other missiles but were slowed down by the waves created by the falling rocks. Yet, slowly, inevitably, they began to catch up with the windsmiths.

'There's no stopping them!' cried Kerne.

An arrow punched into the stern of the canoe, narrowly missing Ogmios. 'Keep rowing!'

Kerne turned his head to see a hail of arrows descend. *This was it!*

Ogmios had his eyes closed and seemed to be humming. A flurry of wind made the canoe rock and all but one arrow go astray. The one arrow hit the windsmith in the shoulder and he dropped his paddle into the river.

'Ogmios!'

The old windsmith roared with pain as he broke the arrow off. He looked at the shaft with contempt and then cast it into the water, breathing heavily.

'Is that bee sting the best you can do?' he bellowed back at the enemy.

Yet with only Kerne paddling they had stopped making much headway. The constant rain had swollen the river. The iron craft drew closer.

'Are you —?'

'I'm alright,' Ogmios replied, clutching his shoulder, gritting his teeth. 'Keep paddling!'

'But what about you?'

Suddenly, there was a gust of wind and Ogmios's paddle flew into his lap. 'The spirits have not left me yet. Go!'

Digging furiously into the water with his paddle again and again Kerne thought his chest would burst. They could not keep this up for ever. His arms felt like lead, starting to shake from the effort. A stitch burned in his side. It was only a matter of seconds before he would have to drop the paddle.

Moments before they came in range once more the flotilla miraculously veered off. Kerne turned to see the iron crabs were turning away from them to the opposite shore – to the base of the White Boar, Tawrk's caer. Like a great grey wave the war craft ran ashore and out poured the cavalry and foot soldiers. They joined their comrades already besieging the caer from the road leading from the hill fort of the White Bull, which remained under heavy assault though stubbornly refusing to yield. Taranis's army was like a swarm of locusts, leaving devastation in their wake. It seemed nothing could stop them.

The windsmiths carried on upriver. Kerne did not slacken the pace, though his hands were blistered. Ogmios assisted as best he could by steering, using his paddle as a rudder. They would not feel safe until they were out of sight of the Iron Army – and then only temporarily. As they passed a tributary on their right, they saw it was bristling with spears from warrior-filled canoes.

'The Tuns!' exclaimed Ogmios as the tin miners poured into the river and rammed the sides of the iron crabs. With spears and hammers and mining tools, the Tuns attacked, driving back the Grey Raiders from the flanks of Caer Henwen. From the battlements Tawrk mocked the enemy. He was in his spiked plate mail, wielding his cleaver and bristling with fury, as dangerous as a cornered boar.

Slowly the hue and cry of battle receded as the windsmiths' canoe made its way around the snaking bends of the river, past the opposing caers of Setanta and Saar, the hound and the deer, towards the temporary sanctuary of Drunemetom. Never had a place looked so inviting. Kerne's hands were raw from the canoeing, his arms and shoulders aching. Ogmios strained at the rudder, jaw set. A bloom of blood stained his blue robe. Slower now, they paddled towards the island of the windsmiths.

Kerne thought of all the warriors and chiefs fighting downriver: the Donn, Macha, Nemain, Tawrk … and here he was fleeing from battle. Ogmios had said he had 'a role to play in this which could turn the tide of battle', but all he felt like at that moment was a coward. He would run away no longer. Here he would make his stand. Here he would make an end of it.

27

Muster at Moot Holm

The stout bulwark of Moot Holm loomed before them, reassuringly impregnable. Yet it had never been intended for defensive purposes, but was a sacred meeting place of peace. Now it was the eye of the storm. It was all that stood between the Iron Horde and the Upper Da'anu. If it was taken, it seemed inevitable the rest of the valley would fall.

For now, at least, it offered sanctuary from the slaughter. Its craggy flanks were bustling with activity as fugitives arrived from fallen homesteads, fallen caers. Warriors who had lost their comrades staggered on to the rocky banks, dropping to the ground with wounds both inner and outer. Another contingent of Saar's green-cloaked healers did what they could, their faces pinched with concern, for their mistress was besieged at Caer Vran. Broth and blankets were handed out to the refugees. A makeshift camp of hides and driftwood had been set up on the side of the crag, vulnerable and exposed around small fires. Everything was sodden from the rain and an air of misery pervaded; everywhere the sounds of agony and loss.

It was midday, though it was hard to tell that in the perpetual darkness.

'This gloom is not natural,' observed Ogmios, leaning heavily on his club as he and Kerne clambered ashore. They were both exhausted from the rowing. The old windsmith wiped his glistening brow with the back of his hand. Kerne noticed the hand was shaking.

'I can sense the cythrawl is close. The rift is widening. We haven't got much time!'

Kerne knew what he meant. He had somehow to reach Madoc and put an end to it before their dual presence ripped HyperEurus apart. He rubbed his side, where a stitch throbbed. He was weak, hungry, terrified by the undead like the rest of them. How was he going to stop a madman who controlled an army? But his first concern was Ogmios. He helped him up the stone steps and it seemed strange to be assisting him. His mentor's strength was gone. The broken shaft of the arrow protruded from his left shoulder blade.

'We need help over here!' Kerne bellowed, and a healer came to them. She did what she could – a basic field dressing of sphagnum moss and hemp binding, for Ogmios refused to have the shaft removed.

'It would take the life from me.'

Kerne was horrified at that blunt statement. Was the arrow wound that serious? The old windsmith masked it well. He still looked so … full of life. Kerne could not imagine him not being there, his mentor. He helped him to a nearby shelter in front of which a spluttering fire defied the rain. They shared its fragile warmth with the silent assent of raggle-taggle bunch of refugees gathered around it: a young mother with babe at her breast; an older girl with her arm protectively over a boy sucking his thumb, his head in her lap, looking seriously at the flames; two grizzled old veterans too weary for war; a young warrior with a bandaged head, pale and saucer-eyed; a fat trader looking miserable and shaking his head in disbelief. They passed around a small flask of liquor to warm their bones. All gazed sullenly into the erratic flames of the fire, hissing from the rain.

Ogmios gripped his club and softly chanted a healing kenning, using the aspen plug fixed into it: *'Cosc lobair.'* This made them all feel better, but it became a struggle to hear it against the growing sounds of drums and bullhorns. The battle drew ever closer. All there were aware of this inescapable fact. There was nowhere left to run.

Along the valley, fires raged and the river bristled with skirmishes. It would not be long before the tide of war engulfed them, but the refugees were too exhausted to run any further, and some deep instinct told them Moot Holm offered their only sanctuary.

When they had caught their breath and devoured a bowl of watery, gristly broth – all that could be mustered from the dwindling supplies – Kerne and Ogmios thanked their hosts and moved off.

'I must join my fellow windsmiths at the Drunemetom,' asserted Ogmios. 'We will need all our strength to defend Moot Holm from this war-host.' He painfully made his way to the winding stair leading up to the oak grove. With Kerne's help he ascended it. When they passed the tree into which Kerne had fallen they paused and laughed raggedly at the memory.

'A strange sound in a time of terror.'

Then they saw the falcon perched in its branches.

'Merlin!' they said together, pleased to see the Feathered One.

'Do not be too glad to see me – I bring bad news.'

The two windsmiths huddled under the shelter of the oak to escape the drumming rain.

'Tell us, wise one, for we must know,' said Ogmios.

The bird looked at them with eyes hard as stone. 'We have lost two more chiefs – Tawrk and Macha.'

'No!' Ogmios sank on to a mossy boulder, letting his club go slack in his hand. It was the first time Kerne had seen him lose hope.

'Caer Findbhennach and Caer Henwen have fallen,' Merlin continued, his voice for once softened. 'Tawrk fought to the bitter end, dying with his men. He was surrounded by a deadly harvest of Grey Raiders. He did not go down to Annwn alone.'

'And how did Macha die?' asked Ogmios weakly.

'She fell valiantly, defending Cyndyn's host as you escaped his fort.'

'What of the Donn and Nemain?' asked Ogmios, tense for the answer.

'They survived – by the skin of their teeth – and made it back to Caer Vran with the remaining Morrigan and Rhianna. They are heavily besieged but are holding out. That fort will not yield so easily. Saar and Cyndyn are also there.'

'It is a grievous loss and I will mourn for Tawrk and Macha,' said Ogmios, 'but we still have many mighty chieftains left: Setanta, Cormac, Eryr, Arthus, Partholon and Brigantia.'

'As well as our ore allies – the Tuns, Copors, Plwms and Arianedd,' reminded Kerne.

'Yes – the day is not lost yet. We still have strength in arms and the light of Ceugant on our side. Come, we must report this to the council.'

'Then quickly, for the Iron Army is almost upon you!' warned Merlin. 'You will need to bring all the survivors to the higher grove. Soon the battle will be at this shore.'

'You report to the windsmiths, Ogmios,' suggested Kerne. 'I will raise the alarm and meet you in the grove as soon as I can.'

Ogmios placed his hand upon Kerne's shoulder and nodded, then continued up the rain-lashed steps.

'And I will check the tide of battle and will find you!' cried Merlin as he flew off, spraying Kerne with raindrop from his feathers and the branches he had disturbed.

In haste Kerne descended and made ready to raise his voice. He had no need – the Iron Army was already attacking and the refugees were either leaving in boats or heading for higher ground. It was chaos. People were falling into the river or being trampled in the hysteria. Overloaded boats capsized as the iron craft disgorged their deadly cargo. Curved swords flashed in the rain, hacking down anything in their path. Moot Holm offered no more sanctuary.

Then from upriver came unexpected help. It happened in a blur of rain and movement. Out of the veil of rain a war party came racing downriver. It was too late for the Grey Raiders to leap out of the way. The assailants let the swollen current smash them into the enemies' side. Iron-armoured warriors were jolted into the cold embrace of the Da'anu. The newcomers leapt ashore and starting cutting through the ranks rushing to meet them. Their wildness was terrifying to behold: like a pack of rabid hounds they ripped apart any in their path. Kerne recognised the shaven-headed leader with the spiky collar and dog-tail mantle: Setanta! His Wardogs' surprise attack had given them the advantage.

Inspired by this new onslaught, white-cloaked Sanctuary Guards rallied to the aid of Setanta's men, cutting into the enemy's blindside, and, together, their combined strength turned the tide. The enemy battalion seemed doomed. The fifty or so survivors formed a defensive circle as the Bronze Warriors surrounded them. Shaking his iron sword at them, Setanta bared his teeth. Kerne could imagine him growling. With the bloodlust on him he would not stop until every one was crow-meat.

Just as Kerne was thinking that it was a good job the dreaded cauldron was on land – and unable to benefit from the slaughter – there was an ominous rumble in the dark heavens and, out of the unearthly penumbra, he saw the Royal Barge approach.

Death would not avoid them for long.

Kerne ran up the winding stair, pushing past the fleeing refugees. He finally made it to the summit of Moot Holm, now overflowing with survivors. The wind howled about them. As Kerne neared the sanctuary, he discerned the sound of chanting carried and snatched by the wind. At the eye of the storm were the white-cloaked windsmiths, standing in a circle in the centre of their grove. They had created a tower of light with their awen. Ogmios was leading his fellows in a windsummoning. They were trying to raise a storm but the cythrawl was jinxing their magic, making it difficult to control. Kerne sensed its malignant vortext poisoning the windsmiths' awen, their intoning drowned out by the howling gale.

A lightning bolt arced down from the black clouds and shattered an oak. The severed branch toppled and, with sickening inevitability, fell on top of two of the windsmiths: Senach, the Donn's priest, and Gwyllt, Cormac's. Kerne was blown over as the chanting abruptly ended, the shockwaves of the deaths shattering the circle.

The tower of light flickered and faded from the grove.

Only the preternatural maelstrom increased in intensity.

Then a falcon fell out of the sky, bedraggled and exhausted. 'It's no good!' screeched Merlin. 'The summoning has failed. The gramarye's been overpowered. It's up to you, Kerne – only *you* can stop this! You know what you must do!'

The windsmith felt the weight of the Webley on his hip. Its iron felt cold.

Suddenly, there was a gunshot.

Below, Moot Holm was assailed by a new wave of the Iron Army. The Wardogs had lost their advantage and were losing the battle. Many had been cast into the angry river to be speared like fish when they clawed for help. Their canoes had been crushed by the crab craft. The Sanctuary Guards had been driven back at heavy cost, their white cloaks torn and bloody. Many lay twisted and cut on the rocks.

The Royal Barge moored and disgorged its contents. Over timbers rapidly deployed by slaves the Cauldron of the Dead was wheeled ashore and behind it was the unmistakable figure of Madoc, iron crowned, bear cloaked, wielding his pistol. He waved the smoking barrel over a body that lay at his feet: Setanta. For a moment, Madoc looked up – and Kerne felt a flicker of cythrawl between them. The crag seemed to tilt and Kerne had to steady himself. Had his nemesis seen him looking down? It was hard to say.

Victorious, Madoc walked into the sanctuary of the Chalk Folk over the body of Setanta, who lay clutching his stomach, dying in a pool of his own blood.

28

The Last Stand

The sky was midnight black flecked with silver veins of lightning. Stinging rain howled around the grim edifice of Moot Holm. Grey Raiders surged up its slopes. Any of them who were cut down by the retreating Sanctuary Guards were picked up and thrown into the cauldron, to emerge as undead.

Refugees huddled on the island's bare summit, exposed to the elements except in the sacred grove, where none could enter except the priests and chiefs, even now. The windsmiths struggled to hold their circle as the maelstrom lashed at them, sending branches crashing down. Two of their number lay crushed underneath a lightning-struck oak; their bird allies, a wren and robin, sat disconsolately on the toppled branches. The storm the circle had summoned had been polluted by the cythrawl and turned into a force of evil. Darkness snaked around the blue-cloaked, white-robed figures, threatening to suck them into Annwn. Despite their grievous loss they had to continue, for the sake of the Chalk Folk, and so the weary magicians steeled themselves once more to the task. Reforming the circle, the eleven remaining windsmiths stretched out their hands and resumed their intoning of the awen. It was drowned out by the sturm und drang around them, but slowly a column of white energy crackled and swirled between them, spiralling upwards amidst the seething chaos – a lighthouse beam in a vast unnatural night.

The survivors on the summit waited for the end, Kerne with them, crouching with his cloak pulled about him hiding the Sam Browne belt with its Webley at his hip in its holster. They could hear the harrowing sounds of the massacre down the dim winding stair.

Suddenly there was silence. Only the wind keened, shredding itself through the twisted branches of the grove. The small circle of human beings huddled closer together. A baby cried, until it was stifled. In the anonymous night both men and women choked back sobs of fear and grief, smothered by the deafening silence, the animal frisson of expectation.

Then up the stairs appeared the War Dead, staggering forward with sickening inevitability. The women and children screamed; the men prayed at their swords, kneeling, preparing to die. What they saw made them tremble, for among their number were Setanta and his slain Wardogs, bloodied corpses brought to life.

'They've turned them into undead!' someone gasped in despair.

The remaining men dropped their weapons. How could they fight their own brothers in arms? And, worse, a similar fate awaited them if they died in battle. The survivors backed away in terror.

With a jerk, the war zombies paused, prevented from entering the sacred grove by the powerful protective hexes placed there by successive windsmiths. Deathly still, eyes glowing amber in the midday murk, they stood sentinel.

Then the ranks of the undead parted and Kerne recognised the silhouette of Madoc as he swaggered forward. Flanking him were the Royal Guard – Kerne recognised the cruel-eyed Horse Nomads in their pointed fur-trimmed helmets and black quilted tunics, their torsos protected by cuirasses of ornate metal squares. With blood-stained scimitars thrust into their wide belts, they jabbed spears towards the Chalk Folk.

Madoc approached the grove.

The survivors flinched back, parting like a sea.

'You know who I am,' he rasped in his ragged voice. Thunder rumbled above, making the young cower back. 'Fear not – I will not slay women and children. I am no savage barbarian, am I Kerne?'

The former brothers in arms locked eyes. Lightning cracked the sky, illuminating their faces with glaring intensity.

Madoc stopped before his navigator and they faced one another, the warlord and the windsmith. The world seemed to shudder, shadows to bend.

'You have become a monster,' Kerne accused.

'Like breeds like, my friend. It seems that strange creatures follow you around.'

The air seemed to bend. Light writhed over their skin. Kerne felt as he had when the chimeras appeared. He quickly backed away.

Madoc laughed raggedly. 'Ever the coward, Kerne. One day you'll learn that to get what you want in any world, you have to fight.'

The ruler of the Forbidden Kingdom went to step across the threshold of the grove. Barring his way was Ogmios, club in hand. Inside the Drunemetom the other windsmiths strove to maintain the circle, but the tower of light was weakening.

'Out of my way, old man,' growled Madoc.

'You may not enter the sacred grove! You will not despoil this sacred place, skyman!'

'You and whose army?'

Behind Madoc the Royal Guard bristled with spears and the undead legion waited in absolute stillness. The Grey Raiders brought up the rear. There was no escape.

'By the gods of this grove, Taranis, you will not pass!'

Madoc lifted his Webley and shot Ogmios point blank in the belly.

'Nooo!' cried Kerne.

The column of light flickered and died, leaving a gaping vacuum. A cataclysmic rumble shook the sky, and a deeper darkness engulfed the summit, leaving only torches guttering in the storm.

'You bastard!' In a blind rage Kerne pulled out his Webley and raised it to shoot Madoc, but in one swift movement a Royal Guard notched and fired an arrow. The arrowhead punched straight into his left hand, knocking the pistol flying. 'Aaarrggh!' Kerne doubled over in pain, the arrow stuck in his hand. He watched in horror as his only weapon was cast over the edge of the summit and plummeted into swirling shadows below.

'Tut-tut, old boy, you wouldn't shoot your old flying partner, would you? After I showed you mercy as well? Didn't I give you that gun back to end your miserable life? Do you want me to do it for you?'

Madoc raised the gun to Kerne's head as he knelt broken in the rain.

'Do it! End this madness!' Kerne cried out, his face twisted in agony as he held his skewered hand. 'Can't you see we're destroying this world? We are not meant to be here! One of us must die – otherwise the cythrawl will overwhelm HyperEurus and the dead will find no peace.'

Madoc looked around him at the zombies, the warriors, the storm, the destruction. 'End this? Why would I do that? Isn't this glorious? If I am the destroyer of the worlds it is only to recreate them anew. We know nothing really ends. We did not die, so I will rule, immortal! No, I won't kill you. I'll let you live, for now. Admit it, Kerne. You're defeated. Give up on this lost cause. It's not too late to join me …'

'I'd rather suffer in Annwn than become what you are!'

'What a pity.'

Madoc turned the Webley in his hand and, holding the barrel, pistol-whipped Kerne. The blow on the side of his head sent him reeling. The world flooded with blood. In a stunned daze he could only watch things unfold in an abstract way. He looked at the arrow stuck in his hand. He felt the hot blood trickling down his face. Everyone was sideways. Sounds faded in and out of his consciousness. Madoc towered over him, shaking his head. Slowly he turned, someone drawing his attention.

The airman lay on the ground next to the body of Ogmios, who was twitching in a widening pool of blood. The old windsmith breathed heavily. Blood bubbled from his mouth but he looked at Kerne with a strange light in his eyes. His gaze cast skywards and Kerne followed it, but saw only blackness.

As he looked up into the rain, into the broiling clouds of shadow, Kerne thought about his life, about all that he had seen. How had he ended up here? Was he to die in this dark and distant land, worlds away from home?

Suddenly, the shape of a falcon caught his eye. There. In a gap in the inky cloud. Yes, it was Merlin!

Somehow, he could see from the falcon's perspective as it soared over the Valley of the Chalk Folk. Was his soul leaving his body? Was this what death felt like? Something was happening below. There was commotion at the edge of Kerne's vision, fragments of conversation.

'More warriors are attacking, my lord!' reported a Grey Warrior.

'Do these Chalklanders never give up? Don't they know when they're beaten?'

A cry went up from the survivors: 'It's Cormac and the lead miners!'

Distantly, Kerne remembered the Wolf Chief. His was the next caer – and by it ran the Plwm stream.

Madoc sighed. 'Undead – attack!' he roared. The legion of zombies turned and began to leap off the cliff – to drop down on top of the attacking Wolf Clan and plaided lead miners. Kerne saw it all from the air through the falcon's keen eyes.

The airman saw the Iron Horde swarm upriver, pushing further and further into the heart of Chalklander territory, razing Caer Blaidd and reaching the walls of Caer Andarta – the Caer of Arthus. This was where the majority of the women, children and elderly sheltered, protected by the mighty Arthus and his Bearshirts – berserkers, fierce and unstoppable in battle. Aided by the remaining forces of Stag, Eagle and Salmon, the Bearshirts kept the enemy at bay. Flame-haired and magnificent in her bronze breastplate, Brigantia commanded the defending forces from her war chariot. Her champion and son Brak led them into battle, with Bronwen his sister fighting by his side. If they were to fall then they would die together in glory. If this was to be the last stand of the Chalk Folk then it would be remembered throughout the worlds.

'More fodder for the cauldron,' sighed Madoc. 'Guards, take this bag of bones and throw him in as well.'

The ten surviving windsmiths wept for their fallen chief, but were held back at spearpoint by the Royal Guard.

As the broken body was lifted up by two mail-clad warriors, Kerne noticed the dying sorcerer make a weak sigil with his fingers. Then he was swept away. But the brief signal had been transmitted: the elder woodword.

What it implied Kerne could not fathom in his pain, but he raised his uninjured hand to bid his mentor farewell. A Royal Guard struck him with a spear butt. The rapport with the falcon snapped. Shadows soaked Kerne's mind and he blacked out.

29

Voice of Thunder

Kerne came to in the oak grove; he was lying on the altar stone in the rain. His head wound throbbed, making him wince with pain. His vision was tainted crimson by the rain-washed blood flowing from where the Royal Guard had struck him. The iron taste of it filled his mouth.

Madoc stood with his back to Kerne, hands linked behind him holding his gun, as he looked out over the war-racked valley, where fires lit the midday darkness. The cythrawl raged about them, lightning arcing in tongues of dragon flame above them, splitting the heavens with jagged cracks followed quickly by deafening rolls of thunder. The surviving ten windsmiths were tied to the oak trees – one to each. One tree lay fallen, the bodies of the two windsmiths beneath it. Two trees of the thirteen remained untouched, standing side by side. It was between these that Madoc gazed at the devastation he had caused.

Kerne groaned in pain and anguish. Blood poured down his arm and on to his chest, into the grooves of his gold breastplate. His hand still had the black-shafted Hun arrow stuck through it, and with returning lucidity reality became increasingly painful.

It truly looked as though all was lost. Four chiefs had fallen, five caers. The Drunemetom had been captured. And Ogmios was dead. Kerne still could not accept that his mentor had been shot point blank by Madoc. The shock left him numb. Yet the last gesture of Ogmios, the elder sigil, echoed through his mind. *Ruis, ruis, ruis* ... Kerne remembered that it represented the end in the beginning and the beginning in the end, but he could see no hope, no rebirth in this day of night. He whispered it to himself, but no revelation came.

'Ah, good, you're awake.' Madoc's hoarse voice mockingly invaded his consciousness. 'I wouldn't want you to miss this, Kerne. My finest hour. Don't you just love the scent of victory, old boy? If only this was the killing fields of Europe – I would have won the day for King and Country. Yet now I command an army of the Hun. Ironic, wouldn't you say? It seems as though I have more than a lick of the Kraut in me, after all. Then so has our royal family, God bless them. And the Normans, what were they originally? The *North*men – Vikings! My ancestors. Perhaps we make enemies of what we don't like in ourselves ... Now that's profound for a biplane pilot, and you the one with your head in the clouds. How's your skull, Kerne? Sorry I had to do that, but you were just about to shoot me.' Madoc turned, lifting the Webley. 'And you the pacifist. Tut-tut.' Madoc's face was momentarily lit up with a sigil of lightning, his eyes gleam-ing with the same fanaticism that had driven them into the Angel Vortex. Eyebrows, lashes, fur cloak – everything glistened and streamed with rain. The bolt had hit one of the oaks. It burst into flames, consum-ing one of the windsmiths, who screamed out in agony.

'Morann!' cried the other wood-priests.

Setanta's windsmith. How many more would die?

'For God's sake, let them go, Madoc! Let me be your sacrifice.'

'And stop all the fun? Not likely!'

The screams of Morann became unbearable.

'Oh, shut up for bally's sake!' Madoc unloaded a bullet into the windsmith's chest and the priest fell silent. The report echoed around the valley like the thunder.

'These heathens deserve to die anyway. What do they worship? Trees? They're savages! Not much better than my old shaman. Oh but didn't Crow-Walker get blown into the pyre meant for you? Now where did that gust of wind come from, I wonder? Who sum-moned the gale? And who has called this storm down upon us?' Ma-doc shouted at the windsmiths. They flinched as he pointed the Webley at them in turn. 'Well, it's the last magic you'll perform, wiz-ards.'

Something caught his eye below. 'Ah, looks like they're just about to throw your friend into the cauldron, Kerne. Waste not, want not, eh? You shouldn't miss this. Here, let me help you.'

Madoc ordered his guards to grab Kerne, lift him up, frogmarch him to the edge of the grove. The cliff plummeted beyond, to the foot of Moot Holm, where torchlit figures were standing guard around the cauldron as Grey Raiders cast in the fallen. The limp, robed body of Ogmios could be seen, his chest and shoulder stained by a bloom of red. Guards went to roughly pick him up.

'The cauldron's ingenious, isn't it?' boasted Madoc. 'I wish I could claim credit for it, but, you see, I have a new shaman now – far brighter than the old fellow ...'

242

Out of the very shadows emerged a figure cloaked in uncanny light. Kerne only caught a fleeting glimpse, but felt the evil that radiated from the wraith. It was humanoid, but undeniably demonic. A stretched skull leered from beneath the spectral shroud. With fangs of flame it seemed to grin malevolently at Kerne before vanishing like a snuffed candle.

'Not much of a talker,' Madoc joked, trying to hide the nervousness in his voice.

It reminded Kerne of the chimera. What the hell was it? But his attention was drawn back to the scene below.

The Grey Raiders cast the windsmith into the cauldron's maw. Kerne collapsed in despair and howled into the storm. Through his fingers he watched his old friend fall into the Annwn portal. The same Void called to him. But as the sickening lurch of vertigo tugged at his guts Kerne blinked.

Ogmios, spread-eagled, was holding on to the edges of the cauldron! Kerne saw that the arrow shaft in the windsmith's shoulder had caught the lip of the vat. His own impaled hand spasmed at the thought of the pain. Then he saw the thick-limbed windsmith push against the edges with all his might, and he was chanting, chanting a woodword.

Madoc also saw this and shouted down to the guards, but the gale snatched his words away.

'Your friend needs some persuading to die!' Madoc raised his Webley and took aim.

'No!' Kerne hauled himself up and lunged against Madoc, whose aim went wild and brought down a guard. The Grey Raiders below looked up and scattered in panic.

'Get out of my way, or you'll be next!' Madoc knocked Kerne violently back with a swipe of his mailed fist. The pilot's teeth were bared and there was a wild look in his eye. Kerne knew he meant what he said. Then the mad king laughed savagely: 'They thought the thundergod had struck down their comrade. And they were right. I am Taranis. I am Speaks-with-Thunder!' he shouted into the rain with his ragged voice, waving his pistol.

Kerne had been momentarily stunned by Madoc's blow. Blood poured from his mouth. He could only watch in horror as the pilot took aim once more and fired. This time his shot hit home, striking Ogmios square on, but with his death-spasm the old windsmith roared, '*Cara bloisc!*' and burst the cauldron asunder.

There was a shockwave of shadow, and then from the implosion monsters of fire streaked outwards. Chimeras! Winged demons, ram-headed serpents, tigers, creatures of every nightmarish shape and combination poured from the space where the cauldron had been, tearing apart everything in their path.

The Grey Raiders nearby never stood a chance.

Ogmios had destroyed the cauldron with his dying breath, uttering the kenning meaning 'friend of cracking', using the hazel wood of the arrow embedded in his shoulder. But had he unleashed Annwn?

The monsters surged around the base of Moot Holm, a rising tide of terror. The broken body of Ogmios was lifted up along with the plates of the cauldron by some invisible force. Slowly the limp, bloody burden was raised towards the summit.

Kerne realised they must be Ogmios's wind dogs, performing one last act of loyalty for their master.

Madoc began firing at them from above. 'Demons, go back to the hell from where you came!'

While Madoc was distracted, suddenly, out of the cythrawl sky Kerne heard a piercing shriek. Looking up, he saw a blur of feathers just as something hard landed in his lap. He looked down: it was his Webley.

Merlin had returned it to him. This was his last chance.

He picked it up and pointed it at Madoc.

'Harry Mallard.'

The shock of hearing his real name made the tyrant turn. In an instant he saw Kerne aiming the Webley and went to fire his own.

'Isamb—'

The barrel flared and tore out Mallard's throat. The impact of the bullet pushed him over the precipice.

Time seemed to dilate as the airman fell backwards, leaving a bloody arc of skull and brain. There was a look of astonishment and accusation on his face, which pierced Kerne to the core.

The wind seemed to toy with Madoc as he plummeted – but no gust blew him into a tree. The pilot's body struck with a sickening thud the rocks where the shattered cauldron and the figure of Ogmios had lain. The wind stopped, leaving a vacuum of sound.

Thunder echoed around the valley, growing louder and louder. The whole world seemed to shake. The chimeras grew frenzied, screaming with a shrill despair, and were suddenly sucked back into a point of singularity, where they vanished with a flash of black fire.

Then the sound of doom overwhelmed them all.

A huge wall of water was thundering down the valley, washing away everything in its path – the Grey Raiders and the Undead – anything not at the level of the caers or the Drunemetom.

Kerne clung to an oak root as Moot Holm was battered by the surging tide, which thrashed against even the summit of the island, ripping away trees and boulders from its flanks. He realised with elation that the deluge was the legacy of the storm summoned by the windsmiths.

The island's foundations trembled as the flood pummelled against its bulwark. Water had fallen on the foothills all day and now it roared down the path of least resistance, scouring Taranis's army from the valley, both quick and undead.

The churning water kept coming, a wave of wrath, unstoppable, filled with the flotsam and jetsam of war – bodies, weapons, boats.

Finally, when it seemed all would be swept away, the flood subsided, an anger dissipating. The thick cowl of clouds parted and shards of sunlight pierced the cythrawl gloom.

Surrounded by the nine surviving windsmiths and the raggle-taggle bunch of Chalk Folk who had taken refuge in the broken grove, Kerne lay slumped in utter exhaustion next to the cold body of Ogmios, the gun warm in his hand and the sound of thunder still ringing in his head.

Book Four

The Ship of Air

30

The Dead Side

It was a brilliant August morning, the mist still burning off from Salisbury Plain, as Kerne waited at the Old Sarum airfield for his pilot to turn up. Harry Mallard was booked to take him up on a trial flight to 'get his wings'.

It had all happened so fast. The events of the last fortnight had gone by in a blur: his return from Brittany, signing up, aptitude tests, initial briefing. Only when Kerne opened the letter from the War Office confirming his placement as an observer in the newly formed Royal Flying Corps did it all seemed real. And today would be his first taste of flying.

Maud was terrified for him, and so he did not bring her along in the Bentley, for she would have made him even more nervous as he sat there deciding whether to stay in the aerodrome and meet his fate, or drive off.

Archie would have loved to have been there. Since Kerne had told his brother of his intentions to 'do the right thing' and enlist, his brother had been full of nothing but praise for his 'baby brother' and had offered relentless advice. Kerne had thanked him, he knew he meant well, but this was his time, his duty. He had to deal with it, as Archie had in his day, by himself. This was his 'alignment', and despite the fact Kerne was a pacifist by nature, if not publicly, and the very thought of going to war filled him with dread, he felt that by offering his surveying skills he would be 'doing his bit'.

Kerne took a deep breath and stepped out of the reassuring cocoon of the Bentley, swinging the door shut behind him. It slammed louder than he had intended and the sound was like a gunshot in the dead morning air.

With the eye of a civil engineer for the GWR and as an amateur antiquarian, Kerne scanned the shrouded fields surrounding the airbase and took heart in the ramparts of Old Sarum looming out of the mist, overlooking the airstrip and the new hangars. In a way that Maud would call 'one of his fanciful notions' he took the proximity of the airbase, hill fort and former site of Salisbury Cathedral as a sign of the convergence of his obsession, profession and destiny. It was said in one tradition that the site of the new cathedral, lower down on the banks of the Avon in the heart of Salisbury, was chosen by shooting an arrow – and that morning Kerne himself felt like he was ready to be shot towards his fate.

As the mist began to slowly rise, Kerne could make out more and more of the small aircraft in neat rows by the airstrip: biplanes covered with tarpaulins to protect the canvas wings from condensation. Blue-overalled ground crew prepared selected machines for take-off. Silhouettes of pilots in bulky flying coats chatted to them, or idled by the mess shack with tin mugs of tea, waiting for orders or for the mist to clear. There was a strange atmosphere of both nonchalance and nervous tension, masked by the sangfroid and cocky bonhomie of the airmen, many of them not much older than schoolboys.

Kerne felt awkward and out of place. Wherever he stood, he seemed to be in the way, and so he waited by his car and hoped his pilot would show up soon. He knew nothing about him other than his name. Blane, the squadron leader whom he had spoke to on the telephone, had said he was one of their crack pilots and would be ideal for what they would be attempting – aerial surveillance of enemy positions. An intensive course in photography was lined up for Kerne in the next week, along with intensive basic training. Everything had to be accelerated, for the 'big push' was scheduled within seven days. The German forces were advancing west over Belgium: the British Expeditionary Force was expected to meet them before they reached France. The crisis had escalated with alarming rapidity, the sleepy status quo of peacetime England ruptured by escalating newspaper reports. Within days of Archduke Ferdinand's assassination Europe was at war. It had overwhelmed them all, and there was no escaping its consequences.

In the distance a rumbling grew, muffled by the mist still hanging heavy on the lower ground. Then there were several noises like gunshots, as though a pheasant shoot was taking place nearby. Kerne turned his head towards the road entrance just in time to see a man on a motorcycle emerge from the befogged hollow. He hooted at the airmen milling about outside the mess, and they raised arms in recognition, even though the figure was clad from head to foot in black leather, with goggles and long lappet headgear. The motorcycle arced around and came to a spluttering stop in front of Kerne. The rider dismounted and lifted the bike on to its stand before lifting up his goggles and freeing one hand from its gauntlet to offer to Kerne.

'Mallard, Harry Mallard, although the boys insist on calling me "Mad Duck". Pleased to meet you.'

Kerne shook his hand, and the grip was as tight as an iron clamp. He looked into the steel blue eyes haloed by the dust of the road. Mallard was in his early twenties but seemed to tower over Kerne. He spoke with a strong Yorkshire accent and had a touch of his Nordic ancestors about him.

'Isambard Kerne. Likewise.'

'It's bally chilly. Let's go in the mess for a mo' and get some Rosy Lee. I'm in need of one before we take to the skies.'

Kerne noticed the shadows under the pilot's eyes, which seemed, on closer inspection, a little bloodshot. And he had forgotten to shave too, by the looks of things. He absent-mindedly scratched his stubble as he led Kerne to the mess. He showed him into the simple corrugated-iron shack with a round, pot-bellied iron fire at one end, on which steamed a large black kettle. Armchairs of all shapes, sizes and stages of deterioration were scattered around it, with oil drums used as tables for card games and mugs. Airman lounged about, boots on the furniture. A gramophone played a saucy music-hall number on a scratched 78. The air was thick with pipe and cigarette smoke, musty clothes and the boozy bonhomie of a gentleman's club, although no liquor appeared to be in sight. A noticeboard was smothered with various memoranda. Images of beautiful women from art books and French postcards adorned the ramshackle walls.

'Oh, who looks like death warmed up,' quipped a red-haired officer with a pipe, upon seeing Mallard enter. 'Wasn't expecting to see you this morning, Mad Duck.'

'Good morning to you as well, Ginger. But not so loudly, if you don't mind. Bit of a pounder this morning. I knew that aqua vitae was a bit of a mistake.' There were a few chuckles as Ginger recounted the drinking match, saying something about Sassenachs not being able to handle their Scotch.

Mallard poured himself some tea, sniffing a pint of milk before adding some, then seemed to remember Kerne, who was standing in the doorway. 'Oh, by the way, lads, this is the new observer chap. Kingdom Brunel, or some such.'

'It's Kerne, Isambard Kerne.'

Everyone glanced over and waved. 'Come on in, old boy, and don't mind Mad Duck. He's got the manners of a goat,' explained Ginger. 'Get yourself a brew and warm the bones – it's going to be freezing up there this morning.'

Mallard handed Kerne a chipped mug. 'Sorry, I'm never myself until I've had a cuppa.' The pilot sloped off to a favourite armchair, and pulled off his motorcycle helmet, revealing a shock of blond hair.

'That's alright. Thanks.' Kerne poured himself some of the thick brown tea and sat down, glad to hold its cupped warmth. He seemed inappropriately dressed compared with the pilots, who all wore various combinations of jumpers, scarves, hats, gloves, thick coats, overalls and boots. Kerne wore his hiking gear, the only thing he'd been able to think of.

'Your first time, is it?' asked a young freckle-faced airman.

'Yes.'

'You'll soon get used to it. It's like sailing. It's the best feeling in the world.'

'Unless you hit turbulence,' added another, and they all guffawed.

'Don't get seasick, do you?'

Kerne shook his head. He wondered whether they were testing him, in their wry way, yet they seemed friendly enough. He looked over at Mallard and was horrified to see him pour something from a small bottle into his mug. When he saw Kerne looking, he raised his tea. 'Cheers.' He smiled defiantly, as if daring Kerne to challenge him. He had a ferocious grin.

'Mad Duck, on the G and tea already?' ribbed Ginger. 'Don't know how you can drink that stuff this time of the day. Turns my stomach.'

'If it stops his hands shaking, then it will mean you're in for a smoother ride,' muttered the young airman, but the record chose to stop at that precise moment and everyone heard.

'And I'm not the only one who needs their medicine, am I?' challenged Mallard.

There was a strained silence. Someone coughed. Others pretended to carry on playing cards.

'Calm down, old boy,' said Ginger, blowing a smoke ring. 'No one's criticising you. You're one of our best testers, and you know it.'

'Mad Duck, seeing red again?' commented a thin-faced man lurking in the shadows. 'You can see why we call him that, can't you?'

'And I think Kerne can guess why we nickname you "the Weasel"?' riposted Mallard.

Someone shouted, 'Mist is clearing.' There was a general sigh of relief, and the airmen began to shuffle to their feet, finishing off tea and taking any remaining tiffin with them.

'Think nothing of it,' said Ginger with a smile, emptying out his pipe. 'They're just like a lot of eagle chicks. The sooner they're airborne, the better. Good luck, Isambard.' They shook hands as he passed on the way out, and Kerne felt reassured.

Mallard downed the rest of his tea and Kerne did the same. He wanted all the warmth in him he could get. 'Come on then, mapman.' Mallard cuffed his shoulder with a flick of his gauntlets. 'You better borrow some overalls, otherwise you'll freeze.'

Putting his leather cap back on, Mallard swaggered over to the ground crew and spoke briefly to a man he called Allingham, a wiry, bright-faced man. The young engineer rummaged about and then passed Kerne some overalls. 'Sorry they're a bit oily.'

'They're fine. Thank you.' Kerne started pulling them on.

'I hear you're from Eastbourne. Me too.'

Kerne asked whereabouts, and they briefly discussed the merits and problems of the town and its districts. The engineer shook hands with Kerne, who mentioned that he was a civil engineer but had no idea how the aeroplanes worked. Trains were about his limit. Allingham chatted amicably as they walked over to the biplane Mallard was standing by.

'Give us a hand,' said the pilot.

Together they pulled back the tarpaulin to reveal the biplane underneath.

'Here she is: a Breguet. Not the fastest flyer in the sky, but a fine old bird.' He banged the fuselage. 'I call her "Sally", after a gal I knew back in York ...' For a moment he looked wistfully at the fuselage, then he gathered himself. 'But this one's far more reliable, I hope. Better give her the once-over.'

Mallard walked around inspecting the biplane, checking the undercarriage, the wings, and that the engine and exhausts were clear. 'We don't want any nesting birds.' he explained. 'Has she got fuel, Ally?'

'Filled her up myself before I put her to bed.'

'Good old Ally. Likes to look after his ladies as much as I do, eh?'

Allingham went red and Mallard laughed. Kerne was reminded of the rough camaraderie of the railway and kept a polite silence.

Mallard climbed into the cockpit and gestured to Kerne to get in. Kerne found it awkward clambering up the stepladder held by Allingham and then arranging himself in the confined space. 'It's a bit tight but you get used to it,' smiled the Eastbourne man.

'Here, you'll need these.' Mallard tossed back some red rubber goggles. 'It gets smoky sometimes and the wind hurts your eyes. Ally, rudders?'

'Check,' replied the engineer, watching the movement of the rudders as Mallard operated the controls.

'Righty-ho, let's take her up.'

Mallard nodded to Allingham, who flipped the propellers and stood back. The engine fired and died. 'Again'. The engineer repeated the action and this time the engine sparked into life. Whipping away the wooden chocks by a tug of the rope attaching them, Allingham stepped clear of the double wings and gave them the thumbs up.

Mallard taxied Sally over the dew-glittering grass towards the end of the airstrip.

Other biplanes were doing the same, each lining up for their turn. Kerne watched with admiration as, one by one, the biplanes took off, on training flights over Salisbury Plain and beyond, gleaming in the August sun like dragonflies.

The air was alive with the throb of the engines. Mallard tried to shout something to him, but Kerne misheard. It sounded like 'rush hour'. Then Mallard's window came, he was given the all-clear by the ground crew waving a flag in front of them, as though at a motor race, and they were off.

At first, Kerne thought the biplane was going to shake to bits as it rattled along the grass airstrip – seemingly as smooth as a cricket pitch from a distance. The whole aircraft seemed frail and ridiculous, a contraption as unlikely to get airborne as his father's skiff. Yet as Mallard gunned the engine and accelerated with alarming rapidity towards the end of the runway the vibrations decreased and suddenly, almost before Kerne realised it, had stopped altogether, to be replaced by an altogether different sensation. The surveyor looked over the side of his passenger seat to see the ground rapidly plummeting away. They were flying! It was a dreamlike sensation, as Kerne had felt on numerous occasions while lying next to Maud in their house at Goodridge Park. He had flown in his dreams and now he was flying in reality!

Mallard turned around and gave Kerne the thumbs up, grinning wildly. He seemed to come alive in the sky, a light came on in his eyes, and the sullen, shadow-eyed wreck in the mess seemed a bad dream. As they soared over the gilded fields, thick with mist-tangled wheat, it seemed that they had left their mortal selves behind and entered the domain of the gods.

'That', shouted Mallard, pointing down to the mess, workshop and offices with a gloved finger, 'is the dead side, and this' – he gestured over the airstrip and beyond – 'is the live side. I know which side I prefer.'

They soared over the earthworks of Old Sarum and Kerne could clearly see the foundations of the original cathedral, even through the rapidly thinning veil of morning mist. Every fold, every green lane, hillock and stream was becoming more defined in the light of the new day. The rolling folds of Salisbury Plain seemed to emerge from a Neolithic slumber, its barrows like islands in a receding sea.

Whether from the icy wind biting into his face, or the sheer exhilaration, Kerne found himself weeping – this God's-eye view of the land was what he had seen in his vision from Glastonbury Tor. In one flash he had seen the 'shining roads' as he'd described them to his fiancé – for that was the day he had proposed to Maud, New Year's Day, 1900 – the alignments criss-crossing the land like a lattice of light. He had suspected as much, having glimpsed the correspondence of one ancient site after another in his fieldwork for the GWR. In surveying a modern railway he had stumbled upon an ancient system of trackways and navigational aids used by the ancestral traveller. Perhaps they had been more than that – processional routes, lines of power, ways to the Otherworld, but his research had been curtailed by the start of the war. Who knew when he would be able to follow those lost roads again, or if?

For now, at least, as he soared past the outskirts of Salisbury, with its great spire at its heart like the hub of a wheel, he felt glad to be alive and to be where he was. He wanted to share his joy with Mallard – but the sheer noise of the engines, wind, rattling and thrumming of the biplane prevented all but the most rudimentary gestures and exchanges. Yet words alone would not do the experience justice. There was an unspoken joy and lightheartedness about it that words would trivialise. Here, all was dominated by the voice of the wind, which obliterated all other thought. The slightest air pocket would make the biplane buck, as though they rode an untamed steed. Mallard was constantly adjusting their flight path into the wind to compensate for the drift caused by the strong easterly. Kerne admired even more the birds of prey, the peregrine falcons he had seen once while walking on the coast of Dorset, which could hover in equilibrium with the wind, true masters of the air.

They headed south on what Mallard had called a 'bit of a spin'. He had promised they would be back in time for elevenses. Soon they were crossing a vast forest, and with excitement Kerne recognised it. The New Forest! He had often walked through it, in search of 'ways through the wood', but now he was flying over it.

Kerne checked the Ordnance Survey map slotted into a glass case in front of him, and it confirmed his supposition. His trained surveyor's eye soon spotted landmarks below: the shape of roads, settlements, the lay of the land. He quickly found his bearings and was delighted to discover his ability to orientate and survey translated extremely well to the skies. He felt as though he had reached a new level he had been grasping for all of his life.

The biplane startled a herd of dapple-haunched fallow deer crossing some heathland rising out of the forest. Suddenly they panicked and were leaping over the yellow gorse and purple heather, away from the noisy intruder. For a moment, it was like looking at a living tapestry. Not surprising, considering the New Forest was still very much a medieval landscape.

The quality of light began to change and Kerne looked ahead, past Mallard's head and the blur of propeller. They were heading towards the sea. It glittered on the horizon, a band of platinum light. The pilot had taken a straight line south from Old Sarum, and Kerne suddenly had an intimation where they were heading. The forest dwindled towards the coast, to be replaced by wetlands and scrubby dunes. Then the land gave away, like a rug pulled from under their feet and they were flying above water. As his gaze dropped to sea level Kerne's stomach plunged with the vertigo.

'Let's hope the engine doesn't pack up,' Mallard shouted back. 'I can't swim!'

This didn't reassure Kerne, although there was no doubt Mallard was a natural pilot. The biplane seemed an extension of him and to respond to his every mood or whim. He nosed her towards the white flanks of the Isle of Wight, a short way over the Solent. It looked like a fabled lost island on that hazy August day. Kerne had seen it in the distance from the so-called Isle of Purbeck when walking on Studland Heath with Maud on their honeymoon, yet he had never visited the place, until now.

Mallard banked the plane towards the west and flew in a wide arc around the stacks known as The Needles, offering his passenger a spectacular view of them, although in his open-topped seat Kerne perhaps appreciated the bird's-eye view less than he should have. Their tiny craft felt so vulnerable above the jagged rocks. Far below, the deep blue waves churned around the rocks, white spumes reaching upwards, as if calling the airmen into their embrace.

Just when Kerne's nerves couldn't take much more the biplane straightened out and headed back inland, bearing north. Once more over terra firma, Kerne felt safer, although he was unnerved by Mallard's constant scanning for suitable crash-landing sites.

'You never know if you're going to stall her. I've had to bring the old bird down a few times in farmers' fields and the like.'

Kerne was glad he saved this anecdote until after they were back, 'on the dead side', in the mess. This time he joined his pilot for glasses of 'G and tea', which they clinked together, Kerne's hand still shaking from the adrenalin.

'Well, here's to us. I've just been informed by Blane that we're to be crewed together on the first run into France. We're going to get on just fine and dandy, aren't we?'

A log shifted in the fire, breaking Kerne's trance-like gaze. How long he had been staring into the flames he did not know. His surroundings were a distant blur of activity. He cast a dead-eyed glance down at the hands hanging loose in his lap, noticing abstractly the bloody bandage around one of them. The congealed blood cracked when he moved the hemp gauze, making him wince with pain. He turned over the hand and saw the other side was equally as bloody – like an RFC roundel, a red ring around a black core. Then he felt a dull throb at his brow and with the other hand gingerly felt another bandage at his temple. Where he had received these wounds he could not immediately remember, or did not want to.

Someone placed a blanket around his shoulders, the grey wool coarse but warm. Kerne looked up and saw a woman in a green robe with a concerned look in her eyes. She seemed to be asking him if he was alright, if she could get him anything.

Kerne tried to gauge his feelings, but he only felt numb. He tried to speak and, at first, he managed nothing but a dry croak. His tongue was thick. His mouth seemed full of dust. He cleared his throat and articulated the request. 'Water. I would like some water, please.' The woman in green nodded and went away.

Other people were sitting around the fire, equally injured and forlorn. Kerne wondered who they were, what terrible thing had befallen them. But an insistent voice, which he tried to deny, hissed the answer: *he had*.

The woman returned with a chipped clay beaker of water. Kerne thanked her with a weak smile. Why was she being kind to him?

When she saw him sip the water she seemed satisfied and left. It was icy and clear, trickling down his throat like a thin waterfall down a bare mountainside. It made his head ache, but it served to awaken him a little. Painfully, awareness of his whereabouts and predicament returned.

He was sitting at a campfire on the banks of the Da'anu, by the blacksmiths' huts, which had become a makeshift field hospital for all the casualties pouring in from up and down the river. The dark waters had subsided since the flood, but still seemed surly, like an angry beast disturbed from its slumber, rankled, slowly settling down. In the red light of the sunset, its surface looked like bronze. Opposite, the dark buttress of Moot Holm brooded, its grove silent, its flanks deathly still. No one had wished to step foot on it since the last stand. All survivors and all activity had converged on the hospital of forges. Yet, as Kerne looked at the bedraggled refugees and casualties, the weary warriors, exhausted healers, and families broken by grief, he wondered if the Children of Da'anu could ever be mended again.

Kerne spotted dark-haired Baramis the Scythian helping to organise things. He exuded a stable strength and confidence amidst the despair and suffering. Not surprising, considering he had witnessed as much inflicted on his own people by the Grey Raiders. If anyone could mend the unmendable, the iron blacksmith could, thought Kerne. He had done something right, at least, in inviting him to the Valley of the Chalk Folk. One white mark then, but so many black.

There was a familiar squawk and the falcon fluttered down on to a wood pile beside him. Kerne ignored the bird at first, jaws set, glaring into the flames.

'How's the great hero then?' asked Merlin.

Kerne remained silent.

'Hmph, looks like you'll live, though it seems you lost your tongue in the battle. Not much of a windsmith without one.'

'For once, hold *your* tongue, Merlin,' Kerne seethed. 'You have said and done enough.'

Merlin seemed nonplussed by Kerne's rage and smoothed his feathers with his beak. 'Yes, I was there when you needed me.'

'There when you needed me!' Kerne spluttered in fury. 'You come and go as you please, then drop that despicable weapon into my lap so I can murder my friend!'

'Your "friend" is he now? Was he your friend, this Madoc, when he shot Setanta or Ogmios?'

The death of Ogmios came back to him in brutal detail. It made him bite his lip and he gripped the edge of the log he sat on, knuckles white.

Merlin awkwardly attempted to speak in more soothing tones. 'Your mentor's loss was great, but his sacrifice was not in vain. He broke the Cauldron of the Dead and closed that particular gateway to Annwn. His memory will live on. And you must be sure it does. Remember what he has taught you, or the chain of tradition will be broken. And remember what he meant to you. Compose him an elegy worthy of a great windsmith. He is to be buried in three days along with the rest of the fallen, in new barrows on the Hills of Peace. Do not let your old friend down. This is the ultimate test for a windsmith. Is your memory stronger than death? Can you make your loved ones live through your song? I do not care if you insult me with silence, but do not insult Ogmios. Perhaps I will see you when you're in a more amenable mood.'

Merlin flapped away into the darkening sky.

The survivors around the fire looked at the airman with fear in their eyes. He had spoken with thunder. Could he now speak for those at peace?

He stood up, a little unsteady on his feet. Those nearest to him flinched back. He looked at them puzzled.

'Why?' His voice carried over the crackle of the fire in the dusk. 'Why are you afraid of me?' Their hollow eyes burnt into him. As he turned to face the circle the blanket fell from his shoulders and he realised what they were staring at.

The Webley sat in its holster – a heavy load at his hip.

Kerne tried to undo the holster clip with his bandaged hand and cursed in pain. Quickly, he pulled out the gun with his other hand. 'This? Is this what you're scared of? This blasted thing?' He waved it violently and the onlookers cowered, eyes wide. 'It's nothing more than a piece of metal.'

By now, half the camp was looking at him, a madman in the twilight with a gun. He realised he must look like Madoc. And for a moment he felt closer to his pilot than to the Chalklanders: his fellow Englishman, the only one to share his experience. Together they had crossed and each had found his destiny waiting. When they had set off on their reconnaissance mission, that fateful August morning so long ago, little had they expected to end up discovering the dark side of their souls.

Kerne saw Baramis watching him, hand resting lightly on his bow.

'Only blacksmiths should handle such iron,' called out Kerne wryly. 'They are used to getting their fingers burnt, isn't that right, my friend?'

The Scythian nodded grimly, watching him with steady intensity, his hand resting lightly on his bow.

And with that Kerne cast the Webley contemptuously into the river. He watched it spin in the air, arcing up and then down to disappear with a splash. The dark waters seemed to whisper, but what they said Kerne could not catch on the wind.

The airman fell to his knees, empty now and numb.

As the waters settled, Kerne reflected sadly that he did not even know if his pilot had had a family. He realised then that he hadn't really known Mallard at all. Had anyone mourned him back in England? A parent, a sibling, a sweetheart, a son? No one would mourn his passing here – that was for certain.

No one, except Kerne.

He did not mourn what Mallard had become, but what he had once been – as innocent as Kerne had been, as innocent as they had all been, before the war.

'Rest in peace, my friend,' he whispered to the dark river. 'And may I, and may I.'

31

Nine Barrows

The barrows had been raised in the three days since the floodwaters had subsided. They stood in a row on the Hills of Peace, pristine chalk packed firm into bell-shaped mounds – one for each party affected to mourn their fallen at. The toll was heavy: Tuan, Tawrk, Macha, Setanta, Ogmios plus the three other windsmiths who had died; a massive tomb for the two hundred and eighty-seven Bronze Warriors who fought so valiantly; and a pair of mounds for the Metenaidd fatalities, the hundred and fifty Tuns and Plwms. They stood in line with the mound of Bron, facing west towards Mount Anu, the White Mother.

On a drear morning at summer's end the survivors from each tribe gathered on the bleak slopes, exhausted from their three days of toil, of mound-building and grieving. The physical exertion had helped them work through the initial shock of bereavement, the soil in their hands had been healing, and the support of their immediate community strengthening. Each tribe raised a mound for its lost; reminding Kerne of something he had written once: 'It may take a village to raise a child, but it may also take a village to bury the dead.' The tribe of Caer Dagda raised a mound for their fallen chief, Tuan. His heir was his nephew – a youth with golden hair called Maddon, who surveyed the proceedings with a moody awareness of his destiny and new status.

The Morrigan raised a mound for their beloved chieftainess, Macha, burying her with a bronze chariot and gold horse trappings. Their horses helped move the earth in giant leather scoops.

The people of Caer Henwen raised a mound for their avuncular chief, Tawrk, wept for by his several wives and children. Their fabled culinary skills would supply the feast for the funeral games to follow.

The remaining Wardogs of Setanta laid to rest their chief in a fine mound. At his side, to accompany him on his journey, lay his faithful hound, Drudwyn – who had been found limp over his body, having dragged him out of the flood's reach, bursting his heart in the process. The warriors howled like dogs pining for their master, and they howled for their fallen comrades washed away in the deluge.

The many Bronze Warriors who had given their lives to save the valley were buried in a mass grave together, for all to mourn at. Every caer had lost a son or daughter in the battle. Though it was not a grave of chieftains, the mound for the warriors was the largest of all, twenty feet high, a hundred feet across. All had helped build it, chieftain and serf alike.

The two tribes of the Metenaidd who had lost men, the Tuns and Plwms, raised their own mounds – for the first time upon the Hills of Peace – helped by their fellows, the Copors and Arianedd. Traditionally, they buried their dead in their own secret valleys. But this war had been bigger than them all and its victims deserved to be buried together, side by side, so this particular corner of the Da'anu Valley would be for ever remembered as the Field of the Five Rivers, to mark where the blood of the five tribes mixed in death.

The four windsmiths who had been lost were buried together in a single mound – Senach, Morann, Gwyllt and Ogmios – raised by the nine remaining wood-priests and their acolytes. Kerne helped as best he could with his wounded hand. Its stigma-like hole was nothing compared with the hole left in his heart by his mentor's death.

Nine barrows: many lives, many threads of fate. Now they stood in a single line, pointing towards the sunset that gilded the inviolate flanks of Mount Anu with blood-gold.

A skirl of pipes played as the great host stood silently in the biting east wind, sharp with the tang of winter. The sun was impaled on the peaks of the Bone Mountains; its dying light leaked over the land, tainting the chalk mounds pink, the hills crimson. Cloaks and blankets flapped in the seething wind. The survivors held one another, arms around shoulders, or holding hands.

Tears fell like a gentle rain, watering the soil. Come the snowmelt of spring, flowers would grow there. The barrows themselves seemed to bloom in the dusk, the remaining light drawn to them so they glowed with preternatural radiance.

Kerne remembered the glowing blooms he had found behind the waterfall shortly after his arrival. He still carried the one he had picked, pressed between the pages of his journal. When he had regained consciousness after the confrontation in the Drunemetom and had seen the body of his mentor lying before him he had wanted to use his flower on Ogmios, but the other windsmiths stop-ped him – for there was a geas against using it on their own kind.

What use then was such power? He hadn't been able to save his mentor, or the many others slain in the War of Metal, as it was already becoming known. Iron had clashed with Bronze and the effect had been as devastating as it must have been in prehistory, the same cycle of horror repeated here in the Afterlands. And the airmen had brought the virus of war. It was Kerne's very own bullets that had slain Setanta, Ogmios and others – fired from Madoc's gun, yes, but *he* had supplied the ammunition. How much blood was on his hands?

Was this the Way of the Windsmith? Merlin had told him he had to choose words, not swords, as his weapon in the fight against Taranis. Yet he had been corrupted by the conflict into what he despised most. Kerne felt anger surge within him. He could hear himself arguing with his old mentor, only to have his questions dissolved by his tough, loving wisdom. Ogmios would mock such doubts, Kerne was sure. Had not the war been won? Had not the valley of the ancestors been saved? If a price had to be paid for that precious peace, then so be it.

Kerne gazed hard at the silent mound. Surrounding it were the remaining windsmiths, wearing tattered blue cloaks over clean white robes put on after the mound-building had finished. They chanted a dirge in deep monotonous voices. They had performed the burial rite for each of the mounds and now they did it for their own. Each windsmith was exhausted and fatigued with grief. Their gaunt faces were wrinkled and stubbly. They all looked years older. Yet each one reminded Kerne of Ogmios. He could see him so clearly whenever he shut his eyes. As the dirge finally faded, Kerne stepped forward to declaim his elegy for Ogmios, which he'd composed in his head over the last three days while the mounds were being raised:

Ogmios Honeytongue, bitter the world without you.
Your death has meant eloquence has died;
No more the ears of men will be chained to your tongue,
No more shall your sunface lighten our darkened minds.
Gone the warrior of words,
Gone the poet of his people.
His club is beneath the mound now;
No longer will its gems shine in the fire circle.
Unstrung is the bow,
Broken are the arrows.
The cauldron is sundered

By your strength.
You plugged the path of the dead
With your body.
Mighty the limbs that cracked the tyrant's bowl,
Mighty the club that cracked the enemy's skull.
Gone now are the words of wisdom,
Gone now the breath of magic.
Silent the sacred grove,
Lightning struck the kingly oak.
It will shed no more acorns,
But its awen will live on.
Your name remembered always,
Ogmios Honeytongue, Ogmios Sunface,
May you find Gwynedd, may you find peace.

Kerne fell silent. Never since his schooldays had he composed a poem, let alone performed in public, and from memory to boot; but he had not been unchanged by his time in HyperEurus. He had learnt the art of the windsmith, though he was aware he had only mastered one wind. Yet now he had found his own windlass – his own key to unlock the gateways. His wife had her songs, while he had his verse. It would be his guide and ally. He had grown up in a household of song and verse, his Welsh Chapel mother singing her hymns and his father reciting Irish legends. Something, it seemed, had rubbed off on him.

It would appear the spirit of Ogmios Honeytongue did indeed live on.

The undead, those which had not been washed into the fathomless Mandorla, Kerne had insisted were given proper burial. The evil enchantment that had animated them had faded, and the battered corpses scattered along the flood line had looked frail and pathetic, so much so that even the Chalk Folk pitied them. Their respect for the dead was deeply ingrained. Once, each cadaver had been someone's father, brother, husband, friend. Their nationality was not important any more; their uniforms were ruined beyond recognition. They had not chosen to fight in this shadow war. They deserved to be laid to rest decently. Some of the survivors still feared them, remembering the horror, but they would not insult the dead, not even their enemy's. They did not want angry ghosts seeking vengeance. All debts were paid, duties discharged in this great levelling. All were united in death – mourning or mourned for. The bones had been piled high and a mass cairn had been raised on Moot Holm, for no tribe wanted it near their caer.

Of Madoc's body nothing was to be found.

All that was left of his existence were the metal plates of the cauldron, broken into their original biplane panels by Ogmios's last effort. The panels had been carefully stored and guarded. All but one had been recovered: the fourteenth, which bore the roundel of the Royal Flying Corps, had been washed away in the flood.

The pipers began to lead the gathered in a spiral procession around the nine barrows. The mourners intertwined like Celtic knotwork, thought Kerne – the chain of life, weaving together, stronger together than alone, the threads of the community rewoven. And in a snaking line, the procession made its sombre way down to the caer of Partholon, where a great feast had been prepared in Salmon Hall.

Between two fires the procession descended in the gathering dusk, like the herd of the Donn driven from their summer pasture to their winter pasture. This year the slaughtered were the people's own kith and kin. This year the feast of the dead would be for their own loved ones, recently departed. The ancestors would be honoured too, as always: their heads would be brought out and given pride of place on the tables, candles lit inside their skulls. Together, the living and the dead would feast.

Kerne had to remind himself that *all* the Chalk Folk were dead, that they were acting out the ceremonies and rituals of their lifetime. The ancestors were mourning their own. He could not avoid a growing sense of guilt, for should he not also be dead? Had not his presence in the Afterlands been paid for by another? His life had been bought with Madoc's death – at his own hands. His wound still ached, his bandage like a badge of blood, a constant reminder of his deed.

Bright fires awaited them. Long tables were adorned with the last of the apples, and rainbows of berries, piles of nuts – the bounty of the thickets and the forests. The guests were offered beakers of spiced ale by Partholon's household. Then all sat down to a banquet of hot broth and freshly baked bread, buttered vegetables and roasted meats, prepared by Tawrk's wives.

The feasting and carousing blurred around Kerne – a forced merriment to banish the shadow of death, to encourage the continuation of life. All were lost in the melancholy dreaming of the music. They played the goltai, one of the Three Strains, the strain of sorrow, haunting and heartbreaking. As the melody faded, other musicians –

tin whistlers and drummers beating crude drums on wooden hoops covered with pigskin – took up the tune and changed it. A man with a bandaged eye played polished bones upon his knee, clicking them together in syncopation to the reel, and the wakers began to sway and dance. Kerne looked at him and thought of Ogmios One-Eye and his sunny demeanour. He had a duty to celebrate his life properly, as befitted a great windsmith. He asked for his mead horn to be filled, stood up and raised a toast.

'To Ogmios!' he roared.

'To Ogmios!'

The battle-wounded watched with a glee as the maidens danced for them, tossing their skirts and hair. All were heroes and all would be favoured by the Goddess that night.

The massive frame of the Donn reared up at the head of the mead bench where he'd been sitting with the remaining chiefs – Brigantia, Nemain, Cormac, Arthus, Saar, Cyndyn, Eryr and the host Partholon – and silence respectfully fell.

The Bull Chief had been scarred across the cheek, and limped from a wound to his thigh, but he was still full of life and mighty of frame.

'Chalk Folk, hear me! We have won a great victory. A victory bought dearly with the lives of our loved ones. The War of Metal is over. This is a peace we must cherish. We have a duty to savour every moment, or we insult their memory. Tonight, celebrate for them. Celebrate because you have made your ancestors proud. Celebrate because you have defended this sacred land we live in. Celebrate tonight, and tomorrow return to your homes to rebuild your lives. We have much work to do to prepare for winter. This is the feast of Samhain – what more fitting time to honour our dead? Let their memory live on through us!'

When the cheers had died down the Donn continued: 'I was chosen your war chief for this battle. I hope I have fulfilled my duties sufficiently. The lives lost will always haunt me. No one could have been prepared for what we faced. We were outnumbered and outmatched. Not only were our weapons inadequate against the iron, but we faced the war zombies. No man could match them, whatever his prowess. And do not deny it, there were many feats of valour: Tawrk's defence of his caer, Macha's last ride at Caer Minas, Setanta's attack on the iron ships, and Cormac's wolf-strike. We are glad you did not get washed away, old friend!'

'Let it be known, this wolf can swim when he needs to!' Cormac replied, and the company roared with laughter.

'And I am glad of that, but, alas, there were many who could not … Both Bronze and Iron were washed away in the flood and we mourn those who fell, but I have no doubt, it was the only way to rid us of that vast army of both the quick and the dead. The windsmiths strategy worked, though they paid a heavy toll also.'

The Donn nodded to the wood-priests, who sat at their own table. They raised their hands to receive his blessing.

'The sacrifice of Ogmios will never be forgotten. Nor the courage of the skyman. Windsmith Kerne, you have proved your mettle. You have the heart of a Da'anun. If we doubted and feared you at first, you cannot blame us, but you showed how different you are from that mad tyrant. You saved us all from destruction. Bron, that mighty stag chief – how I miss him so – would have been proud of you. To Kerne!'

'To Kerne!'

The eyes of the hall were upon him, tankards and mead horns raised, and Kerne was humbled and struck speechless. It was the first time he had been called a windsmith in public. Ogmios would have been proud. A lump came to Kerne's throat. All he could do was nod and raise his own flagon in thanks.

'And let us not forget the deeds of our own chiefs and champions: Arthus, who protected the families; Brigantia and Brak, who helped fend off the legions; Saar, whose tireless efforts eased the suffering of the wounded; Eryr, for his counsel and insight; Nemain, formidable in battle…'

'May I announce that my new champion is Bronwen!' declared the Morrigan battle queen.

A cheer went up. Bronwen blushed – for once not wearing her white warface. She wore instead battle scars on her cheeks. Thwarted from exacting her revenge upon Madoc, she had taken it out on his men. Kerne had seen her at Dagda's Cauldron, culling heads, implacable.

'And of course, thank you', said the Bull Chief, 'to our gracious host, Partholon, and to Cyndyn – for supplying this feast.'

Kerne caught the eye of Partholon on the dais in the smoky shadows across the hall, and the Salmon Chief acknowledged him with a gracious nod.

'Finally, my friends, I have one more duty to perform, and that is to end my duties as your war chief. I am needed no longer. The valley is safe. I gladly relinquish the authority given me. Thank you for placing your trust in me.'

A deafening cheer went up, and everyone stood to toast the Donn, who for once looked abashed.

When the din had died down, Partholon stood up. 'Good people, we have peace and hard won it was, but for how long? The Horse Nomads are leaderless. How long will they stay on their side of the lake?' There was an uneasy murmur as the Salmon Chief looked at them with his watery eyes. 'Will they forget their defeat? We need a high king, to rule over all. Such a king or queen will unify the lands. The chiefs will not lose authority in their own cares, but will pay fealty to the chosen liege. We need to look after the tribes that have lost their chieftains while they recover. We must contribute grain to a relief fund. A high king could oversee this and coordinate the clear-up. What say you?'

There was an awkward silence at first, then Brigantia stood up, resplendent in black and gold, and spoke with a clear voice that rang out across the hall, piercing the hearts of the listeners: 'The wood-priest speaks with hazel-wisdom. If this awful war has taught us anything it is that together we stand, divided we fall. What is a land without a ruler? It is like a body without a head. I, for one, vote for a high king – or queen.' The Caer Chief of Cernunnos sat down in a flurry of reaction, and then one by one the other chieftains slowly gave their assent to the proposal.

A representative of the windsmiths stood up. It was Simias, the surviving eldest of the nine. 'Then we must have a Tarbh Feis to choose the high king. A bull must be slain and one of our number will drink its blood and a broth made from its gore, and then he will prophesy.'

'Very well, it is agreed,' said Partholon. 'When the moon is next full we shall hold a bull feast. For now, eat, drink and be merry! For the dead live through you!'

32

The Bull Feast

The stench of blood and smoke was in the air for days after the bone fires had died down, the herds having been driven through them to ward off bad spirits. The highland cattle were tended by the Donn's Bullmen in times of peace. Every Samhain the herd was brought down from their high summer pasture in the foothills of the Bone Mountains to the rolling downlands by the lake. Those that were not to be kept, whether because of illness or age, were slain and their meat salted. It was a critical time: the lives of the Chalk Folk depended upon storing enough supplies to last the hard winter that would sweep off the Steppe. This year one bull was held back – a magnificent creature of with ochre-dappled white hide. It was the pride of the Donn's herd and it was to be sacrificed for the Tarbh Feis.

In the ruins of the Drunemetom a round wattle hut of the quicken tree was constructed. In this the chosen would sleep off the feast, wrapped in the hide of the bull, and dream of the One Who Must Rule while the windsmiths chanted over him.

The sacred bull was taken to the enclosure. All that remained was for the bull-feaster to be selected.

There was argument among the tribes as to who it should be. Normally, such a duty would be the jurisdiction of the windsmiths, but none of the Chalk Folk trusted another chief's windsmith to be completely unbiased. And the nine remaining windsmiths were reluctant to take on this onerous task: if they were selected as the bull-feaster and did *not* choose their chief as the high king or queen, they might be cursed by their own tribe, yet if they *did* then they might be accused of falsehood – punishable by death. The bull-feaster had to be someone who had no vested interest in one particular tribe winning the kingship. An outsider.

There was only one person it could be. Although Baramis the black-smith archer had been accepted by the Chalk Folk after his gift of swords and the sharing of his craft, and the Donn had gifted him four gold tresses to show their appreciation, it was too soon to let him decide something so momentous. The Scythian was busy overseeing the reconstruction of the forges by Moot Holm. Thanks to him the valley was entering the Iron Age. He would be busy for some time to come.

That left only one other.

It was a biting cold morning as Kerne lay in Ogmios's hut, gazing at the sacred fire he had dutifully kept burning, reminiscing sadly about his one-eyed mentor and meditating on the mysterious last gesture he had made, Ruis – the five-finger sigil for elder, the sign of ancestral memory, of death and rebirth – when there was a horn blast from outside. It was not a bullhorn of battle but it still made Kerne jump out of his skin. Ever since the War of Metal the sound of horns had haunted him.

Scratching his thick beard, wearing the same dun-hued woollen shirt and plaid breeches he had for a week, Kerne got up and, wrapping a mangy fur cloak around his shoulders, went to the entrance.

Wind dogs played about his heels, stirring the dust, excited by his movement. For days he had lain in bed, in the darkness, and not even their antics had been able to amuse him. The death of his mentor had left him bereft and numb. Only in the oldsmith's lodge did Ogmios still feel close, his presence in every object. Kerne had brooded for days on his demise. His sacrifice had destroyed the war cauldron and had saved the Chalk Folk from the legion of undead. Yet why did he have to die so they could live? Had there been another motive behind Ogmios's sacrifice? It had certainly given Kerne sufficient rage to shoot Madoc. He still could not accept what he had done. He had taken a human life. Even worse, the life of someone who had once been his friend. Kerne had reacted instinctively. It had been a crime of passion. And it had been for the survival of his own ancestors the Chalk Folk, and of HyperEurus and all its people, and perhaps even of his own world – for the rift would have overwhelmed Earth eventually, if Llyr and Merlin were to be believed. But this made the pain of his deed no less.

The horn blast still ringing in his ears, Kerne lifted up the hide flap and squinted in the stark winter light. The enclosure was covered in frost. Silhouetted against the blinding glare were the nine remaining windsmiths. They stood in a semicircle, dressed in white, but with thick blue cloaks about their frames. Each wielded a staff made from their respective sacred oak. A gold lunula, horned like the moon, shone on each chest.

Their horn-bearer stepped aside, an acolyte in brown robes.

Curious villagers sidled over to see what was going on, but kept a respectful distance. The windsmiths were feared and needed no guard.

'Windsmith Kerne,' declaimed their newly appointed chief, Simias. 'You have been selected by the grove to partake of the bull feast.'

There was a murmur of surprise from the eavesdropping tribespeople, followed by nods of approval and even pride. The Stag tribe had adopted Kerne as their own; they were proud to have the slayer of Taranis within their walls.

'Do you accept this honour?'

The eyes of the nine bore into him.

Kerne blinked, blearily. He wasn't expecting this. He did not feel worthy of this sacred duty. He had not washed or eaten for days. He scratched at a louse in his greasy beard. Brak and Bronwen had tried to raise his spirits but they had seen that his soul sickened. They assumed Kerne was mourning for Ogmios, as they all were. But that was only part of the story.

Kerne was still haunted by the look on Madoc's eyes as he shot him. *His pilot.* The only other person in this world who shared his experience of coming from the twentieth century, of being alive in the land of the dead. That was why Madoc had to die, he kept telling himself ... Yet, there was no denying, he had his friend's blood upon his hands. His wounded palm would always remind him of that, a stigma he had to bear.

And now the windsmiths expected him to perform this sacred duty. But as he looked at each one of them in turn, seeing their belief in him, in the logic of their choice, he knew it made sense. He had killed one king, so he must find another.

'What is your answer?'

'Yes,' he croaked. Then clearer: 'Yes, I accept this task.'

On the eve of the full moon, three days later, Kerne stood in the remains of the Drunemetom in front of the wattle hut hastily erected for the bull feast. The airman had been washed, his beard shaven off, hair untangled and tied back, face and arms painted with sigils, and his body dressed in a breechclout and a simple white robe. A large fire burned inside the ring of broken oaks. Suspended on a tall metal tripod over it was a cauldron decorated with spiral patterns. The white speckled bull was held by two of the windsmiths, Uscias and Morfessa, by a halter attached to its nose ring. A third, Bladud, wielded a sickle that flashed gold in the firelight. The other six formed a crescent. Behind them stood the surviving chieftains of the Chalk Folk – Brigantia, Arthus, Partholon, Eryr, Cormac, Saar, Nemain, Cyndyn and the Donn – each resplendent in their ancestral regalia.

Simias spoke: 'Isambard Kerne, you are charged with a sacred duty: to choose a high king or queen from the chieftains of the Chalk Folk to rule over the peoples of HyperEurus in peace and wisdom. The sacred bull is tethered. From its pure body a broth shall be brewed, which you must imbibe until you are glutted. Then you must lie down in the hurdle enclosure, wrapped in its bloody hide, and dream of the liege to rule us all. We shall chant the spell of truth over you. When you rise on the morrow, you must speak your prophecy. And let it be known the Bull-Feaster will perish if he speaks false. Do you accept this sacred duty?'

'I do.'

'Then let the Tarbh Feis begin!'

Acolytes lifted the white robe from Kerne's shoulders. He shivered in the chill winter air, now naked but for the breechclout, the green spirals on his chest and the feathers attached to his arms by gut.

Simias nodded at Bladud, who sliced the bull's throat with the sickle. It let out a moan of distress and shook its head as if to rid itself of a stinging insect. The rich lifeblood gushed from its gaping neck to be caught in a bowl beneath. The mighty bull staggered and fell to its knees, as if genuflecting, offering its blood. It let out a long low note, then toppled over, making the ground shudder. It rasped, twitched and then fell still and silent – steaming in the coolness of dusk.

Bald, bare-chested acolytes set to work to butcher the bull and casting its joints into the bubbling water of the cauldron. Soon the stench of boiling meat permeated the damp air. Simias lifted the bowl of blood and took it to Kerne.

'Our sacrifice has been made, in the name of the Lord and Lady of All. Drink of the sacred life force. Let the awen flow.'

Kerne accepted the dark wooden bowl and raised it to his mouth. His stomach churned at the prospect. He had never been fond of red meat, but it was too late for such qualms. The fate of a kingdom was at stake. He took a draught of the hot blood, choking at first, blood spluttering from his mouth. The arch-windsmith looked at him sternly. Drums began to beat in the background. Kerne felt the pressure build. He closed his eyes and drank deep, swallowing all he could until the blood ran down his neck, on to his torso. The hot blood surged within him. He staggered, coughing. Simias took the bowl back and turned it upside down, showing it was empty. The crowd cheered.

Only the entrails and hide of the bull remained steaming on the grass. Thighbones stuck out of the vat, dripping with juice. When the broth was cooked, four acolytes threaded stout staves through the handles, lifted the cauldron off its hook and brought it before Kerne. A silver ladle was placed next to it. Kerne had fasted for three days, and so hunger overcame his repulsion and he began to pluck out meaty ribs and devour them. The cooked flesh burnt his lips at first, but tasted surprisingly good. As the drumming grew louder, and the blood throbbed in his ears, Kerne gorged himself on the hot meat – his hands slippery with blood and grease. Finally, bloated, he slumped to the ground and dropped the ladle. He felt if he ate another mouthful he would throw up. Not an auspicious sign. He tried to stop the grove spinning around him.

Windsmiths brought the bull hide, blood congealed upon its inside, and wrapped him in it. It was warm and sticky but after the initial nausea felt almost comforting.

In a drunken manner, Kerne staggered into the wattle hut and fell on the floor into a deep trance as the dull throb of drumming mixed with the chanting of the spell of truth. The windsmiths seemed to be inside his skull, their incantation reaching into his very soul. It was as if they eavesdropped on his every thought. There was no longer any division between man, bull, windsmith, grove. Kerne felt connected to it all. Skinless, he floated above his body. Looking down, he saw it lying in the bloody hide, shuddering, covered in gore. He felt weight-less and strangely detached from it, with its heavy belly and soiled robe. A shining silver thread connected him to the body and he almost felt tempted to sever that thread, to disown his tainted flesh, and drift off, but he knew he must protect that link. His very life depended on it. The windsmiths had trained him for this. Each had come to him over the three days of his fast, with advice, and to pay their respects to the memory of Ogmios in his dwelling. So now, like a climber, or a deep-sea diver, he ascended as his lifecord was paid out …

Kerne flew over the valley, seeing the caers lit up with hearth fires, the chalk giants illuminated by the moon, the barrows of the dead on the Hills of Peace. He felt a tug of strange homesickness for it all as he passed beyond the valley into the vast night.

The Bone Mountains glowed in the moonlight. Kerne soared towards their peaks, returning upriver to the Da'anu's source, to the horsetail of waterfall, shimmering silver; retracing his steps to the start of his journey in the land of the dead – a land that felt more alive, more vivid, more beautiful and passionate than the world he had known before.

Ascending to the summit of Mount Anu, Kerne saw the whole of HyperEurus spread out below him far as the eye could see into the east – the Da'anu Valley, Lake Mandorla, the Red Hills and, beyond, the Steppe, endless and untamed.

Curious, Kerne looked west, but was dazzled by the moon. There seemed only void beyond the ridge of mountains. The snow-capped peaks shone with reflected radiance. At their centre was a circle of crags. Within it stood a ring of Feathered Ones: tall men in cloaks of shimmering feathers. Kerne recognised the place where he had first emerged from limbo yet this time the ice statues were *alive*. Kerne's heart leapt for joy – among their number he saw Ogmios! Unbroken by death, standing clear-eyed, he glowed with an uncanny light.

Kerne floated down towards them. 'Ogmios, you're alive!'

Ogmios shook his head. '*No, my friend, I have passed on to the inner realms.*' His familiar voice seemed distant and inside Kerne at the same time. '*I have become one of the Guardians. Don't you realise by now? Nothing ever really ends …*'

Another voice came: '*Isambard Kerne, you have been appointed a sacred duty, the Tarbh Feis. You have come here to discover the identity of the One Who Must Rule.*'

Kerne turned to the mightiest of the Feathered Ones. He was fierce to look upon, there was an icy will there, and a wildness in his tangled hair and, beneath dark brows, eyes piercing to the core. Yet there was depthless wisdom there also and disciplined power. Kerne recognised the deep, clear, slightly mocking Scots voice.

'Merlin, is that you?'

The Bird Priest nodded. '*On the inner planes I retain my true form.*'

Kerne recognised Morann, Senach, Gwyllt also – the windsmiths who had fallen in battle. He felt humbled in their presence.

'*You must not dally,*' Ogmios warned. '*Your silver cord dwindles constantly as long as you linger here. If you stay too long you will not be able to return.*'

'Then what is your answer? Who shall be high king?'

'*We have dreamed deeply upon this,*' said the windsmiths. '*It cannot be one of the chieftains, noble as they are.'*

'It must be an outsider,' said Ogmios.

Kerne thought for a moment they meant him. 'I – I cannot accept this duty.' And for the first time, there on the summit of the Bone Mountains, with the world spread out below him, Kerne could see his destiny clearly: to travel to the four corners of Shadow World and master the four winds. This is my alignment, he resolved. And this alone.

'Yes, your destiny lies elsewhere,' replied Merlin, as if he had heard him speak. *'You cannot be the one. It must be someone whom both sides of the lake will respect. The Horse Nomads will never submit to a Chalklander chief, even less to an outlander.'*

'Then who else can it be?'

'Think, Kerne. Whom have you met who most embodied the balance needed to bring these tribes into balance?' asked Ogmios.

Kerne thought back to all whom he had met. Then the answer came, as clear as Mirrormoon itself.

'The King in the Lake! But he's a salmon ...'

'You must find a way to make him remember the man he once was, and prove to him the people of HyperEurus have learned the folly of war.'

The Feathered Ones slowly nodded.

'Now, quickly, go!' bade Ogmios. *'Your life-thread fades!'*

'Farewell, Feathered Ones. May I one day see you all again.'

Kerne began to float off.

'You will, windsmith; you will.'

Kerne fled back over the moonlit mountains, down towards the Valley of the Chalk Folk, past the palisaded silhouettes of the torchlit caers, until he was descending back into the Drunemetom, back into the wattle hut, back into his pale shivering body. A fire burnt outside the quicken enclosure. There he slept, exhausted, until daylight. When he awoke, the grove of windsmiths expectantly awaited his answer.

He was given a cup of water. Kerne wanted to tell them all about the Feathered Ones, but Simias insisted he speak the answer. 'Bull-Feaster, you have visioned. Now speak your truth. Who is to be high king or queen of HyperEurus? Remember, to utter a falsehood is to perish.'

Kerne gazed at the nine windsmiths – pale shadows of the bright Feathered Ones. One day their training would enable them to join their fellows. He gazed at the gathered chieftains. Any one of them would have been adequate to govern the valley, but not to rule all of HyperEurus.

'It must be the leader of the Lake People.'

There was a gasp of astonishment.

'They have no leader,' stated Arthus.

'They have a legend of a wise king who may one day return.'

'Bah! How can we pin the safety of our lands upon a legend,' sneered Cyndyn.

'I have consulted with the Feathered Ones. They said only a leader of the Mandorlans will bring peace to all of HyperEurus. Such a king will rule fairly.'

'Ruled by fishermen?' spat by Cormac. hey do not know how to fight!'

'They keep their neutrality for their own gain,' criticised Cyndyn. 'Where were they when the Iron Army attacked?'

'Silence, my esteemed chieftains,' commanded Partholon. 'There is deep wisdom in this. The Horse Nomads will not respect any of us, but everyone trades with the Mandorlans. The Fisher Folk would not want to upset the balance of things.'

'Yet would they accept the responsibility?' asked the Donn. If he was disappointed he masked it well.

'I remember seeing a sword there ... a sword of old kings,' said Kerne, swaying from his ordeal.

'Glaive: the Sword of Light!' recalled Eryr. 'Yes – it was wielded by their ancestors when once they ruled these lands.'

'Before they renounced violence and worldly struggle,' said Saar softly.

'Yes,' agreed Partholon, 'but they do not need to resume it. The sword is a symbol. If we can persuade their leader to take up the sword in the name of justice and peace ...'

'But who would they listen to?' asked Arthus.

'We will go,' said Simias. 'Kerne has fulfilled his duty. We can ask no more of him.'

The windsmiths gathered in a circle around Kerne. 'The Tarbh Feis is ended,' declared Simias. 'The high king has been chosen. His name is Ollav Fola, of whom the legends speak. Let the Bull-Feaster be released from his quicken hut alive, and let the Sword of Light be drawn in peace!'

33

The Cauldron

The Journal of Isambard Kerne
Anagantios 6th, Waxing Atenoux

This is the first chance I have had to catch up with my journal since the end of the war. I am still reeling from the bull feast, and so are my guts! I have laid off red meat for a while, not that there is an abundance to go around, now winter is setting in. The caer survives off its stores of salted meat, fish and what its hunters can catch in Wight Wood. Yet I have been made comfortable. All I need is brought to me. Brigantia ensures I am being well looked after. I feel she would do more for me herself if she were not chief of this tribe.

I still mourn Ogmios, whose dwelling and mantle it seems I have taken over. And the death of Madoc hangs heavily on me. Brak calls in now and again to try to lift my spirits, and even Bronwen, when she is back visiting from the Morrigan camp. They have both changed so much. We all have.

The valley isn't the same either. Every caer has suffered loss. It will take years for the Chalk Folk to fully recover. I doubt I shall see that ... I don't know how much longer I will remain here. I feel my time here is drawing to an end, but my work is not yet complete.

The windsmiths have returned from their council with the Mandorlans. After long and fraught discussion the Fisher Folk finally agreed to the proposal – that the King in the Lake should be awoken. The lake village was seriously battered by the flood, but has survived and something has been stirred. Their neutrality has been tested. They can't remain an island any more ... And the Mandorlan Elders said the time was auspicious – the Salmon is coming into alignment with the Sword at the time of the winter solstice. So that is when Ollav Fola will be summoned. Whether he chooses to heed our calling is another matter. The elders suggest that an offering needs to be made, an offering of some considerable value and meaning. Ollav Fola will need evidence that the peoples of the lake have learnt their many lessons and are finally willing to live in peace.

A Drunemetom was held at which I was asked to attend. I was nervous about returning there after the Tarbh Feis and I did experience a little nausea at first as the memory of the bull feast returned, churning my bowels. It was debated what offering would be appropriate. Also, there was the matter of Madoc's cauldron to discuss. Since the battle it had been stored in pieces, one plate in each caer. It was agreed this was the safest option until its final fate was decided. Never again could it be assembled. No one wanted to risk the dead walking again.

At first, several rich gifts were discussed. The finest bulls, hides and furs, shields and swords, vats of mead, metalwork from the Metenaidd – but none seemed sufficient. How would any such things persuade Ollav Fola that the people of HyperEurus had learnt their lesson?

Then, in a wave of awen, I had an idea that would reconcile the problems of the offering and the cauldron's safe disposal: to make each of the thirteen plates depict a scene from recent history, and let that be the gift! It seemed simple, obvious even, and perfect. We had the finest metalsmiths on our doorstep and, as for the content, well, that could be a combination of what the Chalk Folk deem sacred and important. I saw it all in a flash – a richly decorated cauldron, broken, and ritually deposited in the lake. It reminded me of something, but at the moment I still cannot recall what. Perhaps that faint memory, whatever it is, suggested this idea … Who knows? As soon as it was forwarded the wood-priests gave it their blessing. It seems a most elegant solution to these loose threads – the final part of this tapestry.

I have been chosen to supervise the creation of the Cauldron of Legends, as we have started to call it – if only for the simple reason that no one from the Chalk Folk wishes to handle the 'cursed' metal that caused so much suffering. More than that, it is my vision that will shape this offering to the King in the Lake. After all of the thirteen pieces had been collected from the respective caers a meeting was held with the Metenaidd elders. Their skilful input will ensure they will be looked upon favourably by the future high king. Among the Metenaidd elders gathered at Moot Holm were some whom I recognised from the Samhain rites. Grualen Grimalkin, the Copor elder, is stocky with a long red moustache, fiery eyes and dark brows. The Plwm headman is simply known as 'the MacCracken'; he is dour and large-limbed and has a black-grey mane and blue eyes. The Tun elder, Tavey Mevagissey, pale and lanky, long-faced and flaxen-haired, was sucking on a clay pipe with a mischievous gleam in his eye. And Fandar Grey represented the Arianedd – silver-haired, grey-eyed, garbed in black.

I mooted the involvement of Baramis, but his blacksmith skills would not be needed in this project. I look forward to catching up with him when there's time. But we had the deadline of the solstice to work to and so every moment was precious.

It was decided among the Metenaidd that the best technique would be to coat the metal plates with silver. It is an art mastered only by the Arianedd, the silversmiths, and the best among them was Fandar Grey. He was charged with supervising the work upon the plates. Time was against us; there was less than six weeks until the winter solstice alignment. Fandar Grey accepted the task with gentle humility. He quickly brought together a team of the finest craftsmen he could find – thirteen in all, one for each plate. They set up camp in the remote mountain valley of the Arianedd and I stayed there with them to oversee the work. With my gold breastplate and mace of office I was once more seen as a figure of authority, though I was surrounded by men more knowledgeable than me about their craft. However, as a railway engineer I did have experience in overseeing large projects with gangs of men: the digging of cuttings, the laying of tracks, the meeting of deadlines, and so on.

In the lodge of the Arianedd chief – a simple but comfortable roundhouse, warmed by womenfolk, hounds and children – I related all of my recent experiences. He listened intently as I told him of the death of Bron and the abduction of Bronwen; of Brak in the guise of Cernunnos, talking to the animals; of the stag, wolf pack and chimeras; of Taranis, the burning giants and the iron mines; of being borne across the lake on the back of Llyr; of the beauty of Brigantia; of the powerful grace of Macha and her Rhianna; of the might of the Donn; of the

278

Horse Nomads and Grey Raiders; of the bull feast; and of the Cauldron of the Dead.

With charcoal plucked from a dead fire, the master craftsman began rendering the scenes upon rolls of birch bark. My time in HyperEurus came alive before my eyes, told in a powerful symbolic fashion – roughly a plate for each month of my presence here. A whole year in Shadow World! Fandar made the odd alteration here and there, under my guidance, until I nodded my approval. At the end of the first day we had outlines of thirteen scenes – or 'tableaux' as they would be called in my world. These were handed to the thirteen craftsmen the next morning, with detailed instruction from Fandar. The craftsmen pored over them with intense interest and excitement. The designs were intricate, but in the style developed by the Metenaidd guilds over the centuries. It would normally take months to complete such a project. We had five weeks.

Fandar ordered the thirteen plates from the biplane to be flattened out and scoured until they were perfectly smooth and unblemished. Then they were brushed with quicksilver by workers thickly gloved and masked. This was to help the silver to stick when it was melted on to the plates in the forges, the quicksilver burning away in the process. When they had cooled, the blackened plates were scrubbed clean and burnished until the silver shone in the sharp winter sun.

This took all of the first day. Even when the shadows lengthened down the slopes of the Bone Mountains, Fandar Grey would not rest, though he was keen for his workers to do so. They would need their strength, he said. They slumped by the fire, huddled together for warmth, but in good spirits, the broth and ale flowing freely. The men had been selected from the four Metenaidd tribes, and each had their own guild secrets, yet they had been brought together for a common cause and found camaraderie and mutual respect among their fellow craftsmen.

I envied them a little as I watched them from the edge of the fire circle. I did not find such rapport in my previous life. I was unable to share the complexities of my research except with the odd antiquarian colleague, whom I might see once in a blue moon, though always with a slight nervousness at revealing our secret worlds. The windsmiths offer a new brotherhood, yet I know I have to look further for instruction. I cannot remain in the valley, resting on my laurels, comfortable as my new status may be. My studies have not been completed. I have much still to learn.

The light in Fandar Grey's lodge did not go out all night. I called in on him. He was feverishly transferring the design on to what would be the base plate – that of the bull feast. Firstly, he made the silvered plate sticky with a nub of wax. Then he pricked tiny holes in the birch bark along the charcoal outline of the design. After this an extra line of charcoal was applied, which passed through the holes on to the plate. He lifted away the birch bark to reveal the Tarbh Feis design. He picked up a pointed tool, breathed a prayer on to it and began tapping out the lines. I watched in fascination as the plate of the cauldron was transformed from an object of war into a work of art.

I left the master absorbed in his task and went to my hut, glad to get under the furs. That night I dreamt of the thirteen designs: they swirled about in my mind's eye, coming alive, drawn with fire in the darkness.

I awoke bleary-eyed to a camp already at work. Some porridge-like substance was still bubbling away, which I helped myself to as I watched the Metenaidd at work. Thirteen bronze troughs had been carried under the awning and were being filled with a pitch-like mixture made in a massive vat from a tar-like substance mixed with pine resin, tallow and chalk dust. This hardened when cold but could be easily shaped when warmed up. Fandar explained that this was to provide a working surface for the plates that was hard, absorbent and steady.

The plates were placed on to the troughs and rubbed with wax, and the birch drawings transferred as I had seen the previous night. One by one the pieces of bark were lifted away and the images were revealed. Prayers were breathed on to the tools and the craftsmen set to work, the workshop filling with the sound of tapping.

The next day, the plates were lifted off the pitch, cleaned and reversed, the corners bent down in the opposite direction with a rawhide mallet so they fitted snugly on their bed. The image, clearly visible, was now pushed out – into the pitch, so it made a relief. Again the plate was lifted off and cleaned, and then the indentations were filled with pitch, which was warmed with torches until it melted into every crevice. When this cooled and hardened, it provided support for the embossed design that was placed – with the relief facing out – back on to the bed. The final stage was the chasing of the design with fine tools to decorate the surface with an intricate series of dots and stripes, leaves and spirals.

This process was repeated several times over the next few weeks as the designs became increasingly complex and refined.

The grove of the smiths echoed with the tapping of hammers, like woodpeckers in spring. The workshop was partly covered against the gently falling snow. A fire was kept going by assistants, so the craftsmen could thaw out their fingers and have a hot cup of barley brew now and again. The silver-laden stream, the Tears of the Moon, as it was kenned, gurgled by, its edges frozen. Nearby were our stone beehive cells where we slept wrapped in thick furs. It was not an unpleasant place to stay and work for a moon's turning. Yet constantly were we aware of the deadline. Work commenced at first light and finished at dusk but in those winter months the days were not long. In fact, we cursed at how short they were. There was never enough time.

Painstakingly slowly, the designs increased in complexity, reflecting the patterns created by the ice crystals, the snow on the branches of the pines and birch, the frost on the Metenaidd's beards. On the plates the main players of the war loomed large, like gods compared with the soldiers, the lesser mortals at their mercy. Strange creatures haunted the edges of the plates; so fantastical they looked, yet I had seen them with my own eyes. The rift was healed – no more would pass through – but at what cost?

The days shortened as our time ran out. The workshop became buried under a snowdrift and we had to dig our way in to work. Hands were blackened with frostbite. The craftsmen were in constant fear of losing their fingers. We covered our skin in animal fat and stitched ourselves into our clothing to keep warm – it was too cold to change our garb – so we stank and constantly scratched ourselves.

Each week a windsmith would visit to check on progress. They were nervous about missing the alignment, but were pleased with what they saw. The plates were looking impressive, shining now they had been silvered. They looked as though they had been 'kissed by the moon', the wood-priests said.

One of the final additions to the cauldron plates were eyes of blue glass for the god-forms. Holes were bored in the metal, and the beads, traded by Cyndyn from the Mandorlans, were secured in place. As each pair was added, the gods came alive before us, staring at us with an uncanny presence. The cauldron seemed alive. The ghosts of its memory stirred within the metal, filling the workshop with a numinous atmosphere. At night the scenes came vividly to life in our dreams. We had lived and breathed them and given the new legends life.

Then finally, three days before the solstice, the plates were ready. And for the first time I remembered where I had seen them before. They are identical in design to the plates of the Gundestrup Cauldron, found in a bog in Denmark, where it had been ritually broken up and deposited sometime in the Iron Age. How can this be? Fandar Grey created the designs based upon my experiences in the War of Metal. Which cauldron came first, this one or the Danish one? And which one is the shadow? Or are they somehow one and the same? The fact is that ours' fate is to be deposited in a watery place also. The Fisher Folk say that Lake Mandorla is bottomless … Is it a gateway back to Earth, as all springs, wells, pools and caves here are said to be entrances to the Otherworld?

Forged from the very metal we crossed over in, is the Cauldron destined to 'return' to Earth, or to arrive there for the first time? Either way, how did I cause it to be created? The idea, the images, all came to me in a flash of inspiration. Was I subconsciously channelling its forgotten details, or did it already exist in some way outside the circle of the Earth and Shadow World?

I will have to ask Merlin about these mysteries, but for now I was just relieved that it was complete – the 'Cauldron of Legends', the Metenaidd call it – though it will never be put together again, I am sure of that. Folded in soft felt, it is to be transported by canoe to the windsmiths, then to the lake in time for the alignment.

There was a great celebration in the grove of the smiths that night. We have all become good friends during these five tough weeks. Lifetime friendships have been forged; the links between the Metenaidd guilds are stronger. The craftsmen will be richly rewarded, but for now they were all glad to return to their families and grab some rest before the grand ceremony.

The next morning I bade farewell to Fandar. We had become firm friends during the intense period of the project. It has been a pleasure to watch such a skilled craftsman at work, and to talk to such an intelligent soul. I will always remember his dedication. It highlights to me how devotion to a particular path leads to excellence. I run the risk of becoming just a jack-of-all-trades, unless I resolve to pursue the way of the windsmith to the four corners of the world. I feel I owe it to Ogmios. And I owe it to myself.

'May the King in the Lake accept our offering and may he bring peace to this land. And may Nuadha bless your path, Isambard.' Fandar embraced me with a bear hug on the banks of the silvering rill. Having placed my important cargo before me in the canoe, I waved farewell to the Arianedd who lined the bank to see me go, and set off downstream.

34

Offerings

Upon the frozen lake the dwellings were scattered either side of the Mandorlans' floating village, now locked into the ice. It was the dusk of the shortest day. The sky was a fiery red, the pale sun impaled on the horns of the Bone Mountains, and the representatives of the Chalk Folk and Horse Nomads had gathered on their respective sides of Sword Rock.

The tribes of HyperEurus had been arriving since the beginning of the week, erecting their felt-lined gers, or crude shelters. Black-maned horses were tethered to stakes driven into the ice, which was thick enough to light fires upon. Arguments over fishing holes and water supplies had erupted occasionally, until resolved by the diplomatic Mandorlans. Everyone heeded their governance of the lake. All were bound by ancient truce laws, but the peace was as fragile as the ground upon which they stood. This was the first time the opposing tribes had confronted one another since the decisive battle of the Da'anu. The Horse Nomads' numbers were greatly diminished, but the Chalk Folk were not at their full strength either. Many warriors from each side lay beneath the lake, swept down by the flood, along with the undead and all the detritus of war, and this was the only chance for a peaceful future. Now the lake presented an inviolate shield of white, *like a fresh sheet of paper*, thought Kerne, wondering what he would do now that only half a dozen pages of his journal were left.

A hole was being cut in the ice by the grey-robed Mandorlans, as graceful on the ice as on water. The assembled tribes found it difficult to remain upright. The nine windsmiths, immaculate in white, wielding their oak staves, tried to stay as still as possible – and looked very solemn. With them were the chieftains and champions of the Children of Da'anu in all their richest array, and limping Baramis, nervous to be meeting his slave-masters for the first time since his escape. His presence had been requested because his knowledge of the Forbidden Kingdom gave the Chalk Folk an advantage, and the champions of the caers assured him that the Horse Nomads would have *them* to deal with if they tried anything. And since the end of the War of Metal more iron swords had been forged in the rebuilt smithies, arming more of the Chalklander warriors with confidence.

Opposite them, scowling and cruel-eyed, haughty and suspicious in their furs and pointed hats, were the Horse Nomads. At their head was a new leader: a short but powerfully built man with a long black moustache he kept stroking. Richly attired in ornate armour and flanked by a brutal-looking bodyguard, he made Kerne think of Attila the Hun, but Baramis whispered that his name was Roas. The Scythian remembered him all too well – his own missing kneecap was a constant reminder.

In between the two parties officiated the elders of the lake, in long robes and thin sandals, seemingly oblivious of the freezing cold. Willowy framed and wispily bearded, as if a sudden gust would blow them away, the Mandorlans looked the most balanced of all, sure-footed and serene. The assembled crowd stood in silence while the ice hole was cut out using the jagged-toothed jawbone of what looked like an ichthyosaur. Had its fossilised remains been discovered, Kerne speculated, or were such creatures still alive in this ancestral realm? The Horse Nomads had their tarpan. Why should there not be other lost species? Did animals have ancestors too? It was an exciting but faintly worrying thought. What other monsters lurked beneath the ice?

The cutting completed, the lid of ice was lifted from the hole. Many such holes pocked the surface of the lake for fishing purposes but the Mandorlan elders felt it necessary to cut a new one – out of respect for the sacred duty they were about to perform. Mandorlan priests now came forward to bless the opening, smudging it with incense. Dried flowers woven into a garland were placed about its edges, along with precious fruit, shells, beads and other offerings. Next, an entourage of Horse Nomads came forward, led by a filthy, black-toothed shamanka, who beat her skin drum low to the ice, swaying as she walked.

With a shudder Kerne recalled the demon ally of Madoc's he had seen briefly on the Drunemetom. What had that been? Had it been responsible for the creation of the Cauldron of the Dead? Where was the feathered magician when one had a question to ask?

The Horse Nomads led a tarpan to the hole. It protested, perhaps sensing its doom, and had to be soothed with soft voices and

285

strokes. It skidded on the ice like a freshly dropped foal. The shamanka kissed its ears, eyes and nose, before hammering a spike into its temple. She guided the jet of dark blood into the hole of water. The tarpan let out a moan, staggered and slumped on to its side, steaming and twitching. Beside it the Horse Nomads placed jars of oil and koumiss, knives and a pair of exquisitely embroidered fur-lined boots. The shamanka screeched her dedication of the sacrifice to the King in the Lake.

Finally, the windsmiths moved forward; with the nine walked Kerne, bearing the cauldron in its soft leather bundle. He wore the signs of his office, the breastplate and mace, and a thick fur cloak about his shoulders. He was glad of his officer's boots upon his feet. With great ceremony he unravelled the bundle and revealed the plates. There was a gasp of admiration as the thirteen silvered panels caught the dying rays of the setting sun. The images burnt into all who gazed upon the plates. The Horse Nomads nodded, recognising certain images: angry Taranis with his iron wheel; the chimeras; the Cauldron of War. Delighted to see themselves, horse-mounted warriors, represented, they struck their chests and beamed.

Kerne hoped that the King in the Lake would be equally pleased.

One by one the plates were held aloft, glinting in the light, then were cast into the icy water. Thirteen plates taken from the Breguet biplane in which Kerne and his pilot had passed through the Angel Gate, hammered into a cauldron that brought the dead to life, and now changed beyond recognition into a beautiful work of art and skill, dropped slowly to the bottom of the lake, turning over and over through the murky depths; offerings to the lake and its sleeping king …

Then the Head Priest of the Mandorlans, the Steward of the Sword, who bore the Sword of the King in its scabbard, stepped into the circle and spoke: 'Mighty Llyr, King in the Lake, accept these gifts. May they prove to you that we have changed our ways, learned our lessons and wish for peace. Return to us, O great King. Return to us and unite our lands, Ollav Fola!'

A chant of the King's name was taken up: sung gently by the Mandorlans at a high pitch, intoned like the awen by the windsmiths in tenor fashion and droned by the Horse Nomads in long bass notes. The three strains intertwined and vibrated together, creating harmonics that the ice echoed back, vibrating beneath their feet.

The ice cracked slightly, as if breathing out, then stilled in silence. Fires were lit as the last light faded and the temperature plummeted.

'It's going to be a long night,' said Brak.

'The longest,' replied Kerne, gazing up at the darkening sky.

The stars came out in all their splendour that night, dwarfing the tiny constellation of humans dotting the frozen lake. The gathered tribes looked up in awe to see the Sword align with the Salmon. And all hoped and prayed that Ollav Fola, lost king of the Mandorlans, would return to unite them. If he made no appearance it would not bode well for the security of the region. In the vacuum left by Taranis's defeat who could know what chaos would ensue unless a good king returned whom all respected? Even the Horse Nomads had their own legends of this wise king. He had always been generous and respectful to their people and many boasted descent from his royal line.

The chanting and drumming continued all night – hypnotic and haunting as they carried across the ice. The shamanka led her followers in an endless dance about the fire circles, their stamping spiral casting phantom shadows out into the half-light radiating from the whiteness.

The windsmiths performed their own ceremony, maintaining a chant of power all night in overlapping exhalations of sound.

The warriors present were constantly aware of one another across the ice. They paced restlessly up and down, played gwyddbwyll – a form of chess – drank hot grog, sang marching songs or recounted anecdotes from the war, but even they were subdued.

The night was deathly still. Eurus did not stir in the east. Perhaps even he was aware of the great events afoot. No one slept a wink thanks to the insomniac combination of intense cold and tension.

Rationally, Kerne knew they were pinning their hopes on something absurd: a legend of a king turned into a giant fish. But this was the Otherworld. Had not he conversed with a magician in the form of a falcon? And had not he ridden on the salmon's back? He still remembered every word he'd shared with Llyr. If the salmon were to change shape and return, would he remember anything of his time below the lake? Of their conversation? Of his previous existence centuries ago?

In the dead of night, when the cold and darkness had stripped away everything, all that remained were the stars burning with fierce intensity. The starfield filled the vision of all those on the lake that night, and dominating the sky was the alignment prophesied by the Mandorlans, of the Sword and the Salmon. The conjunction seemed to point directly down to Sword Rock, as if its pinnacle focused all celestial energies, and it became the focus of everyone's prayers, a dark needle above the white.

Just before dawn, when all was deathly still, the Windeye stirred, and the gongs of the citadel were rung, booming across the frozen world.

The sunrise came late but was bright as a polished sword, piercing the gloom of the mist-covered lake. The tribes were cold, damp and exhausted from their vigil. A common respect had grown overnight, since they had shared this ordeal and shared the new dawn. Both sides were freezing; both were mortal; both wished for hope to emerge from the water that morning.

Questions and fears had carried in whispers through the night. Had Llyr noticed the offerings? Had he viewed the plates of the broken cauldron? Had he understood the scenes depicted? Or had it all been in vain? Had all of that skill and effort been wasted? A priceless treasure had been cast into the water … as perhaps had Kerne's last chance of returning to the land of the living. If the dead had passed through from no-man's-land, could he not pass back? But it was not worth the risk. He could not justify the risk of unleashing Annwn again; his presence had done enough damage. *Perhaps* this one last gesture would make amends. Yet Kerne shared everyone's concern: was this sacrifice adequate to prick a king's conscience, or stir his mercy?

All eyes were upon the hole in the ice. The drumming and chanting crescendoed, then stopped simultaneously, as if by common consent. The sun had breached the Red Hills. It was now or never.

The lake filled with silence. Baramis gritted his teeth. If this failed, would he be forced to go back? And many others there had similar fears and doubts. The unspoken question hung in the frozen air: would there ever be peace?

Then the waters gurgled and from the hole exploded a human form. He was lean and ragged, with hair long, beard dripping, eyes shining. He gasped for air. Blinking, he pulled himself up and, with the help of Kerne and Baramis, out of the water – until he stood naked astride the hole, glistening with rainbow scales still clinging to his skin.

'Lo! Ollav Fola has returned!' declaimed the Mandorlan elder. 'Hail to the High King!'

The lake erupted with cheering. Robes of great splendour were placed about the King's shivering shoulders and he stepped into the fur-lined boots offered by the Horse Nomads. The Steward of the

Sword stepped forward with the fabled blade upon a cushion and knelt before his liege. The King, with wise sad eyes, gazed down upon the sword gleaming in the light of the new day and cast a glance across the gathered tribes. He caught Kerne's eye and smiled, then lifted up the blade and held it aloft. It seemed to capture the sharp light of sunrise and send it into all of their hearts.

'Long live Ollav Fola – King of HyperEurus!' declared the Steward.

Everyone fell to their knees; Horse Nomad, Mandorlan and Chalklander alike. The reborn sun rose over the white lake and the King surveyed his people. Finally, he spoke, slowly at first, as if remembering the faculty of human speech, but then with clarity, authority and conviction: 'Let these lands be united in peace. I wield the sword of justice, not in might, but in mercy. All men are equal and all women too. Share the riches you have been blessed with, help your neighbour, love your fellow man, and let peace rule!'

35

Last Leaves

Journal of Isambard Kerne
Ogronios 7th, Waning Atenoux

This could be my last entry: these are the last few pages of my journal. My trusty companion; I don't know what I'll do when it runs out … There's no stationers around here! In this world where everyone seems to revert to an ancestral state of being, paper hasn't been invented yet. With their oral culture, the Chalk Folk have no need for it. They have no writing other than the secret alphabet of the windsmiths, the woodwords, which is conveyed either verbally or with hand gestures or in runic engravings. Though I have learnt and mastered several of the sigils, many I gleaned from the Void still remain a mystery to me. I need to talk about these mysteries with the grove. There is no library to consult here … How I long sometimes for a copy of Shakespeare, Dickens, Mallory or the Bible. Just one book would mean the world to me. All I have is my own and it's rapidly ending, although what that end will bring who knows? New adventures?

I could try to make some paper, I suppose – it can't be that difficult. Yet, do I even want to continue a journal? So many things have happened, it is difficult to keep it up sometimes, or do the events justice. But I feel it is important to record these events, to remember the lessons of this last year, this year in the Afterlands.

As I fill these last pages the snow begins to melt, the thawing gaps on the white hills like ink marks on paper, heralding my departure. Over these last three months, since the return of Ollav Fola, I have been snowbound, like the rest of the valley's people, and forced to stay within the caer, except for brief hunting trips with Brak. He will never make me a good hunter, but at least now I am proficient enough with the bow and spear not to starve in the wilderness. And soon I shall have to fend for myself. My clumsiness should have discouraged Brak from allowing me to join his hunting parties, but I sensed he wished to spend as much time with me as possible. Perhaps he misses his father's presence ... Whatever the reason, we have become close over the last year, as much as his warrior's bluster allows. He knows my plans, as do all the caer, but maybe he also wanted to show me the beauty and bounty of his land in an attempt to persuade me to stay. Certainly, the rugged grandeur of the foothills of the Bone Mountains, of Wight Wood and the Hills of Peace and of the perennial Da'anu, glittering through all, has made a lasting impression upon me.

But I can feel the spring's quickening in my blood and it calls me.

Before I leave the Chalk Folk I wish to record some of the skills I have gleaned this past remarkable year. I have been consolidating my research into the sigils: visualising, meditating and intoning each one, carefully recording its effect and preserving its wisdom in a mnemonic poem, a good old Welsh englyn, a form familiar to me from the eisteddfodau I attended, and sometimes reluctantly performed in, as a schoolboy in the Marches. This is very much in keeping with the bardic culture of the windsmiths – but a dramatic departure from that is my creation of a *written* alphabet from the sigils. The geometric patterns I first visualised in the Void I have now transcribed in their entirety – twenty-five in total, five more than their existing system.

This alphabet I have named in honour of its pioneer: Ogham, after Ogmios, so that his memory and wisdom will live on. I called a meeting of the windsmith council at which I unveiled my creation – the 'window' of five concentric circles containing the letters, as I first glimpsed in the Void. At first there was silence, then argument. Some thought it sacrilege and even dangerous. This is the secret alphabet of the windsmiths, handed down from master to initiate through a process of rigorous training. What if it were to fall into the wrong hands? I said that in my world writing is for everyone. Literacy is not global, but is rapidly improving with advances in education and welfare. Even the children of the poorest families now have a right and opportunity to write.

I showed them my journal and explained how it captures

my thoughts and shares them with whoever can read them; that it tells a story without speech when I'm not there. This impressed them. They have the finger-based sign language that allows them to communicate with one another across a moot in the 'dark speech' only decipherable to the initiate. This system of signs – variations of sticks upon a central bar – is also ideal for leaving clues and messages in nature. Broken twigs placed strategically can convey much to those who can read them. It is a system said to have been inspired by the patterns made by the crane as it migrates – and so their kenning for it is 'the crane-knowledge' and the windsmith keeps his magic in a bag made from craneskin. But the idea of preserving wisdom that does not require immediate communication, that will last longer than a night in the forest, fascinated them. They are all walking libraries of wisdom but what if they had *all* died in the battle of the Da'anu? Their wisdom might have been lost for ever. Some said such a fate was not their 'tuirgen', their soul-path, but that if it had been they could not have argued with the Creator. But others saw the wisdom in what I said. Many had wished Ogmios had left his ideas behind – I said he had done so and his wisdom would be honoured through the alphabet named after him. I instructed them all in it and gave them all copies written on birch bark to study. In a noncommittal manner they said they would 'consider it' – but all thanked me.

Afterwards, Partholon came to me and said I should forgive the older windsmiths for being set in their ways. By their very nature and calling they were embodiments and guardians of tradition. Change would not happen overnight, but he saw value in what I had offered them. 'Give them time,' he said.

Meanwhile, the rest of the world moves on. With the thaw, freed Chalklander slaves have been returning across Lake Mandorla with tales of how the harsh regime of the Forbidden Kingdom has been collapsing in the absence of its tyrannical King. In the turmoil created as rival horse tribes fought for control, the iron mines were left unguarded and the slaves just walked free. As soon as the Ironwound Pass was free of snow they made their way home. Some of Baramis's people have come too, rather than return to their distant Scythian homelands. Word had spread of how the blacksmith stood defiantly on the ice of the lake and was treated as an equal by the Chalk

Folk. These refugees have been allowed to make a new settlement on the flanks of Caer Epona, which they have helped rebuild. With them they have brought tarpan, their own horse totem.

Families torn apart by the raids have been reunited and there's been much celebration. I have been invited as guest of honour to many feasts up and down the valley. Through fear of causing offence, I have attended as many as I can.

At Caer Andarta I met my father again. We hugged – overjoyed to see one another alive. As the drunken revelry roared around us we caught up and shared an ale or three. It was so good to see the old man. He was frailer than when I'd last seen him – the winter has been tough on all of us. Like many of the elderly, he had taken refuge in Arthus' caer, though it had piqued him that he was not young enough to fight. Instead he'd helped enhance the defences with the rest of his gang who'd been unable to wield a sword. 'Not too feeble to handle a spade!' he rumbled. He talked of what we would do in the summer together, fishing trips and fires under the stars. I found it difficult to break the news, but when he noticed my silence he made me speak what was on my mind. I told him my plans to travel.

'Where do you have to go?' he asked, exasperated. 'This is home. Your people are here. This is where you belong. Where else is there?'

Then I broke the news: I do not belong here, in this valley, or in this world, for I am not dead. That my presence has threatened the existence of all. That I have to master the four winds to find a way back home: to Earth, to the land of the living.

The old man sighed heavily, and puffed for a while on his pipe; then he brightened up and said, 'Well, one day you'll be back here, son, and I hope I'm not a heap of bones by then!'

I hope so too … Who knows how long my quest will take? And I've noticed the prevalence of superannuated citizens here. It seems there is something about this valley which keeps its inhabitants alive longer than usual, absent warfare and acts of God. Maybe the old man *will* still be here, after all, when I finally breathe my last.

I have winds to master before then: a seemingly impossible task – except that help has come in an unexpected fashion.

The High King, Ollav Fola, has summoned me several times over the winter. He has treated me as his confidante. He finds reassurance in talking to me. As the last person to talk to him before his transformation, perhaps I offer a link that helps him to reconcile his two lives. Perhaps he sees me as another fish out of water. We have become good friends. He treats me as as much of an equal as protocol allows. We talk away the long nights discussing our past and present worlds. He seems glad to be inhabiting a human body again and finds great delight in the slightest sensation – the wind upon his skin, snowflakes on his hands, warm broth, freshly baked bread, a woollen blanket, clothes against his skin, the play of firelight, the laughter of a girl, the majesty of a woman. It seems that we and we alone share an awareness of different worlds. Yet he admires how distinctive are the different tribes, how synonymous they are with their own locality, as if they are genius loci themselves. The King talked longingly of the wide oceans he has crossed, the wonders he has beheld. He is having sea charts made while his memory is fresh, charts drafted on vellum. When I talked of my desire to visit the four corners of the world to master the four winds he looked at me with a strange twinkle in his eye. He said he would see what he could do.

It was only later that I discovered he was having a seaworthy vessel constructed for me as a token of his esteem, and of his appreciation of the craftsmanship poured into the cauldron plates. Their beauty and symbolism had awoken him from his salmon-sleep and persuaded him to surface and resume the body and duties of a king. He believes I freed him and so he feels obliged to help me find freedom. He knows I am 'other': that I was alive in the land of the dead and will remain so until I have mastered the four winds and become a master windsmith, able to navigate my way, finally, back home to England. Who knows *what* I will find there, or *when* I will achieve my goal. It may not be for years ... I cannot expect Maud to be waiting for me – I made her let me go – or even the land I love, Logres, to still be as I left it ... But Ollav Fola, of all men, knows the instinct that makes you want to find your way home, back to the source – even if you must cross oceans and aeons to do so.

So he had his shipwrights set to work. He promised that the vessel would be 'ready by spring'. Only the river was still passable in this time of ice – it was my thoroughfare to the King, to Sword Rock, still icebound. Upon my return I was welcomed at every caer, often hailed from the riverbank by Chalk Folk who would insist I enjoy their hospitality – it would be an insult not to do so. Thus, it usually takes me days to return to Caer Cernunnos, where the welcome is always warm.

Brigantia has often asked me to her hall. I sense her desire for me to stay. They need a new windsmith. Who will replace Ogmios? I cannot step into my mentor's shoes. His lodge has been set up as a place to study the new alphabet – the first school in the Valley of the Chalk Folk. I have left a legacy that will ensure his wisdom would live on, but nevertheless I feel a little guilty, as though I am abandoning them. And Brigantia's beauty and spirit are sorely tempting too! There have been cold nights when I wished I was wrapped in a lover' embrace. I have to keep reminding myself she is my ancestor, taboo, and my destiny lies elsewhere. Come spring she will have a number of suitors bringing tribute to her hearth fire. She has respected my wishes, though often she has made light of my plans to sail 'into the abyss'. None of her tribe, or of any of the Chalk Folk, has journeyed beyond the lake and its hinterlands. The valley is the whole world to them; nowhere else exists. And perhaps it doesn't – for them. This is the world of my ancestors. What lies beyond it even I am uncertain. Will my presence affect other Afterlands?

Maybe there are as many Afterlands as ancestors … Could I pass through other afterlives without some connection? Are these realms shaped only by our past – or could they be shaped by our future as well? By future ancestors? Anything is possible in this world outside time. Yet it operates by rules familiar to those who live in it. They maintain their customs and perhaps shape their paradigm through their expectations. What we expect of the afterlife shapes it, but, as I have found out, in most unexpected ways.

At least the cycle of seasons stays constant. I have had to wait for snowmelt, as everybody does in this land: life is put on hold for a quarter of the year. But, inexorably, the melt has started. Only today I saw my first snowdrops, in a patch of melted snow. Life returns, even in the land of the dead.

36

Llyr

The snows finally melted and it was time for Kerne to go. This spring the raiding parties were replaced by traders from the Horse Nomads – who brought iron to barter for tin and silver, copper and lead. They were welcomed cautiously, but Cyndyn was happy to trade with them on behalf of the Metenaidd, and Baramis offered his expertise to making sure they were bartered the best pig iron.

Kerne's blacksmith friend had carved himself out a privileged niche in the valley, overseeing the forges and passing on his skills. He had several apprentices working under him, and their families reimbursed the master generously for his precious time and skill. They hoped he would pass on his magic touch: his ability to bend the strongest metal to his will. Many viewed him with awe, for he wielded the secrets of iron and had escaped from the Forbidden Kingdom. It made Kerne happy to see the dark-moustached Scythian doing so well. Baramis deserved it more than most, after what he'd endured. Women seemed drawn to him like metal to a lodestone and Kerne was sure it would not be long before he had a wife – he had no filial taboo to obstruct him.

Kerne's bed was still empty. It had been a long while since he had felt the loving touch of a woman.

Everything has its season, a familiar voice seemed to whisper – or was it the wind dogs, ever restless?

'Ogmios, is that you?'

Kerne awoke. He had slept one last night in Ogmios's hut, dreaming of the old man, imagining him with the Feathered Ones. He had told Kerne to 'follow the wind'. The old magician's blessing meant much to Kerne.

He hoped to receive a message from Merlin, but the mercurial bird was nowhere to be seen. Typical of the old curmudgeon, though Kerne. He comes and goes at his own choosing and asks no one for their leave. Yet Kerne was slightly disappointed. Even that irascible magician must have been pleased with how far he had come since he'd first staggered down the mountain.

And now, a year's turning later, it was the moon of Cutios again, the time of winds, the time to be travelling. He felt the restless energy in the air, the same that called pilgrims to travel each spring throughout Eurasia, Earth's HyperEurus.

On a bright spring morning Kerne packed his few belongings into a bundle and said a sad goodbye to the lodge of Ogmios. He was bidden farewell by the people of Caer Cernunnos, Aneurin the Bard singing his praises, and many paying tribute. So different from his reception there a year before. There was no disputing that he belonged now, that he was one of the Children of Danu.

There was a silence as the gathered crowd waited for him to say something. Kerne looked at their faces. They were tough people, they had lost much, but their hearts were still open. He felt a deep sense of connection with them, a web of love and joy.

He tried to summon the words to express what he felt: 'What can I say, other than thank you, thank you, thank you ... You may not understand why I go ... I have a quest to complete. My heart calls me ...' The words dried in his mouth.

Kerne looked longingly at his friends, his family. If this was not home, then where was? Was this not the Afterlands of his ancestors? Yes, but he was alive and belonged in the land of the living, in England. Logres called, his own lodestone. There was a long and hazardous path ahead of him, and there was no guarantee he would make it. Who, after all, could master the winds?

It felt then that he was giving up something solid and supportive for the ethereal and elusive – as though he was stepping into thin air.

He could turn back now. It would be easier, safer, saner ...

Then he caught the encouraging gleam in the eyes of the caer chief and her champion. 'Go, follow your star, Isambard Kerne,' said Brigantia, her breath freezing in the air. 'You will always be welcome within these walls you have helped defend. Say farewell if you must, but with the blessings of Cernunnos!'

Kerne bowed low and turned to leave, though he did not leave alone. Brak and Brigantia were to escort him to Sword Rock and see him off. As the tribe looked on from the ramparts, they walked with him down to the riverbank.

Kerne stopped at the foot of the Stag Lord to pay his respects: 'Mighty Cernunnos, protect this tribe always with your strength and wisdom.'

They climbed aboard the chieftain's canoe and pushed off. In awkward silence – words did not seem adequate – the company sailed on, paddled by two warriors, one at either end. The canoe silently passed Caer Andarta with its white bear, Caer Blaidd of the white wolf, Caer Enid of the white deer and Caer Cynon of the hound.

Then, up ahead, loomed Moot Holm.

The canoe pulled into its dark embrace.

Kerne looked puzzled.

'Your presence has been requested at the Drunemetom,' said Brigantia with the ghost of a smile. 'We shall wait here.'

'But don't take for ever talking to the trees,' Brak jibed.

Kerne nodded and climbed on to the craggy quay, then let Sanctuary Guards escort him to the grove above. The island had felt bleaker since the War of Metal. There was a haunted quality about the place, and Chalk Folk passing it on the river gave it a wide berth. He passed the cairn of the War Dead and stood for a moment in respect. It was the first time he had returned to Moot Holm since he had helped build the memorial with his own hands.

The blue-cloaked, white-robed windsmiths waited within the circle of oaks, now budding into life. Even the lightning-damaged ones were half in leaf.

'Welcome, Isambard Kerne.' Simias spoke for them all. 'We are glad you could visit the grove one last time before you go. You departure should not sadden us, for we know you follow your destiny – but your presence in the valley shall be missed. You have brought much to us, and left behind wisdom. We will not forget.'

Kerne took the ceremonial mace from his knapsack and placed it upon the altar with a bow. 'I return the Mace of the Maker. My work here is done.'

Uscias stepped forward with a silk-wrapped bundle. Silk was the most precious fabric – rare and expensive, traded from the Horse Nomads. 'This is a token of our esteem.'

Kerne wasn't expecting this and was genuinely touched. He reached out and accepted the bundle – it was round, hard and heavy. He looked up with comprehension and delight. The windsmiths smiled. Kerne pulled off the silk to reveal the Eye of the Moon.

'Ogmios would have wanted you to have it,' said Simias.

'I don't know what to say.'

'It is good to be speechless sometimes … Silence is sacred. Use the Eye to help you in your quest.'

'And perhaps check on the valley now and again.'

'I shall. Thank you, wise ones. I will not forget your wisdom.'

'Nor we yours.' Another stepped forward, Orddu, and unrolled a tapestry. It was the Ogham, embroidered in the design of the five concentric circles he had witnessed in the Void.

'Ogmios's alphabet!'

'Yes, the council has decided to adopt it. We shall begin using it in our instruction of any who wish to learn, taking turns to instruct in Ogmios's lodge to keep his flame alight. Thanks to you, his wood-wisdom will live on.'

Kerne smiled at this. It seemed a fitting way to honour the old windsmith.

'Now go, while the wind is with you. And may the awen always flow.'

Kerne wrapped up the Eye and bowed low.

'Blessings upon this grove,' said Kerne, feeling the gramarye in the words.

He looked one last time at the nine windsmiths, white and blue among the budding trees, wielding their staves, standing immutable like the Feathered Ones in the Bone Mountains. They would endure, he was certain. They had all been made stronger by the maelstrom. It had tested them all and these nine had survived, though changed for ever. In a thoughtful mood Kerne descended the rock-cut steps, wondering whether he would ever set foot on them again. He joined the others waiting in the boat and they set off once more.

'What do you have there?' asked Brak.

'A gift from Ogmios,' smiled Kerne.

So they carried on down the river, past the other caers. Silently Kerne bade farewell to the chalk giants and all they represented: gods, ancestors, land and tribe.

Finally, their craft emerged on to Lake Mandorla. By now other canoes were escorting them, and Kerne recognised the other chiefs. This was an escort of honour.

It was a bright day upon the lake and there was a fair breeze. The air was filled with possibility. They moored at Sword Rock, where they were welcomed by a royal entourage including Ollav Fola himself, tall and graceful in purple robes.

'Come; let me show her to you!'

The King led his guests to the royal boathouse where the ship had been constructed. It now waited in the harbour; sleek and long, with a tall mast. Ollav Fola called it a 'birlinn', but it was a fine yacht by anyone's standards.

'I name her *Llyr*. She'll sail where I once swam.'

'A fitting name. She's beautiful.'

'Let me show you aboard.'

The wooden interior was beautifully illuminated by the portholes. There was a bunk with storage beneath, a small toilet, a saloon area with a fold-up table and fitted bench with cushions, and a galley with a wood-burning stove, a small sink and cupboards filled with supplies. The vessel was fully kitted out with all Kerne needed for his sea-bound voyage. At a desk were vellum maps rolled into a rack. Ollav Fola pulled out one and unrolled it with pride.

'Isn't it magnificent?'

Kerne's eyes feasted on the detail rendered in coloured inks. The whole of the Otherworld's oceans were revealed to him, although the landmasses were featureless except for rivers and the legendary names of the continents: HyperZephyrus in the west, HyperNotus in the south and HyberBorea in the north. Strange creatures appeared at the fringes and Kerne realised what the map reminded him of: the fourteenth-century Mappa Mundi he had once seen in Hereford Cathedral as a schoolboy. It had fired his imagination with its fantastical medieval imagining of unknown places populated with a bizarre bestiary and clues as to what lay beyond the rim of the world of mortals: the gates of paradise, ranks of angels, God on high, the Devil and his minions tormenting the damned.

With a ringed finger Ollav Fola traced the route he had marked on it. 'Follow this current, the Spiceway, across the Wyndark Sea and you can't go wrong. Once you reach the open ocean, let the good east wind blow you westwards and take you to the Isles of the Blessed.'

Kerne read the name of the island: Ashalantë.

'It has many names. That is the one I heard sung by the merfolk. Watch them; they can be tricky characters, and their song can be maddening!'

Replacing the map, the King showed Kerne the blank scrolls also stored there. 'I thought you would like some extra vellum ... There are charcoal and ink for writing with, in case you feel like doing a little – what did you call it? – "cartography" of your own. There are still many lands to explore.'

Kerne was overwhelmed. Without thinking he embraced the King, then realised his faux pas, but Ollav Fola accepted the gesture with grace. Here, out of sight, such informality was permissible. Embarrassed, Kerne backed away and straightened up. 'Thank you, Your Highness.'

'Now come, while the wind is in your favour.'

They stepped on to the deck – into the bright sunlight. From the quayside it seemed the whole of the floating village was watching. And emerging from the crowd were familiar and much-loved faces.

'Baramis! Fandar Grey! Brak! Brigantia!'

Stepping ashore with the King, Kerne embraced them one by one, tears welling in his eyes.

'We had to see you off, windwalker,' beamed the blacksmith. He was dressed in baggy breeches, sandals and a sleeveless leather jerkin revealing his muscled arms. One gold tress dangled from his beard, two from the ends of his long moustache, and the other tied back his wiry black mane in a ponytail. 'Here, take this; it's a simple gift.' Baramis thrust something into Kerne's hand and hobbled back.

The gift was a small effigy carved from amber.

'It's Thagimasadas, our god of water and horses. May he protect your travels and speed your passage.'

Kerne tried to thank the blacksmith, but Baramis insisted that Kerne had given him so much.

Then Fandar Grey stepped forward, draped in black and silver, white hair blowing in the breeze that rolled off the lake. 'And I have had this made so you can navigate by the stars.' The Arianedd mastersmith produced a disc of metal. Upon it were circles and dots. Around its edges were regular markings. 'These are the Bright Daughters. Keep them in sight and you can't go wrong.'

Kerne accepted the disc and examined its markings. The cluster of dots reminded him of the Pleiades. 'It is beautiful. You truly are a master of your craft.'

'I had help: the Mandorlans advised me with their star-lore and Gofannon the coppersmith lent me his skill. Keep it safe in this felt bag and may it guide you well.'

Kerne bowed low and then turned to the chieftain and champion of Caer Cernunnos.

The windsmith and the warrior looked at one another awkwardly.

'Farewell, skyman. Don't let all those gifts go to your head.'

'Goodbye, Brak. It was an honour to fight with you. You helped me to find my inner warrior.'

'But perhaps not your hunter,' Brak joked.

'No, but I think I'm a better fisherman,' Kerne laughed, gesturing to the King.

They gripped forearms. 'Sword-brothers, always,' Brak affirmed with a nod and a grin. For a moment there was a look of vulnerability in his eyes. Kerne let him hide it in a bearlike hug.

'Mighty Bron would be proud of you, Champion of Cernunnos.'

Brak pulled away. 'See you in the sky-hunt, my friend.'

Then Brigantia was before him in all her magnificence. 'You are indeed a better fisherman, Kerne. Good enough to fish for a king.'

'But not a queen ...'

'You will always be welcome at Caer Cernunnos, Isambard.'

'Thank you. I have felt more at home there than anywhere for longer than I can remember. I shall never forget your hospitality and generosity, or your courage and nobility.'

'Make me a song,' she said with a smile, kissing him upon the brow, before she stepped back, a look of inscrutable intensity upon her face.

Humbled, Kerne stood before them – Ollav Fola, Baramis, Fandar Grey, Brak and Brigantia – the dearest friends he had made during his time in HyperEurus. Yet there were important gaps ... Kerne noted sadly the absence of his father. He had not come to say farewell, had insisted that if his son wanted to see him again he'd have to return. Instead, he had sent a message via the windsmiths: 'There's no such thing as goodbye to those you love – just good riddance to those you don't!'

There was one other, whose absence saddened him most of all.

As if reading his mind, a tawny owl landed on the prow of the boat. 'Blodeuwedd!'

The owl watched him with enigmatic eyes. Kerne bowed to the bird. 'Send my salutations to your master.'

It hooted and flew off towards the Bone Mountains. Kerne watched it dwindle towards the cloud-feathered heights of Mount Anu.

The Windeye swung southwest and chimed dolorously. A brisk northeasterly was picking up, ideal for the way Kerne was heading.

'Time to go, my friend,' Ollav Fola said softly.

Kerne boarded *Llyr*, which seemed to be pulling at her moorings.

'She hears the call of the ocean,' called out the King. 'Let her go where I can no longer and may the roads of the sea take you to your destiny.'

Mandorlans threw Kerne the ropes. Set loose, the ship bobbed in the white-capped waves. Remembering what his father would do on their trips on the Severn in the *Kingfisher*, he set to work, unfurling the blue canvas sail painted with the silver overlapping circles of the vesica piscis and tacking into the wind. The image on the sail had been adopted on the national flag, symbolising the two peoples of

HyperEurus united as one through Ollav Fola.

Manning the rudder, Kerne nosed *Llyr* out into the bottomless lake. He waved at the entourage upon the shore: Brigantia and Ollav Fola shining in their royal regalia; Brak resplendent in his gold torcs and champion's mantle; and the metalsmiths, Baramis and Fandar Grey, as distinctive as iron and silver. He fixed the image of them in his mind and then put out.

The cheers of the well-wishers faded behind him. As the ship was rocked by the waves the realisation finally sank in: he was at the helm of his own vessel; it was up to him and him alone to steer his path.

Wind dogs whished around the boat, nudging the craft along, adjusting the sail-arm like an invisible crew. Occasionally, Kerne tossed them scraps of food – he'd made sure he had a good bag of them handy. He didn't want his crew mutinying!

Llyr was followed by a flotilla of canoes. In them he recognised contingents from the different caers. In one he thought he saw flame-haired Bronwen among the black-garbed Morrigan. They all hailed him as he steered his vessel along the length of the lake. The Salmon King's craft handled beautifully, like a sword through grass.

Soon she was outdistancing the canoe-riders, who turned back with a final wave of valedictions. The sounds of the farewell receded until there was only the thrumming of the wind beating against the sail, and the hiss of the water on the keel. The sun rose high to port as he pushed south.

Finally, he was alone.

He felt humbled by many blessings. He did not feel he really deserved them. He should have felt exonerated, but deep down in his heart Kerne knew he would have to go a long way to wash the blood of Mallard from his hands. The spindrift from the prow stung his face and that felt purifying. It was inside that he still felt tainted – but he had done what he did to save HyperEurus, hadn't he?

Suddenly there was a screech overhead and out of the sun a falcon flew – and landed on the wheel.

'Merlin! I thought you had not forgiven me. I'm sorry.'

'Never mind that. A fool as usual, Kerne, despite your accolades. Our paths have far to go before they part. Like it or not, our destinies are entwined ...'

'That's fine by me, Merlin. I am happy to have your company.'

'Don't think it's because I like you, Kerne!'

'Oh no, of course not. I wouldn't dream of it!'

'Good. As long as we understand one another ... You've got to put up with me until you can master enough magic to release me from this form.'

'And enough magic to find my own freedom.'

'Agreed. Besides, I need to keep an eye on you,' added Merlin with a glint. 'A little knowledge can be a dangerous thing.'

'What do you mean? I'm no fool!'

'Aren't you? You nearly destroyed Shadow World and you killed your fellow countryman. Did you plan that, O wise one? Could you have prevented the death of Ogmios?'

Kerne felt like he had been punched by the falcon's cruel words.

'No, you couldn't have. So, don't drag any useless guilt around with you, do you understand?'

The airman looked at the palm of his left hand: the scar could still be seen in its centre.

'Do you understand?'

'Yes,' said Kerne weakly.

'But the fact remains that it is not over. There are forces out there that will test your weakness, that will want you to fail and fall.'

Kerne looked up. 'Who do you talk of? I thought the enemy was defeated, the war over.'

'Nothing is so clear-cut, not in Shadow World.'

Kerne rubbed his brow. His head throbbed.

'Did you ever stop to wonder where Madoc got his idea for the Cauldron of the Dead? That was strong magic far beyond the skills of his shamanka. Think! In that dull mind of yours you know of whom I speak ...'

Kerne racked his brains. He did not have the slightest notion. 'Wait a minute.' The image flashed before his eyes. That elongated skull, a demon in the rain. 'On Drunemetom, just before ... the end, I thought I saw a creature behind Madoc. What was it? A hallucination?'

Merlin sighed. 'Unfortunately not. It was an Agent of Discord. Don't ask me to explain, for that is all I have discovered so far, and that name has cost me dear. You wondered what I have been doing these last few months. Now you know.'

Kerne could see for the first time that the falcon looked burdened.

'I have seen them before, but had not realised it until that day on Moot Holm,' continued Merlin. 'They have a way of making you forget, but they have been there all along, mark my words; behind the scenes, orchestrating tragedies and strife. They unravelled my dream of Camelot, and were there at the bloody end: that cursed snake on the fatal field of Camlann ... Who or what they are, and where they come from, I know not. But I fear we have not seen the last of them.'

Merlin's ominous words haunted Kerne as they sailed on across the bottomless lake in silence.

Lyr nosed south, towards the river that would take them to the Wyndark Sea. The ropes sang in the wind, making the ship seem like a stringed instrument, and indeed her hull was shaped like a lyre. The music of wind, wave, rope and sail played together as Isambard Kerne, fledgling windsmith, sunlight gleaming on his gold breast-plate, headed into the unknown. How far he would have to wander, how long before he would finally find peace, perhaps only the Eye of the Moon knew. And he would have to watch every step he took from now on, for malevolent forces waited in the wings.

The shores of Lake Mandorla curved inwards to the point where the great river it became, the Achyron, snaked through a narrow shadowed gorge. South – to the sea and all its myriad possibilities. Kerne carefully guided *Lyr* through the defile, the boundary of HyperEurus, and out of sight.

And perhaps it was a trick of the light on the water, a fata morgana, but it seemed a white shadow followed the ship as it disappeared into the dark chasm.

The Ballad of the Two Brothers

How comes that blood on the point of your sword
My son come and tell me?
Oh it is the blood of a little song bird
That sat in yonder tree, tree, tree
That sat in yonder tree.

But a little bird's blood was never so red
My son come and tell to me.
Oh it is the blood of my own greyhound
That would not run for me, me, me
That would not run for me.

But a greyhound's blood it was never so rare
My son come tell to me.
Oh it is the blood of my grey, grey mare
That would not ride for me, me, me
That would not ride for me.

But a grey mare's blood was never so clear
My son come tell to me.
Oh it is the blood of my brother dear
That rode away with me, me, me
That rode away with me.

And what did you two fall out about
My son come tell to me?
Oh it was that he plucked up a hazel bush
That should have grown to a tree, tree, tree
That should have grown to a tree.

And what will you do when your father comes to know
My son come tell to me?
Oh I'll set foot in a bottomless boat
And sail across the sea
And sail across the sea.

And when will you be coming back again
My son come and tell to me?
When moon and sun dance in yonder hill
And that will never be, be, be
And that will never be.

Traditional ballad, Britain / North America

THE WINDSMITH ELEGY
CONTINUES IN ...

VOLUME 3: THE WELL UNDER THE SEA

Appendices

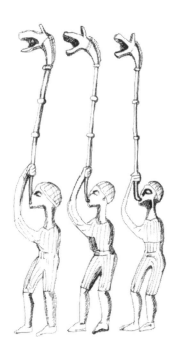

(i) Writing *Windsmith*

Although this book is a work of the imagination I have endeavoured to base the world of *Windsmith* on facts, unlikely as that may seem for a 'fantasy' story.

For me the delight of writing is, apart from the crafting of words into a satisfying form, this journeying and charting. One feels like an explorer in an unknown world. The further in, the deeper you go, the more there is to discover. There is a real frisson in being such a pioneer in a virgin land. For a while, during the initial drafting stage, this world is yours and yours alone. It is indescribably nourishing and rewarding to be able to create a private dreamtime one can return to again and again, over the course of months, years even, during the writing process. One can see why Tolkien didn't want to let Middle Earth go – even being reticent about getting *The Lord of the Rings* published. What had started out as a series of adventures for his son, Christopher, became very much the story he wanted to tell to himself and we are inestimably richer for it.

For the other delight in such imagineering is in sharing one's world. I can but dream of Tolkien's talent, skill and success, but I hope you enjoy exploring this Afterland as much as I have. And it's only just begun! Shadow World is a big place and has room for many realms, many wonderlands, maybe even your own. I have only depicted the ancestral realms of Kerne and Madoc. Perhaps there are as many worlds as there are people, as many Afterlands as there are lives, each one creating its own quantum reality? If they overlap, who knows, but the universe is a big place. There's room for all. The Zapatista slogan echoes this: 'for a world in which there is room for many worlds'. My cosmology is egalitarian. It does not deny the possibility of other narratives – of many heavens, hells and otherworlds.

Here, in *Windsmith*, the focus is primarily on the Celtic – specifically the Irish and Welsh traditions, but also with influences from Gaul and further east. The Celtic culture is not exclusively racial, but rather a pan-European diaspora of languages, art, beliefs, social structures and monuments stretching from the Black Sea, across the Carpathians (via the Danube Valley), across Europe and into the West. I have based the Chalk Folk (aka the Children of Da'anu) partly on the Tuatha De Danann – the Irish aboriginal aristocracy, the Lordly Ones who retired to the hollow hills – but also on their cultural forebears: the salt-mining Hallstatt Culture, overlooking Hallstatt's deep Austrian lake, the cradle, or perhaps cauldron, of what we think of as the Celts today.

Being fascinated by the 'what ifs' and the negative spaces in our knowledge, I have extrapolated upon what might have been a totem-based clan system on the chalk downlands of England – Britain's own 'lost tribes'. Of course, there is evidence of Celtic tribes throughout Britain, but I am interested in the localised phenomenon of the chalk giants, and whether the cluster we have left of ancient originals (the White Horse of Uffington, Cerne Abbas, the Long Man of Wilmington) may be the fragments of an indigenous pantheon or whether each represented the tribal totem of its area. I wondered what others have been lost – could each clan have had its own? Visible from miles around, and appearing on its coins, such a bold effigy would be the tribe's 'logo', immediately recognisable to neighbouring tribes like the costumes, face and body paint, songs and customs of the First Nations people in North America. Another comparison might be to the sacred landscape of the Australian Aboriginal nations, each with their Dreamtime animal carved into the land by the windings of the Rainbow Serpent.

I have tried to recreate something of the clash between the late Bronze Age and the early Iron Age – when bronze swords met iron on the battlefield, and the victory went to the stronger weapon. This is paralleled by a shift in usage of hilltop enclosures (e.g. Cadbury Castle) from ceremonial spaces to defensive purposes, and the construction of enhanced fortifications (e.g. at Maiden Castle), often of great size and complexity – a killing maze requiring enormous manpower to build. It is tempting to conclude that the many stories in the fairy traditions of the People of Peace's aversion to iron is a result of this: that such stories represent a folk memory of a subjugated people driven 'under the hills', or into hiding, by an aggressor with more advanced technology. This may be too prosaic an explanation for some, but it did provide the grit in the oyster for my story. What if the iron was a gun? Imagine the devastating consequences … What if my trespassers in paradise brought their own doom with them?

To end on a positive note, I wanted to celebrate the amazing heritage we have. If nothing else I hope *Windsmith* will inspire you to look more deeply into history, into the Celtic and Steppe cultures and others. For me, these mythic histories are not along a distant line into the far past, but happening right now, right next to us. They are our shadow (or perhaps we are theirs) and we cannot deny or disown them. Our ancestors live on through us. I wished to honour some of the ancestors of this incredible land called the British Isles. I hope, after reading this, you may feel inclined to do the same.

(ii) The Tale of Dru the Windsmith

When the monks of Wilmington had finished building their priory they set about their next task – to construct a windmill. For they had much good land thereabouts, and from it they reaped fine grain, and so they needed a mill to grind it, to make their flour, to bake their bread.

The prior, who was a wise old man, thought it might be as well to invoke the offices of the Windsmith, the surveyor of windmills. There was one who lived up on the Downs, named Dru. He was a curious fellow – tall and thin, wearing a threadbare but clean white

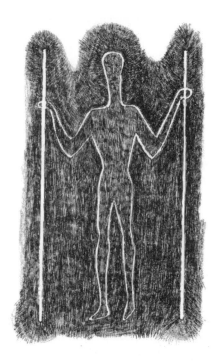

smock, and a straw hat upon his head, wreathed with an oak garland. He wielded a staff in each hand, his sighting poles, and roamed the Downs, living on beechmast, berries and water from dew ponds. He was seldom seen, except when his services were required.

At this the sub-prior, who was zealous and ambitious, cried out in anger. He condemned that vagabond of the Downs for not attending Mass, calling him idolater and one of the Devil's own. Now, the old prior practised the tolerance he preached, and thought it best to build bridges with those who walk other ways. But the sub-prior petitioned his fellow monks and with their support persuaded the prior not to seek the Windsmith's help.

So the monks set about building their mill, siting it without consulting the Windsmith, and when it was finished they were pleased with their handiwork. All was in place, and on the next windy day the prior made the sign of the Holy Cross and with loud cheers from the villagers the miller-monk struck home the striking rod. But the sails did not move, which was odd, for there was a fair breeze blowing. The monks tried to get them going by hand, but still the sails would not turn. The windmill was examined from top to bottom and everything seemed to be in working order. They were baffled and out of breath.

Then the prior took matters in hand, sending a monk to find the Windsmith. The brother returned to say that Dru would come in a week to ten days, which is an old English way of saying he would come in his own good time! But Dru had warned the monk that no crucifixes or bells were to be rung. 'They upset my ears and eyes,' he said.

A fortnight later Dru the Windsmith came striding down Windover Hill and without a word set to work. He walked about the windmill, shaking his head, then started to pace back and forth across the hay meadow: plunging a staff into the soft soil here, then another one there – and sighting between the two. He would squint, tilt his head, stand on one leg, lick his finger, test the air, then start all over again. Dru did this all day long, until the sun was low over the Weald and the shadows were long. Then finally he found the spot and plunged in one of his poles. Hanging his oak garland over it, he walked off with the other – back up Windover, not asking for reward.

The monks ascertained from this strange behaviour that the new location had been dowsed, and so, with great reluctance, they dismantled their lovely mill, and rebuilt it, brick by brick and beam by beam, on the spot marked by the staff and oak leaves.

The mill was finished, and on a windy day the striking pin was struck home – and this time the cogs span and the millstones ground together. Success! Quickly, the hoppers were filled with grain – which rattled down between the stones, coming out as good white flour. The prior ordered that the bells of Wilmington be rung out in thanks, but as soon as their peal was heard over the meadow the windmill ground to a halt. One by one the monks returned to the mill to see what the trouble was – and as soon as the ringing stopped, the sails started to turn once more.

This was proof enough for the sub-prior that the windmill was indeed the Devil's work. But the monks needed their flour, and so a compromise was reached – no milling at High Mass. This extraordinary situation became the routine – though little it pleased the sub-prior – and so things were for a whole year, until the old prior, ill in health, passed away. The sub-prior took over his mantle, and he hated the sight of the windmill. It mocked him from the meadow, a symbol of Satan on his doorstep.

One night as he tossed and turned in vexation he had a vision –

of Saint Boniface, or 'Bishop Boniface' as he was back then, famed for cutting down the pagan groves. He would send for Boniface, and the next day this is what he did. Seven days later a great ecclesiastical host was seen approaching from the west, and at their head was Bishop Boniface himself, in his bishop's mitre, wielding his golden crozier. The new prior welcomed his esteemed guest, lavishing upon him the best food and wine from the stores. After dinner, the situation was explained in full, and Boniface said, 'This shall require only a minor miracle – but, first, we need to celebrate High Mass!' The new prior wanted to explain that the windmill would not work if the bells were rung – but he wasn't going to argue with a bishop, was he?

As the bells pealed across the meadow Boniface strode to the mill. 'Strike home the striking rod!' he commanded, and struck the rod with his golden crozier. Immediately, the sails began to turn. Rejoicing, the monks poured their grain into the hoppers and out of the millstones came good white flour. They filled sack after sack, until all the grain was gone. Then the striking rod was pulled out – but to their horror the windmill would not stop! The sails turned, the cogs span and the millstones ground together – scattering sparks on to the flour-covered floor, threatening to set the whole thing on fire! They had to keep the stones cool, and so a human chain was formed from the well in the Priory, and pails of water were passed along it to douse them. But the monks could not keep that up for ever! What were they to do? For once, Bishop Boniface seemed powerless.

Then from down Windover Hill came Dru the Windsmith. He stood on the edge of the meadow, shaking his head.

'Back, Devil's own!' warned Boniface.

Dru just shrugged and watched as the passage of water along the line came to a halt.

'The well is dry!' someone cried out.

Red in the face, Boniface knew he had to ask for help. 'Remove your curse!'

Dru just stood there and smiled. The windmill was beginning to catch fire.

'Remove your curse – and ask your price,' Boniface spat in disgust.

Dru watched him, impassive.

Boniface was desperate now. 'Remove your curse and I will make sure you shall be remembered long after we are all dust!'

Dru seemed to consider this, but wavered. 'You know I am a man of my word. By the cloth I do as I say!' Then he stepped forward, raising his staff, looking angry in the firelight. Boniface flinched, but Dru ignored him and began walking backwards around the windmill. Three times he circled it, faster and faster, until he stopped dead and struck his staff against the mill. The stick split in two and the sails creaked to a standstill. Then a great gust of wind blew out all the flames and knocked the monks off their feet. Dru looked pale and shrunken. He gazed at them sadly with his green eyes, then walked away up the windswept downs – never to be seen again.

After the mill was repaired and working once more, Bishop Boniface honoured his agreement with the Windsmith. He ordered the monks of Wilmington to cut out his shape on the side of Windover Hill, removing the turf to reveal the chalk beneath. And there he stands to this day – remembered long after Boniface and his kind became ashes and dust.

Extract from Kevan Manwaring, *The Long Woman*, Awen, *2016*

(iii) The Angel of Mons

This fascinating phenomenon, which I recreate in *Windsmith*'s prologue ('The Angel of No-Man's-Land'), arises from an incident said to have taken place in the opening battle of the First World War, at Mons, Belgium, on 23 August 1914; part of the larger Battle of the Frontiers. It is interesting that this event occurred at such a critical time, in a liminal space when the world could have taken a different path. A modern equivalent might be the outcome of the Bush–Gore US election debacle and the aftermath of 9/11. It is clear the world has taken the path of the sword since then, not learning the lessons of history. In 1914 Europe was about to embark on its bloodiest and most futile war to date, when millions of soldiers would needlessly lose their lives. Events rapidly escalated out of control from the moment Archduke Franz Ferdinand was assassinated, yet at any moment each individual had a choice and collectively they could have stopped the juggernaut of war. I believe the Angel of Mons represented our last chance to turn back in 1914, a divine warning even. Alas, it became the point of no return.

One of the most famous episodes of angelic intervention [was] the supposedly widely reported descent of an angelic army in

August 1914, which came to the aid of the British forces
against the Germans in Mons ... The angelic host's assistance
could not have come at a more propitious moment as the British were being driven back by the relentless German advance.
(Matthew Bunson, *Angels A to Z*, Crown, 1996)

The fascinating thing about the incident is that is seems to have
been witnessed by troops on both sides, though no one could agree
on exactly what was seen, as though each saw what he needed or
dreaded to see:

During the Great War thousands came to believe that a miracle had happened during the British Army's first desperate
clash with the advancing Germans at Mons in Belgium. In
some versions a vision of St George and phantom bowmen
halted the Kaiser's troops, while others claimed angels had
thrown a protective curtain around the British, saving them
from disaster ... within weeks the 'angel of Mons' had entered
the realms of legend. By the end of the war it became unpatri-
otic, even treasonable, to doubt the claims were based on fact.
(www.forteantimes.com)

The legend grew like an urban myth and inspired artwork, musi-
cals and wild theories! As writer Arthur Machen said, claiming himself to be responsible for the legend: 'The snowball of rumour was
set rolling until it was swollen to a monstrous size.'
Bunson cites other visions

corroborated by German prisoners describing a force of phan-
toms armed with bows and arrows and led by a towering figure
on a shining white horse who spurred on English forces during
an assault on German trenches. Another story spoke of three
angelic beings seen by the British, hovering in the air over
German lines, providing a source of deep inspiration for them.
Aside from these beings, Bunson states that soldiers later
claimed to have seen St. Michael the Archangel, the Virgin
Mary, even Joan of Arc. (Alan S. Coulson & Michael E.
Hanlon, 'The Case of the Elusive Angel of Mons')

This culture of fervent credulity I explore in *The Long Woman*, set
mainly after the war, when many bereaved souls sought consolation

in spiritualism or hedonism; even Sir Arthur Conan Doyle succumbed to the glamour of the Cottingley Fairies.

To add to the fascinating matrix of fact and fiction, Arthur Machen, a popular writer of the times, claimed to have inspired the whole legend with his short story, 'The Bowmen', which describes a phantom English army, led by Saint George, coming from Agincourt to the aid of beleagured British troops. Yet Machen's story was not published until September 1914, in the *London Evening News*, a month *after* the Battle of Mons. How could it have inspired the troops on the ground? It may have caught the zeitgeist, even helped shape it afterwards, as all good art does (and maybe the British public developed a false memory syndrome, confusing fiction with fact) but to say it inspired the event in the first place is putting the cart before the horse. *Something* happened that day, which the fog of war obscured and amplified, like the 'glory' phenomenon when one's shadow is projected on to thick mist, and its nebulous quality made it all the more susceptible to projection. We fill such 'gaps in reality' with whatever we need: science, religion, human fallibility, the unexplained.

The Angel of Mons is one corner of reality which hasn't been tidied away, and I am glad of it. 'There are more things in heaven and earth than are dreamt of in most people's philosophy', after all, and the world would be a duller place without such mystery. Furthermore, I think it is humbling to accept that we cannot explain everything away; that humanity cannot fully comprehend the vast complexity of the universe, only gaze in wonder – what Keats called 'negative capability'.

Although I discount Machen's 'The Bowmen' hypothesis, it tickles me to think of a piece of fiction having such an impact. Another example is the famous incident in the 1930s when that master fabulist Orson Welles broadcast H.G. Wells's *War of the Worlds* on the radio, causing mass panic because people thought it was really happening. I am also intrigued by the bowmen's resonance with the Amesbury Archer, who features indirectly in *Windsmith* (see below). Does it stretch this resonance too far to remember that the English longbow, such an important weapon, was always made of yew – a tree known for growing in churchyards (or for having churches and cemeteries sited around it) and said to grow through the mouths of the dead? It is a tree connected with the underworld and the afterlife. A suitable tree to make an appearance at this gateway between the worlds ...

(iv) Bush Barrow Man

This rich burial discovered at Bush Barrow, Normanton Down, near Stonehenge, dating from c. 1600–1500 B.C.E. and exhibited in the Wiltshire Heritage Museum, Devizes (a real gem of a museum), inspired both me and Kerne! It is first mentioned in *The Long Woman*, when Kerne is overwhelmed by a feeling of déjà vu, or something else, while walking on the down one summer solstice morning with his wife, Maud.

One idea is that 'Bush Barrow Man' was one of the architects (of one phase) of Stonehenge, and that his mace is a symbol of his office – a magical mason? This gave me the idea to link him to Kerne, who was a surveyor for the GWR in his civilian life back in England before the First World War.

Aileen Fox, in *Southwest England, 3,500 BC–AD 600* (David & Charles, 1973) calls it 'One of the richest of the Wessex chieftains graves'. She goes on to describe 'the perforated stone mace head which is a pebble of Devonian limestone from the Teignmouth district: together with the remarkable bone mounted wand or sceptre which has affinities in the Mycenean shaft-graves'. Fox surmises, 'It was probably part of a royal insignia.'

The milky white orb and mace could be the equivalent of the monarch's sceptre and orb – symbol of secular and sacred power – but the orb seems similar to a crystal ball, and in *Windsmith* I imagined it being used for scrying. Brigantia, Brak and Bronwen gift the breastplate, buckle and brooch to Kerne; the Donn lends him the mace to oversee the construction of the earthworks and escape road; and finally the windsmiths give him the milky stone (the Eye of the Moon) as a leaving present, with which he can check in on the valley of his ancestors now and again.

(v) The Amesbury Archer

I have based the figure of Baramis the Scythian blacksmith on this real person, to whom I found myself connected when I was asked to pose as him in costume for the Wessex Archaeological Trust's website! I have taken some artistic liberties with his context – placing him in the early Iron Age (as replayed in my Otherworld) and making

him hail from slightly further east – yet the most remarkable elements about him I did not need to amend or embellish: missing one kneecap, he had made a remarkable journey from Central Europe to Britain, bringing with him the magical knowledge of metallurgy, which made him a feared and revered figure (as blacksmiths were in many cultures). He is virtually the archetypal crippled blacksmith: a Celtic Vulcan, Hephaestus or Wayland.

From the information given on the Wessex Archaeological Trust website we may infer that not only did the crippled blacksmith accomplish his epic journey, but he also assimilated so well into a local tribe that he had a son and that both were buried with high status. A stranger in a strange land, he must have made a big impression on the natives to have been treated with such respect.

The BBC made an excellent *Meet the Ancestors* programme about this incredible figure ('King of Stonehenge', screened 19 February 2003), which reconstructed him brilliantly. Worth watching if you can source it.

(vi) List of Characters

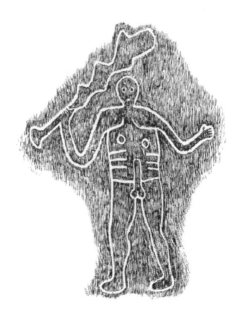

Anu: the White Mother, the highest of the Bone Mountains, seen as the source of life.

Archibald (Archie) Kerne: Isambard's brother and Boer War veteran.

Arthus: Bear Chief of Caer Andarta.

Baramis: the crippled Scythian blacksmith archer who helps Isambard.

Bladud: windsmith of Caer Henwen.

Blodeuwedd: the owl bird-ally of Ogmios, whose name means 'flower-face' in Welsh (from 'Math and Mathonwy' in *The Mabinogion*).

Brak: the son of Bron and Brigantia.

Brigantia: the wife of Bron, and subsequent chief.

Brighid: the Celtic goddess of poetry, smithcraft and war.

Bran: A mighty chief of Welsh mythology, connected to alders and ravens. According to legend his singing head was buried beneath the White Mound (the Tower of London) only to be dug up again by King Arthur.

Bron: chief of Caer Cernunnos.

Bronwen: the daughter of Bron and Brigantia.

Cernunnos: the Celtic Lord of the Animals, the Horned One.

Cormac: Wolf Chief of Caer Blaidd.

Cyndyn: Ram Chief of Caer Minas.

Dagda: the Good God, connected with fertility and a prodigious appetite.

Donn Cooley: known as 'the Donn': Bull Chief of Caer Findbhennach.

Eryr: Eagle Chief of Caer Ewilod, lord of the college of windsmiths.

Esias: windsmith of Caer Enid.

Fandar Grey: master silversmith of the Arianedd.

Finegas: windsmith of Caer Fintan.

Gwydion: windsmith of Caer Epona.

Gwyllt: windsmith of Caer Blaidd.

Harry Mallard: aka Madoc, Speaks-with-Thunder, Taranis: First World War pilot of the Royal Flying Corps. Missing in action since the Battle of Mons.

Isambard Kerne: antiquarian and Royal Flying Corps surveillance officer, of Irish and Welsh ancestry. Missing in action since the Battle of Mons.

Macha: Horse Chief of Caer Epona.

Maddon: Tuan's youthful successor.

Martha Kerne: Isambard's Welsh mother.

Maud Kerne: wife of Isambard (see *The Long Woman*).

Merlin: aka Myrddin Wyllt: Isambard's unpredictable bird-ally, the great wizard of legend turned into the eponymous falcon by 'a woman'.

Morann: windsmith of Caer Cynon.

Morfessa: windsmith of Caer Vran.

Nemain: Raven Chief of Caer Vran, training college for warriors.

Nubi: the Kernes' lurcher, Anubis.

Ogmios: windsmith of Caer Cernunnos; also the Celtic god of eloquence, aka Ogma (known by various epithets including Ogmios Honeytongued and Ogmios Honey-face), depicted with chains from his tongue to men's ears and with a club.

Ollav Fola: the King in the Lake, wise and loved former ruler of the Lake People.

Partholon: Salmon Chief of Caer Fintan.

Patrick (Paddy) Kerne: Isambard's father.

Roas: chosen chief of the Horse Nomads.

Ruadan: windsmith of Caer Minas.

Saar: Deer Chief of Caer Enid.

Senach: windsmith of Caer Findbhennach.

Setanta: Hound Chief of Caer Cynon.

Simias: windsmith of Caer Dagda.

Taranis: the Celtic god of thunder, associated with wheels and cruel sacrifice.

Tawrk: Boar Chief of Caer Henwen.

Tuan: Chief of Caer Dagda/Brighid.

Tuns: tin miners and smiths.

Urswick: windsmith of Caer Andarta.

Uscias: windsmith of Caer Ewilod.

(vii) Ogham – the Celtic Tree Alphabet

The Ogham was known as 'the secret language of the poets'. It was a secret system of signs and correspondences used by the druids and was known as the 'Dark Speech', which only initiates understood. The twenty-five tree-letters were divided into four categories or ranks. (As you can see, there are more than twenty-five, because there are variations on the specific trees included, perhaps indicating regional variation.)

I.   Chieftain (oak, hazel, holly, yew, ash, pine, apple)
II. Peasant (alder, willow, hawthorn, rowan, birch, elm, beech)
III. Shrub (blackthorn, elder, aspen, juniper, box, reed)
IV. Bramble (dogrose, bramble, broom, heather, ivy, vine, honeysuckle, fern, spindle)

This hierarchy is brilliantly illustrated in the ancient Celtic poem 'Cad Goddeu: The Battle of the Trees' (see Robert Graves's *The White Goddess*, Faber & Faber, 1951). An even more practical categorisation was into five groups of five, corresponding to vowels, consonants, consonant-based diphthongs and vowel-based diphthongs:

1. B, L, F, S, N   2. H, D, T, C, Q   3. M, G, NG, STR, R
4. A, O, U, E, I   5. EA, OI, UI, IO, AE

This gives us the strongest evidence that the Ogham was used in the oral tradition.

It was also a means of non-verbal communication through the use of hand signals (illustrating the idea of a secret language) – ideal for sending surreptitious messages across a court or mead hall. It could also be used for leaving messages in the wild (famously in *The Tain*, where Cuchullain leaves oghams in the trees). Less transiently, the Ogham has been used for inscriptions upon stones, thus paving the way for writing.

Perhaps the Ogham exists not to follow religiously, but to act as an approach to developing an intimate familiarity and harmony with nature, for the important thing is not to impose a system upon nature, but to develop a close and sustainable relationship with it, one in which we are sensitised to its energies and the lessons it can teach us. I suggest one finds one's own correspondences by observing and working with the trees over the seasons.

There are a couple of 'glossaries' that give us a clue to Ogham interpretation. John Matthews has translated the list of Morann mac Main in *Taliesin: Shamanism and the Bardic Mysteries in Britain and Ireland* (Aquarian Press, 1991). The chart overleaf is my interpretation based upon the Mac ind Oic word oghams.

It occurred to me that these word oghams would make excellent spells or incantations, and so I have used them as a magical system in *Windsmith*. They may well have been used in a magical way, and certainly there are layers of magical wisdom inherent within them.

OGHAM	LETTER	TREE	WORD OGHAMS	KENNING	MEANING
Beithe	b	Birch	Glaisium cnis	Most silvery skin	Salmon wisdom
Luis	l	Rowan	Cara ceathra	Friend of cattle	Gentleness
Fearn	f	Alder	Comet lachta	Guarding of milk	Protection
Saile	s	Willow	Luth bech	Activity of bees	Business
Nuin	n	Ash	Bag Ban	Flight of women	Cowardice?
(H)uathe	h	Hawthorn	Banadh Gnuisi	Blanching of face	Terror
Duir	d	Oak	Gres Sair	Carpenter's work	Construction/joining
Tinne	t	Holly	Smir guaili	Fires of coal	Constant heat/stamina
Coll	c	Hazel	Cara bloisc	Friend of cracking	Inspiration
Quert	q or kw	Apple	Brigh annum	Force of the men	Strength
Muinn	m	Vine	Aruusc n-arrligh	Condition of slaughter	Battle frenzy
Gort	g	Ivy	Mednercc	Trunk-binder	Entanglement
Negetal	ng	Broom/fern	Etiud midach	Robe of physicians	Healing touch
Straif	str	Blackthorn	Moridrun	Increasing of secrets	Concealment
Ruis	r	Elder	Ruamna dreach	Redness of faces	Embarrassment/satire
Ailm	a	Fir/pine	Tosach fregra	Beginning of an answer	Clue
Ohn	o	Gorse/furze	Feithim saire	Smoothest of work	Ease/effortlessness
Ur	u	Thorn/heather	Siladh clan	Growing of plants	Expansion/profusion
Edhadh	e	Aspen	Comainm carat	Synonym for a friend	Trust
Ido/Ioho	i	Yew	Chinem feada	Most withered of wood	Decay
Ebadh	eba	Aspen	Cosc Iobair	Corrective of a sick man	Health
Oir	oi	Spindle	Li crotha	Beauty of form	Attraction
Uilleand	ui	Ivy/honeysuckle	Cubat n-oll	Great equal length	Balance
Iphin	io	Pine	Amram blais	Wonderful of taste	Love/nourishment
Phagos	ae	Beech	None recorded	None recorded	Teaching

Fionn's Window

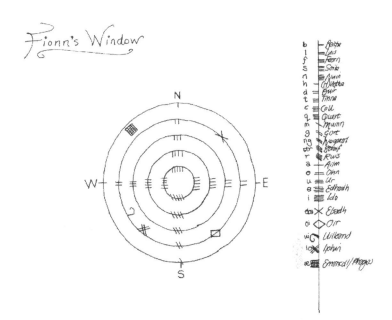

b	Beithe
l	Luis
f	Fearn
s	Sail
n	Nuin
h	(H)Uatha
d	Duir
t	Tinne
c	Coll
q	Quert
m	Muinn
g	Gort
ng	Ngeatal
str	Straif
r	Ruis
a	Ailm
o	Onn
u	Ur
e	Edhadh
i	Ido
ea	Ebadh
oi	Oir
ui	Uilleand
io	Iphin
ae	Emancoll / Phagos

Kerne 'discovers' the last five (aka 'koad', 'tharan', 'uilleand', 'phagos', 'mor') in the Void, extending the 'woodwords' of the windsmiths to twenty-five. It is generally thought that these last five letters were added later to the alphabet, although when and why remain a mystery. In this gap of knowledge I have spun my tale. It is a quintessential part of Kerne's quest to unlock the secret of each of these extra oghams. Robert Graves suggests they are alluded to in a collection of ancient Irish poems called *Dunaire Fionn*, a riddling inventory of the craneskin bag once belonging to Manannan mac Lir. The unusual shapes of the five extra letters (compared with the rest of the Ogham) seem to symbolise their legendary content – thus providing a visual aide-memoire. Whether they are otherworldly hallows, real treasures or a shaman's toolkit is a matter of debate or perhaps personal study.

(viii) The Gundestrup Cauldron

A glory of Celtic civilisation, the Gundestrup Cauldron is a richly decorated silver-gilt vessel thought to date from the La Tène period of Celtic art in the second or first century B.C.E. It was found in a peat bog near Gundestrup in Himmerland, Denmark, in 1891. It is now kept in the National Museum of Copenhagen. Made of fourteen plates, it was found dismantled (with one plate missing) in a dry section of peat bog, suggesting it was a ritual deposit. The style and technique suggest it could have originated on the shores of the Black Sea, an area of Thrace well known for its fine metalwork, especially in silver-gilt. However, the images (one round base plate, five shorter inner plates, seven longer ones facing outwards) are tantalising glimpses into the cosmology of the Celts. The larger figures dominating smaller humans suggest the relationship between gods and mortals. The tableaux are filled with strange monsters, which gave me the idea for the chimeras: the firecats, serpent and valkyries:

Most famous are the scenes depicting a horned man sitting cross-legged and holding a ram-headed serpent in one hand and a torc in the other, and the ranks of soldiers seemingly being offered to a cauldron. The pantheon of Celtic deities seems represented, including a fierce-looking Taranis – whose wheel is being held, or stopped, by a smaller horned figure. These fascinating windows into the Celtic world inspired many elements of the novel. I endeavoured to create a narrative around them as a way of unlocking their mystery and empathising with the paradigm of the people it represents in such an iconic way.

Base Plate

The round base plate is dominated by a bull. On its back is a leaping man wielding a spear, attacking it. Two dogs are also shown, one over the bull's head, and a#nother under its hooves.

Exterior Plates

Each of the seven exterior plates centrally depicts a bust, probably of a deity. Plates a, b, c and d show bearded male figures, while the remaining three are female.

- On plate a, the bearded figure in each hand holds a much smaller man by the arm. Each of the two men reach upward towards a small boar. Under the feet of the men (on the shoulders of the god) are a dog on the left side and a winged horse on the right side.
- The god on plate b holds in each hand a sea-horse or dragon. The god has been associated with the Irish sea-god Manannan.
- On plate c, the god raises his empty fists. On his right shoulder is a man in a 'boxing' position, and on his left shoulder a leaping figure with a small horseman underneath.
- Plate d shows a bearded god holding a stag by the hind quarters in each hand.
- The goddess on plate e is flanked by two smaller male busts.
- On plate f, the goddess holds a bird in her upraised right hand. Her left arm is horizontal, supporting a man and a dog lying on its back. She is flanked by two birds of prey on either side of her head. Her hair is being plaited by a small woman on the right.
- On plate g, the goddess has her arms crossed. On her right shoulder, a scene of a man fighting a lion is shown. On her left shoulder is a leaping figure similar to the one on plate c.

Interior Plates

Plate A: Horned God

Plate A centrally shows a horned male figure in a seated position, usually identified with Cernunnos. In its right hand, the figure is holding a torque, and with its left hand, it grips a

328

horned serpent by the head. To the left is a stag with antlers very similar to the god's. Other animals surround the scene, canine, feline, bovine, and a human figure riding a fish or a dolphin. The scene has been compared to the Pashupati 'lord of animals' of the Indus Valley Civilisation.

Plate B: Goddess with Wheels

Plate B shows the bust of a goddess, flanked by two six-spoked wheels and by mythical animals: two elephant-like creatures and two griffins. Under the bust is a large hound.

Plate C: Broken Wheel

Plate C shows the bust of a bearded god holding on to a broken wheel. A smaller leaping figure with a horned helmet is also holding the rim of the wheel. Under the leaping figure is a horned serpent. The group is surrounded by elephants and griffins similar to those on plate B. The god has been associated with the Irish Dagda.

Plate D: Bull Sacrifice

Plate D shows a scene of bull-slaying. Three bulls are depicted in a row, facing right. Each bull is attacked by a man with a sword. Under the hooves of each bull is a dog running to the right, and over the back of each bull is a cat, also running to the right.

Plate E: Warrior Initiation

Plate E apparently displays a sort of initiation ritual. In the lower half, a line of warriors bearing spears and shields, accompanied by carnyx players march to the left. On the left side, a large figure is immersing a man in a cauldron. In the upper half, heading away from the cauldron, and probably having completed the initiation ritual are warriors on horseback. Interestingly, later Celtic myth features resurrection themes based on immersion of dead warriors in cauldrons.

Description of plates from www.wikipedia.com

(ix) The Strettweg Chariot

Although a lot smaller and probably designed for ceremonial use, the magnificent Strettweg Chariot, and other similar Celtic wheeled chariots, inspired Madoc's war chariot made from the panels of the crashed Breguet biplane. The panels are transformed from a Cauldron of War (inspired by the Cauldron of Rebirth in 'Bran and Branwen' in *The Mabinogion*) to a Cauldron of Art by Kerne and Fandar Grey, before being ritually deposited in Lake Mandorla – to emerge in a bog in Denmark!

(x) Pronunciation Guide

Since I am more familiar with Welsh pronunciation, I have stuck to this, rather than Irish, throughout the book. Kerne grew up on the Welsh borders with a Welsh-speaking mother, Anglo-Welsh peers and Welsh placenames, so he would have been more attuned to it, even though he had an Irish father and grandparents. This pronunciation guide is based on that given in the Penguin Classics version of *The Mabinogion*, translated by Jeffrey Gantz.

Consonants as in English, but:
c as in *c*ane
ch as in lo*ch*
dd as in *th*en
ff as in *f*urze
g as in *g*irl
ll as if *hl* with a hissing *h*
rh as if *hr* with a hissing *h*
s as in *s*in.
th as in *th*istle

Vowels:
a as in f*a*ther
e as in m*e*t
i as in p*i*n
o as in n*o*t
u as in p*i*n or French t*u*
w as in n*oo*k
y as in p*i*n

Dipthongs:
ae, ei, eu, ey as in t*i*ger
aw as in o*u*t
oe as in o*i*l
wy as in d*ewy*

Stress on the penultimate syllable.

(xi) Glossary

Abred: (Welsh) The circle of rebirth: the **Afterlands** where *Windsmith* is set. 'The circles or spiral of Abred: emerging life – up to the human' (D.J. Roderic = DJR). 'Where the dead is stronger than the living, and where every principal existence is derived from the dead, and man has traversed it.' From the *Barddas* of Io-lo Morganwg (IM), a questionable but fascinating reinvention of bardic lore by the eccentric eighteenth-century Welsh druidic revivalist.

Afterlands: the different realms of the ancestors within **Shadow World**.

Agents of Discord: mysterious and sinister beings with elongated skulls and malevolence in mind.

Andraste: Icenian goddess of victory and revenge. British warrior queen Boudicca famously released a hare in her name to prophesy the outcome of battle.

Annwn: (Welsh) Cymric land of the dead, where our world seems mirrored, albeit through a glass darkly (see **Shadow World**). The 'source'; the first stirrings of life – a primeval state of existence. 'The outermost from God, not abyss but outer darkness' (IM). The Void that Kerne first inhabits when caught in limbo between the worlds.

Arianedd: silver miners and smiths.

Awen: (Welsh) bardic word for inspiration; literally 'flowing spirit'.

Bard: (Welsh) a master storyteller, poet, musician and remembrancer for their respective community or court, with a huge repertoire (350 songs and stories) and an extensive knowledge of the genealogies and landrights of the ruling families. The bard's mandate was to compose elegies for their noble patron and to record famous events (like battles). Their satires were feared and their praise was sought. Their extensive training in British bardic colleges took twelve years. Caesar records of this high-status Celtic caste, 'The Bards celebrated the brave deeds of their gods in verse.'

Barrow: Bronze Age burial mound of varying shapes and sizes: bell, saucer, ring.

Bird-ally: sentient totem animal-spirits associated exclusively with one **windsmith** and maintaining a telepathic link with them. As individual as their masters, e.g. **Merlin, Blodeuwedd**.

Bobac: small mammal of the Steppe, whose flesh is prized by hunters.

Bronze Age: the period from about 2000 to 700 B.C.E. that usually followed the Neolithic and preceded the Iron Age, corresponding to the introduction of metallurgy, notably bronze-working, for making tools, weapons and ceremonial objects.

Caer: an Iron Age hill fort. The largest hill forts are referred to as 'oppida' (small townships). Many started out before the Iron Age (e.g. Neolithic Windmill Hill) and possibly were sacred enclosures, their fortifications being developed during periods of warfare.

Cerne Abbas Giant: the ithyphallic chalk giant wielding a club who stands proud over the eponymous Dorset village. Of unknown date, although he has been associated with Bel, Herakles and even Oliver Cromwell. However, **Ogmios** was depicted wielding a club and the **Dagda** was equally well endowed!

Ceugant: The seat of the Godhead. 'The radiating sphere of the divine' (DJR). 'One falls, yet returns to the centre, the divine Ceugant' (IM). The soul strives to return to this source yet, paradoxically, only God can dwell there.

Chalk giant: a symbolic figure carved out of the turf to reveal the chalk beneath, unique to the chalk downlands of England. See **Long Man**, **Cerne Abbas** and **White Horse**.

Chimera: fiery monster from **Annwn**, released by the rift created by the presence of the two living men in the **Afterlands**.

Coelbren: a wood-carved alphabet. A runic development of the **Ogham** with more elaborate letter-forms. Said to have been (re)invented by outlawed **bards** when King Henry V forbade the use of paper after the death of Owain Glyndwr: 'Then was remembered, and brought into use, the ancient custom of the Bards of the Isles of Britain; namely, the cutting of letters, which they prepared for the purpose, called Coelbren of the Bards – and thus it was done' (Ross Nichols, *The Book of Druidry*, Thorsons, 1992).

Copors: copper miners and smiths.

Cromlech: the former entrance to a Neolithic burial chamber, eroded away to leave only the entrance stones, normally three, capped with a lintel. Aka 'quoit' in Cornwall, e.g. Lanyon's Quoit.

Cythrawl: Iolo Morgannwg's dark element of chaos and evil, said to dwell in **Annwn**. In *Windsmith* this is a malevolent force threatening to overwhelm the worlds.

Da'anu: river flowing from the Bone Mountains, whose source is a waterfall below Mount Anu, the White Mother. Akin to the river Danube, whose valley cradled early Celtic civilisation. Its valley is the ancestral homeland (**Afterland**) of the Chalk Folk.

Dark Speech: another name for the **Ogham**, also referred to as 'the secret language of poets'. Essentially a code only the **druid** caste were able to interpret (like Latin to the Christian priesthood).

Druid: Celtic priest, judge and master of ceremonies; literally 'oak-priest'.

Drunemetom: the sacred meeting place of the Iron Age Galatians of Asia Minor. Etymologically connected with 'druid' and 'nemeton' – the sacred enclosure of the **druids**, or the 'sacred oak enclosure'.

Gramarye: word-magic, literally 'grammar'. The magic of the **windsmiths**.

Grey Warrior: a Thracian scale-armoured scimitar-wielding foot soldier of the Steppe.

Gwynvyd: aka Gwynfid: the white life/place – 'where the living is stronger than the dead, and where every principle existence is derived from the living and life, that is God, and man shall traverse it; nor will man attain to perfect knowledge, until he shall have fully traversed the circle of Gwynvyd, for no absolute knowledge can be obtained but by the experiences of the senses, from having born and suffered every condition and incident' (IM). The realm of earthly existence, akin to the Buddhist Wheel of Life.

Huns: nomadic tribes of the Steppe, renowned for their horsemanship and archery skills. The most famous was the warlord Attila. Also derogatory slang for German soldiers in the First World War.

Iron Age: the period between the end of the Bronze Age (c. 700 B.C.E.) and the expansion of the Roman Empire. The main era of Celtic civilisation, in which iron replaced bronze for tools and weapons.

Karma-serfs: Celts who work off debts of honour and wealth in the Otherworld.

Kenning: an Anglo-Saxon concept of describing something in a poetic way to avoid using its direct name, e.g. 'whale-road' (sea). Possibly connected to a predilection for riddles and fondness for thinking laterally. It is likely the Celts had a similar practice.

Kurgan: Scythian name for a royal burial chamber.

Long Man of Wilmington: chalk giant of West Sussex; a mysterious featureless figure wielding two staves, on Windover Hill in the South Downs.

Mandorlans: the peaceful Fisher Folk of Lake Mandorla.

Metenaidd: the four Ore Tribes of the Da'anu Valley, who live along tributaries rich in the metal they mine, work and trade.

Ogham: the Celtic tree alphabet, each of whose twenty-five letters represents a native species, with its corresponding sigil and gloss. See also **Dark Speech** and **Coelbren**.

Plwms: lead miners and smiths.

Saiga: antelope species of the Steppe.

Scimitar: curved sword of Asiatic warriors.

Scythian: tribes of nomads that originated in Iran and inhabited the Eurasian steppe in the first millennium B.C.E. The ancient Greek name 'Scythians' probably derives from the Iranian word 'skuta' (archers).

Shadow World: Otherworld connected to Earth symbiotically.

Sigil: a sign or seal. The entoptic patterns Kerne sees in the Void, 'letters of fire', are a development of the system of **woodwords** used by the **windsmiths**. They are in effect mnemonic symbols for words of power.

Steppe: an ecosystem in temperate regions in which grasses and herbaceous plants are the dominant vegetation. The term is commonly used to refer to the treeless, undulating plains that extend from Hungary and the lower regions of the Danube basin, through Ukraine and southern Russia, into northern Kazakhstan and Siberia as far as the foothills of the Altai Mountains. Other steppe regions lie further east in Mongolia and northeastern China. The width of the Eurasian steppe belt varies between about three hundred and a thousand kilometres.

Tarpan: short, stocky black-maned horses native to the Steppe, extinct since 1919.

Thrace: country to the north of Greece inhabited by people generally reputed to be warlike (aka Cimmerians), but also the homeland of the master-bard Orpheus, who famously entered the realm of Hades to win back his beloved.

Torc: a gold neck, arm or wrist bracelet bestowing high status upon the wearer. Neck-torcs were a sign of chieftainship. Many have been found in graves and ritually deposited in pools, wells and springs.

Tuirgen: cyclical Celtic notion of destiny, analogous to the Anglo-Saxon concept of 'wyrd'.

Tugen: 'shamanic' feathered cloak worn by Celtic poet-priests.

Underworld: realm of the ancestors and chthonic deities, akin to **Annwn**.

White Horse of Uffington: stylised chalk-cut horse overlooking the Vale of the White Horse, Oxfordshire. Recently discovered to be three thousand years old. Above it is the Iron Age Uffington Castle.

Windsmith: a magician of **gramarye** able to summon the wind. Each windsmith is associated with a particular **caer** and has a **bird-ally**.

Wood-priest: another name for **windsmith**; effectively, a **druid**.
Woodword: a kenning for an **Ogham** name.

This is one of the woodwords Kerne discovers: 'oir' (aka 'tharan'), which he uses the raise the east wind. Connected to the spindle tree (symbolic of the weaver of life), it is interpreted as meaning sudden sweetness/intelligence – symbolised by the lightning of Tharan, Thunder – the flash of illumination that Kerne beholds in the vast expanse of the Steppe, the domain of Eurus. It was interpreted by Robert Graves in *The White Goddess* as representing one of the treasures in Manannan mac Lir's craneskin bag.

(xii) The Coligny Calendar

This important document dates from the early first century C.E. or late first century B.C.E. John Matthews in *Taliesin* explains, 'The Coligny Calendar was discovered in 1897 near Bourg in France. It consists of a number of bronze tablets, stamped with an intricate series of notation which has been interpreted as precise astronomical observance.' Experts are still deciphering it, but so far the following has been gleaned.

The calendar shows sixteen columns, covering a five-year period. Each month is divided into two blocks of days, called 'atenoux': one of fifteen days; the second of fourteen or fifteen days = 29.5 days on average. These two periods correspond to the waxing and waning moon, both numbered from 1; thus Waning Atenoux (1–15) and Waxing Atenoux (1–14/15). It is a luni-solar calendrical system, giving an annual lunar year of 355 days. The ten days' loss are compensated by the insertion of an intercalary month of thirty days every two-and-a-half years. This gives a total of 1835 days per five years: just over nine days extra – perhaps these would be 'holy days'?

Although the calendar is written in Latin it is undoubtedly a Celtic system, as the Gaulish names attest, evoking the annual cycle and the mindset of the tribes who used it. It gives us a tantalising glimpse into their lives. Each month was marked 'MAT' (good) or 'ANM' (not good), as were the days – the druid astrologers determined days favourable or ill-omened for certain endeavours (marriages, battles, raising monuments, journeys, even births). It is the system used by Kerne's Celtic ancestors and some modern pagans.

Samionos	Seed fall	Oct/Nov
Dumannios	Darkest depths	Nov/Dec
Riuros	Cold time	Dec/Jan
Anagantios	Stay-home time	Jan/Feb
Ogronios	Time of ice	Feb/Mar
Cutios	Time of winds	Mar/Apr
Giamonios	Shoots show	Apr/May
Samivisionos	Time of brightness	May/Jun
Equos	Horse time	Jun/Jul
Elembiuos	Claim time	Jul/Aug
Edrinios	Arbitration time	Aug/Sep
Cantlos	Song time	Sep/Oct

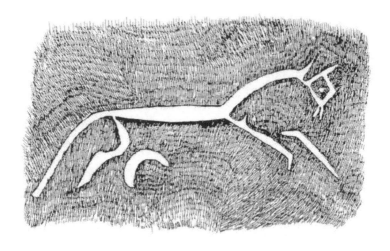

Acknowledgements

Thank you to:

Nimue Brown, for your windsmithery.
Steve Hambidge, for your stunning cover.
Moyra Caldecott, feedback from a much-missed friend.
Anthony Nanson, for keeping the awen flowing.
Robin Acton, for flying lessons.
John of Spraysparks, for a day at the forge.
Chris Joliffe, for advice from a swordmaster.
Gregoire the silversmith, on the art of cauldron-making.
Derek the storyteller at ELF.
Ronald Millar, for the story of 'Dru the Windsmith'
Skip Palmer, for originally setting the book in ink.
& Ian Davidson, for enabling it to first take wing.

The photograph of the author as the Amesbury Archer is by M. Leverett for Wessex Archaeological Trust.

The main image of Gundestrup Cauldron is from Nationalmuseet, licensed under the Creative Commons.

Images of interior plates of Gundestrup Cauldron are reproduced by permission of Sacred Source (www.sacredsource.com). Sacred Source is a source for images of the divine and seeks to spread healing archetypes to every corner of modern culture.

The drawing of the Strettweg Chariot is by Friedrich Drexel.

www.awenpublications.co.uk

Also available from Awen Publications:

The Long Woman
Kevan Manwaring

An antiquarian's widow discovers her husband's lost journals and sets out on a journey of remembrance across 1920s England and France, retracing his steps in search of healing and independence. Along alignments of place and memory she meets mystic Dion Fortune, ley-line pioneer Alfred Watkins, and a Sir Arthur Conan Doyle obsessed with the Cottingley Fairies. From Glastonbury to Carnac, she visits the ancient sites that obsessed her husband and, tested by both earthly and unearthly forces, she discovers a power within herself.

'A beautiful book, filled with the quiet of dawn, and the first cool breaths of new life, it reveals how the poignance of real humanity is ever sprinkled with magic.' *Emma Restall Orr*

Fiction ISBN 978-1-906900-44-1 £9.99
The Windsmith Elegy Volume 1

The Well Under the Sea
Kevan Manwaring

Imagine an island at the crossroads of time where lost souls find each other … Having learnt the secrets of the East Wind, Isambard Kerne must sail beyond the West Wind to the fabled Island of the Blessed, Ashalantë, where the visions of Plato, Da Vinci, and Brunel have come to life. Here he meets the legendary aviatrix Amelia Earhart, who is assigned to instruct him in the art of flying, but they find themselves falling in forbidden love. Torn between duty and desire, the two become embroiled in a tragic chain of events that threaten to destroy not only this otherworldly paradise but also its shadow: Earth.

Fiction ISBN 978-1-906900-48-9 £9.99
The Windsmith Elegy Volume 3

The Burning Path
Kevan Manwaring

Three strangers meet in a nameless desert and must come to terms with their past before they can escape it: a First World War airman, an American aviatrix of the 1930s, and a French poet of the skies from the Second World War. They are the lost of history and must go into the desert to find themselves. To find peace they must walk the burning path. Each is forced to confront the question: What are you prepared to sacrifice for the one you love?

Fiction ISBN 978-1-906900-49-6 £9.99
The Windsmith Elegy Volume 4

This Fearful Tempest
Kevan Manwaring

In an alternative 1940s Great Britain, Isambard Kerne is confronted by a dystopian wasteland ruled by the fascist army of the White Dragon. If he is to defeat Aveldra and the Agents of Discord once and for all, he must undertake a perilous journey into the far north to become the Lord of the Winds. The spirit of the Battle of Britain is kindled as the fate of a kingdom is fought for in the air between Spitfires and fire-breathing dragons. In the hour of his country's greatest need, a king returns to fulfil an ancient prophecy – but is it too late? The lost of history clash in this epic finale of The Windsmith Elegy.

Fiction ISBN 978-1-906900-50-2 £9.99
The Windsmith Elegy Volume 5

The Firekeeper's Daughter
Karola Renard

From the vastness of Stone Age Siberia to a minefield in today's Angola, from the black beaches of Iceland to the African savannah and a Jewish-German cemetery, Karola Renard tells thirteen mythic stories of initiation featuring twenty-first-century kelpies, sirens, and holy fools, a river of tears and a girl who dances on fire, a maiden shaman of ice, a witch in a secret garden, Queen Guinevere's mirror, and a woman who swallows the moon. The red thread running through them all is a deep faith in life and the need to find truth and meaning even in the greatest of ordeals.

Fiction ISBN 978-1-906900-46-5 £9.99

Mysteries
Chrissy Derbyshire

This enchanting and exquisitely crafted collection by Chrissy Derbyshire will whet your appetite for more from this budding wordsmith. Her short stories interlaced with poems depict chimeras, femmes fatales, mountebanks, absinthe addicts, changelings, derelict warlocks, and persons foolhardy enough to stray into the beguiling world of Faerie. Let the sirens' song seduce you into the Underworld ...

Fiction/Poetry ISBN 978-1-906900-45-8 £8.99

Exotic Excursions
Anthony Nanson

In these stories Anthony Nanson charts the territory between travel writing and magic realism to confront the exotic and the enigmatic. Here are epiphanies of solitude, twilight and initiation. A lover's true self unveiled by a mountain mist ... a memory of the lost land in the western sea ... a traveller's surrender to the allure of ancient gods ... a quest for primeval beings on the edge of extinction. In transcending the line between the written and the spoken word, between the familiar and the unfamiliar, between the actual and the imagined, these tales send sparks across the gap of desire.

Fiction/Travel ISBN 987-0-9546137-7-8 £7.99

The Immanent Moment
Kevan Manwaring

The sound of snow falling on a Somerset hillside, the evanescence of a waterspout on a remote Scottish island, the invisible view from a Welsh mountain, the light on the Grand Canal in Venice, the fire in a Bedouin camel-herder's eyes ... These poems consider the little epiphanies of life and capture such fleeting pulses of consciousness in sinuous, euphonic language. A meditation on time, mortality, transience, and place, this collection celebrates the beauty of both the natural and the man-made, the familiar and the exotic, and the interstices and intimacy of love.

Poetry ISBN 978-1-906900-41-0 £8.99

Words of Re-enchantment: writings on storytelling, myth, and ecological desire
Anthony Nanson

The time-honoured art of storytelling – ancestor of all narrative media – is finding new pathways of relevance in education, consciousness-raising, and the journey of transformation. Storytellers are reinterpreting ancient myths and communicating the new stories we need in our challenging times. This book brings together the best of Anthony Nanson's incisive writings about the ways that story can re-enchant our lives and the world we live in. Grounded in his practice as a storyteller, the essays range from the myths of Arthur, Arcadia, and the voyage west, to true tales of the past, science-fiction visions of the future, and the big questions of politics and spirituality such stories raise. The book contains full texts of exemplar stories and will stimulate the thinking of anyone interested in storytelling or in the use of myth in fiction and film.

'This excellent book is written with a storyteller's cadence and understanding of language. Passionate, fascinating and wise.' *Hamish Fyfe*

Storytelling/Mythology/Environment ISBN 978-1-906900-15-1 £9.99

Glossing the Spoils
Charlotte Hussey

Each poem in *Glossing the Spoils* works like an intricate time-travel machine, carrying the reader back to the beginnings of Western European literature. Like an ancient clapper bridge with its unmortared slabs of flat sandstone, these poems step us across the choppy currents of the past 1500 years. Anchored at one end in the deep past and at the other in the turbulent present, they explore interconnections between historical, personal, psychological, and mythic states. Plundering their opening passages from such early texts as *Beowulf*, *The Mabinogion*, and *The Tain*, these glosas address eternal themes of love and war and give voice to the surreal potency of the Western European imagination.

'The author is not only a gifted poet, but also well versed in Celtic mythology. She writes from a spiritual perspective that brings these ancient stories alive and relevant to our world today.' *Abena*

Poetry ISBN 978-1-906900-52-6 £8.99

The Fifth Quarter

Richard Selby

The Fifth Quarter is Romney Marsh, as defined by the Revd Richard Harris Barham in *The Ingoldsby Legends*: 'The World, according to the best geographers, is divided into Europe, Asia, Africa, America and Romney Marsh.' It is a place apart, almost another world. This collection of stories and poems explores its ancient and modern landscapes, wonders at its past, and reflects upon its present. Richard Selby has known Romney Marsh all his life. His writing reflects the uniqueness of The Marsh through prose, poetry, and written versions of stories he performs as a storyteller.

Fiction/Poetry ISBN 978-0-9546137-9-2 £9.99

Tidal Shift: selected poems

Mary Palmer

Knowing her end was near, Mary Palmer worked on her poems, compiling her very best and writing new ones with a feverish intensity. This is the result, published here with her full cooperation and consent. These are poems from the extreme edge and very centre of life – words of light that defy death's shadow with a startling intensity, clarity, and honesty. Containing poems from across Mary's career, selected by Jay Ramsay, *Tidal Shift* is an impressive legacy from a poet of soul and insight.

Poetry ISBN 978-1-906900-09-0 £9.99

Iona

Mary Palmer

What do you do when you are torn apart by your 'selves'? The pilgrim poet, rebel Mordec and tweedy Aelia set sail for Iona – a thin place, an island on the edge. It's a journey between worlds, back to the roots of their culture. On the Height of Storm they relive a Viking massacre, at Port of the Coracle encounter vipers. They meet Morrighan, a bloodthirsty goddess, and Abbot Dominic with his concubine nuns. There are omens, chants, curses … During her stay Mordec learns that words can heal or destroy, and the poet writes her way out of darkness. A powerful story, celebrating a journey to wholeness, from an accomplished poet.

Poetry ISBN 978-0-9546137-8-5 £6.99

Made in the USA
Columbia, SC
05 July 2017